AN
EMBROIDERY
OF
SOULS

An Embroidery of Souls

Ruby Martinez

ALFRED A. KNOPF
NEW YORK

A Borzoi Book published by Alfred A. Knopf
An imprint of Random House Children's Books
A division of Penguin Random House LLC
1745 Broadway, New York, NY 10019
penguinrandomhouse.com
rhcbooks.com

Text copyright © 2025 by Ruby Martinez
Jacket art copyright © 2025 by Anna Stead

Penguin Random House values and supports copyright. Copyright fuels creativity, encourages
diverse voices, promotes free speech, and creates a vibrant culture. Thank you for buying an
authorized edition of this book and for complying with copyright laws by not reproducing,
scanning, or distributing any part of it in any form without permission. You are supporting
writers and allowing Penguin Random House to continue to publish books for every reader.
Please note that no part of this book may be used or reproduced in any manner for the purpose
of training artificial intelligence technologies or systems.

Knopf, Borzoi Books, and the colophon are registered trademarks of
Penguin Random House LLC.

Editor: Gianna Lakenauth
Cover Designer: Angela Carlino
Interior Designer: Ken Crossland
Production Editor: Melinda Ackell
Managing Editor: Jake Eldred
Production Manager: Liz Sutton

Library of Congress Cataloging-in-Publication Data is available upon request.
ISBN 978-0-593-90103-8 (hardcover) — ISBN 978-0-593-90105-2 (ebook)

The text of this book is set in 11-point Adobe Caslon Pro.

Manufactured in the United States of America
1st Printing

The authorized representative in the EU for product safety and compliance is
Penguin Random House Ireland, Morrison Chambers, 32 Nassau Street,
Dublin D02 YH68, Ireland, https://eu-contact.penguin.ie.

Random House Children's Books supports the
First Amendment and celebrates the right to read.

For Natan, my partner in life, parenting, and *Stardew Valley*.
This one's for you.

And for all the worry warriors out there. You're far braver
than you know, and more capable than you can imagine.

AN EMBROIDERY OF SOULS

PART ONE

CHAPTER ONE

JADE

I CAN KILL A MAN WITH NOTHING MORE THAN A NEEDLE, THREAD, and a lock of his hair.

My skills allow me to stitch love, embroider away death, and unspool memories. Even the most wonderful gifts aren't out of my grasp. Beauty. Courage. Happiness. I can bestow them as I choose, or steal them away as I see fit.

And yet, for all my talents, I can't get through tea with the queen—or anyone, for that matter—without my hands shaking.

The teacup rattles as I return it to the saucer, and though it can't be loud, to me it's a blaring screech. Queen María-Celese Ríos sits across from me in a dress of verdant green stitched with all nature of flora, from honeysuckle to marigolds. Her gown is glorious—no doubt made of the finest Caldistan silk—and the chambers we're seated in are just as lovely. Thick leather sofas and chairs, azure tiles, and walls painted to look like the jungle outside the city gates. It's absolutely stunning.

I hate it. Hate that it's not my small, *safe* cabin. My skin itches just being in this unknown place with this unfamiliar person. The fact that the queen is supposedly descended from Oro, king of Devociónism's many gods, only makes my anxiety worse. His blood runs in her veins, and while the blood of a god has never bestowed any powers, it certainly grants status, of which the queen has reached the pinnacle. Now that status makes me squirm under her gaze, sharper than a fresh needle.

It takes everything inside me not to flinch. We've already exchanged pleasantries, and I've spent the past minute debating what to say before tossing every foolish idea aside. What do I say to a queen, of all people?

In the end, she breaks the silence. "I brought you here to ask some questions, if you would be so obliged."

My eyes dart up to meet hers, much too abruptly, which spurs more panic. Did she notice? Is she upset with me? Her soul hovers about her, a rainbow of fragments, and my eyes stick on the burnt orange impatience before I remember she asked a question. My throat tightens, and I barely manage to cough out my next words. "Of course, Your Majesty."

She glances at the wall, almost unsure of herself, then leans back and waves a dismissive hand. "Please, call me Celese. It's what all my closest confidants use."

My collar is suddenly too tight, the stitching on my ivory cotton dress unbearably itchy. I can't imagine a world where I'm one of the queen's closest confidants—I've only just met her. My mother has worked with her, but not me. Never me.

What do I even say to that?

"Yes. I mean, okay . . . Celese."

Gods, I'm making a fool of myself—in front of the queen, no less. She studies me a beat too long, then says, "Let's start with your mother. Have you heard from her recently?"

I think I might vomit all over the queen's pretty dress. I know where this is going, and I don't like it.

"No." My palms are clammy as I bring them together. "No, nothing since she disappeared. I filed a report with the polesa."

Her brow furrows, and my eyes skitter to another hue in her soul, a bright, judgmental citrine. "Didn't you file that report three months ago?"

The blood drains from my face, both from the queen's assessing gaze and from the reminder of *that* morning, when I last saw my mother—ninety-two days ago now.

I nearly crack then, under the weight of missing her. I still remember our last morning together so clearly—how I found her sitting at the kitchen table, face ashen, an article on the recent murders spread out in front of her. When I asked what was wrong, she said nothing, but an hour later she hugged me tighter than normal, told me she loved me, and whispered into my ear, *Don't fret, but I have to run some errands. Pack your things. When I get back, you and I need to talk.*

What about, I might never know, because she didn't return. Not that day, or any after.

I still haven't been able to bring myself to unpack that trunk. It's foolish, but if I do . . . it somehow makes this real, means that she's gone, and I—I don't think I can face a world without my mother in it. I'm not sure I want to live in that world at all.

My eyes sting, and I startle when the queen clears her throat, reminding me that she said something.

"Yes—sorry, you're right. Three months." My voice is little more than a strained hiss. I should say more, but there doesn't seem to be any air left inside me.

"You must know what this means, Jade." She pauses, and

everything inside me tenses. "The Crown needs a thread speaker, and with your mother gone . . ."

I'll be expected to take her place.

And of course I will. Thread speaking doesn't follow bloodlines—it's random and rare. There are barely more than a dozen of us alive today, and in the queendom of Mérecal we're obligated to serve the Crown. To gift them health, spin them happiness, stitch their intelligence.

To kill their enemies with the tug of a thread.

The prospect has me dizzy, and I absently reach for the pendant at my throat, imagining everything my new role will entail. Leaving the house, public appearances, crowds.

Crowds.

For a moment, I'm no longer with the queen but ensnared in a memory. In it, the cool stone of the courthouse steps digs into my back while a frenzy of hands pulls at my limbs, my clothes, my hair. I'm trapped in a fog of their breath, drowning beneath the crush of their bodies. In reality, my throat begins to close up, a warning sign that one of my episodes is impending, and—

"Jade?"

The queen's voice is the mental slap I need. She's looking at me, and her hand twitches, fingers spinning her signet ring. The symbol there catches my eye, familiar after years of seeing it on my mother's desk, stamped in wax on the queen's letters. A crescent moon over a river, haloed in a ring of feathers. A mark each: feathers for the god she's descended from, a moon for the one she's named after, and a river for her surname—Ríos.

Her movement abruptly stops, and I realize I've been staring. "What were we talking about again?"

My voice squeaks, and another wave of nausea rolls through. What if I upset her? I fight a wince as she bites her lip, appearing almost . . . uncomfortable as she studies me. "I need a thread speaker."

I shrink at what she's implying, realize I'm squeezing my pendant, and drop my hand to my lap. "But my mother will be back soon."

You are strong, capable, and wonderful. Don't ever forget it. My mother used to tell me that. She may have adopted me after learning of our shared gifts, but she loved me for me. Even so, she was wrong—I'm not any of those things, least of all strong. I'm too afraid of the world to ever truly join it.

The queen's next words are gentle, a kindness I wouldn't have expected from her. "If she was coming back, she would've returned by now."

At first I don't recognize the strange, creaking sound. Then I realize it's *me*, a sob twisting its way out of my throat. I clamp a hand over my mouth, but it's too late. The queen's already heard.

Her eyes flick to the wall again, and the lilac compassion in her soul pulses before she looks back at me. "Perhaps I could grant you an extension."

It should be a relief. It *is* a relief. Any extra time is a gift. And yet days, weeks, years . . . it doesn't change the fact that my mother is gone. I can't afford to sound ungrateful, though, so I nod, and the queen's voice is soft as she replies.

"How about sixty days? If your mother isn't back by then, you'll assume her duties."

Sixty days. It's not nearly enough time to prepare. Logically, I've always known I'd be called on to take my mother's place, but that's always been a far-off concept. I never thought I'd be in this position at seventeen.

But Queen María-Celese has already budged—a truly surprising concession. My mother didn't reveal much about her work with the queen, but she did offer one piece of advice: to *never* disobey her. Which is why even as my stomach gives a sudden, violent twist, I nod. "Of course. I understand."

What else can I say? That I'd run away to avoid these duties, if only the prospect of leaving wasn't so terrifying? Sixty days, though. That's not nothing. Perhaps my mother will return.

Or maybe I could find her.

It's not like I haven't already tried. I've written letters to the hospitals, morgues, even prisons, searching for her. But all my efforts have been in vain, and none have required me to leave the safety of my home.

Every night I dream of finding my mother, bringing her back. But come sunrise, when reality hits, I've always been too afraid. Cowardly. This deadline, though . . . Soon I won't have an option. If I don't search for my mother now, there won't be time later, not as thread speaker to the Crown.

"There's another matter."

The queen's tone is unexpectedly soft, and something about it makes me lift my head, look at *her* and not simply the soul hovering around her. She's young for a queen, still in her early thirties. She was only sixteen when a fire ravaged her home, killing her parents and older sister. The official story claims it was nothing more than a horrible tragedy, but the rumors . . . they speak of something more malicious. Of a killer and ill intent. Personally, I'm not sure what I believe, but regardless, the result was the same. Celese became the queen, one of the last remaining monarchs in a world increasingly possessed by democracy.

The years since have transformed her into the woman in front of me. She's clearly well pampered, all manner of creams and powders applied to her face, smoothing her skin and making her dark eyes glisten. But it's strange. There's no luster to her hair. Her nose has an unexpected bump. The blades of her cheeks aren't quite as sharp as I would've predicted.

Perhaps I'm superficial, but I expected her to be more beautiful, in the way only those altered by thread speaking can achieve. Her face on the dineda coins certainly suggests as much, and I could've sworn my mother stitched her beauty years ago. I must be thinking of someone else, though; it's a common request, after all.

She shifts in her seat, almost . . . *nervous*, but that can't be right. "I also wanted to discuss the murders."

Oh.

The words settle between us like a lead weight, and too much silence passes before I realize I should've said something by now.

"What about them?"

My voice comes out too high, but the queen graciously ignores my awkwardness. "I was hoping you might be able to aid in the investigation. The polesa are doing everything they can, but it's been months, and they still have no suspects. I understand this is a stretch, but I wondered if your unique talents might lend themselves to the case. At this point we're desperate for any help we can get."

Oh. I hadn't expected that, though I can see why she'd ask. I've been reading the papers, absorbing the details of the case the same way roots might soak up poisoned water. The bodies have been discovered across Mérecal, their eyes gouged out, bloody tears striping their cheeks. No one is safe. Peasants, businessmen, preachers, even a member of the polesa have been killed, and anyone could be next.

The polesa insist the killer's a madman, the reporters speculate the murders are tied to gang activity, but the people whisper. They say it's the wrath of the old gods. That Vada's become greedy, and her dog is running amok. That Oro's disappointed in our declining faith, and that's why he isn't stopping her.

Me, though? I don't know what to think, or whom to believe. All I know is that my mother's been missing for ninety-two days, and in every quiet moment I wonder if she was one of the victims.

Just the thought steals my breath every time. Grief. Panic. It's surprising how sometimes they hit much the same. A vicious tide, drawing you ever deeper into the abyss.

Normally I avoid using my talents, preferring to remain safe at home, but on this I wish I could do something. *Anything* but sit helplessly by, secure in my cabin while in the city, innocent people are killed, and my mother remains missing.

It's unfortunate, then, that I can't do much.

"I'm afraid I don't see how my services can be useful here," I tell the queen. "Not without a suspect or a murder weapon."

She's fidgeting with her ring again. "But you could help? If we brought you something?"

"Maybe."

It's not a simple yes or no. If an object is held dear to someone, their soul will leave an imprint on it. One I could see, if the murder weapon was a treasured knife or pistol. As for the victims, it's not so different. Even in death our souls remain tethered to our bodies for a time, a fading mark slipping into the afterlife bit by bit, day by day. If the perpetrator has a strong bond with the people they're killing, little pieces of their soul might imprint on their victims the same way they could an object. Possible, but unlikely.

I explain all this to the queen, stumbling at several points. She nods when I'm finished, then leans back. "Okay. If evidence is uncovered, I'll have the polesa call you in. Perhaps we'll even have you inspect one of the bodies. We need to stop these murders."

I squeeze my eyes shut. The urge to vomit is back, and though it's not unusual around others, it's worse today.

"Of course, Your Majesty—I mean, Celese." And because bile's rising in my throat with no signs of stopping, I ask, "Is that all, or may I be excused?"

I half expect her to demand another service of me. Surely she didn't ask me here simply to inquire if I could help with the murders, only to let it go so easily? Fortunately, though, a quick study of my pale face has her nodding. "Yes, you can go. I'll send a messenger if we need you."

The words have barely left her mouth before I'm scurrying away, a lizard escaping the eagle, but not fast enough. I'm a mere three steps from the door when my panic tips over the edge and I heave up everything inside my stomach. Ochre vomit screams against the azure tiles, and for a second all I can do is stare at it in disbelief.

Oh gods. I just vomited in front of the queen. It's not the first time my nerves made me sick, but I was *leaving*, almost through this.

"I—I'm so sorry." I face her, trembling. "I didn't mean to; it was an accident, I swear."

For her part the queen is also staring at my bile, but now she shakes her head and looks at me. "It's, um. It's fine. Would you like to visit the medical wing?"

I'm fairly certain there's nothing I'd enjoy less.

"N-no. It's fine. I'll be fine. I'd just like to go home now, if that's okay."

She's wringing her hands but crosses her arms when she catches me staring. "Yes, that's okay. I'll be in touch."

I practically dash to the door, already planning my route home. It'd be faster if I went straight through the Joyal—Sallenda's wealthiest district—but it's always loud and bustling. There are too many shops, bakeries, and once-empty temples now bursting with people terrified by the recent murders and seeking safety in their faith. If I cut south through Mugra, though . . . It's a district steeped in poverty, but it's quieter.

Still, all that requires me to actually get *out* of the palace. Not a difficult feat for most, but just like at the temples, people have clustered outside, hoping for a glimpse of their queen. Praying that Oro's descendant will save them from these murders. I'll need to find a back door. Someplace quieter . . . away from the crowd.

All this passes through my mind in a flash, and my hand's already on the doorknob when the queen punctures the silence.

"And, Jade?"

I wince but turn back to her. She looks almost apologetic, but that doesn't stop her next words.

"Don't forget. Sixty days."

CHAPTER TWO

LUKAS

I SHOULD ROB THE DEAD MAN. MY STOMACH GROWLS ITS AGREEment. If I'm lucky, what's in his pockets could feed my family for a week, maybe even two.

But as I look at the corpse, I can barely bring myself to move.

He's splayed across the dirt of the alley, clothes rumpled and neck twisted at an unnatural angle. His mouth is slack, his scream forever trapped in death, never to reach another soul. None of that is what startled me, though. Dead bodies aren't wholly unusual in this part of town. No, the real frightening aspect—the one that made me flinch—is his eyes.

Or lack thereof.

They've been gouged out completely—by what, I can't tell. The space where they should be is just two bloody, pulpy holes.

I silently thank god for my strong stomach, or I might've tossed my breakfast. I can't afford to lose any more sustenance. When I've collected myself, I bend over the man—not to steal his wallet, but to pull up the sleeve covering his right forearm.

The skin is smooth. Tanned.

Blank.

No snake twisting toward his elbow with two heads and four glittering eyes. Whoever he is, he wasn't a Serpensa. They prefer to investigate their own murders, especially with the queen's vendetta against them. Touching one of their bodies is a bad idea. But this man isn't marked, so they won't come knocking on my door if I report this.

Good.

I'm just about to call out for someone when I notice a spot of yellow peeking from the cotton of his sleeve. I lift it farther, stomach twisting at what I see there.

Thread stitched onto the man's arm in an odd zagging pattern, a tattoo of fiber instead of ink. I let his sleeve fall with a shake of my head, disgusted.

In this part of town, the mark can only be a fake; the real thing's far too costly. Thread speakers charge upward of ten thousand dineda for something like this, no matter how desperate you are for their help. The thought heats my cheeks with a familiar flash of anger, because I was once one of those people, pleading at the feet of a thread speaker.

Begging her to save my sister.

I'm sorry, she said, staring down at me as I kneeled on her porch, *but you can't afford it.* Then she slammed the door in my face.

I bite my tongue, shake the memory off, and wipe away the burning wetness of my eyes. Feet thud on the nearby street, a young boy passing the alley. I whistle at him. "Hey! Call the polesa. Someone's been murdered."

His eyes shift to the corpse. The fact that he doesn't appear rattled speaks volumes.

"Serpensa?"

I shake my head. "No."

"What's in it for me?"

I look at the body. I don't *want* to take his money. In Mérecal, the common religion—Devociónism—includes an entire pantheon with dozens of gods, whereas in my home country, Kabrück, most people follow the faith of Dreimann, which worships one triple god, divine in his trinity. Vastly different faiths, but they have their similarities. For instance, they both condemn stealing—which is unfortunate, because maybe then I wouldn't feel so bad about the thievery.

Then again, my faith hasn't been too strong in recent years. I sigh.

I'm being foolish, wasting money when my family's well-being is on the line. Five years ago I promised my father I'd care for them, and I intend to do just that. Even if, in the pitch black of night, I dream of faraway places and people. Of wind in my hair and coins in my pocket, of no responsibilities on my shoulders save for the ones I've placed there myself.

Selfish dreams for a selfish person, and I wave them aside as I riffle through the man's pockets. Soon I find what I'm looking for. His purse is faded black satin, filled with a few disappointing coins, no more than ten dineda. I hold it up for the boy to see. "If you fetch them, I'll give you half of what's in here."

The rest I'll take home. The sin can't be good for my soul, but so be it. I'll damn myself before I let my family starve. Honor's for the rich.

The boy looks at me, speculative. "How much is in there?"

"Does it matter?"

He studies me a moment longer, then shrugs. "I'll go get the polesa."

That's what I thought.

I wait for him to scamper off, then return my focus to the

dead man, those bloody tears. I trace the lines down his cheeks, find the reddish flecks on his tattered clothes, the brown dirt clotted beneath his fingernails. And then, strangely, the black shafting through his clenched fist. Curious, I pry his hand open.

It's filled with a clump of matted hair—except that's not right. The texture is a shade off, the feel a touch too oily, the consistency a bit too dense.

Not hair, but *fur*.

I flinch, then hurry to put everything back as I found it. Fur. That can't be correct—I must be mistaken.

Still, I've heard the whispers, an ever-present buzz. They claim there's a monster roaming the streets, indiscriminate in who it chooses, hungry for souls. That Mérecal's old gods have unleashed it upon us, punishment for the growing tide rushing away from Devociónism. For the rumbles of displeasure directed at the monarchy and the queen, the last of Oro's descendants.

Some people have even taken to killing dogs, fearful they're the beast the rumors speak of.

I never believed any of it, but staring at the man's empty sockets, I can't deny at least one part of it must be true.

A monster is loose in Mérecal, and anyone could be next.

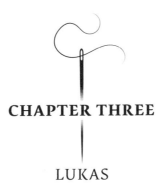

CHAPTER THREE

LUKAS

MOST BODIES HERE DON'T DRAW ATTENTION. OVERDOSES, REvenge, starvation—the people of this district have seen it all, and a stray corpse or two isn't cause for concern. When the nature of *this* body gets out, though, it's different. He's the fourteenth person in as many weeks to die with his eyes clawed out, and that's just in Sallenda alone. While the rest of Mérecal has seen its share of murders too, the killer must prefer it here. Most of the deaths have occurred in Sallenda, and a mixture of fear and disbelief clouds the air.

Whispers abound, spouting the most popular rumors. The killer is Vada, goddess of death, punishing us for our lack of faith. Or perhaps he's the Unseen Death, as the papers refer to him, a madman on a rampage. Those brave enough speculate it's gang activity, Serpensas on the loose.

I ignore all of it, making my way down the dirt streets, a zigzag through the dense cluster of squat adobe buildings and away from the dead man.

As promised, the boy fetched the polesa. Unfortunately, news of another victim brought the expected chaos with it. The narrow streets are now clotted with people straining to get *away*. All terrified the murderer still lingers, waiting for them. And maybe they're right. Perhaps the killer *is* waiting. The gods, gangsters, or simply someone dangerous on a rampage.

Their fear I can understand and respect, even if I'm in a rush. Their hostility, though, and the fact they're not moving, *that* boils my blood. My face heats as I struggle to push through the crowd, pinned between a mess of shoulders, chests, and necks craning to see the corpse.

Two different groups appear to be facing off: dissidents proudly displaying posters emblazoned with large black letters, demanding the end of the monarchy, and their religious counterparts, clergy, worshippers, and the like, desperately handing out pamphlets imploring citizens to return to Devociónism. Claiming it's the only way to stop the murders.

And all of them—every single one—blocking my way.

Great.

"Excuse me." I try to push past one of the religious members, a woman with graying hair and a pinched mouth. "I really need to get by."

"Are you sure you don't have a minute to discuss the gods?" And of course, without asking, she shoves a pamphlet into my chest. When I don't grab it, she frowns. "These murders, they're punishment for straying from the gods, the queen! You could be next!"

Fortunately or not, I'm saved from replying when a protestor, a burly man with a robust mustache, notices the interaction. "That's horseshit! Your precious queen can't save us—she's a menace to this country."

Privately I agree with the man. The queen *is* a menace. Mérecal isn't a true monarchy, with its council of nine elected officials—the

Regela—in charge of writing our laws, which the queen then approves or denies. Unfortunately, her role still affords her a lot of power. Enough to make her citizens, including my family, miserable.

It's why I'm in such a rush. By day, I'm employed on a fishing boat, but my earnings are no longer enough. If I don't find a second job today, my family will go hungry tonight. Perhaps they wouldn't have to if the queen had approved a minimum wage, but she refused. Because of her, there are no jobs, no assistance for the starving—not even proper healthcare. Six months ago she refused further trade with Valsarra after a perceived insult from their minister. Now Mérecal goes without all the necessary medication they provided us.

The woman doesn't acknowledge this, though, or perhaps she doesn't care. Her cheeks flush as she faces off with the protestor. "The queen is the last descendant of Oro—true royalty! To spurn her is to spurn your faith and invite Vada to your door."

Luckily, in her distraction, the woman's dropped her hand from my chest. I begin to slide away unnoticed, though not before the man spits out a fiery retort. "The queen is poison who should've died in that fire with her family. If only that killer had gotten her."

That gets the woman going. Her shrieks echo across the alley. Of course she claims the fire was nothing more than a tragedy, though most know better. The aftermath of the blaze smelled like turpentine, and no one else survived the inferno. An assassination, clearly, though the perpetrator was never caught.

And unfortunately, María-Celese survived.

Now, sixteen years later, Mérecal is a country divided. The murders have only added more fodder to the flames.

But that's not my problem, and I wiggle through the crowd, ignoring the pamphlets and posters shoved my way. Soon I'm back in the crush of frightened citizens rushing by, but I haven't made it far when I hear it. Not the fearful chatter, nor the gentle scuff of feet on dirt roads, but a keening wail that slices through it all. The ragged breath of someone in distress.

Don't worry about them, I instruct myself. *I've already been sidetracked enough today.* But when I turn the corner and see her, my feet move of their own accord. I can't help it—she looks so fragile. Arms curled around her legs, back pressed against an adobe wall, face streaked with tears. She reminds me so much of Adelina, the breath is knocked right out of me.

It's not the way she looks. Where Adelina was fair, this girl has eyes of glittering garnet, hair of raven silk. It's not even her size. Lina was only ten when she died, but this girl, though thin, must be near my eighteen years. I think it's something about the way she's sitting. The gasping pain, the trembling shoulders, the shattered defeat. Lina would get that way sometimes, especially near the end. And though everything inside me demands I focus on the family I have left, I see Lina in this girl. I can't turn away.

Before I know it, I'm kneeling in front of her. Slowly, so as not to startle her.

"It's okay." I keep my voice as low and soothing as I can. "Don't worry, it's okay. You're safe."

She doesn't appear to hear me. I resist the urge to tuck a lock of her hair back, then try again. "Just breathe," I tell her. "Breathe, you're safe."

JADE

My episodes are how I've always imagined drowning to be. It's perhaps why I'm so afraid of the water. I see the ocean and can think of nothing but how it must feel to be trapped beneath the obsidian waves, fighting toward the surface, unable to breathe.

Most days when the panic takes me, I come out of it cold. Trembling.

Alone.

But today I'm gently guided free by a voice, pulled to the surface, sputtering.

The first thing I notice is his eyes. Calm. Bronze-flecked. Green, the color of courage.

My gaze locks on his, and for a moment I simply let myself exist here, enveloped in a strange sense of safety—the first I've felt in months. The boy watches me, his lips twitched in a half smile. "I'm glad you're feeling a little better."

His voice is warm, the vowels rounded with the hint of an accent. Kabrückian?

"I—"

I'm not sure what to say, and I abruptly snap my mouth shut. Gods, I must look like a fool. I cut through Mugra thinking it would be quieter, but it was chaotic, people swarming around, gossiping about a body in the streets.

I tried using my thread tattoo—which grants stealth, speed, and agility—to escape, but I must have been too panicked. I don't even remember collapsing, and it's hitting me that this stranger saw me in my most vulnerable state. Normally I'd be embarrassed he witnessed me this way, but all I can manage is relief. This boy wants to help me; someone else might've taken advantage.

"Thank you," I finally cough out.

"You're welcome." His eyes, so earnest and beautiful, are still on mine. "You reminded me of someone I love. Someone I miss. It wasn't a problem at all."

Who? It's on the tip of my tongue before I swallow it. I barely know this boy—man? If I asked, he'd probably think me rude.

An awkward beat of silence passes before the boy offers me his hand. "Would you like me to walk you home?"

I'm about to say no when I look at him. *Really* look at him, and not just his features, though admittedly it's hard not to notice those. He's handsome with blond hair, fair skin, and cheekbones that could slice you open, and while he's not large or broad, his forearms tell me he's most likely covered in a layer of lean muscle.

But while his outer shell may be appealing, it's his soul that draws me in. Waves of rich, nurturing green embrace vines of burgundy, a love so intense it takes my breath away. Shimmers of violet intelligence flicker, while the kindness of coffee brown abounds. I witness the same courage of his eyes, flashes of crimson anger, charcoal strength, and silver health. Woven through all of it, though, are spikes of ebony sorrow, so deep and dark my own heart clenches at the pain his soul reveals.

It's beautiful—and *familiar,* almost as if I know his soul, have stitched his portrait. But that's ridiculous. I've never seen this boy in my life; I'd remember someone like him.

He clears his throat, and I realize I've been staring. "So would you like me to walk you home?"

I force myself to speak before I talk myself out of it. "Yes."

I can see it in his soul: This boy won't hurt me, and maybe this could even be . . . nice. I can't remember the last time I voluntarily spoke with anyone other than my mother, and the weather's perfect for a stroll. Granted, the weather's nearly always perfect in central Mérecal, never too hot like our southern province or a touch chilly like the northern one, but still. I can do this. I *can,* and warmth spreads through me as I clasp the boy's hand. For a moment he doesn't move, and I'm trapped in his eyes until he stands and gently pulls me up with him.

His hand lingers in mine, pleasantly callused, before he drops it and steps back. "Which way?"

I lead him back the direction I came. Silence stretches between us, and while it's not exactly comfortable, it's not pained either. He doesn't ask me why I was cowering, and I don't press on who I remind him of.

Together we wend our way through the city, until the streets are once again cobblestone and lined with palm trees. Their fronds flap in the salty ocean breeze, shading the shops below, no longer a rusty adobe but colored in a variety of pastels. A periwinkle storefront nearby boasts a medley of sugared treats in the window, and my mouth waters at the smell of shortbread, though my stomach quickly sours when I notice the stall next door. At it a man displays his wares, totems to Segira, goddess of safety. Some depict her likeness directly, while others display her symbol, a violet-eyed raven.

A few months ago his business likely wouldn't have attracted many customers, but today there's a line more than ten people deep, everyone desperate for any sense of safety they can latch onto.

My heart twists as I watch one of the customers select a Segira totem, along with a golden feather necklace stamped with the crown—a mark of Oro and the queen both. I hate that it's come to this, that people are relying on totems and trinkets for a false sense of security, but what can I do? This killer is out of my control, and I know the tang of fear better than most. A false sense of safety is better than terror, at least.

I shake my head free of the morbid thoughts as we approach the Eastern District's edge. My mother and I live a ways outside the city in a little cabin, in a location secret from everyone save for us, the queen, a few of her most trusted messengers, and the Regela. It's safer that way.

"Thank you." I turn on my heel in what I hope clearly signals I wish to stop. "For helping me. I can get home from here."

"Are you sure?" He glances over my shoulder. "We can't be far now. I don't mind taking you the rest of the way."

"Yes, quite— Oh!" A thought occurs to me. "Did you want me to pay you?"

The Eastern District isn't exactly the Joyal, but it's nice, and I'm walking with a boy from Mugra. He could probably use a few dineda, and I have more than I know what to do with.

"What? No!" His cheeks color, a delicious coral, the hue of affection. "That's not why I offered. I just wanted to help, that's all."

Now *I'm* blushing.

"I'm sorry. I didn't mean to offend you. I just— I thought . . . Well, you're from Mugra, and I'm from here, and you've been so kind, and I—" Oh *gods*. I'm making a fool of myself. "I'm sorry— just . . . Here. Please. Take it."

I shove my coin purse at him, desperate now. If he doesn't take this, I might combust. "Please. What you did today meant more than you know."

The boy studies my purse before his eyes lift to mine, and I abruptly drop my gaze. Still, I feel his on me, almost as heavy as his next words. "If I take the money, will that make you happy?"

"Yes."

My answer comes out breathless, and I tense at the gentle brushing of his fingers against mine before the purse is released from my grasp.

"Thank you." His voice is deep. Earnest.

I can't summon the willpower to respond, so I turn and scamper away. I haven't gotten far when the boy's voice rings out.

"Wait."

I pause, then slowly look over my shoulder, daring myself to meet those courageous eyes. They're so intent on mine, and I wonder if he's a thread speaker too, reading my soul just as I did his.

"I never got your name," he says.

I swallow. With my gift I can gather a person's deepest nature with a simple glance. What I can't do is discern emotions. Those are far more fleeting, and thus out of my grasp.

I've never been more frustrated by that fact as I meet the boy's gaze, summon a bravery I didn't know was there, and say, simply, "Jade."

"Jade." He rolls it around his tongue. Tastes it. "I like that."

Fire bursts through me, unwarranted but not unexpected.

"And yours?"

I don't know what's possessed me to speak like this, but I can't say I don't like it.

"Lukas," he answers after a moment, lips kicked up in a half smile.

"Lukas." I test his name just as he did mine, savoring it. "It was nice to meet you."

Then, the rest of my bravery spent, I turn around and march all the way home.

CHAPTER FOUR

LUKAS

I'M BARELY ONE STEP THROUGH THE DOOR BEFORE EMMA RIPS THE parcel from my hands.

"Excuse me, what is *that*?"

I shrug, sheepish, as she opens the paper bag and more of the heavenly smell slips out. A loaf of sweet bread and three shortbread cookies stare back at her. "I made a little more than I expected today and thought we all deserved a treat."

Which is technically true, even if I'm leaving Jade out. I think I stood there a full minute, watching her walk away, before I remembered myself and opened her coin purse. Then I stood there another minute, mutely staring at the contents.

There were over a hundred dineda in there. Enough to feed my family for the month at least. If I was a better person, I would've insisted she take it back. But the truth is I'm not a good person, I'm a desperate one. As those coins shimmered between my fingers, I couldn't shake the desire to return home victorious for once.

It's been months since we've eaten anything other than canned beans or corn cake; a few cookies are deserved. Or at least I thought so—Emma clearly disagrees. She frowns, light brown hair sliding across her cheek before she tucks it back.

"We can't afford this, Lukas. You know that."

She's not wrong. Three years my junior, Emma's been working just as hard as I have to put food on the table. We live in the heart of Mugra, where the houses are so close together, I can stand between two, stretch my arms, and brush both with the tips of my fingers. We're lucky to have a single bedroom, where Mom and Artur sleep at night, but our surroundings are a stark reminder of how little we have. Barren walls. Low ceiling. Dirt floors. The whole space is dim, lit by a single window, necessary now that we can't afford oil for our lamps.

Every day I look at what we have, what we *don't* have, and burn with a churning mixture of shame and nostalgia. Shame because I should be providing more than this. Nostalgia because things weren't always this way. Back when we lived across the Jimonne Ocean, in Kabrück, we were happy. Never had much but always enough, our stomachs full at the end of each day. There my father could support us on his lumberjack wages, bringing in the timber Kabrück is known for. An entire family comfortable on a single income.

That's no longer the case; it hasn't been since we immigrated to Mérecal. Emma's right. Of course we can't afford this. And yet . . .

I grab one of the cookies and wave it under her nose. "Come on, Em. You can't say you don't want it."

She doesn't take it, but she doesn't swat it away either. "I don't, if it means we won't have enough to eat the rest of the week."

"It doesn't." I reach into my pocket and hold up Jade's purse. "I came into some money today. We'll be fine." I jingle it for emphasis, the coins rattling inside.

Still, she doesn't take the cookie.

"Did you steal that?"

"No."

"Gamble for it?"

"With what money?"

She gives me a pointed look. "Then how did you get it?"

I flash her my most saccharine grin. "Would you believe me if I said I rescued a damsel in distress?"

Emma's returning look is flat. Then, "No."

"Fine." I shake the biscuit. "Just trust that I came into it honestly and eat your damn dessert."

"You're the worst." But despite her unkind words, she takes the cookie, breaks it in half, and offers me a section. "Because I know you didn't get one for yourself."

I take it, groaning when the sugar hits my tongue. It's been too long since my family's had sweets, and for a moment I wish it was a big slice of apple cake. Or perhaps gingerbread. Something that tasted of home. Even so, I'm still savoring it when the door flings open and Artur bursts in, followed by our mother.

He just about screeches when I hold up a cookie.

"Lukas! Give it to me!"

I'm tempted to make him jump for it. He's short still, only six years old, and while I'd love to mess with him, my resolve crumbles at the eager flush of his cheeks. He snatches the cookie the second it's within his reach, a mumbled thank-you passing his lips before he scurries off to the bedroom. My eyes water a bit, watching him. This kind of thing should be a weekly occurrence. It hurts that it's not.

My mother watches Artur go, her mask of sadness cracking before she turns her brown eyes my way.

"We could afford that?"

I nod. "Yes."

My mother doesn't bother with an interrogation. I don't think she's troubled herself with our finances in years—not since Lina died.

"Good." She shakes her head, looks around the room, anywhere but at me and Em. "I should go rest. It's been a long day."

"Wait." I pluck the final shortbread from the bag and offer it to her. "For you."

The moment becomes unbearably silent, and my heart stumbles as my mother simply stares at the cookie. But the second passes, and when she takes it, her eyes are wet. "Thank you, Lukas."

My throat aches. "You're welcome, Mom."

A moment later she slips behind her bedroom door. She spends most of her time in there, sleeping or staring at the walls. Missing Dad and Lina. Letting the world pass her by, because it's not one she wants to live in anymore, no longer complete. It can't be, not without them in it. So she isolates herself in her grief, because at least in her pain, a fragment of them remains. Letting go of it feels like letting go of them.

There's an ache in my chest as I watch her slide back into her personal abyss, and I'm almost grateful when Emma turns her signature glare on me a moment later. "Right. So, you might've come into money today, but what about a job? You know we need something long-term."

My day flashes through my mind. Visiting the tannery, the bank, the railway station, everywhere. I even tried the Western District, all the factories lined up in a row, smoke blotting the sky while coal dust clung to my boots. Cotton, matches, buttons. It didn't matter where I went, the answer was always a different version of the same thing: *We're not looking for anyone right now. You don't qualify for this position. I'm afraid you're not the best fit.*

No, in other words. Which is what I should tell Emma, but somehow that's not what comes out of my mouth. "Yes, actually. The tannery said I could come in afternoons once I'm done on the ship."

She scrutinizes me, her gaze narrowed and discerning. "Really?"

"Really."

Her brown eyes go even slimmer. "Because Benito Salgado applied there last week, and they told him they had nothing."

I'm not surprised. There aren't enough jobs; it's as simple as that. Not under the queen's rule, when she refuses to pass a minimum wage and everyone needs multiple incomes just to get by. The protestors are right. The queen, this monarchy . . . it's crushing us.

I shrug. "Maybe they just wanted to let him down easy."

Emma studies me a second longer, then sighs. Her next words are so quiet, I have to lean in to catch them. "You know, Lukas . . . you don't have to be perfect. He wasn't either."

He. I nearly flinch at the mention of our father. Emma and I have an unspoken understanding that we don't talk about him, not since our argument three years ago when she suggested his death might not have been natural. That perhaps he was involved in something that got him killed. She wasn't there when he died, though, didn't know him quite like I did. Our dad *never* would've done something to jeopardize his safety, not when we depended on him. He wouldn't have been so selfish.

My voice is edged in malice, a hint of warning there. "Maybe not, but he wasn't what you're insinuating either."

Emma shakes her head, but thankfully she lets the topic drift away. "Well, regardless, thank god you found something today. I was just beginning to worry you wouldn't."

I force a grin, hoping she can't see the tension in it. "Me too,"

I say, but what I'm really thinking is that now I need a job more than ever.

If the thought of Emma beating my ass isn't enough to get me out of bed in the dead of night, imagining Artur's gaunt, starved face definitely is. I could pretend I don't know what possessed me to lie to Emma, but there's no point fooling myself. It's the same reason I'm navigating Mugra's dirt streets at three in the morning.

If I don't find something soon, we'll be in trouble once the month is out. Jade's gift was a needed relief, but a temporary one. I've searched everywhere in the city, and nothing's available—which is why I'm no longer searching *in* the city.

I'm going to look under it.

Gradually my surroundings change as I reach Sallenda's Comerqueda District, a place of trade and merchants. The dirt streets become cobbled, the clay buildings replaced with limestone that glows in the moonlight. It's still a far cry from the Joyal but wealthy enough to have shops, paved streets, and—most important—sewers. You'd think all of Sallenda, as Mérecal's capital, would be this nice. If only.

The one constant between this district and Mugra is the flyers peppering the walls and alleyways. Everywhere I turn, there's a warning. *BEWARE,* most of them proclaim, a black dog with glowing red eyes beneath the dripping letters. Other posters urge citizens to repent or else risk their souls. Unsurprisingly, a handful of them have been covered by *Down with the Monarchy* handouts, decrying the queen's failure to protect her citizens.

I guess there's a lesson hidden in there, somewhere. Divided as we are, we share our fear.

All those posters, pamphlets, and warnings flutter in the breeze as I glance in every direction. I'm alone, and of course I am. The city streets were never so bare before, even at this hour, but people are terrified of the killer. I don't blame them. If I didn't need the money, I wouldn't be out here either.

But I do, so I lift the sewer grate, a wheezy creak filling the night. I tense, searching for threats anew. When none reveal themselves, I release my breath, then lower myself into Sallenda's true underbelly.

It reeks of sewage, salty brine, and the whiff of bad decisions. Rats skitter when my feet hit the ground, and the tang of sulfur slices the air when I strike a match. It's difficult not to wince at the use—we only have three left now—but I banish the thought as I carefully light the lumpy candle I brought along, then pocket the remaining matches.

The view it reveals isn't a pretty one. Long, dark tunnels, seemingly endless. Water creeping down the walls, dripping over sleek stone, framing a space bare of everything save for dirt and grime . . . I've entered the abyss. And, judging by the two-headed snake etched into the wall, Serpensa territory.

Perfect.

For a brief moment I'm struck by an image of Jade down here with me. Of all her pristine perfection and the way it misaligns with my current predicament. I'm overcome by a sudden, foolish desire to see her again before I shake it off.

I'm being ridiculous. I don't know her, will *never* know her or fit into her world.

No. This is where I belong.

My strides are purposeful, and I try to ignore the wetness in my shoes as I make my way through the maze, candle guttering. I've only been walking a few minutes when, to my relief, a hood is thrown over my head from behind, followed by a stiff arm around my throat. Musty air hits my skin when my sleeve is abruptly rolled back. Though my world has gone dark, I know what it reveals. A smooth forearm, absent of any Serpensa markings.

The arm at my throat tightens, and a voice follows. Low. Menacing. Definitely male. "What business do you have here?"

"I want to speak with Cora."

My assailant stills. "Do you have a death wish?"

It's a reasonable question. Cora Ramos is more vicious than the twin-headed snake tattooed on every Serpensa; her reputation is razored, and she's often referred to as the underqueen. Many believe she's more powerful than the actual queen, who's limited by the whims of the Regela. Some whispers even claim the Regela's been looking to unseat the queen, sick of her constantly blocking their proposed laws. Ones that would help people like me and my family.

But with Cora, there's no rule or group that can bind her. The more ridiculous rumors claim she's descended from Serpensa herself, Mérecal's old goddess of trickery, just as the queen is a descendant of Oro. Personally, I've always thought Cora's symbol was clever branding and nothing more. Other whispers claim she's only biding her time on a throne beneath the surface, preparing to take the one above.

And the newest rumors? Well, they claim Cora and her Serpensas are responsible for the killing spree. Motivated by what, no one's sure. The only certainty is Cora's vicious enough to do it.

I swallow, resisting the urge to fiddle with my sleeves. True or not, I have to tread carefully.

"No. Simply a wish to join your ranks."

Cora may be brutal, but it's common knowledge she takes good care of her people *and* their families.

The man barks a laugh. "A pretty boy like you? Cora'll eat you alive before she lets you in."

"Maybe." I straighten. "But all the same, I'd like to see her."

There's a pause in the air, the potential of a fresh inhale. I imagine the man shaking his head before he responds. "All right. It's been a slow night. I could use the entertainment."

I blink once the hood is ripped off, doing my best to discreetly study Cora's chambers. They're exactly how I would've pictured the dwelling of some underworld god.

By my estimate, my captor and I walked at least a mile, maybe two, and it's led us to some kind of underground chamber, a meeting of several tunnels. The room is spacious, misery cloaked in finery. Grimy walls peek out between lush tapestries. Crystal chandeliers dangle from cracked ceilings, glittering in the candlelight. Rich perfume lilies the air, masking the dank sewer smell, though not completely.

And at the center of it all, perched atop a throne forged of rusted knives, decommissioned pistols, and blackened iron, is Cora Ramos herself.

A queen in her own right.

Her smile is crooked, cunning, *powerful.* I shiver when she turns the full force of it on me.

"Manuel, *what* have you brought me?"

Manuel—my captor—steps back.

"Found him wandering around the tunnels. He asked to speak with you."

"Did he now?" Cora's smile turns up, and unbidden, the words *devious perfection* enter my mind. It's true, though. She's older than me, likely in her thirties, and gorgeous. A perfect clash of creamy skin, midnight hair, and lips of wicked red. Despite all that, it's her eyes I can't look away from. A cool hazel, almost gold, they glow in the low light and burn even brighter when they land on me.

"Come here. I wish to look at you."

I can't exactly say no. She's flanked by six Serpensas, not including Manuel. One step out of line and my last act will be feeding the snakes.

My heart hammers harder with each step I take, until I'm barely a foot away from her. This close, I can see the shimmer of blue in her dark hair, the flecks of green in her eyes, and, when I look down, her Serpensa tattoo. Like the others, it's twisted along her right forearm, only hers isn't made of simple ink.

It's stitched of thread so black it's like staring into a void.

And unlike the dead man's tattoo this morning, I have no doubt Cora's is real, laced with some unknown quality.

"Look at me." Her voice is low, almost hypnotizing, as her fingers lift my chin, featherlight, razor sharp.

I swallow, then meet her eyes. Cora smiles. "You risked your life coming here, which means whatever you want you must desire a great deal."

I think of Emma, Artur, Mom. Remember the way it felt to cradle Lina's body, the icy brush of her skin. I can't let the same thing happen to the people I have left.

"Yes." The word scrapes. "I do."

My breathing stutters when Cora drops her hand and leans closer, her lips hovering at my ear. "Tell me, then. What do you want?"

Emma would scoff to see me like this, more flustered than a schoolboy. I shake my head. By now Cora's leaned back, which is helpful, as I'm no longer enveloped by her lily perfume. "I'd like to join your crew. To be a Serpensa."

"Why?"

Everything else she's said has been airy—soft—but this word rings of steel.

"I need to provide for my family," I say simply. "And you're the only one hiring."

"I see." She circles me, her gaze lifting up and down, examining every inch. "I could put you in the Sweet House. You certainly have the features for it."

My gut clenches. The Sweet House is Mugra's seediest brothel. While I'd never judge anyone for working there, I'm not sure if I could stomach it.

"Do you have anything else available?"

Irritation flickers across Cora's face. "You came here asking for a job. I've offered you one. Are you saying you don't want it?"

"I—no. No. If that's all you have, I'll take it." Blood rushes to my cheeks, because I mean it too. "I was merely wondering if you have anything else. Something you're struggling to find someone for."

I swear my heart stops beating. Cora pauses. Stills. Looks at me, expression inscrutable. I can't tell if she intends to honor my request or slit my throat. Perhaps both.

Finally she breaks the silence. "There is one thing. You wouldn't be a Serpensa right away, but if you succeed, I'd bring you in afterward. Find you a good position, much better than the Sweet House."

Relief is a warm, heady feeling. "Yes, anything."

Cora studies me a second longer. "I assume you're familiar with the recent string of murders. That someone's clawing out eyes."

An image of the man from this morning flashes inside my skull.

"Yes."

"Wonderful." Cora's serpentine grin is back. "I need you to find whoever's responsible and bring them to me."

CHAPTER FIVE

JADE

A PRICK OF THE NEEDLE, AND BLOOD WELLS ON MY FINGERTIP, A brilliant ruby bead. One shade off passion, a few down from anger, and a far cry from the first blush of affection, it's not a color that represents any aspect of a soul. It is, however, necessary for my work. Because to strip someone of their basest qualities, I first need to stitch their soul portrait. A kaleidoscope of shapes and colors, uniquely them, laid out in thread. Not active, though, not yet.

Not until I bring it to life.

First, with a piece of them. A lock of hair. A drop of blood. A stray fingernail clipping. Anything will do, and once their essence is woven into the portrait, the last thing I add is a little piece of myself. It's those fragments of us that turn the portrait from mere thread into something *more*. Something magic.

From there it's a simple matter of unraveling the qualities in their soul I'm required to take—stored forevermore in the thread that contains it. A spool of beauty. A length of intelligence. A snare of passion. Removed from their soul just as you could pluck a tooth from their jaw, a piece of them no longer.

Hence why I'm sitting in my living room, dyeing thread with my blood. It's been six days since my disastrous visit with the queen, and I've felt each of them acutely. Only fifty-four left to find my mother before I'm chained to the throne and no longer have time. So far my new efforts have been spent in our attic, riffling through my mother's old documents, hoping to find a clue. And while I did come across a truly disturbing journal, it contained nothing helpful, which is why I've returned to my embroidery kit. I hoped the busywork would calm my mind enough to focus on other, more important things.

It hasn't.

My brain's still buzzing, even after I tuck the final thread into the metal case beside me. I look around the room, at the bright woven rug, coarse beneath my feet; at my mother's spectacles, left on her desk, wire frames collecting dust next to the sewing machine the queen sent us, unaware it's incompatible with our magic. Sunlight filters through the windows, reflecting on the glass of the embroidery portraits lining the walls, each stitched by my mother's hand, depicting friends and loved ones, their souls rainbowed around them. And on the mantel, her most prized totems.

Mavida, goddess of life, depicted as a pregnant woman. A small, bright sun for Solera, goddess of light and hope. And of course Oro's there too, a magnificent golden eagle.

Every night she prayed to them, always devout, a trait that never rubbed off on me. Still, there was comfort in it, listening to her evening prayers. Witnessing her belief.

My heart squeezes. My mother should be here.

This place . . . it's not home without her.

But she's gone, and now I'm left to pick up the pieces of her life, this job, one that I learned the toll of long ago. I was only twelve, after all, when my mother gifted me a lock of hair and insisted I stitch the portrait of the soul it contained. Still so clueless, padded in baby fat and innocence, when she gathered me and that portrait, walked us down to the docks, and pointed to the man it belonged to.

I recall the heaviness of her silver gaze, the first stirrings of my confusion when she looked at me.

To be a thread speaker is to bear the burden of responsibility. The price of pain. She pierced my palm with a needle then. *Use your blood. Bring his portrait to life. And when you're finished, remove his life thread.*

Kill him, in other words. An untraceable death.

I was only twelve.

A knock at the door jolts me from the memory. I freeze, wondering if I could've heard correctly, when the second knock occurs. Oh gods. Someone is *here.*

My fingers tremble as I unholster my pistol and point it forward. A knock at the door can mean one of three things.

One, the queen has sent a royal messenger.

Two, my mother has returned.

Or three, someone else has found me, and if that's the case, surely they don't mean well.

I need to be careful, especially if it's the third possibility, which is why my steps are whisper soft as I approach the door, pistol raised. Thank the gods I know how to use it. I've been trained extensively by the polesa captain in combat, self-defense, all of it. A favor to my mother and an effort to alleviate some of my fear after the courthouse incident left me strangled in it.

Now all that training might be what saves me.

I swallow. *Run,* everything inside me screams, *hide, wait for them to leave!*

Instead, I lift my shaking hand to the door, take a deep breath, fling it open, and—

It's *Lukas.*

I nearly put a bullet right between his eyes. My finger twitches, and I'm not sure if it's from the shock of seeing him or if that shock is what stays my hand. Perhaps both. I think we must stand there a solid ten seconds, staring at each other slack-jawed.

Lukas breaks the silence. "*Jade?* What are you doing here?"

"What am I doing here?" My tone lacks the bite of suspicion. I'm merely repeating his words as a chance to catch my breath.

"Yes." Lukas tilts his head and peers around the gun I've yet to lower. "I wasn't expecting you, and I'm wondering why you're here."

His tone is oddly practical, and that practicality somehow brings me back to the present. I blink at him but don't lower the pistol. For all I'm aware, he knew who I was that day in the streets. He could've deliberately tracked me down, followed me home, *watched* me.

My stomach lurches dangerously, and accusation lines my next words, a jagged edge. "I live here. What are *you* doing here? And how did you find my house?"

He shouldn't know where I live. A few odd passersby have stumbled upon our cabin over the years, but in those instances my mother unspooled their memories of that day.

He winces, like he knows I've caught him in a bad act. "I found it when I was young, exploring in the woods. I never told anyone, so my memory of it wasn't erased."

It's plausible, but it clarifies much too little, and I keep my pistol steady. "That still doesn't explain why you're here."

To my frustration, he ignores my question and looks past me, into the house. "Are you the maid? I wouldn't have thought she'd have one."

"I—" What?

"Jade." Lukas meets my eyes. "I know this visit is unexpected, but please, I need your help. Could you fetch the thread speaker for me?"

"I could shoot you."

I'm not sure why I say it, perhaps because someone needs to acknowledge the glaring fact. Lukas certainly hasn't, but now his eyes stray to the gun, then back to my face. "I'm aware."

"And that doesn't bother you?" My cheeks are hot, my mind spinning.

"I mean, yes, it does. Of course it does. But will you put the gun down if I ask?"

I mull his question over. "No." I still don't know if I can trust him, or why he's really here.

"I didn't think so. And are you planning on shooting me?"

I'm beginning to understand why his eyes are such a courageous viridian.

"No." The word comes out as a mix between a groan and a sigh. "Not unless you attack me."

"Good." He nods. "Because I wasn't planning on attacking anyone. I just want to talk with the thread speaker, that's all."

I could tell him she's not here. He'd probably leave peacefully if I did, considering he hasn't realized I'm also a thread speaker.

But eventually he'd come back. Either that or I'd have to erase his memories of this place, and the idea puts a bitter taste in my mouth. Removing memories is tricky business, with the potential for heartbreaking error, and despite the fact that his intrusion is unwelcome, I can still remember his voice the other day. *Don't worry, it's okay. You're safe. Breathe, you're safe.*

I don't know much about Lukas, but I do know this: He helped me when I was hurting, he has a good soul, and now he's in need of my aid. Turning him away would be easy, and if it were anyone else, that's exactly what I'd do.

But he's not anyone else, so while I don't drop my pistol, I do step aside. "You can sit on the couch."

"Thank you." He sounds genuine, and the wood floors groan as he slowly enters my home, then lowers himself onto the leather sofa. I take the rocking chair across from him and carefully rest the gun next to my leg. Still pointing at him so the message is clear.

I let him in, but I don't trust him fully.

"Okay then. What do you need from the thread speaker?"

I'm not sure what I'm playing at, acting like I'm not her, but Lukas answers right away.

"I need her help tracking down the killer taking people's eyes—the Unseen Death, as people have been calling him."

"You *what?*" I sputter. "Why?"

"The killer," Lukas explains again. "I need the thread speaker's help finding them. As for why, I promised Cora Ramos I would."

It takes me a moment to process his words, not because I don't understand them but because they're ludicrous. Lukas doesn't seem like the sort to report to Cora, and once I've caught my breath, I nod toward his arm. "Please lift up your sleeve."

He obeys, revealing clean skin, no tattoo.

Not a Serpensa, then. I'm not sure if I'm more or less confused. Lukas must read my expression, because he explains.

"I'm trying to become a Serpensa. It's not ideal, but I need to, or I won't be able to feed my family. If I can catch the killer, Cora will welcome me in."

My eyes linger on his soul, and I study all the colors pulsing there, especially the burgundy love. Given how intensely Lukas feels, I'm not surprised he'd go to such lengths to protect his family, but it strikes me as odd that Cora would want him to. Why task some random person with finding the killer? Surely she has more qualified members in her gang?

Lukas must read the confusion on my face, because he answers my unspoken question, self-consciously rubbing the back of his neck as he does.

"I know—I don't get it either, why she'd trust me with this. The only answer I can think of is that I'm desperate, and desperate people are willing to do things others aren't. I'd do anything to feed my family."

Perhaps. It's not as if either of us can pretend to understand Cora's motives, and I shake my head, no longer trying, my chest lightening as I do. Because Lukas said it himself. He's not desperate to become a Serpensa but to feed his family, and while catching a killer might be a tall order, money's easy.

"Forget Cora Ramos; I'll give you all the dineda you need. Then you won't have to worry about the killer."

It's Lukas's turn to look flabbergasted. "How? Surely the thread speaker doesn't pay you *that* much?"

I'm not sure if it's the pistol giving me confidence or perhaps something about Lukas himself, but my next words are uncharacteristically cocky. "No, actually, she doesn't pay me at all. I earn my money the same way she does." And in case it's not clear enough, I nudge the embroidery kit at my feet.

"I—you—what?"

Scarlet floods Lukas's cheeks, and I almost smile when I explain it as simply as I can.

"I'm a thread speaker too, Lukas. You came here looking for my mother, but perhaps I can help you instead."

CHAPTER SIX

LUKAS

I'M A STUPID, DESPERATE FOOL FOR GOING TO CORA RAMOS and expecting a fair deal, and doubly so for accepting said deal. Find the murderer who's been evading the polesa for months. I mean—god of three—I really thought I was cut out for this? I would've been better off at the Sweet House.

And now I'm a stupid, desperate fool thrice over. This time for seeking help from a thread speaker, then being too obtuse to realize Jade *is* a thread speaker. Perhaps I didn't want to believe it. She opened that door, gorgeous in her floral skirt and cotton blouse, and I couldn't reconcile the fact this beautiful girl is someone I revile.

And unfortunately, someone I need.

I've spent the past six days desperately trying to find clues. Staying up nights, patrolling the streets, hoping to come across another body. Lurking outside the polesa building, praying one of them will drop something about the case while I'm in earshot. I even asked citizens about the so-called monster wandering the streets. One woman described a large black creature she'd seen from her window, prowling about at night. The next morning a body had been found a few streets over, eyes gouged out and, according to the rumors, claw marks on its chest.

When I asked the woman what she thought she saw, her answer was simple.

Sero, the goddess of death's dog, sent to collect souls.

Frightening, certainly. A legitimate lead? I'm not sure.

Personally, at this point I'm inclined to believe what the papers speculate, that it's a madman. The Unseen Death, as they like to call him. *That* seems more plausible than a monster. And yet there have been no reports of a man lingering about the corpses.

What I do know is this: All my efforts have left me with no options and brought me here, to a house I shouldn't know how to find. One I discovered as a child. A secret well-kept until I returned three years ago, desperate to save Lina. The porch outside is where I begged Jade's mother to save Lina's life. Where I stood while, back in the city, Lina took her final breaths.

She was already cold when I returned.

I'm not sure why Jade's mother left my memories intact, but I do know what brought me back. Foolishness, definitely. Desperation, absolutely. But above all, hope that perhaps a thread speaker's skills—*Jade's* skills—can somehow solve this mystery.

I look into Jade's eyes now, and any warmth I might've had for her evaporates. Perhaps I'm not being fair. She's not her mother— I'm not even sure she knows about my encounter with her mom— but she's a thread speaker all the same, with too much power for her own good. That anger might be why I say what I do next.

"I can't take your dineda." My voice comes out cold, and I ignore the slight twinge inside me when Jade's face crumples.

"What? Why not?"

"Because it won't do any good. I made a deal with Cora Ramos, and I can't back out now. She'd kill me."

Which is true, but it's not why I'm heated. I could've told her kindly—she *did* just offer me money—but my ire is born of festering wounds.

My fingers twitch when Jade's eyes go misty. Ten minutes ago I would've been furious with myself for making her cry. Now I remind myself of all the tears I shed after Lina died.

"If you don't want money, I'm not sure I can help you."

Her voice wobbles, which only irritates me more. I'm the one with nothing, and she's crying?

"You mean you don't *want* to help me."

"No—I . . ." She chokes on her words.

You what? I hold myself back, though, giving her a second to compose herself. I came here for her help. Upsetting her isn't the best route to secure it.

"Jade?" I force my voice into something soft, and she releases a shaky breath.

"I mean it, that I want to help you—more than you realize probably. I just don't see how I can."

Her gaze is on her lap, her hair a silky curtain, blocking her face from view. I lean forward and dip my chin so I can study her features, even if she refuses to look at me.

"I'm not sure I understand," I say, my words carefully measured. She wraps her free arm around herself.

"I can do great things, terrible things, but I can't do everything." She meets my eyes, her own glassier than before. "I can't simply tell you who did this. If you brought me the killer, I could read their soul and look for a lack of certain traits, like compassion or empathy. If I had a murder weapon, I could maybe, *maybe,* match it to the guilty party if I saw them. And if I saw a body . . . it's unlikely, but if the victim was close with their assailant, it's possible that some of the murderer's soul would have imprinted on them, and that I could match it back. But those are all big ifs." She takes a deep, shuddering breath. "I wasn't lying earlier. I wish I could help you, Lukas—I really do, but I can't. I'm sorry. Truly."

She seems genuine, but of course she does. So did her mother when she apologized—right before she slammed the door in my face. To be honest, I was expecting much the same today, but as I'd run out of options, the visit seemed worth the effort. Now I'm not sure what's worse: her mother's cool lack of interest in helping me or Jade's inability to see how she can.

It's an effort to keep my voice level, all the anger from the past threatening to seep in.

"You can, though. Everything you just listed, those are all things that I can't do. Help me, please."

"How?" Her fingers twitch, jittery. "Do you have a murder weapon? A suspect?"

Of course I don't, and it's only then that it hits me. Perhaps the reason she seems genuine is because she's telling the truth. Maybe she really can't help me. I came here so desperate, I hadn't considered that even a thread speaker is limited in what they can do. God, if Jade could solve these murders, the polesa would've already secured her aid.

If I was simply doing this for myself, I'd let it go right about now. But I'm not here for myself, and who knows what Cora will do if I fail her. She's not the one gouging people's eyes out—why have me investigate if she was?—but she's still dangerous. Her retaliation might not be limited to me; she could hurt my family too. That more than anything is what makes me stay and face Jade.

"No," I admit, "but I could get a body."

If I found one the other day, I can find another now.

Jade blinks. "Where are you going to get a body?"

I shrug, false nonchalance. "Don't worry about that. It's my job. What I want to know is, if I find one, can you help me?"

She hesitates a long time. Bites her lower lip, which distracts me way more than it should. But her eyes are no longer glassy, and her voice is steady again. "Not unless the murderer was deeply involved with the victim. It would have to be a crime of intense passion, and these murders seem somewhat random."

She pauses, and I don't dare interrupt the silence that stretches.

"But maybe," she finally adds. "It's possible."

To most people, possible might be a small thing, but for me, it's my first bit of hope since I left Cora's chambers six days ago. Possible is beautiful, and wonderful, and exciting. For a moment I forget all my anger with Jade, because right now she's everything possible is and more.

"So you'll do it? You'll help me?"

"Well—I—I . . ."

I wait for her to say more, but she abruptly shuts her mouth and looks at her lap. Her free hand lifts to her throat and rubs a faint bump beneath the collar of her blouse—some kind of pendant most likely. When a minute passes in silence, I prod gently, careful not to startle her.

"Please? I'll do anything, I swear."

Jade's voice is so soft, I almost miss it.

"Anything?"

"Yes, anything. I promise, whatever you need, if it's in my power, I'll do it for you."

The words sting. I hate that I'm once again baring my throat to a thread speaker, but what choice do I have? I wait, tense as she continues to stroke that pendant, until she stills.

49

"Okay." She lifts her head, tucks a lock of that silky hair behind her ear, but still doesn't meet my eyes. "In fifty-four days I'll become the Crown's official thread speaker, which means I'll have to visit the palace monthly for appointments, and the courthouse weekly to collect punishments. I would like it very much if you could escort me to each."

I blink. "That's all you want?"

"Yes." Her voice squeaks. "That's all."

Warmth floods me. I expected her to ask for something difficult, impossible even. This, though, is easy. It might mean spending time with her, a thread speaker, but for my family, I can do it.

"Okay. Yes. Absolutely."

"Good. Good." She repeats it as if she can't believe it, then takes a deep breath and holds my gaze. "Fetch me when you find a body, and I'll examine it for you. In return, you'll escort me into the city when I have need, even if I don't find any evidence to help you." She stands, leaving the gun on the chair, approaches, and offers me her hand. "Do we have a deal?"

I eye her slender fingers, then grasp them firmly in my own. "We do."

CHAPTER SEVEN

JADE

I PULL MY WOOL COAT TIGHTER, PROTECTION FROM THE COOL ocean breeze as I follow Lukas through Mugra's streets, heart in my throat.

Terrified because he's leading me to a body.

Moonlight cascades from above, transforming our shadows into fearsome, spindly creatures, and I absently reach for the pendant beneath my shirt. It's quiet out here—*too* quiet—and while I don't have a proper frame of reference for what it's normally like at this hour, I can't imagine the roads are typically this bare.

It's unnervingly easy to imagine a killer, a monster, a madman lurking about, this Unseen Death we're all so terrified of, and I yelp when in the distance a shadow *moves*. A pool of oily black, slithering deeper into the darkness.

"Jade!" Lukas is there a second later, his hand at my elbow. There's not exactly warmth in his gaze, but concern laces his features. "What is it? Are you okay?"

I shake my head, staring at the road ahead of us, where, I

swear, just moments ago a shadow moved. But nothing's there now. Nothing abnormal at all, save for the posters flapping in the breeze, slathered on walls and pinned to doors.

Most of them declare *BEWARE* in large crimson letters, a shaggy black dog beneath with its teeth bared, eyes a heated vermillion. The rest contain a simple message:

PROTECT YOUR SOUL FROM THE BEAST! REPENT TODAY!

Atypical, yes. But they were already present when we arrived.

"It's nothing." I shake my head, trying to dispel the lingering fear, but it clings to me, coalesced in all my hollow places. "Just my imagination getting the best of me. Come on, we should keep going."

Accepting this job was foolish, and I've spent the past seven days spiraling between panic and determination. But the simple truth is I was out of options, had almost given up on finding my mother. Sitting there with Lukas, though, I realized that maybe this was my chance. Maybe I can get her back. I've always thought her disappearance could be connected to the murders, and if it is . . .

What if she knew something? Had figured it out somehow, but the killer got to her before she could reveal it? It would explain why she wanted me to pack—she needed to flee for her life and couldn't leave me behind.

It's a long shot, but it's my only one.

I can't afford to let it pass me by, not if I want to see my mom again, because if I fail . . . in forty-seven days I'll be confined to my mother's role as the royal thread speaker, with no time left to search for her, and it's not as if I can request an extension. Doing so would risk the queen's displeasure, which my mother warned me is dangerous. And even if she hadn't, it's common knowledge the queen can be . . . difficult when she doesn't get her way. Servants she commonly disposes of, but me?

I imagine she could make my life quite miserable.

At least this way, even if Lukas and I don't catch the killer, I'll have his help navigating the city when I step into my mother's role. And not only that, but if there's even a small chance my gifts *can* stop this killer, shouldn't I help? I don't know whether I could agree to more, but Lukas only requested that I view the body.

It's why when he asked for my assistance, I couldn't refuse. For my mother. For myself. For Mérecal.

Lukas is my only option.

Which is unfortunate, considering that option led me *here*. I've been so stressed, I've barely slept, and judging by the purple bruises beneath Lukas's eyes, he hasn't either. But whatever he's been doing, it's led him to a body. That was all he said at my door, and I've been quietly following him since.

Now he pauses, hand twitching at his side before he turns to me. "It's down there." He nods to a darkened alley.

My stomach twists. There's a corpse mere paces from where we stand. A real dead body. One that I'm going to examine. Gods, I could get into so much trouble. What if the queen discovers I did this without consulting her?

"Jade." Lukas's tone is soft, the same one he used the day we met. "It's okay. I'll be with you the whole time, and I won't let anything happen to you, I promise."

When I was thirteen, I stole a shot of tequila from my mother's liquor cabinet, and Lukas's words feel much the same. A wild, burning sensation, followed by a gradual warming.

I lift my head, look at Lukas, and anchor myself. A dead body can't hurt me—it's the living ones I'm afraid of.

"Let's go."

He studies my face a second longer before leading me into the alley. It's narrow, and I wince at the small space, the sensation of the walls closing in. There's a smear of graffiti on the adobe, dripping black letters proclaiming that a just god wouldn't punish us this way, but I can't help but think this is exactly that. A punishment. It certainly feels like one.

My breath comes in heavy little pants while my stomach roils, but I push on. *For my mother,* I remind myself. *This could help me save her.*

"It's right here." Lukas crouches near a dark lump, cloaked in shadow and covered in a patchy quilt. Only a hand protrudes from the fabric. Dirty nails and delicate fingers clutching, of all things, one of the *BEWARE* posters, those glowing eyes staring right at me.

I shiver. It's an ominous warning if there ever was one. But I've already come this far; there's no going back now, so I nod for Lukas to continue, then bite my lip as he slowly lifts the blanket.

When I see what's hidden beneath, I violently flinch backward, a scream caught in my throat. Bile rushes up, sudden and hot, and before I can stop myself, I'm retching all over the dirt streets.

"It's okay." Barely a blink and Lukas is there, crowding my vision, hiding the corpse from view. "It's okay, breathe. I know. It startled me too."

But it didn't, not in the same way. Because Lukas and I aren't reacting to the same things. He looked at the body, the *woman,* and saw cracked lips spread in a silent shriek. Matted hair clotted around her in a frenzied halo. And of course, bloody tears. Ruined eyes.

And all of that's horrible, terrifying, inhumane, but it's not what has my throat closing up, the first waves of an episode pounding through me. Because all of that I could handle. But not this. Never this.

"Lukas." I gasp his name right before the panic drags me under. "That body—it doesn't have a soul."

CHAPTER EIGHT

LUKAS

I DON'T WAIT AROUND FOR JADE'S REACTION TO GET WORSE. Bodies, souls—I don't know much about either, but it's clear they shouldn't be separated, even in death. Whatever befell this woman, I can't let it happen to me or Jade. I crouch so I'm at her level, as she's since slumped to the ground.

"Jade."

She whimpers, and my heart pinches. It's like that first day, the moment she reminded me of Lina.

I force myself to push those thoughts out. Jade and Lina aren't the same—far from it. Fear's the only link between them, but that's where the similarities end. Jade's a thread speaker, a woman nearly, and Lina never had the chance to be anything more than a girl.

"We need to get out of here. Can you walk?"

She doesn't look at me, her body trembling, racked with shivers. *Remember what her mother did to you,* I think, *how she turned you away.* But it's hard when Jade's like this, so vulnerable.

"I'm going to pick you up," I say carefully. Slowly. "I'm going to get us out of here."

I don't think she could respond if she wanted to. Her breathing's too fast, erratic even, and her eyes are squeezed shut, face caked in tears. Though I try to remain stoic, it's difficult when I slide my arms beneath her calves and cradle her to my chest. She softens against me, tucking her head into my neck. For a moment I can't breathe. The silky fall of her hair swishes over my knuckles, and I catch the faint aroma of roses on her skin. A foolish urge to protect her rises up, and even though I push it aside, my arms still curl tighter around her.

It's easier to get out of here that way.

"It's okay," I say softly, just as I did that first day. "It's okay, breathe. I won't let anything happen to you."

Even with our history, the unfortunate truth is that I need her.

We've lingered long enough, and I march us from that alley through Sallenda's silvered streets. At this hour they're largely empty, but Jade flinches as we pass through a crowd outside a white marble temple. It's all curved domes and sturdy pillars, dedicated to one of Mérecal's many gods—Celese, I think? Their moon goddess?

A few months ago I doubt it would've gathered this many worshippers, but with these murders everyone's out in droves— the only place they dare venture at night. People spill out the doors and down the steps, even to the foot of the temple, where several of its wealthier patrons have parked their coaches. On the surface the sight isn't particularly abnormal. Just citizens gathered to worship. But a closer inspection reveals the nervous looks cast over shoulders, guns holstered at hips, everyone clustered near the doors and in the light.

Terrified they'll be next.

Jade tucks her head into my shoulder as we pass, the rapid panting of her breath growing even more frantic. I pick up my pace, and soon we're at the city gates, though we still have another hour before we reach Jade's cabin. By now her trembling has dampened some, and I duck my head so the shell of her ear is near my lips. "Can you walk now, if I put you down?"

She nods mutely, and I carefully lower her to the street, backing away once I'm certain she won't fall. A few seconds slide by with Jade standing there like a newborn fawn. I hate that I'm tempted to scoop her back up.

She's pretty, and she smells good. I'm not so proud I can't admit I'm attracted to her, but any desire is purely physical. That's all it'll ever be.

"I'll walk you home," I tell her, since it doesn't seem like she's capable of speaking yet. "You can explain there, where it's safe."

The rest of our journey passes in silence. When we arrive at Jade's cabin, the sun is rising, gilding the jungle in dawn. Somehow the sight makes my limbs heavier, exhaustion settling in. Every morning since I met Jade, I've been up with the sun, out on the sea, fishing to feed my family. And every night has been spent walking Mugra's streets, hoping I'd be the first to find a body.

I'm no longer sure it was worth it, and dread brews in my gut as we enter her home. Because she still appears to be in shock, I guide Jade to the couch, then gently sit down next to her. The thread portraits on the walls seem to watch us, eerily lifelike. I repress a shiver.

A minute passes. Two. Five. Ten. I sense that I won't get anything from her if I press, and nearly thirty minutes pass before Jade clears her throat.

"That body didn't have a soul."

I wait a second. When she doesn't add anything, I say carefully, "I take it that's not normal."

"No." Jade meets my eyes. "It's not normal, at least for a body this fresh. It's . . . Our lives end. Our existence ends. But our souls? They're eternal. Even after we pass, their imprints linger on our remains, fading as our souls slip into the beyond. I'm not sure what you believe about death or the afterlife, but I'm guessing it hinges on having a soul. So to have it stolen like that . . ."

My gut clenches, clarity finally dawning. In my faith, when you die, your soul is judged by the triple god on the three characteristics he embodies: purity, strength, and wisdom. If you're found worthy on all counts, he welcomes you into Parliese, his afterlife paradise. Unworthy, and you descend, either to a middle realm or to Dunkolter, a place of eternal torture.

It's not too different in Mérecal. Here people believe that each god owns a domain within the afterlife, and that your soul enters the realm of the one you most align with.

Regardless, both religions have one key belief in common: You're not going anywhere without your soul.

My next words are barely above a whisper. "There would be nothing left. Death would be it. Permanently."

Jade nods. "There's only one punishment crueler than death, and that's to have your soul taken."

I get it now, Jade's reaction in the alley. If I'd known the danger we were in—*god.* Everyone in Mérecal's risking their soul just being here, and nobody knows it. I need to get my family out, tell people, do *something.*

Stop. Breathe. I follow my own advice. I can't do anything if I don't know what's reaping souls, and I try to hide my panic as I meet Jade's eyes. "How does someone even steal a soul?"

"No." Jade shakes her head. "Not some*one.* Some*thing.*"

Goose bumps prickle my skin. This wasn't at all what I'd pictured when I asked for her help.

"What kind of thing?"

We tip into silence. Somewhere in the house a clock ticks, the only sound.

"Jade?"

I need to know what's putting Sallenda—all of Mérecal, really—in danger.

"I'll be right back." Jade scurries up the stairs before I even have time to blink. She returns a minute later, a dusty volume in her arms, the pages worn and wrinkled.

"What's this?" My eyebrows rise as I study the book. Its cover is brown and faded, no title to be seen.

Jade sits back down and flips it open, revealing handwritten notes, the letters cramped and running together. And the *language*—it's Kabrückian.

"I found this in the attic not long ago," she explains. "It must've belonged to my mother, though the handwriting doesn't match hers, so I'm not sure who wrote it, or why she had it."

"And you actually read it? I mean—you were able to?"

My words contain a nip of surprise. I had no idea Jade spoke my language.

She nods. "My mother spent years in Kabrück, training under a thread speaker there. And this cabin . . . it can be stifling, sometimes, when you rarely leave it. So I asked her to teach me, another way to pass the time."

Her admission rocks me. We don't even speak Kabrückian much at home any longer, and I never have cause to use it anywhere else. It's rare here to find someone who speaks my language. Kabrück and Mérecal don't often mix. Not with an ocean between them.

The urge to speak with Jade in my native tongue rises, but I shake it off. We have more important things to focus on right now.

I scan the journal again, my eyes catching on the heading,

underlined for emphasis. *How to Create a Sievech*. My stomach sours, the little food I had earlier churning violently.

Whatever this is, it can't be good.

"So this sievech, it's related to that woman's missing soul?"

"It is." Jade pauses and takes a deep breath. "People think that as a thread speaker, I'm transferring qualities—beauty, charm, intelligence—but that's not true. What I'm really exchanging are pieces of souls that embody those qualities. And it stands to reason that if I can take a piece of someone's soul . . ."

"You can take the entirety of it too," I finish for her.

"Yes." Her voice is hoarse. "I can kill a man by unspooling his life thread or damn him by stripping away everything else." She taps the journal. "This details how to do exactly that."

My head is spinning, all the new information knotting inside it like a snarled clump of Jade's precious thread. "I don't understand. If a thread speaker did this, what does a sievech have to do with it? And what even *is* a sievech?"

Jade's fingers twist in her lap. "You see, it's— Well, what thread speakers can do is— It works like—"

I nearly place a comforting hand on her forearm before I remember who she is and stop myself. Still, I need this information, and I try to make my voice soothing. "It's okay. There's no rush—just breathe."

Her breathing gradually slows. This time when she explains, it goes much better. "Everything with a heart has a soul, which means anything with a heart can become a sievech—a monster with the ability to consume souls. To make one, a thread speaker simply has to strip every thread from a creature's soul *except* for the lifeline. Apparently, though, when you do this, the sievech isn't much of a threat, and will wander aimlessly until it dies, usually of dehydration."

I think of that woman's corpse, still splayed in the alley, eyes gouged out. Of all the bodies strewn across Sallenda the past few months.

"But this one isn't wandering aimlessly, is it?"

"No." Jade shakes her head. "This one isn't, because I believe it's bound."

My eyebrows lift. "Bound?"

"Yes." She flips through the journal, landing on a page halfway through before she offers it to me.

I grimace at the illustration there, a crude drawing of a thread tattoo. Beneath it there's a caption.

> *Binding the sievech requires stitching core pieces of the subject's soul onto your own skin, or that of whomever you wish to bind it to. Once bound, the sievech will be a puppet, subject to the whims of its master.*

"Sieveche can be tethered by the speaker who made them," Jade adds, then nods at my hip, where my father's gun is holstered. "Your pistol is deadly, but without you, it's just a hunk of metal. The sievech is similar. Just a weapon, controlled by whoever's wielding it."

Slowly the knot of confusion begins to unravel.

"And *that's* how the sievech relates. It's the weapon, created and bound by a thread speaker."

Jade's jaw is tight. Grim. "According to the journal, yes. Exactly."

Silence descends as I mull over everything Jade's shared, until one possibility becomes glaringly obvious.

"Do you think your *mother* did this?"

"No!" Fire kindles in her gaze. "My mother would never kill an innocent person, let alone create a sievech and order it to gouge out people's eyes!"

Jade's conviction speaks for itself, but that doesn't mean she's right. My blood heats. In the entire world there are maybe a dozen thread speakers. Maybe. And of those, only two live in Sallenda, or even near it. Unless Jade's an incredible actress, she's not guilty, but that doesn't mean her mother's innocent.

Suggesting that will only get me burned, though, so I latch onto a different piece of what she said.

"Sieveche don't always go for the eyes?"

She stares at me a second, then deflates. "No, or at least I don't think so. When sieveche are controlled and made to kill, they typically do so by consuming the soul, and that shouldn't leave a mark."

Well, *that* doesn't make any sense. "Why take the eyes, then?" Without their absence the deaths could be passed off as tragic but natural.

Jade shrugs. "Maybe the killer wants people to know it's murder?"

It's a plausible suggestion, especially if they want to stir up fear. Even so, it leaves unanswered questions.

"Probably," I agree. "Their method is pretty specific, though. I mean, they could be slicing throats or spilling guts, but instead they're taking eyes. It almost seems symbolic."

"What kind of symbol do you think— Oh my gods." Jade's mouth has dropped open. "Lukas, I think that's it."

"What's it?"

But I've barely gotten the words out before she's sprinting up the stairs again. She returns a minute later with yet another book, the pages yellowed with age. It thuds into her lap as she sits down. I have just enough time to read the title—*A Taxonomy of the Gods*—before she flips it open, dust wafting from the paper.

"What are you—"

"Just wait," she cuts me off, and I nearly startle. She's never this brusque, but I can see it now, the determined tilt to her chin. She's onto something, and I watch silently as she flips through the pages. Entries slide by, all with detailed illustrations rendered in ink. Strellita, their star goddess, followed by Ventoso, god of winds. Gods and goddesses for crops and beauty, destruction and love, anything and everything.

Eventually, her hands still, and she settles.

"Yes, *gods,* I think this explains it." She offers me the book, and my blood ices at the illustration contained within. The image is of a rainforest. One that might have been peaceful, if not for the corpses piled between the trees, each with their eyes gouged out. A woman stands at the center of the carnage, sleek and beautiful, accompanied by a snarling dog, its fangs tipped in blood.

The caption beneath it is simple.

Vada pictured with her dog, Sero.

When you live in Sallenda, it's impossible not to become familiar with their religion. They have hundreds of gods, and while I don't know all of them, I'm familiar with the core pantheon. Vada's an important part of it.

The goddess of death.

She's charged to rule the underworld, but legend claims that sometimes she'll become greedy and send her dog to the surface to reap souls. Unlike sieveche, though, Sero does this by consuming the eyes of his victims.

"Holy shit." The words gust out of me. "What do you think this means?"

Jade's quiet for a minute, her gaze sharp on the page. When she finally speaks, the words come slowly. "I think it means that our killer wants people to believe Vada's responsible. As to why . . ." Her eyes lift to mine. "My best guess is to cause a religious panic. It's no secret that worship has declined these past few decades, but ever since the murders started, the temples have been set to burst. People are scared."

She's right. And it's not just the temples, either. It's the people in the streets, heckling others to return to their faith. Handing out pamphlets and proclaiming only religion can save them. It's in all the whispers too, the ones claiming Vada's responsible for the killings, but the stories go further than that. All the way up to Oro, the king of their gods. People believe he's unhappy with them, and that's why he's letting Vada run rampant. I never lent the whispers any credence until now.

"So whoever's doing this . . . they must be some kind of religious leader benefitting from the influx of worshippers."

"That," Jade agrees, "or perhaps they're simply a true believer. Someone upset by the declining faith who's determined to set things right—by their standards, at least."

Her answer is solemn, and an uneasy quiet slinks in, all while my thoughts race. This killer doesn't need to steal souls. It's easy enough to make it look that way without actually damning people, and the fact they've gone to such lengths suggests some twisted need for punishment. Mérecal's in danger, and regardless of motive, we need to focus on what really matters: stopping this.

I clear my throat. "How do we kill it, then? The sievech, I mean."

"You can't." Jade's voice is flat. "It's bound to its master. You can temporarily disable it, but unless you kill whoever it's bound to, the sievech will heal in a matter of hours."

God, this is growing more convoluted by the second.

"So if I kill the master, I kill the sievech?"

Jade bites her lip. My eyes lower to her mouth before I mentally slap myself. *Purely physical,* I remind myself. *Confusing situation, nothing more.*

Fortunately, Jade seems oblivious to my inner turmoil, wincing as she likely goes through her own.

"Whatever it is, you can tell me." I lace my voice with the honey drip of earnestness. It does the trick.

"Yes and no," Jade explains. "If the master's killed, the sievech dies too. The only thing is, *you* can't murder the master." She pauses, fingers tapping her thighs. Though it kills me, I wait quietly. "Well—see—it's . . . How it works is—" She drops her gaze. "I'm sorry, it's just—this is difficult. I'm trying, I promise."

"I know," I say, because I believe her. And purely because I need this answer, I lift a hand, letting it hover over her own. When she doesn't flinch or move away, I lower my arm and wrap her fingers in mine.

Jade shudders.

"What I was trying to explain is that the master has to die a true death. When they bind themselves to the sievech, their soul begins to rot and change, and in turn, it changes them. You can't kill them with a bullet, or a knife, or even a sword, not permanently. You can incapacitate them for a time, but once they join with the sievech, they become close to immortal. The only way to properly stop them is with a needle." She pauses, her meaning sinking in. "*You* can't kill them, but *I* could unspool their lifeline."

Oh. *Oh.*

It suddenly makes sense why she couldn't get the words out. I squeeze her hand. Just a gentle pressure, a way to show I understand. "Will you help me?"

Jade's quiet for a long time. Waiting for her answer is agony, but this isn't a process I can interrupt. I'm asking her to risk not just her life but her soul. If she says no—*nope. I'm not going there.*

I nearly startle when she speaks again, voice soft. "You think my mother's the killer."

She's not wrong. After I found Jade here instead, I asked around. Apparently, Jade's mother hasn't been seen in months. The official story is she's taking a sabbatical, but it seems unlikely her break would begin shortly after the murders began. And if Jade really is primed to become the official thread speaker, that means her mother isn't coming back.

"You're right," I admit, "I do."

I expect my answer to spark her earlier fire, but it has the opposite effect. Her shoulders slump and she sighs.

"She isn't. You probably think I'm foolish, but I would've known if it was her. The rot in her soul would be obvious. Whoever the killer is, I haven't seen them, at least not recently." She blinks and shakes her head. "But that's not the point I'm trying to make. Because even if I couldn't spot the killer on sight, I'd still know she's not guilty."

You haven't seen your mother recently, I want to say, but I swallow the words. Jade's clearly building to a point, so I help her.

"And how would you know it's not her?"

Jade has a habit of looking down, away, even over my shoulder. Always a few shades off my eyes, nervous of holding my gaze. She holds it now, though, her own inflamed with passion.

"Because she's good, plain and simple. She'd never do something like this, and if she were here right now, she wouldn't hesitate to help you. Because that's how she is, *who* she is. My mother's the kind of person who would risk her soul to save others."

Then why did she let my sister die? Why keep that journal? The questions burn my tongue, but a far more important one takes precedence.

"And what about you? Are you that kind of person?"

She bites her lip so hard, blood rubies the surface, staining her teeth. The entire moment freezes—I don't think either of us breathes. The only movement is Jade's thumb, swishing over the fabric at her collarbone, against the pendant beneath it. Finally she shudders, her eyes locking on mine.

"Our first step will be luring a sievech to us. That should tell us who created it."

Stars burst in my vision as I let myself take a breath, hardly able to believe what I'm hearing.

"You'll do it, then? You'll help me?"

She wipes the blood that has since dripped onto her chin. A gesture that, given the circumstances, strikes me as oddly heroic.

"You asked me if I'm the kind of person who'd risk my soul to save others. The truth is I'm not." She takes a ragged breath, her hand nearly white now, she's clutching the pendant so tightly. Her fingers flex one more time before she releases her grip, steadying herself. "I think my mother would've liked me to be, though, so yes. For better or worse, I'll help you stop this killer."

CHAPTER NINE

JADE

"THIS WILL REALLY LURE IT IN?"

Lukas holds the thread portrait I stitched up to his face, as if the extra proximity can give him answers. He's seated on the ground, close enough that our legs nearly brush, and the jungle frames him, a riot of emerald leaves and fresh, earthy scents. We woke with the dawn and hiked to an even more remote part of the forest, far enough from Sallenda and my cabin that no one will be caught in the cross fire should our experiment go awry.

And it very well could.

It's a risk I can't believe I'm taking, but I meant what I told Lukas. My mother would've wanted me to be the kind of person who fights for others.

It's a bit shameful, really. I'm doing this for her. If I was a good person, I'd help Lukas simply because it's the right thing, because the people of Mérecal need me. I wouldn't require any extra push. But I'm too cowardly to be truly good, and so I'm helping for selfish reasons: to honor my mother.

Mérecal deserves better.

"Jade?" Lukas prods, and I realize I never answered his question. "It should bring the sievech right to us," I tell him, "if the journal is accurate."

"Hmm."

He frowns, and my stomach twists. Preparing this soul was a costly matter, in part because of thread speaking's cardinal rule: In order to give, first you must take. *Nothing* is free.

To heal sickness, I steal health. To bestow beauty, I must first make a crone. Happiness, intelligence, creativity—gifting them to one means thieving them from another. Nothing can be manufactured, produced, or freely given, and the true power of thread speaking isn't creation but redistribution.

Hence the costliness. I had to use thread already imbued with soul bits, all purchased from the royal stores. People assume that as a thread speaker, I own the traits I collect, but that couldn't be further from the truth. In reality, I'm merely a broker for the Crown. Harvesting bits of people's souls on collection days, turning them over to the palace officials, then stitching thread tattoos as requested when someone wealthy has purchased a quality from the stores. And if I want soul-imbued thread? I have to buy it just like everyone else.

Thousands of dineda went into this portrait, which I finished just minutes ago, a precaution against luring the sievech in earlier than intended.

The result is a kaleidoscope of color—lavender swaths of contentment, canary starbursts of charm, coffee-brown eddies of kindness. An entire rainbow of waves, spikes, smooth edges, and jagged points. Because really, there's only one thing a sievech truly wants.

A soul.

The fact that this one's untethered should make it more appealing to the beast, but for some reason Lukas is frowning at it.

I begin to sweat. "What's wrong?"

He twists it, as if that will allow him to see it more clearly. "Why'd you stitch it on leather? Wouldn't fabric be easier?"

It's an easy question to answer, and I tap the portrait's edge for emphasis. "It's a tenet of thread speaking. Portraits can only come alive when they're stitched on something that is or once was alive. Some fabrics can technically work, but most have been manipulated so much in the process of their creation that the magic is diluted. Leather works best, or sometimes a pliable tree bark if needed."

"Oh."

But he's still frowning, so I prod a bit further. "Is that all?"

"No. I don't know." He rubs his neck, nervous almost. "Is this really what a soul looks like?"

He's not the first to ask, and some of my nerves bleed away. "Were you expecting something different?"

"I don't know. I thought maybe it would be . . . shinier?"

My mouth twitches, a grin tugging the corners. My first in months. "You expected it to be shiny?"

"I don't know!" He lowers it, cheeks that delightful shade of coral I'm growing to enjoy. "To be honest, I'm not sure what I pictured."

When his eyes stray to the portrait again, I know what he's thinking. "And now you're wondering what yours looks like."

"Well . . . yeah."

He's oddly sheepish, his eyes downcast, fingers absently fiddling with the portrait. It's nice, seeing him this way. Something about his demeanor changed when he discovered I was a thread speaker, and while I didn't appreciate it, I also can't blame him. If Lukas harbors resentment toward us, he's far from the only one—I learned that lesson on the courthouse steps, and my chest tightens at the memory.

"Jade?" Lukas brings me back to the present. "You still there?"

I shift my eyes to his, then around him, to the subject of his question. By now souls are so commonplace for me that usually they fade into the background quickly, but it's hard not to focus on his. It's beautiful, and that odd sense of familiarity tugs at me again before I dismiss it. I've never stitched Lukas's soul; I'd remember if I had.

"I am," I finally answer. "And you should know your soul is lovely."

I don't mean it as a flirtation—far from it. His soul *is* lovely, but when his lips twitch, I can't hold myself back anymore. Because despite everything, with Lukas it's impossible not to smile.

LUKAS

God.

It's getting harder to hate Jade. When she says things like that, when she *smiles* at me, with the entirety of her face lit up?

She's absolutely radiant.

Stop it, I chide myself. *She's a thread speaker.* I need to remember what that means.

"Okay, well." I clear my throat. What do you say to someone who just complimented your soul? "We should get into position. We don't want to be caught unawares when the sievech arrives."

Jade's demeanor instantly shifts, her spine straightening, posture rigid. She stands, and it's an effort to keep my eyes firmly on her face. Because while she's usually dressed in all manner of loose, embroidered dresses, today she went with a button-up shirt, form-fitting slacks, and knee-high boots for our hike.

I swallow. "How should we position ourselves?"

Placing the thread portrait is easy work, and we leave it on the ground in a small clearing. Positioning ourselves, however, is more difficult. We're both armed with pistols, but somehow, with our souls at risk, a gun doesn't feel like sufficient protection.

I look around, searching for any kind of option, until my eyes alight on a tree with a couple of low-hanging branches.

"What if we climb that?" I point at it. "We'll have cover, we won't be in its line of sight, and if the sievech wants to reach us, it'll have to come up."

Jade pales, but she doesn't immediately reject the idea. "And if it can fly?"

God, it's becoming clearer with each passing second how poorly this plan was thought out. "Look, all we have to do is hit it," I say, attempting to project some confidence. "If it can fly, we'll just shoot it out of the sky."

I glance at the pistol holstered at Jade's hip. She knows how to use it, that much was obvious when she first pointed it at me, an image that has remained disturbingly present in my mind.

I'm fairly certain something's wrong with me.

"Okay." Jade lifts her eyes to mine as if finding something there. "Okay. We'll wait in the tree."

She doesn't sound confident, though, and a thin sheen of sweat glistens on her brow. Something's bothering her, and it's pretty obvious what.

"You don't know how to climb, do you?"

"No, it's not that." She shakes her head. "I reckon I can climb quite well, actually."

Her phrasing's a bit odd, but I decide not to comment on it.

"So then what's bothering you?"

She cranes her neck, taking in the length of the tree, before her gaze drops to her feet. "What if I fall?" She winces. "I'm sorry. I know I'm being a nuisance."

Is that how I've made her feel? A wave of shame rolls over me. The history between our families may be fraught, but Jade's out here risking her soul to keep people safe. The least I can do is hide my attitude about her.

"You're not being a nuisance," I tell her, "and you won't fall. I'll be here the entire time looking out for you. Okay?"

Her lip trembles, but she nods. "Okay."

Hauling myself up is simple. Jade, however, is a different story. It's not her skill that's the issue. She "reckoned" correctly. She's actually quite good at this, moving with a deftness that surprises me.

No, what's difficult is my unexpected rush of emotion every time she winds her fingers through mine. For a moment I wonder how things would be if she wasn't a thread speaker. If she was just a normal girl without wicked gifts.

If it hadn't been her mother who turned me away.

The truth is, I don't know her well enough to say. Would we have been friends, lovers, adversaries? I can't answer that, but I do know this: If Jade wasn't a thread speaker, and I wasn't some dirty boy from Mugra, I would *want* to get to know her better.

And somehow that makes holding her hand all the more painful. It burns more than the rough bark beneath my palms, more than my aching muscles as I pull myself onto that final branch, then reach to assist Jade. She doesn't need my help, but she still grasps my hand and allows me to lift her to the spot next to mine.

I must be imagining it, but I swear her fingers linger a touch longer than necessary before she lets go. But that's ridiculous. Impossible.

"Thank you," she whispers, blushing.

"You're welcome."

I scan her, searching for any scrapes or bruises, before I realize what I'm doing and stop myself. She's fine, and even if she wasn't, she can afford Sallenda's best doctors. God, she could stitch her own health if she wanted. I need to stop worrying about her and remember why we're here today.

Chastened, I shift my focus and unholster the pistol at my ankle. The mother-of-pearl inlay glows in the soft light filtering through the leaves, and I brush my fingers over the inlaid initials: *EK.*

"That's a beautiful weapon."

I almost flinch. For a moment I forgot Jade was here.

"Thank you." My throat is oddly tight. I try without success to swallow the knot that's formed there.

"EK?"

There's no reason to share this with Jade, and even if there was, this isn't the kind of memory I care to relive.

"It was my father's," I say simply. "Before he died."

I should've sold it a thousand times over by now too. God knows we could've used the money.

Jade must sense my reluctance, because she doesn't press further. She simply lays her hand over mine and whispers softly, "I'm sorry, Lukas."

My eyes burn, and I struggle to hold back the threatening tears. I'm not sure if it's Jade's tenderness that unwinds me or the memories surfacing of the day five years ago when my father gave me this gun. What it means.

If something happens to me, I need you to take care of the family, Lukas. You have to put them first.

He pressed it into my palm then, green eyes fervent. Just days earlier someone had blown up a statue of the queen, and looking back, I think he feared what the impending chaos might deliver.

Three days later he was dead.

Wetness beads on my chin, followed by a sudden softness brushing my hand. I look down to the silk kerchief pressed to my palm.

"Keep it." Jade's eyes are earnest, her voice unusually deep.

"Thank you." The words chafe, but the fabric is soothing on my damp cheeks. I'm not sure whether her kindness is welcome or not. In an effort to distract myself, I change the conversation. "How did you get so good at climbing? You seemed uncertain about yourself, but you didn't need my help."

Jade brushes the branch beneath us, almost like she's surprised too. "It's this thread tattoo I have. A few years ago there was a woman robbing mansions, and when she was caught, the judge ordered me to strip some of her traits. Stealth. Sure-footedness. Her ability to scale buildings. So I did, but instead of turning them over to the court, I purchased them for myself."

Of course she would have a thread tattoo—would feel entitled to that woman's traits. I can't believe I nearly thought her kind. My skin heats when she rolls up her sleeve and reveals the mark on her biceps, whorls of blue and green embroidered into her skin. Jade continues, oblivious to my irritation. "This is what helped me. I haven't used it to climb before, but it was pretty simple. I willed it to activate, and all those traits became mine."

"Oh, wow. How fortunate for you."

My words have a bite, one Jade doesn't miss. "You don't like that I have a thread tattoo?"

Of course I don't, I want to snap. *You took advantage of someone at their lowest.*

But we're about to face the sievech. I can't afford to rattle her.

"No. I just think we should wait in silence."

Jade flinches but doesn't argue, and we turn our attention to the clearing, where the soul portrait rests.

We have no idea how long it'll be before the sievech arrives. We don't know what it is, or where it was, except near Sallenda. It could be minutes, but it will most likely be hours.

So we sit in the tree, and we wait. Silent, so that when the creature arrives, it's not alerted to our presence. Midmorning shifts into early afternoon without any sight of it. With each minute that passes, the weight on my chest grows, a boulder of hopelessness crushing my lungs. I'm just beginning to wonder if we should take a break when the jungle goes frighteningly silent.

The birds stop their cawing. The monkeys quiet their shrieking. Even the bugs go mute, the ever-present hum of the rainforest abruptly cut off. Jade tenses beside me, and we study the clearing with a newfound energy, jolted by the snapping of twigs under a heavy tread. Sweat beads on my skin. I suck in a deep breath, an effort to calm my racing heart.

Relax. It'll be fine. All I have to do is shoot it.

But when the monster emerges from the underbrush, I'm not prepared in the least.

CHAPTER TEN

JADE

OH GODS.

The sievech is somehow exactly what I expected and so much worse at the same time.

It's the largest dog I've ever seen, with paws the size of saucers and legs nearly as long as mine. Black, matted fur clumps on its back, while yellow fangs drip saliva onto the jungle floor. What must have been kind dog eyes have since become inky pits, and the space around the sievech that should be filled with a soul is horribly, disconcertingly empty.

And while all of that's terrifying, it's the feel of the monster that has me in knots. I can only describe it as a *wrongness* permeating the air, like the smell of a corpse overtaking a field of poppies. My skin prickles, hundreds of imaginary ants skittering across it, and my stomach takes an abrupt turn. The little breakfast I managed threatens to reappear, and I clamp a hand over my mouth.

No. This can't be happening. I cannot retch violently in the presence of a ferocious, soul-eating monster.

I grip Lukas's arm, then jerk my head in the sievech's direction. He scans me with those viridian eyes before I bob my head again. *Shoot the damn thing.*

Fortunately, Lukas gets the message. He lifts his arm slowly. Silently. Aims his gun at the clearing, right where I left the potential soul, and my stomach lurches anew as the sievech gets closer . . . closer.

Closer.

I heave everything in my stomach the same moment Lukas pulls the trigger.

"Shit! Jade, are you okay?"

I can't see past the curtain of my hair.

"That depends. Did you hit it?"

"See for yourself."

I shift my gaze to the clearing, where the sievech lies, murky blood pooling near its throat. Its eyes are still wide, tongue lolling out, and for all intents and purposes, it appears dead.

It won't stay that way long, though. We have an hour before it wakes, maybe two, which Lukas well knows, because he brushes his hand across my arm. "You stay here. I want to be sure we got it."

I don't protest, and Lukas slips from the tree, underbrush swishing when he lands on the ground. His steps are careful, gun raised as he approaches the sievech, then nudges it with his foot.

In that moment, time slows.

The sievech twitches. My breath catches, heart stumbling. *Lukas!* I would warn him, if there was time.

But there's not.

The sievech lunges up, swipes Lukas with its giant claws, and tackles him to the ground. The gun goes off, a violent pop, but misses its mark. Soon the sievech smacks it from Lukas's hand.

It takes me a moment to process what's happening. That Lukas is on the ground, grappling with the sievech—that he'll lose his soul if I don't act soon.

The panic's here too, creeping up, bitter acid coating my tongue. I can already feel my breath coming in rapid pants, shivers rippling across my skin.

If I don't do something now, Lukas will die.

The thought isn't calming, but it sheds the splinter of clarity that I need, and I aim my pistol at the sievech.

If they'd only stay still—

But they won't. They're a tangle of writhing limbs and screeching howls.

"Jade! Shoot it! Hurry!"

There isn't time to think, and my biceps heats as my thread tattoo comes to life. I'm silent as I scramble down the tree, feet light on the branches. The jungle is filled with bramble, but my steps are quick, quiet, perfectly placed, and I don't make a sound as I creep behind the sievech.

I couldn't get a clear shot from the tree. Here, though, it's a simple matter of placing my gun to the beast's temple.

The pistol screams, the sievech jerks, and the world goes silent.

"Lukas!" I crouch to where he's sprawled on the ground, covered in hulking dog carcass. "Gods, Lukas! Are you okay?"

He stares at me, eyes glassy, not with death but with shock. "Jade?"

"Lukas." I almost sob. His soul is still there, hovering around him. "Hang on."

I throw my weight against the beast, grunting as it rolls off Lukas. The blood drains from my face at the sight it reveals. It's like a carmine flower has bloomed across the creamy linen of Lukas's shirt, while a gash slices from his left temple down his cheek.

My voice wobbles. "Lukas, I'm so sorry. I didn't— I don't . . . Gods."

"It's okay." He winces as he sits up. "It hurts, but they're just surface wounds. I should be fine. I just want to get out of here."

"Of course." I glance at the sievech. It's still—for now. "I only need a moment."

Lukas watches as I slip the knife from my boot and slice away a swatch of the sievech's fur, faint soul traces of the thread speaker who made it clinging to the strands. Once it's securely tucked away, I retrieve the portrait we used as bait, then stand and offer Lukas my hand.

"Come on, let's get you to my place. We need to clean out that wound first; then *I think* I know someone who can stitch you up."

The journey back home isn't an easy one. It's clear Lukas is in more pain than he's letting on, but he doesn't complain, and I usher him onto the couch the second we get through the door. Lukas hisses as he hits the cushion, while I rush upstairs to retrieve a small vial of opium tincture from my bedside drawer.

It's old, recommended by the apothecary after the courthouse assault ended with my arm broken, but it should still work.

"For the pain," I say simply when I offer up a spoonful of the medicine, and he swallows it without a word.

It's foolish, but my cheeks flush when I realize what needs to happen next, and they're only burning hotter once I fetch my thread kit, some towels, and a bottle of my mom's favorite tequila. I stand in the doorway a moment, procrastinating the inevitable. Lukas studies me, his gaze foggy beneath the medication.

And because social graces have never been my strong suit, I say, ridiculously, "You're wounded."

As if he doesn't already know.

"I am," Lukas agrees.

And because *he's* high on opium, he doesn't add anything else that will help.

Okay then.

"Please take off your shirt."

Lukas's lips spread into a wide, mischievous grin. "Psssh. You don't want that. I'm just a dirty boy from Mugra."

Why would he say that? Why would he *believe* it? I cross the room, sit beside him, and meet his eyes.

"I don't care about that. I just want to help you get better, and if you weren't loopy from the opium, you'd know that too."

My skin prickles when he holds my gaze.

Finally, he replies, "Jade, I only took the medicine minutes ago. There's no way it's kicked in yet."

Oh. I'm a fool.

"The blood loss, though," he concedes. "*That* might be making my brain a little funny."

So maybe less of a fool, then. Still, I suspect the blush in my cheeks is here to stay, and it's an effort to get my next words out. "It probably is, which is why I need you to take off your shirt." Then, when I realize I might've come across too pushy, I add, "Please."

The I've-lost-a-concerning-amount-of-blood grin is back. "You don't have to ask me twice."

"I literally just did."

I'm not sure where I got the confidence to speak like that, but wherever it springs from, Lukas seems to like it, because he giggles.

Actually giggles.

"Okay, okay. For you, I'll do it."

I forget how to breathe when Lukas unbuttons his shirt. Not in an awestruck, muted-by-his-beauty kind of way, more in an oh-gods-how-do-I-behave-around-someone-who-isn't-wearing-a-shirt? sort of fashion. I've never been near someone half naked before. Do the rules change? Will I offend him if I look too much? If I don't look enough?

In the end I stare firmly at the cushions behind Lukas, and somehow that also feels like the wrong call.

"Jade?"

"Yes?"

My voice is so small, I'm surprised he hears me.

"Did you want to stitch me up?"

A valid inquiry, considering I didn't bring him here just to stare at the couch.

"Correct. Wait—no. I mean, that doesn't answer your question." I take a deep breath and organize my thoughts. "Yes. I'm going to suture your wounds."

I cast a glance at Lukas, only to find a grin curving his lips, probably because I'm such a fool. To be honest, I can't blame him, and my cheeks heat as I dip my gaze to his chest, because this is medical, I *have* to look at him, and anything is better than studying his face right now. Unfortunately, this results in me once again being struck breathless—this time because of all the blood.

Three gashes cross his chest, from his pectorals down his ribs, and while they don't look deep, they've certainly bled a fair amount.

A wave of terror clogs my throat and sets my fingers shaking. *I can't do this. He's going to die. It's going to be all my fault. I—* No.

Lukas needs me. He put himself on the line for me today, and I'm not going to let him bleed out on my couch. *I can do this.*

83

I force my breathing to slow as I pick up a damp towel and blot away the sticky layer of blood. Lukas hisses but doesn't object when I clean his wounds with the tequila, then gently wipe him down with a fresh towel. Soon he's prepared, and when I can no longer delay the inevitable, I meet his eyes.

"This is going to hurt. Are you ready?"

He holds my gaze until my heart races, then nods. "Yes."

Okay. Okay, I can do this. It takes me only seconds to prep the needle and thread, and once they're set to go, I swallow the lump in my throat and face the first of his gashes. Jagged, but not deep. Frightening, but not deadly. And if there's one thing in this world I'm good at, it's sewing.

"Here I go." My fingers are gentle as I place them on Lukas's chest, warm to the touch. "Relax," I tell him. "It'll hurt less that way."

Then I push the needle through his skin.

He flinches, but my grip remains steady, and I begin the slow process of suturing him up. Tension radiates through him, and his heart pounds so violently, I can feel it through his chest. The pain medication either hasn't kicked in or wasn't strong enough, and horror leaks in, an icy rush when I realize I'm hurting him. In an effort to distract both of us, I do the one thing I can think of that might help.

I talk to him.

"Thank you." My voice cracks the silence, and I almost flinch, which is absurd, because how can a person surprise themselves?

"You're thanking me?"

My eyes are firm on my task, but I can somehow feel Lukas's gaze.

"I am. For checking on the sievech. If you hadn't . . ." I'm not sure what would've happened.

Lukas quiets for so long that I pause to look at him, only to find him staring at me.

"What is it?" I ask. Did I say something wrong? Did I offend him somehow? Was I looking at him too much?

"Nothing," Lukas eventually answers, and I can breathe again. "I was just thinking, you saved me."

"I . . . yes. I guess."

He's still staring at me, and I resume my task, if only to avoid meeting his eyes.

"You were in a tree," he continues, "and then you were on the ground, and you shot the sievech. You killed it—well. Kind of. You kind of killed it. Almost killed it?"

The opium must be kicking in, and some of my fear slips away. It's easier talking to him like this, when his pain is lessened and his memories are blurred, so that come morning this interaction won't be much more than a smudge across his mind. "I did."

"You did. Hmm." There's a slight thump as his head hits the cushions. "You used your tattoo. I was mad at that tattoo, but I guess I can forgive it now."

He says it nonchalantly, but I freeze. He was mad at me? I'd thought as much, but then everything happened . . .

"Why were you angry?"

He chuckles drunkenly, a sign the elixir has *definitely* kicked in. "Because it's not fair. People shouldn't—" He hiccups. "People shouldn't have to give up parts of their souls because you want them."

She didn't give it up because I wanted it, though, I long to point out. *She gave it up because she committed a crime.*

It's a common punishment, in Mérecal and elsewhere, when someone's attribute helps them commit their misconduct. Remove that quality—stealth from a thief, quick wit from a scammer—and the risk of recidivism goes down. And even the criminals who aren't court ordered to give up bits of their soul often do, as a way to pay off pieces of their sentence.

The thief knew the risks, the rules, and yet she still broke them. If anything caused the loss of her traits, it was her own choices.

Or at least that's what I'd like to believe, but is it truly accurate? Because if the goal was solely punishment, why turn around and sell the traits? And even if we didn't sell them, would that really make it fair? That kind of change alters someone irrevocably, often in unpredictable and damaging ways. If it didn't, I would've had my fear unspooled long ago. But stealing bits of someone's soul . . .

It's stealing pieces of *them*.

I shiver. For the first time, I wish I had more control over my thread speaking. I don't, though. In Mérecal, the Crown controls any thread speakers. And it's not as if I can simply *leave*. For one thing, it's forbidden by the queen, and even if it weren't, where would I go? Most countries require thread speakers to serve the ruling government, with the exception of Echia, where they practically worship us, and most estates in Kabrück, where we're afforded some freedom. Even so, getting to those places would be no simple matter, and if I were to be caught disobeying the queen?

The consequences wouldn't be deadly—I'm too valuable to her for that—but they'd certainly be frightening and painful. An existence of complete isolation, most likely, locked away in some barren cell, still forced to use my skills, but with the rest of my life stripped from me.

I have no choice but to use my skills a certain way, and even if I hadn't purchased my tattoo, someone else would've. For the first time, I'm truly sickened by my position, and the guilt rolls in, a nauseating tide. Maybe all those protestors are right. Maybe we do need to stop the queen and all these horrible laws she supports.

"You're right," I whisper. "I guess I just wanted to feel safe, and I thought this tattoo would help. I reasoned it was okay since the thief was court ordered to lose them, but I don't know. Maybe it wasn't."

Perhaps I should've simply purchased bravery from someone— but that doesn't feel much better. No one sells bits of their soul unless they're desperate, and desperation can't be a source of true consent.

I bite my lip, ashamed. This shouldn't be the first time I'm entertaining these notions. I've been so wrapped up in the fear my role brings, I didn't consider it, but I should've realized sooner—

"Jade." Lukas interrupts my thoughts, a welcome intervention. When he doesn't say anything else, I pause my work and force myself to meet his eyes, which are piercing. Clearer than they've been all night. "It's okay," he says. "You used it for good, and I think that matters. Thank you."

"But—"

"No. No buts." He gently lifts my hands off his chest and leans forward, our faces only inches apart now. "It's okay. *It's okay.* Just breathe, in through your nose, out through your mouth. Slowly."

It's only then that I realize how rapidly my chest is moving, and I take his advice, pulling in an unsteady breath. Gradually some calm returns, and I shake my head.

"Thank you."

"You're welcome." Lukas's face is still close to mine, and for a moment I consider what it would be like to kiss him. To lean forward and brush my lips to his. Sink my hands into his hair. I wonder what he would taste like, what he would *feel* like, or if—

Gods. Why am I thinking this? And what if he can see my thoughts on my face? I abruptly jerk back, look at the floor, and gesture to his chest. "I should finish."

For a second Lukas doesn't move. I can't see him, but I can feel his presence. The weight of his gaze, the heat of his skin, a fog in the air. Finally he leans back, a silent agreement. I return my hands to his chest, although now I'm having all sorts of inappropriate thoughts about what it would be like to touch him in a different way.

Curiosity, I tell myself. *It's just a natural wondering. Nothing more.*

"What's your favorite color?" Lukas's voice jars me from my thoughts.

"My favorite color?"

"Yes, you know." A vein of amusement tints his words. "The color you like most."

"I . . ." I'm about to ask him why he wants to know when it occurs to me: He's distracting me, just like I did him.

"Red," I respond. "A rich, dark red, like wine." And because something about Lukas makes me feel safe, and brave, I add, "It's the color of love in a soul. Of deep, enduring love."

What I don't add is there's quite a lot of it in his soul.

Lukas grins, and from there the conversation flows. It's the first time I've talked to someone like this in . . . ever. My mother's the only person I've been comfortable with before, and even with her, it's not the same. Something about this feels more . . . charged, and as the night goes on, I shed a few of my inhibitions. By the time the sky's an inky black spill, Lukas is fully stitched up, and an odd sense of calm has come over me, the first in months. It stays, too, after I tuck him in on the couch and slip into my bed, a smile on my lips.

Because everything is out of control. A mess. Terrible. But since I've met Lukas, I have hope that maybe, with some time, I can get back to my comfortable place.

CHAPTER ELEVEN

LUKAS

I THINK I'D BE IN LESS PAIN IF SOMEONE WERE GRINDING AN AX into my skull, and I moan as I begin to wake up. *What happened last night?* I roll over, eyes squeezed shut against the encroaching dawn, shove my face into the couch cushions, and promptly freeze.

The couch. I'm sleeping on a couch, not the pile of ragged blankets at home, and—

Oh.

Yesterday comes back to me in a rush. The jungle, the sievech, nearly dying.

And Jade. So much Jade. The way her hands felt, palms soft but fingers callused as I pulled her into the tree. Her face after she shot the sievech, bone white, but eyes on me. And of course, right here as she stitched me up. Her fingers brushing my skin. The way she talked to me so easily.

If I'm being honest, I liked it more than I should've, like *Jade* more than I should. I can no longer pretend she reminds me of Lina in any way. Perhaps they both have fear, but Jade is fierce, even if she doesn't know it. Beautiful in a way I'm sick of trying—and failing—to ignore. Even my anger with her is a losing battle, the final winter snow as it enters the spring thaw.

It's not that I've fallen for her. Not even close. It's the fact that, given time, I could—*maybe*—see myself falling for her.

And that's not an option.

I need to put as much distance between myself and Jade as possible and, when I do see her, as determined by our agreement, to keep things strictly professional. Because perhaps Jade isn't her mother, but letting this go any further than a passing fondness would be an insult to Lina's memory.

But before I can do any of that, I need to get what I came here for. With that in mind, I crack my eyes open, then promptly regret it. The sun isn't filtering through the windows so much as spearing through them. Perhaps if I didn't have a raging headache, the gold cast to the room would be pleasant. As it is, my temple gives an especially painful throb, but I force myself to sit up and look around.

The space is largely the same as the first time I was here, which is to say oddly normal. The portraits displayed on the walls still make me shiver—it just feels like they're *watching* me. But this time, instead of looking away, I study the art. Each piece is a masterful work of embroidery. While many detail ordinary images—flowers, parrots, nature scenes—surprisingly, it's the people who draw me in the most. Their faces are stitched in a minutia of detail, while fragmented rainbows hover around them, cast in all sorts of shades. I'm still studying them when the stairs creak a few minutes later.

"Is this really how you see people?" I can't keep the awe from my voice as I turn to face Jade, who's on the landing now, watching me.

Her gaze slides past me to the portrait I was studying, then promptly drops to her feet.

"It is. I know it's odd—"

"No." My stitches burn as I cross the room. Soon I'm standing mere inches from her, internally daring her to meet my eyes. "It's wonderful."

I didn't understand it fully yesterday—the soul she had stitched seemed so disjoined from a person—but now, seeing these portraits, everything has shifted.

I meant what I said. It *is* wonderful, but it's frightening too. Knowing she can see the truth of somebody like that, the truth of me. My impulse earlier was right. I need to get the clue from yesterday, then put distance between us. It's the only way to proceed.

"Thank you." Jade finally looks at me, dark eyes boring into mine. "How are you? How are your wounds?"

"Sore. Tender. But thanks to you, I'll live." She blushes, and my foolish heart skips a beat. Damn it. I try to move the conversation along. "And how are you feeling?"

"Me?" Her eyebrows bunch up, which is somehow, frustratingly, adorable.

"Yes, you." I nod toward her stomach. "You got sick yesterday, after the sievech showed up."

"Oh, that." She winces and looks away. "I've been thinking about it, actually. It happened with the corpse too, the one without a soul. At first I thought it was my anxiety, but I don't know. It's almost like the . . . the *wrongness* of the situation set me off somehow."

"But you feel better now?" I mentally slap myself for pushing. It shouldn't matter to me this much.

"I do."

An awkward silence falls, and I clear my throat. "So, yesterday. Were you able to get what you needed?"

She lifts her hand, and I notice she's holding a small swatch of cloth. She unfolds it, revealing what I now recognize as a soul stitched there, all manner of hues staring back at me. It's not as full as the one she left for the sievech, but it's something.

"I did. After you went to bed, I stitched the soul clinging to the fur I clipped yesterday. It belongs to the thread speaker who created the sievech."

Which is useful to exactly one person. Judging from Jade's tone, I already know the answer to my next question.

"Do you recognize it?"

"No." She shakes her head. "The only other thread speaker I know is my mother, and this doesn't match her. I have no idea who this belongs to."

A week ago I would've thought her a liar. Now, though, I believe Jade. Still, something about the soul tickles with familiarity, and I reach my hand out.

"Can I see that?"

Jade passes it wordlessly. I squint, taking in the colors she stitched. Caramel swirls, blue dots, jagged zags of red, and smooth lines of brown. I hold it closer to my face, then farther away, that tickle of familiarity growing to a rumble. I've *seen* this before— seen it recently.

"Lukas?" Jade's voice burns with curiosity. "What is it?"

I don't answer her but quietly lower the portrait and cross the room to a picture hanging just left of the couch. Like all the artwork here, it's not a creation of ink or paint but one of cotton. In it two figures stand, their arms slung around one another. The first I recognize. It's Jade's mother, Zamora, her lips pulled in a sly grin, eyes a stormy gray. The space around her is absent of a soul, as if she didn't want to stitch her own truth.

It's the man on her left I'm interested in, though. Hair of shimmery copper threads, blue eyes, and his soul resplendent around him. It's fuller than the one Jade stitched. More complete, as if her mother had a clearer picture, but still. It's all there. The caramel swirls, blue dots, jagged zags of red, and smooth lines of brown.

It *matches.*

"Oh," Jade breaths beside me. *"Oh."*

"I know." I swallow and step back from the portrait, though I can't take my eyes off it. "It looks like we found our suspect."

CHAPTER TWELVE

LUKAS

JOHANN SCHÄFER OF DREIDEN, KABRÜCK. FIVE WORDS. ONE name. Two clues. It was stitched at the bottom of the thread portrait with the soul match. At the very least, Johann created the sievech. At most, he's our killer.

After our discovery, Jade and I spent the rest of the morning searching her attic, looking for any additional information. When that yielded nothing, I went to the Registrar's Office and searched the public immigration records—still no clues.

What we found will have to be enough.

My heart thumps, the pounding of a drum as I lower myself into Sallenda's sewers. Moonlight cascades from above, a shaft of silver in the blackness, but it fades to a sliver, then nothing, as I replace the grate. A second later a match sparks to life—one from the full pack Jade gifted me. I light the greasy tallow candle I brought along and wait.

Just like last time, it's Manuel who finds me.

"You again?" He scratches his head when I come into view. "I thought we'd seen the last of you."

"Cora gave me a job," I say simply, "and I'm here to do it."

He blows air out his nose, clearly skeptical, but holds up a hood. "Come on, I'll take you to her."

If anyone could kill with a smile, it would be Cora Ramos. Something about it pierces me the second the hood is lifted, and my heart wobbles, unsteady.

"Lukas." That grin twitches, just a hair. "I didn't expect you back so soon."

Once again she's sitting on her underworld throne, flanked by six Serpensas. This time, though, there's a puddle of blood at her feet, a glint of gold inside it.

My stomach lurches when I realize what I'm staring at. It's a pin detailing a wreath of gold feathers surrounding two crossed swords. A symbol of the queen's guard, a branch of elite soldiers charged with protecting María-Celese.

"See something interesting?"

Cora's words are sharper than a blade, and I jerk my gaze back to hers.

"No. Absolutely nothing at all."

Whatever Cora's doing with queen's guards, it's none of my business.

She studies me a moment, her chin tilted. A gown of the deepest black clings to her, shimmering faintly in the light, as if it's made of scales instead of silk. A dark mimic of how I imagine the actual queen to look. I'm reminded again of all those rumors claiming Cora's after the throne. Perhaps more than rumors, if she's killing queen's guards.

"Good," she eventually says, curt. "Now tell me what brings you back."

I take a deep breath. Everything hinges on this moment. If what I have isn't enough—

I don't want to consider that possibility.

"Johann Schäfer," I say. "He's your murderer. The one gouging out people's eyes. The Unseen Death."

Or at least he likely is, but that won't be enough for Cora. Hopefully, this little stretch of the truth doesn't come back to bite me.

"Johann Schäfer." Cora rolls it around her tongue. Coming from her, it sounds like honey. Her gaze cuts to mine. "What do you know about him?"

Embarrassingly little, but I can't exactly admit that.

"He's from Dreiden, a small village in Kabrück." *And he's a thread speaker.*

I don't add that last part, though. It could lead to questions I can't answer without discussing Jade, and she doesn't want her name dragged into any Serpensa business.

"That's all?" Cora's eyes narrow, displeasure written in the firm line of her mouth.

"That, and he's the murderer."

A pathetic offering. I know it, and Cora does too.

"So you claim." Her words are barbed. "But you have no proof, know almost nothing about him. How are you sure he's the killer?"

Fortunately, I came prepared with a lie.

"Because I saw him," I say, watching her for any reaction. Of course she gives nothing away. "I've been staying out all night, patrolling the streets, hoping I'd be the first to find a body and the clues that came with it. I got lucky, though, and instead of finding a corpse, I witnessed a murder. The man looked Kabrückian, and all those immigration records are available to the public, so I went to the Registrar's Office and checked documents until I found his picture. Johann Schäfer. I don't know why he's doing this, but he's the one you want."

Cora looks at me so long that my skin goose-bumps. Finally she says, tone deceptively level, "You must've been very lucky to witness that, and without him seeing you too."

I swallow and force myself to meet her eyes. "I was."

A curtain of silence sweeps in. The air is thick with tension and disbelief, difficult to drag into my lungs. Cora doesn't believe me, that much is clear, but neither does she know what I'm hiding. Sweat drips down my neck. Still, I hold her gaze.

When she does speak, a chill ripples down my spine.

"Do you know what drives one person to kill another in such a horrid way?"

I've never been less certain how to answer a question. It must show, too, because Cora chuckles.

"I can see that you don't. Lucky boy. Let me tell you, then. There are two motives for killers like this." She lifts a finger, the start of her count. "One, pleasure. They're twisted. Sadistic. They enjoy watching the pain they cause. Or two, power." She raises another finger, and her gaze drops to her thread tattoo. She traces it before her eyes lift back to mine. "Securing more of it. Keeping what they have. Regardless, only a strong motive can bring about such strong actions."

My stomach turns. "What are you saying, exactly?"

Earlier, I thought Cora Ramos could kill with a smile, but a grin is far from her deadliest expression. Her eyes burn with intensity now, as if she can see right through me. For a second I understand why some people believe she's descended from the goddess Serpensa.

"I'm merely suggesting you consider whether your suspect meets either of these requirements. Your case, as it stands, is thin."

It occurs to me that Cora fits both those descriptions—not that I say so.

I bow my head. "Understood."

Cora's next words punch me harder than a bullet.

"Then you understand that we had a deal, and you haven't delivered your end. You swore to bring me the killer, but you've merely delivered his name. Do I need to remind you what happens to those who break their promises to me?"

I swallow and look down. I know what happens, and it's nothing good. "You don't. I remember."

"Good." Cora's steps echo as she stands and approaches me, until I can see the length of her shimmery black dress. Her hand comes up, and the image of her tattoo flashes across my vision before her fingers press into my chin. I wince as her nail pierces flesh, warm blood sliding down my neck. Her eyes spark at the sight. She watches it, then lifts her gaze back to mine. "Bring me Johann Schäfer, but be quick about it. Now that I have his name, you won't be the only one looking."

I fight a grimace when she rips her hand away, slicing me deeper in the process. The back of her dress is open, her shoulder blades shifting, twin sickles as she walks away and sits on her throne, one nail stained red.

There are so many things I want to say as I meet those golden eyes, but I value my life, which is why I hold her gaze and say simply, "Of course."

The hood is slipped back over my head. I'm nearly out of there when Cora calls to me. "And, Lukas?"

I pause, along with the Serpensa gripping my arm. I can't see Cora, but I can imagine the tilt of her chin. All that spiked poise.

"You better hope you're right, and that Johann is the killer."

I'm so fucked.

That's the only thought running through my mind as I retrieve my gun, stashed beneath some dead palm fronds in an alley a few streets away. A soft rain began while I was underground, and I absently wish I'd brought an umbrella. At least then I'd be dry. I shiver as several droplets soak into the cotton of my shirt, fill the streets with their fresh scent, and slide over the pearl inlays on my pistol. *EK.*

Egon Keller.

My father.

When he was around, things weren't always perfect, but they were good. Better. The finances may have been leaner than the math would suggest, especially when he got a second job working nights, but Emma was wrong when she suspected he was skimming funds for something nefarious. My dad would never do that, and though the accounts were slim, we never struggled like we do now.

I'd hoped to improve our circumstances tonight, but I failed. Because I may have lied earlier about witnessing a murder, but I told the truth about going to the Registrar's Office. The only problem was that there was no record of Johann Schäfer.

Most likely he's still in Kabrück. According to Jade, he can control the sievech from anywhere once it's bound to him, even from an ocean away.

So I can look all I want, but I won't find him, not in Sallenda. I'll have to travel to Kabrück.

My heart clenches at the thought, a wave of homesickness washing over me before I push it down. I can't leave my family, but I can't abandon this mission and risk Cora's retaliation either.

Hence, I'm fucked.

The roads of the Comerqueda District are hard, unforgiving beneath the worn soles of my boots as I make my way back home. Soon I'm splashing through the muddy puddles of Mugra. The breeze sweeps a soggy pamphlet past my ankles, another one of those *Down with the Monarchy* posters the dissidents like to hand out, runny ink detailing how we'd be better off without a queen. I stomp past it, through alleys swirling with fog, ghostly in the darkness. As I go, I get the strangest sensation, like I'm walking through an adobe graveyard. The houses are so small, squat, and pressed together, like a cluster of mausoleums, and the streets are quiet.

Too quiet.

Like in that jungle clearing when all the wildlife suddenly went silent. The only sound is the fluttering of paper, a *BEWARE* poster rippling in the breeze, the red-eyed dog staring back at me. Ominous. A warning, almost as if—

A strangled cry rips from my throat as the sievech hurtles at me, seemingly from nowhere. Hard ground punches my back. Starbursts flash in my vision, and then it's right there. At my face, inkblot eyes boring into mine. Hot breath washes over me, and it's like all the stars wink out at once. Fear pools inside me, because this time Jade isn't in a tree with a gun.

I'm alone.

The sievech growls, a hairsbreadth away now, and *speaks.* "You two thought you could catch me? *Fools.*"

If I could find any air, surely I'd be screaming. The voice is horrifying, high and jagged and *chilling.* The sievech actually chuckles as it lifts a single claw to my brow, poised to gouge out my eyes and steal my soul.

That realization rouses me more than anything. Icy cold

adrenaline floods my veins. The world turns hazy as I kick, scream, thrash, and bite.

And reach lower. To my waist, fingers closing around my pistol.

Hot blood dribbles down my face as the claw sinks in, reopening my cut—

Crack.

A bullet rips from my gun and tears into the sievech's abdomen. The creature shrieks once before I fire another round, and it slumps, as close to dead as it can be.

Get up! Run! Leave before it wakes up and finishes the job! my brain screams, but it's faint, like my head is plugged with wool. For a while I simply lie there, ears ringing, rain drizzling around me. The world feels distant, muted in color and quality. It's almost like I'm above myself looking down. Just a boy crushed by a monster.

Twice in two days. That's how many times I've almost lost my soul, and this time the sievech actually talked. What did it say? I try to filter through the haze, imagining the creature's eyes, the stench of its breath.

You two thought you could catch me? Fools.

Clarity slices through, painful and quick, but necessary. *You two.* The sievech wasn't just talking about me, and if it was able to track me down—

"Jade."

Her name is the shallow whisper of a cruel realization. One breath, and then I spring into action, wrestle the sievech off me, and sprint through Sallenda's streets.

Hoping I'm not too late.

CHAPTER THIRTEEN

JADE

MY FINGERS TREMBLE AS I ATTEMPT TO THREAD A NEEDLE FOR THE third time. It's dark, the sun long since set, my room cast in the warm glow of the oil lamp on my bedside table, revealing rumpled sheets from the hours I spent trying—and failing—to sleep. The wooden walls creak, rain pings on the windows, and the rosewater on my dresser florals the air. Peaceful, or at least it should be.

I give up my embroidery with a groan.

All I can think about is these murders, and I'm not the only one. The crinkled newspaper on my nightstand certainly has ideas, its top headline proclaiming in large, bolded letters: "The Unseen Death Strikes Again! Polesa Speculate the Killings Are the Actions of a Madman."

Even the smaller stories beneath it relate to the deaths. A woman who swears she overheard Cora Ramos and her Serpensas planning the most recent attack. Sightings of a large, dark beast prowling the streets at night—the sievech, certainly, though the reporters don't know that. And beneath those, an article I read with interest: "Pressures Rise for Regela to Resolve Tension with Queen as Murders Show No Signs of Stopping."

All of it, every story, related to these attacks, though none mention Johann Schäfer—the man involved in this mess.

Someone my mother knows, with whom she was friends, if that portrait is any evidence. The journal must've belonged to him, and my mother probably figured it out, and then . . . what? Did she confront him? Did he track her down and kill her? Or—as I'm hoping—capture her?

Only Johann knows, and I'm more determined than ever to solve this case.

I still have forty-four days left to find her, and Lukas is out securing Cora Ramos's aid right now. With her on our side, maybe I'll get my mother back before the queen's deadline passes and I no longer have time to save her. Maybe I'll have the chance to save others too—an opportunity to actually do some good with my skills and stop this killer.

The house creaks again, louder this time, as if echoing my fear. It reminds me of a similar evening ten years ago, my first night in this room following my adoption. I'd been ripped apart by a terrible episode, triggered by the whiny walls and unfamiliar house.

My mother sat with me until I calmed, then she disappeared, only to return with three shortbread cookies. She held me in her lap as I ate them, singing me a gentle song, and from then on, whenever I was scared or upset, she was there with some shortbread and her lullaby. It echoes inside my skull now, my eyes burning as I remember it.

From the meadows to the mountains, from the valleys
to the sea,
My love for you is endless, eclipses everything for me.

*As the sun glides cross the sky, and day fades into
     night,
You are always in my mind, shining, burning, bright.
And I wish that I could hold you, I wish that you were
     mine,
But should that never come to pass, I wish for you to
     find
Happiness for yourself, even if it's not with me,
A love that goes from meadows to mountains, from
     valleys to the sea.*

I swallow the aching pressure in my throat as I imagine her voice fading on the final note. I miss her so much it hurts, and another eddy of panic threatens to choke me before I stand abruptly, snatch the oil lamp, and then march from my room. My mother might not be here, but I still have shortbread. Resolved, I head down the stairs.

And promptly freeze.

There's a man in my living room. A golden feather glitters at his throat, a pendant meant to symbolize Oro, but nothing about him is holy. He's unfamiliar and tall, older than me—perhaps in his thirties. His hair is dark, his eyes are shadowed, and his soul's nefarious in a way that makes me quake. A cacophony of colors pulses about him, but only a few stand out. Spikes of vermillion cruelty, veins of minty greed, all of it anchored in frightening mounds of charcoal strength. Even the burgundy love has soured, intertwined with threads of chartreuse jealousy.

I'm petrified, unable to scream. The lamp in my hand flickers, and the light traces him, illuminating thin lips kicked up in a crooked grin. "Hello, Jade," he says. "I hear you've been doing some snooping."

"I—"

I can't breathe. It's like my blood has been replaced with bile, my bones with rubber, and—

Oh gods.

What if he's Johann's henchman?

Who are you? rumbles through my head, but my tongue is too heavy, and I can't get the words out. The man, undeterred by my silence, chuckles and lifts a gun I hadn't noticed. It clicks as he cocks it, the barrel black, menacing, and pointed right between my eyes.

I'm going to erupt out of my skin. The man, however, sounds perfectly calm. "Come without a fight, and you won't be harmed."

My self-defense training kicks in, and I'm reminded of my tutor's first lesson: Never, *ever* go to a secondary location with a predator. To avoid that, though, I'll have to lean on my second lesson.

Use the resources at your disposal.

I'm in my nightdress. No shoes, no armor, and certainly no weapons—my pistol and knife are upstairs, locked in my chest. I have nothing save for the lamp in my hand.

It will have to do.

Heart pounding, I duck, then fling the light at my attacker's feet. He howls and leaps back, but it's already too late. The flames are a hungry beast, freed and fattened on oil, and there's no stopping them. They crackle in delight and slither up the walls, but I don't pause to watch. I turn on my heel and sprint toward the front door, bare feet scraping the wool rug, and—

I crash to the floor, head banging into the armchair. My vision flashes and blood fills my mouth where I've bitten my tongue. The man is on me, all his hard edges pressed into my back. If it weren't for my training, the shock would have collapsed me. But through all the terror, one word blares at the forefront of my mind.

Fight.

I kick and scream, writhe and scrabble. The man hisses as he flips me over and sits on my chest, his weight stealing my breath even as my nails rake into him, drawing hot blood. A ripping fills the air when I tear his shirt wide open, and my fingertips snag on something—*thread.*

And then I see it. The tattoo stitched across his chest. Huge. Bear shaped. Enough colors to send my heart screaming. The man follows my gaze, sees what I do, and smiles. A horrendous sight, lit by the ravaging flames. "So you understand now, little dove."

I shriek, punch, and flail, but somehow he pins my arms to the floor. The air is oven hot, and though it's irrational, I briefly wonder if this was what the royal family felt when they died. If they screamed and writhed as they burned alive; if I'll succumb to the same fate.

Those thoughts scatter when the man leans over me and whispers, "Just accept it—you can't escape."

I turn my head, unable to meet his eyes, and that's when I see it. Beneath the armchair, a thick metal case, edges sharp.

My thread kit.

I'm smaller than this man, but he's lithe, not large, and I've been taught well. So when I buck my hips suddenly, then lift my legs and wrap them around his throat from behind, he's shocked. Surprised enough that his grip on my arms loosens.

It's all the chance I need.

My arm darts out, and I yank the thread kit away by the handle, then smash it right into my assailant's face. He howls and flinches backward, and I scurry out from beneath him, thread kit still in hand.

Cool rain soothes my heated skin as I sprint outside, fresh air a relief as my home collapses behind me, devoured by flames. But there's no time to cry now, no space for fear, and jungle underbrush smacks my calves as I rush through the forest. My thread tattoo heats when I will it to activate, lending me the gifts of speed and stealth. I'm going to need them after what I saw on that man's chest. The colors of his tattoo.

The periwinkle of heightened sight.

A mustard yellow for a sharp sense of smell.

Indigo for stealth, the silence of a midnight footfall.

Splices of blood-orange attentiveness.

And all of them swirled together and molded into the shape of a bear, melded for one purpose.

To create the perfect tracker.

Wherever I go, that man will find me. His skills are inhuman, grafted from animal souls, an uncommon practice but not an impossible one. From him there's no escape, there's simply moving faster.

But I can only go so fast for so long before I double over, stomach squeezing as I vomit up the remnants of my dinner. I need to rest, and my chest heaves as I pull myself behind a particularly thick trunk, shivering as the rain soaks my thin nightdress. The metal of the thread kit is cool to the touch, but that doesn't stop me from clutching it to myself.

Hoping. Waiting. Breathing.

Until I hear him.

Not the crush of his feet on the jungle floor, nor the swiping of plants across his legs. He's too good for that. No, what I hear is his voice, because he wants me to know he's here, hunting me.

"Come out, little dove," he croons. "You saw my tattoo, so you know hiding is futile."

And he's right. He *will* find me. I could probably climb this tree, but then what? I'd have to come down eventually. No, my only hope is surprise, to kill him before he can take me.

I shudder, bile rising up—I swallow it. I can't afford to have an episode now, and I refuse to let this play out the same way it did on those courthouse steps.

Fight.

It's all I can do.

"Come on, Jade." The tracker's voice cuts through the patter of rain. "Come out."

And I do.

The jungle's dark, lit only by the spires of moonlight that have managed to pierce the clouds and foliage. It's enough, though, to see the tracker. I lunge at him, screaming, all my fear and rage balled into that one sound. My thread tattoo lends me swiftness as I lift my kit and swing it right at the tracker's head—aiming to kill this time.

I don't get that far.

His vision is better than mine, his reflexes just as quick, and I yelp when his fingers circle my wrist. I lift my other hand to smack him, but he's there just as fast, clenching me in an iron grasp.

Dark eyes bore into mine, thin lips curved in that wicked grin. "Gotcha."

Then he squeezes, his grip bone crushing, until I'm forced to drop the thread kit. "Good." He kicks it away and lowers his head, his lips brushing my ear. "As much as I've enjoyed our games, my employer's waiting, so play nice now, or I can't promise you won't get hurt."

I whimper. I'm caught, and in the absence of action, an episode hits me full force. My chest is tight, I can't breathe, and nausea roils inside my gut. It's like I'm on those courthouse steps again, helpless, and I can do nothing but stand there, trembling, while the tracker removes a coil of twine from his side and binds my wrists. He's just finishing the knot when the crack of a twig slices the air, followed by the click of a gun.

"Let her go."

My heart leaps to my throat. *Lukas.*

When I turn my head, there he is, emerging from the darkened jungle. I can barely make out his eyes, but I swear the courage in them sparks.

"Lu—"

Swift as an eagle, the tracker wraps his arm around my throat and yanks me to him. The barrel of his gun follows soon after, cold and hard against my temple.

I swallow a whimper. Lukas clenches his jaw.

"I'm afraid I can't do that," the tracker says. "What I can do is abstain from shooting her—if you leave now."

Lukas's hand wavers, and his eyes flash to mine, searching for an answer.

For so long, I've lived my life paralyzed by fear of nearly everything. I've never been brave, because I've never really had to be.

I have to be now, though. Anything else risks capture, and my soul by extension, which is why I give an oh-so-slight shake of my head. *Don't give in,* it says.

Lukas gets the message, and a renewed certainty fills his voice. "I'm not going anywhere without Jade."

The gun presses harder into my skull. "Leave," the tracker warns. "I won't ask you again."

Lukas ignores him and comes even closer, gun never lowering. "Shoot her, and I promise, you're the next to fall. Let her go, and we can all leave here with our lives. What's it going to be?"

What pass next are the most petrifying moments of my life.

109

Rain smacking the jungle. Muzzle digging into my temple. My heart speeding faster than a monsoon river. The tension's so palpable, I could slice it open, then watch it bleed, but all I have eyes for is Lukas.

Save me, save me, please save me.

The moment shatters when the tracker speaks.

"No, because you see—"

I shriek when he shoves me at Lukas mid-sentence.

The next few seconds are chaos, a mash-up of the tracker sprinting away, me falling into Lukas while he shouts, then his arm circling my waist, pulling me behind him. He doesn't lower his gun, facing the direction the tracker fled, even as I heave, releasing nothing but bile and panic. Eventually my tremors cease, and when it becomes clear the tracker won't return, Lukas is there, his hands freeing me from the twine bonds, then lifting to my face, his eyes meeting mine. "Are you hurt?"

I numbly shake my head. I have all manner of scrapes and bumps, but nothing that won't heal.

"Can you tell me what happened?"

His voice is soft, and I think that's what breaks me. I crack open, a mess of tears and snot, but through it all, Lukas is patient. He carefully lowers us to the forest floor, pulls me to his chest, and rocks me gently. "Shhh," he whispers. "It's okay. It's okay. Just breathe. You can tell me whenever you're ready."

His words shake loose any control I had. Tears slide down my cheeks, my story and pain and anger spilling out of me like blood from a vein. It's only when I'm finished recounting everything that I realize he came here prepared, almost as if he knew I was in danger. I slide off his lap so I can get a better look at him, and for the first time I notice that the gash above his eye has reopened slightly, blood crusted in a steady drip pattern down his face.

"What happened?" Dread hollows my words, and Lukas's jaw clenches.

"I was attacked too. Near my home, by the sievech."

I gasp, and for once I'm too horrified to worry about how foolish I must look.

"Are you okay?"

It's his turn to share a story, and it rushes out, alarm pooling in my stomach as he finishes his tale, because one thing is clear.

We're being hunted.

The sievech is more sentient than we realized, and now we have a soul-stealing beast and a gifted tracker onto us. Or, in other words, there's no escape.

"What do we do?"

My voice is a hopeless mumble, and Lukas sucks in a tight breath. "I don't know," he admits. "I honestly have no idea."

For a while we simply sit there, the rain having cleared now, until the first rays of dawn sift through the foliage, a bounty of emerald washed in shades of pink. Around us, the birds chitter and chirp, rising with the sun.

A peaceful moment amid the chaos and, most likely, our last.

My house is in ashes, my life as I knew it in cinders. A killer is after me—is after Lukas too—and with what we know, it's doubtful Johann Schäfer will give up his pursuit anytime soon. Every day we don't stop him, we risk our souls more.

You are strong, capable, and wonderful. Don't ever forget it. My mother's words are a beautiful haunting I ache to believe. I'm not one for adventures, though. All I want is to return to my old life, in my cabin with her, the days slow but peaceful. Comfortable. But unless we do something about this threat, that will never happen. The polesa can't protect me. The queen can't shelter me. They could try, for a time, but there's no killing a sievech.

So I could stand down, give up, but then what? Lukas and I won't be safe. My mother will still be missing—captive to Johann, if my suspicions are correct. Sallenda's people will keep dying.

Fight.

It puts a knot in my stomach, but it's the only option, and I reach for my pendant. The reminder of everything I've been too afraid to do, and all the ways I've missed out because of it. It fills me with an odd wave of calm, and I'm strangely composed when I face Lukas and say, "We have to go to Dreiden, find Johann Schäfer, and bring him back." *And save my mother,* I don't add.

It's certainly a risk. Not only because we'll be hunting a dangerous, potentially soul-thieving killer, but also because of the queen's deadline. As of the sunrise, I have forty-three days before I need to present myself to her. Crossing the ocean will itself take eleven days by steamship in each direction, not to mention time allotted for inland travel.

It'll be tight, but we can make it if we leave today and encounter no issues.

"*What?*" Lukas reels back as if I've just suggested something repugnant, which I suppose I have.

"It's our only option," I explain. "You can't go home with that thing after you, and the tracker *will* find me again, and again, until he's successful. We need to end this."

I don't add that maybe—just maybe—Johann knows what happened to my mother. That perhaps he's holding her somewhere, hoping she'll aid his nefarious schemes, and this is my only way to get her back.

His shoulders slump. "But my family . . . I can't leave them, Jade. I *can't.*"

My heart snags, and my gaze drifts to his soul, to all that burgundy love.

"You have to," I say, my own voice shaking. "The sievech made a point to attack you specifically. If it comes after you again, your family could get caught in the cross fire. The only way to keep them safe is to stop the killer, and the only way to do that is to help me."

The words are bitter on my tongue. They feel like a manipulation, but they're true. Lukas must know it too, because he's quiet for a long time.

His shoulders are stiff, his gaze distant, but if he's searching for a scenario where we get to remain here, he comes up empty.

"Are you absolutely sure Schäfer's in Dreiden? That he isn't hiding somewhere in Sallenda?"

For once, the tightness in my chest isn't fear but a strange mixture of guilt and affection.

"No," I answer him honestly. "That's what the picture said, though, and it's our best bet. If he's here, chances are he'll catch us before we locate him. But if he's across an ocean, that gives us the opportunity to lose the tracker and the sievech before we find him, so I'm hoping he's there."

Not one to give up easily, Lukas offers another protest. "And you're sure Schäfer's the killer? We don't know anything about him, or why he'd do this. Maybe we're wrong."

"We could be," I admit, "but even if he's not, we need him. Either he is our murderer or he created the sievech for our murderer. Regardless, Schäfer's our next step."

A fact Lukas well knows, but I sense he needs the reminder. Because while I'm leaving nothing and no one behind, Lukas . . . he has his family to think of.

"I just—" His lip trembles, some of his earlier defeat leaking in. "I can't let them down again."

It's clear he's speaking about his family, and I grab his hand. His gaze darts to mine, sharpened by surprise, and for a moment

I simply meet it. I haven't known Lukas long, but I do know this: Lukas is *good*, plain and simple. Decent in a way most people will never be, so deep it's imprinted on the core of his soul.

I don't just believe it, I see it, which is why my next words are confident. "You could never let anyone down."

"Jade." His gaze is heavy before he looks away, pulls his hand from mine, and wipes his eyes. "You're wrong about that, but you're right about Schäfer. We need to find him."

My breath catches. "Does that mean you'll go to Dreiden with me?"

He's still hesitant, but some of that peels away as he shrugs. "You have to understand, I need to keep my family safe. They can't stay in that house while we're gone, not if the killer might know where I live."

He's right. Fortunately, this is a problem easily solved.

"My mother and I have a small apartment in the city, one we've kept secret from everyone, even the queen. There's a spare key in our safety-deposit box. If we fetch it, they can stay there."

My mother purchased the little one-bedroom unit years ago as a place to sleep on the nights her work kept her in the city late. I never really use it, preferring to remain far from most people, but now I'm thankful to have it.

That appears to calm Lukas some, and the tension around his mouth softens. "That would be perfect. Thank you."

We're silent for a moment, wreathed in early-morning bird-song, before I state what we're both thinking. "So that's it? We're doing this?"

Lukas blinks. Sighs. Faces me.

"Yes. Let's go find that son of a bitch."

PART TWO

CHAPTER FOURTEEN

LUKAS

I NEVER THOUGHT I'D FETCH TEA FOR A THREAD SPEAKER. I NEVER thought I'd care for one either, and yet here I am. Navigating the midnight halls of the *Plamara*, lantern in one hand and a steaming mug of ginger tea in the other.

It's been six days since we escaped Sallenda, and Jade's been sick for all of them. It's a bit ironic. We're on a steamship named after the goddess of happiness, love, and pleasure, but Jade's been nothing but miserable. She locked herself in our cabin that first day and hasn't left since.

I feel awful. About it. Everything.

If it wasn't for me, she wouldn't be in this mess. My guilt frightens me, not because it's wrong but because it's revealing. As much as I want to deny it, I feel this inextricable pull toward Jade despite what she is. *Who* she is.

Her mother let my sister die.

But Jade isn't her mother, and the more I get to know her, the harder it becomes to hold on to those familiar hates—like the day we left.

I was resolved in my decision to leave, despite the distress it would cause my family. This was the best way to keep them safe. I knew that, but still I worried. Not just about the sievech—about their finances too. But Jade thought of that. The day we left, she took us to the bank, where she ensured Emma would receive her apartment key and *half the funds in her account.* Not because I asked her. Not because I wouldn't come if she didn't. But because she knew they needed it.

It was that simple.

I left a letter for Emma explaining how to retrieve the funds, and sharing that I'd be gone for a time, though I didn't specify why or where. The less they know, the safer they are. It felt awful not saying goodbye, but I didn't want to risk luring the sievech to our door. And they'll be fine, or at least that's what I tell myself. Thanks to Jade, they may even be better off.

I owe Jade so much, but I don't know how to repay her, and right now this ginger tea is my best effort. Needless to say, I'm not welling with ideas, but hopefully this'll at least help Jade's constant seasickness. I knock gently when I reach our door, then open it.

Our cabin is tiny, though we're lucky to have it at all. Cargo steamships like this don't normally take on passengers, and with the murders, people are starting to flee town. But Jade and I got the last room, and I'm grateful for it, despite the fact it only holds a single narrow bed. Jade's splayed across it, one arm thrown over her eyes, the other across her belly. An oil lamp flickers nearby, hung from a gimbal to account for the ship's rocking, while waves silvered in moonlight sway outside the porthole.

I pause a moment on the threshold, stomach clamping with guilt, before I shut the door and lean against it. "Hi," I say quietly when Jade remains silent. "How are you feeling?"

It's a stupid question—she's clearly not well. Despite this, Jade lowers her arm, meets my eyes, and attempts to make me believe otherwise. "I'm okay."

She's so unconvincing, it borders on endearing, and a grin tugs at my mouth. "Liar."

It's the wrong thing to say. Immediately, Jade looks away, chewing her bottom lip. She sounds so damn guilty when she responds. "I'm sorry. I shouldn't have lied."

"Jade." Somewhere inside me a coil of affection is winding dangerously, foolishly tighter. "I was joking—it's *fine.*" When she doesn't seem convinced, I sit at the foot of the bed, then offer her the mug. "Here, I got it from the kitchens. Ginger tea. The cook says it'll help with your nausea."

I just hope it works. It's been a while since I've had anything with ginger. Mérecal doesn't grow much, and no doubt this was shipped in from Echia. It's kind of the crew to share it with us.

To my relief, Jade sits up and takes it, glancing at me from beneath her lashes. "Thank you."

"You're welcome."

That damn coil twists tighter as she takes a sip, her eyes widening a moment after she does. She looks at the tea like it's made from liquid gold instead of simple roots. I chuckle. "I assume it's working."

"Yes, *thank you.*" She sounds so grateful that my heart warms, akin to the way it does when I bring Artur a sugary treat or wrestle a smile from Emma.

Similar, yet different, and it's strange. I hate that I had to leave my family, but at the same time—I don't know. Setting off on this adventure with Jade feels like my first breath of freedom since my father died.

The stab of guilt is swift. I shouldn't be thinking like this. Jade distracts me from it, though, when she slurps down the rest of her tea, dregs and all. Her gaze flits to mine once she's finished, and her cheeks pinken in a way I like much more than I should.

When it becomes clear she isn't going to say anything, I break the silence. "I have more than tea," I offer. "Something else that'll make you feel better."

Jade's instantly suspicious, and her hand drifts to her chest, where a chain disappears beneath the collar of her shirt. "What is it?"

I offer her my hand, heart beating fast now, *hoping*. "Come with me and find out."

JADE

I've never seen this many stars. Galaxies burn in front of my eyes, filling me with wonder. So endless, and hopeful, and *beautiful*.

I hesitated when Lukas offered me his hand. I knew he wanted to get me out of that cabin and into fresh air. This entire journey he hasn't pushed me to leave our room once, as if he can sense what it means, but tonight's been different. It's not that he pressured me, simply that he asked.

Come with me and find out. And then, when he saw the longing in my gaze, and the fear: *I promise I won't let anything happen to you.*

I believed him. Do believe him.

Lukas and I are blessedly alone, and I inhale the briny ocean scent, drink in the crystal sky, and revel in the gentle slapping of waves against the metal of the ship's hull, the breeze tousling my hair. Steam trails behind us, funneling out of the *Plamara*'s smokestack, a pale cloud against a granite sky.

Peaceful.

Six days we've been aboard this ship, and I've spent all of them cooped up in a muggy room, all because I was too terrified to leave.

Because of the water, partially, but also because of the tracker and what happens when he inevitably finds us.

If Lukas hadn't pushed me, I would've spent the remaining time there too. The thought fills me with a familiar tug of emotion, and it threatens to pull me under before Lukas breaks the silence.

"What does it mean?"

"What does what mean?" I look at him, bewildered, until he gestures at the hand I've unknowingly brought to my chest, placed over my pendant.

"Your necklace. You're always touching it, and I wondered why."

"I—"

Nerves explode inside me. It's not like I'm confessing some horrible sin, but somehow this feels just as personal, and a memory of that day flashes to my mind. The giggling of children. The sun shining down, burning my bare neck. The tickle of grass against my ankles, and of course a strip of aqua-blue ocean in the distance, beautiful but out of reach.

"It's okay." Lukas is quick to soothe me when he notices my hesitation. "You don't have to share if you don't want to."

And it's those words—the understanding, the lack of pressure—that convince me.

Slowly, I remove the pendant from beneath my shirt, a purple seashell polished to shine, spiraling toward the center.

"My mother hasn't always been my mother," I begin. "I was left at an orphanage as an infant, probably by my parents. The first seven years of my life were spent there. Sometimes I'd get sent home with a family, but it never worked out; they never wanted me, I guess."

What I don't add is that I was always too scared. Too boring. Too timid. When I wasn't the fun, vivacious daughter they'd hoped for, they brought me back. As a babe I was colicky, and as a child I was . . .

I don't know what I was, but I certainly wasn't desirable.

"A few times a year," I continue, "the sisters who ran the home would take everyone on field trips. Usually I'd stay back, too nervous to attend, but one day they announced the next trip would be to the ocean, and I wanted to go. Something about it mesmerized me. So when it came time to leave, I went."

I swallow. I don't know what it is about this day, this memory, that refuses to unglue from my brain. It's become such a pained shard of me, and I briefly wonder if it's ingrained in my soul, barbs of ebony sorrow coiled in veins of sour yellow fear. I'm not sure—thread speakers can't see their own souls, and to be honest, I've never wanted to see mine. I don't think I'd like what it reveals.

Regardless, this memory is a part of me, and Lukas might not realize it, but letting him witness this means something.

"It was a hot day," I remember aloud. "A dozen of us crammed into a cart, the rest of the kids chattering while I squeezed myself into a corner. But I was excited—I was going to see the *ocean*. And then we pulled up, and . . ."

My throat squeezes at the memory. *Panic.* It struck like lightning, filled my veins with acid, set my heart scrambling. The other kids shrieked in delight, while I drowned in my own fear.

What if there are sharks in the water?

What if a wave sweeps me out to sea?

What if they forget me here, and I'm lost?

What if . . .

What if . . . ?

WHAT IF?

"I couldn't do it," I say simply. "Couldn't make myself go out into the water, something I'd been looking forward to for weeks. I stayed back and watched while the other kids had fun. There was another girl, Gloria, who returned with this shell." I lift it higher for emphasis. "And she was so proud of it. Showing it off to everyone the entire way home, sleeping with it under her pillow, and I just got—I don't know—I was jealous. Every day I'd sneak into our room while the other kids played, open her chest, and hold it. I wanted it to be mine."

I wait for Lukas's judgment. *So you stole it,* I imagine him saying, *from that poor orphan girl.*

But there's no judgment in his gaze, only warmth, compassion almost.

"You wanted what she had," he murmurs, and tears spring to my eyes because he understands. I didn't want the shell but all of it, everything Gloria had that I didn't. A life lived without the taint of these poison thoughts. To be brave, and happy, and lovable.

"So badly," I whisper, words burning.

When I couldn't take any of that, I stole the shell instead.

I don't have to share the rest. How the day my mother adopted me, I packed all my belongings, then went straight to Gloria's chest and plucked the shell from the top. That I've kept it on my person ever since, a reminder of everything I'll never have because I'm too afraid to take it.

I don't have to share, because Lukas already knows. I can't say how I'm certain of that, only that I am. He understands.

The silence holds, spreads, and though my eyes are glued to my leather boots, I can feel Lukas studying me. I'm attuned to his every breath, enraptured with the weight of his presence, so I don't miss it when he moves, so soft and gentle, his hands cradling my cheeks, thumbs swiping away my tears. He doesn't say anything, simply lifts my gaze to his and holds it, his expression free of disappointment or disgust. *I see you,* he almost seems to say, and that's perhaps why I do what I do next.

Before I can think better of it, I wrap Lukas in a firm hug, placing my face on his chest. He grunts a bit, clearly surprised, but his arms follow a second later.

"Thank you," I mumble into his shirt. *For seeing me,* I want to add, but that feels too personal, which is why I say instead, "For everything."

He chuckles. "Thank me? Thank *you.* I'll never be able to repay everything you've done for me."

You already have.

I almost say it but hold back. I don't want to scare him away, not when he's the only friend I've had in, well, *ever.* It's tempting to stay locked in his embrace, to feel the beat of his heart, but I've already held on too long.

My wrist brushes against the holster of his gun as I pull away, and I nod to it, an effort to change the subject. "And how about you? Your pistol?"

That day in the jungle, he looked at his weapon like it was something precious, and though I know it belonged to his father, I suspect there's something more to it. I've woken a few nights to find him polishing it, gently stroking the initials.

Lukas's cheeks puff with air before he slowly releases it. "You already know it was my father's. That he died."

"I remember."

I try to make my voice soft the way his was with me. So he knows he can share but that he doesn't have to.

I'm pretty sure I fail, which of course sets my heart thumping. "I'm sorry, I'm being pushy. You don't have to share—really.

I shouldn't have asked. I just thought—I don't know what I thought, and—"

"Jade." Lukas's voice is low. Soothing. "It's okay, really. I don't mind talking about him."

I wait, holding my breath because I'm scared of what'll come out if I open my mouth again.

"I'm not really sure there's much to say," Lukas begins, and though I doubt that, I let him continue. "I lived in Kabrück until I was ten, in a small village not unlike the one we're headed to. It was a happy childhood, and my father made good money, but my sister Lina—" He pauses, coughs, and continues. "She wasn't well. Always ill, longer and more intensely than the rest of us. We moved to Sallenda when the doctors told us she wouldn't survive another harsh winter, but things were harder there. We didn't have much, but my dad, he always kept us afloat—until he couldn't anymore."

A few tears slide down his cheeks, then drip from his chin, and I'm gripped by the sharp desire to fold him into my arms, but I'm not sure he would like that, so I remain rooted to the spot. Still, I ask quietly, "What happened?"

"He died." Lukas lifts an arm and wipes his face with a rough jerk. "We don't know what happened. His heart, we suspect, but he was healthy. I'm not sure. All I know is that one minute he was at the docks, fresh in from a day of fishing, unloading the day's haul, and the next he was flat out on the planks, dead. No warning. No struggle. Just dead. Gone."

No.

Oh gods. Please no.

A high-pitched whine fills my ears, one only I can hear, and though I'm frozen, Lukas continues, lost in his own pain.

He pats the pistol. "He gave me this before he died. Told me

I was getting older, that if anything happened to him, the family would be my responsibility. A few days later, he was gone, and I . . ."

He shakes his head, his distant gaze focusing again, and looks at me. Even though there's no mirror, I know what he sees. My trembling hands, pale skin, eyes wide and hollow and wet.

"Jade? What's the matter?"

His voice is endlessly soft, achingly kind.

I wish he'd scream at me.

"How long ago?" The words scrape, but I push them out. "How many years ago did he die?"

He studies me a moment, then answers slowly, "Five."

I'm going to be sick.

It makes sense, suddenly, why Lukas's soul is familiar. His kindness, compassion, love, all of that is new, purely Lukas, but there are other parts I've seen before. Those shimmers of violet intelligence. Sparks of crimson anger. Swirls of ochre wisdom, and butter-yellow pads of curiosity. Those I know, have stitched with my own hands.

To be a thread speaker is to bear the burden of responsibility. The price of pain. Those were the words my mother whispered to me five years ago, standing at the piers, thread portrait in my hands. One I had stitched lovingly, only to learn its purpose was to steal a life.

The life of Lukas's father.

CHAPTER FIFTEEN

LUKAS

I DON'T KNOW WHAT HAPPENED. ONE MINUTE I WAS TELLING JADE about my father, and the next she had this panicked look in her eyes, her chest moving far too rapidly. By now the pattern has become familiar, and I bend down so I'm at her level.

"It's okay—you're safe. Just breathe."

I repeat the message until she's calmed some, her breathing slowed and trembling ceased. There's no telling what exactly set her off, and I gently guide her back to our room, my hand on her arm. She doesn't say a word the entire time, throat bobbing as I lead her to the bed, then shut the door with a soft click.

The worst of the wave has crested, but it's clear something's still bothering Jade. She's seated on the bed, arms wrapped around herself, eyes misty and downturned.

Just watching her makes my heart squeeze. I wish I could reverse my decision to take her to the deck. Even if I couldn't breathe for a second, watching her look at the stars. My actions have harmed her.

I ask, voice measured, "Do you want to talk about it?"

She doesn't answer right away, but a tear trickles out and slides down her nose, where it hovers before tumbling to the floor. Another follows, then a third, and by the fourth I can't take it anymore.

"Jade, I'm so sorry. I didn't mean—"

"No." The bite to her voice surprises me, and her dark eyes are intent on mine. "No, Lukas, *please*. Don't apologize; you did nothing wrong. I just—" As quickly as it lifted, her gaze shifts back to her feet. "I was just worried about my mom. Learning how your father passed unexpectedly . . . it reminded me I might never get her back."

Oh.

There I was talking about my father, completely forgetting everything she's been going through with her mother.

Longing kindles inside me. A desire to take Jade's hand, pull her into my chest, and whisper comforts in her ear. I might've, too, if this was a different world, or I was a different person. But Jade and I are leagues apart. Once this is over, she'll be a gem of Sallenda, while I'll be nothing more than her escort.

So I don't reach for her hand or scoot closer. I can't even apologize—she asked me not to—and I settle on a paltry offering.

"I can't say for sure that your mother's fine, but if she's not with Johann, I can promise to do everything in my power to help you find her when this is all over. If you need me on this, I'll be there for you, I swear it."

I'm not sure how I'll manage it, since I'll be a Serpensa if we succeed, but I'll figure something out.

That said, I'm not even sure Jade wants my help, especially when she starts crying harder. "I'm sorry." She hiccups and wipes the tears. "I'm sorry." Then she meets my eyes, her own red and swollen. Despite all that, her next words are clear. Crisp. "Lukas Keller, you are far too good, but I can't let you help me any more than you already have."

My heart sinks. This time with Jade feels like freedom. It hurts knowing I won't get much of it. It's better this way, though, and I remind myself of my resolution to keep my distance. Right. With that in mind, I stand and give her some space.

"It's late. I'll let you get to sleep."

Quiet settles, thick as molasses. I practically have to wade through it as I reach beneath the bed and remove the spare pillow and blanket stored there. I haven't gotten far before Jade stops me.

"Wait."

I meet her eyes, my chest tight. *I spoke too quickly,* I imagine her saying. *Of course I want your help.*

But that's not what comes out of her mouth.

"You should take the bed," she insists. "You deserve it, and besides, it's your turn. You've taken the floor the past six nights."

"No." The refusal is automatic. "I don't mind the floor; I'm used to it."

I expect Jade to back down, but she surprises me. "All the more reason for you to have it. Come on." She stands and pats the mattress. "Take it." When I hesitate, she adds, *"Please."*

That's harder to say no to. Still, the thought of her on those hard planks, shivering with the chill—no. I can't leave her to it, but I also don't want to refuse her, which is perhaps how I come to my next suggestion.

"Why don't we share the bed? It might be a little tight, but at least it'll be warm."

Okay, so maybe my idea wasn't *entirely* because I couldn't refuse her.

Jade hesitates, and my face heats. What was I thinking? Of course she doesn't want to share a bed with me. "I'm sorry, forget about it, it's not—"

"Okay," Jade interrupts me, cheeks pink. "Let's do it."

I freeze. Did I hear correctly? "Really? Are you sure? We don't have to."

"I'm sure." She nods, overly prim. "It's a fair compromise, and you're right. We'll be warm."

Warmth—yes, right. A strictly logical reason to share. For Jade, it's probably the only reason she agreed. If only I could say the same.

Keep your distance, I remind myself. But it's impossible when Jade takes off her shoes, slips beneath the covers, then peels them back for me. Her legs stretch along the mattress, impossibly slender, even in her slacks.

I rip my gaze away.

"Lukas?"

God, I'm acting like a fool. Unfortunately, knowing that fact doesn't help me change it, and my mouth is dry as I slip off my shoes. Jade watches me, her expression tight. Slowly, I sit down on the mattress, then pull the blanket over our legs.

"Right," I say.

"Okay," Jade agrees, as if we've just signed some social contract.

We look at each other a moment. For once, I'm the first to drop my gaze, afraid of what she might read there. The mattress creaks as I lie back, and soon Jade follows suit.

I've never been so aware of my own body. The way my heart beats, much too rapidly. The flush creeping over my skin, a burning tide. The breath filling my lungs, each exhale tight with something like excitement.

And of course, every inch of me touching a piece of Jade. From my shoulder down my arm, a break where Jade's waist curves away from mine. Then the long, warm length of her leg, pressing against my thigh, my calf. Locks of her silky, rose-scented hair fan out, tickling my neck, my cheek.

I'm never going to make it to the morning—I'll erupt from my skin long before then. *Gone too soon,* my gravestone will read. *Couldn't survive lying next to a pretty girl.*

Though *pretty* would be putting it mildly.

"Lukas?" Jade interrupts my thoughts. I swear she sounds a little breathless too, though no doubt I'm imagining it. "Should we extinguish the light?"

Of course, yes, the light. I quickly blow it out, and a shroud of darkness falls, tendrils of silver moonlight stroking the shadows. We're eclipsed in a new kind of silence before Jade breaks it. "Good night, Lukas."

It shouldn't have an effect on me, but hearing her say my name—

I shiver.

"Good night, Jade," I whisper, and settle in.

It's going to be a long night.

I wake up with the scent of roses in my nose, softness pressed against me, and warmth straight down to my soul.

I wake up tangled in Jade.

It's a fuzzy realization, lacking the sharp bite of awareness. It feels good, comfortable, *right,* and I revel in the sensation of Jade against me. Her face, nuzzled into the crook of my neck, warm leg thrown over my pelvis, easy to place with me on my back. Her arm draped over my chest, hair spilling down her back, over her cheeks, the strands creating a swath of blue-black midnight. She's so close, her breath tickles the ridge of my collarbone, while her heart beats against my chest, a steady current.

And she's not the only artist in this dance. At some point I must've unconsciously pulled her to me. My left arm is beneath her, cradling her to my chest, while my right latches over, snug in the swell of her hip.

For the past six days I've heard her in the night. The bed creaking as she tossed and turned, unable to find peace or slumber. Now, though, with me, she's peaceful.

A mad urge to pull her closer grips me. To lean into this, if only for a few moments. It's been such a long time since I've been held. Been touched like this, with tenderness, even unintentionally.

And if I'm being honest with myself, it's not merely the human contact I enjoy. It's the fact Jade's the one providing it.

No.

This is dangerous, *unacceptable* territory. Jade doesn't want me, and even if she did, this could never happen. Not with the history between our families.

Chastened, I force my attention away from Jade, onto our surroundings. Dawn light seeps through the window, while waves lap against the steamship, a peaceful hum—the only sound.

It's quiet.

Too quiet.

A chill ripples down my spine.

By now our cabin should be filled with the sounds of the crew above us, their boots scuffling on the deck, muted chatter wafting through the floorboards. The smell of porridge should tinge the salty ocean air, and smoke should be clouding in the sky as we plod along. But when I tilt my gaze to peek out the window, there's nothing save a pristine blue.

Something's wrong.

My pulse kicks up. Slowly, I disentangle myself from Jade, if only to spare her the embarrassment of waking up entwined in me. She reaches for me as I pull away, all drowsy innocence, and my heart snags. If this were a different life, different place, if we were different people, then maybe it would be possible. Maybe I could let her reel me back, dig my hands into that hair, kiss her awake and more.

But we're in this life, this place, these roles. And in this reality, what we've taken is already too much.

The reminders sear me as I stand, slip on my shoes, then turn away from Jade and quietly open the chest at the foot of the bed. It's filled with a few changes of clothes, Jade's thread kit, and—most importantly—two pistols. I take them both out and holster mine, Jade's in hand as I crouch next to the mattress, reach for her wrist, and gently shake it.

"Jade," I say when her eyes blink open, "I need you to wake up." She hears all the hard edges in my voice and sits abruptly. "Lukas? What's going on?"

Her eyes are wide, breath already a bit erratic. Though I shouldn't, I squeeze her hand. "I think something's wrong." Then I explain why. All the missing sights and sounds and smells.

Before I can stop her, Jade lifts her free hand and smacks herself hard across the face.

"What—" My breath comes out in a hiss. "Why? What are—"

"Because I'm feeling panicked," she answers, voice a shade too high, "and I don't think there's time for it right now."

Then she slaps herself again.

Something is seriously wrong with me, because now I want to kiss her even more. I nearly smack myself too, because Jade's right—we don't have time for this.

133

"I'm leaving to scope things out." I offer Jade her pistol. "Keep this pointed at the door. I'll knock when I come back. Two fast beats, a pause, then another, like this." I demonstrate the pattern on the floor. "If anyone comes in who isn't me or the crew, shoot them. Do you understand?"

There's a fire raging inside me, screaming to protect her. It crackles at Jade's next words.

"Yes. I understand." She reaches for the pistol, fingers lingering on the metal before she pulls it from my grasp.

Stay safe. I don't know what I'd do if something happened to you. My tongue burns, but I swallow the words down. "I'll be back soon," I say instead. Inadequate. Necessary.

I turn for the door, fully prepared to leave, but Jade stops me, hand warm around my wrist. "Lukas, wait."

I'm not sure what I want her to say, but hope clogs my throat all the same.

"Shouldn't we stick together?" she asks, eyes glittering, a faint tremble in her voice.

This girl.

She's *dangerous.* Maybe not to others, but to me.

It's unnatural, unwise, illogical; and I imagine what Emma would say if she knew. How she'd chastise me for pining over a girl I just met, whose mother let Lina die. Hot coals of shame spark inside me. I shouldn't feel this way about anyone, but especially not Jade. Caring for her is selfish. It'll only distract me from a family that needs me, one I promised to provide for always, above everything.

And yet.

"I'll be back," I whisper. "I promise."

Then I slip out the door, determined to protect this girl I have no business caring for.

CHAPTER SIXTEEN

JADE

I'M A HORRIBLE PERSON.

First, for not sharing my history with Lukas's father, and second, for lying about it.

I should've told Lukas. I wanted to, even if only to get this off my chest, but every time I entertained the possibility, my throat closed up. Lukas is the first friend I've had, and perhaps the only one I'll ever get, so the thought of him pushing me away . . .

I couldn't bear it. Which is why I lied. Then somehow we ended up sharing the bed, and now Lukas is out there, searching for threats, trying to protect me.

I'm a horrible person—third, because I let him.

The gun trembles in my fingers, only partially due to my fear. The icy cold chill of one of my episodes threatens, but I focus on my breathing, the feel of the mattress below me, and the metal of the pistol, damp in my sweaty hands. Remind myself that I can't let it take me, if only for Lukas. What if something's wrong and he needs me?

That more than anything keeps me grounded. If there's danger, he'll need me functioning, not a quivering husk.

So I sit.

And I wait.

And wait.

Until the door flies open. No knock—it just swings violently on its hinges.

Fire! a disjointed part of my brain shrieks. *Shoot! Lukas warned you about this!*

But the panic makes me sluggish, and in the seconds that spread, the silence grows.

Because no one's there.

Wetness trickles down my cheeks, and my hands shake, but that doesn't stop me from lifting my gun. *Breathe,* I imagine Lukas saying, *just breathe, it's okay.*

But it's not. Something is horribly, terribly wrong, and my words tremble. "Who's there?"

A familiar voice answers, just a few steps left of my door. "It's only me, little dove."

The tracker.

I nearly vomit. I try to steady my gun in the direction his voice came from, but I'm shaking so hard, I don't know how I'll squeeze off a shot, and the tracker speaks before I get the chance.

"Now, I suspect you're having violent thoughts, perhaps wanting to fight me again. I have to say that wouldn't be wise."

Then he slinks into the doorway, vermillion cruelty inside his soul gleaming. If it were just him, I'd empty my bullets right into his chest, but he's not alone.

The captain's here too. I recognize him from when Lukas bartered our passage on his steamboat. Then he was a cheery man. Now he just looks terrified.

My horror must show, because the tracker's grin widens. "That's right. I have you again, and this time there's no place to run, and I don't see your boy swooping in to save you. Now." He nods to my hand, a greenish white, I'm clutching the pistol so tightly. "Put that down, or an innocent man dies. Is that what you want?"

No. My mind races. Going with the tracker means untold horrors, but fighting him? Most likely I'll fail, and the captain will die for nothing.

Slowly I lower my weapon to the bed, a sob threatening. The last dregs of my hope leak away as the tracker instructs the captain to take my gun and empty it of bullets. When that's finished, he forces a rag of something foul smelling beneath the captain's nose until his eyes roll back in his head. Satisfied, he lets the body slump to the floor, then faces me, eyes alight with malice. "Time to take a trip."

LUKAS

Our situation is bleak.

We've been boarded by pirates with a lot more firepower than us. I almost ran into a couple of them on the stairs, and was only saved by quickly ducking into an empty closet. Now I lie on the steamship's bridge roof, hidden behind one of the smokestacks, with a bird's-eye view of the front deck.

It's littered with a mix of crew and passengers, more being led out as I watch. They're cowed but alive, though I'm not sure they'll stay that way much longer. A horde of pirates surrounds them, guns leveled, eyes unblinking. Their boat bobs nearby, a steamship like ours, but larger and sleeker.

It's too late to put up any real fight. I have my pistol, but against their dozens, aggression will earn me nothing more than an early death.

Shit.

I need to keep my head, but I can't stop thinking of Jade, alone and terrified in our room. Whatever's happening, I suspect it's related to our search for Johann Schäfer, and my chest constricts, almost to the point of pain. Because this is all my fault. I tangled Jade in this. If something happens, it'll be on me.

We can't fight our way out of this, but maybe we can hide. Smuggling compartments aren't uncommon in cargo ships like this, and if we can just find one—

A familiar whimper rips my world in two. *Jade.*

My stomach churns as she appears on deck, face streaked with tears, led by none other than the tracker. His gun is pressed to her back, and she's clutching the thread kit to her chest.

A curtain of red cloaks my world. I taste blood, and for a moment I consider putting a bullet right through his skull.

I could, too. I'm a good shot, and the tracker isn't far. I'd hit my mark.

But it would come at a cost.

No doubt chaos would erupt along with the tracker's skull. And while I'm safe up here, Jade would be caught in the cross fire. But what to do?

Not long ago I would've considered leaving Jade behind. She's the one they're after, and I have my family to care for. I wouldn't have abandoned them, not for a girl I've known for a few weeks.

And yet.

Jade isn't just some girl. She's my family's stability, the reason they're fed and housed right now.

For me, though—I think, maybe, she's my freedom.

And I'm not ready to give her up.

"Stop!" I barely recognize my own voice, it's so sharp. "Let her go!"

It doesn't matter that I can't realistically save her, because I *can* go with her. If not as a free man, then as a prisoner.

I stand with that in mind, looking down my nose at the tracker, my pistol raised even as two dozen more point directly at me. Only the tracker's remains on Jade, though he does lift his gaze to mine, his grin barbed.

"You again. I figured you'd be lurking around here somewhere."

I don't know what I'm doing, only that I can't leave Jade behind.

"Let. Her. Go."

"Or what?" The tracker raises his eyebrows. "You'll shoot me? Look around, peasant boy. You have no hopes of winning. Do you really want her to see you die?"

He pulls Jade closer for emphasis, making her wince.

"Lukas, please, don't do this. Don't sacrifice yourself for me." Her voice wavers, slicing right through me. If anything, it has the opposite of her desired effect.

God, I'm being a fool. I should listen. But the time for that has passed. I'm either a prisoner or a dead man now.

As if reading my thoughts, the tracker glances at his crew, then back at me. "Take him, too."

"*NO!*" Jade's shriek is vicious. Animalistic. So unlike her it's jarring. She thrashes against the tracker despite his gun to her spine. "No! Leave him—you don't want him. Take me, just let him be! I can make it worth your while."

The tracker holds up a hand, and the men who've been approaching the stairs to apprehend me freeze. "Go on," he says to Jade. "I'm listening."

A tide of goose bumps ripples over my skin. This is *wrong*. I can't let Jade sacrifice herself. "Jade, please—"

"Quiet!" the tracker's voice booms, punctuated by the click of several dozen pistols. "Let her speak."

I swallow but back down. I can't go with Jade if I'm dead. Horrified, I watch as she leans closer to the tracker, then whispers something in his ear.

Whatever she says, he appears to mull it over, expression thoughtful before that wicked grin slicks back into place. "Thank you," he tells her, "but no thank you."

"No!" She struggles anew, but the tracker must be tired of her games, because he forces a rag beneath her nose. Jade crumples in his arms, ashen. I howl, everything inside me demanding that I lift my gun and put a bullet between his eyes. I would, too, if a lick of sense didn't worm its way in.

If I fight, I die, and if I die, Jade and my family have no one. It's that simple. Surrender is my only option.

My heart pounds as I set the gun at my feet, then raise my arms above my head.

I'm sorry, Dad. I've failed the family.

"Perfect." The tracker's eyes are chips of glittering obsidian, his gaze on me even as he addresses his crew. "Bring him in."

CHAPTER SEVENTEEN

JADE

I THINK MY HEAD MIGHT EXPLODE. IT THROBS WITH A VIOLENT ache, and I must groan, because suddenly Lukas's voice is there.

"Jade? Are you okay? How badly are you hurt?"

He sounds frantic, and the undiluted fear in his tone makes me open my eyes, despite the fact I want nothing more than to return to my black oblivion. At least in there my reality wasn't terrifying.

"Lukas?"

His name scrapes my throat, and I wince as I lift my lids, dim light making my head pulse harder.

I'm in a cell aboard an unfamiliar ship. That much is obvious from the lattice of bars in front of me. Cold seeps into me from the floorboards, and my stomach squeezes at the gentle bob of the ocean, its briny scent thick in the air. Slowly, my memories filter back. The too-quiet morning, the tracker, and then Lukas, standing tall on the ship's roof, eyes blazing that courageous viridian, pistol pointed down.

"Jade?" Lukas's voice cracks. "I was so worried."

He's never sounded so small, and my heart constricts as I take him in. The brig has only a few visible cells, and Lukas has been placed in the one across from me, his skin pale and shadowed in the flickering burn of the oil lamps. A gash slices his lip, now crusted in blood, and a bruise darkens his eye.

"Gods, Lukas." My voice shakes as what he did sinks in. "Are *you* okay?"

Why did you do that? I want to scream. *I don't deserve it, not since I put the final stitch in your father's portrait!*

But even after everything he's done for me, I still can't bring myself to share that venomous truth—or to be upset that he's here. In all honesty, I . . . I think I'm *glad* he's with me, which surely makes me even more horrible.

Lukas brushes off his injuries like they're nothing. "I'm fine— they just had a little fun dragging me in. You, though . . ."

His eyes stray to my face, and my head beats with an extra persistent throb. "How long was I unconscious?"

Lukas's breath shudders out of him. "A few hours maybe."

Quiet settles between us as the reality of our situation creeps in. The tracker found us and is taking us gods only know where to do gods only know what. There's no escaping him, and my heart pounds, the first sign of an impending episode. It only intensifies when I realize there's no way I'll make the queen's deadline now, my chance to rescue my mother cut short.

I could just . . . miss the queen's deadline. The thought occurs, barely a wisp of a thing, before I bat it away. In all her time working for the queen, my mother defied her twice—though she succeeded only once. In that singular instance she risked herself to shield me from the darkest parts of our profession. She would've been punished had the queen ever learned of her deception. Luckily, it remained secret.

On the other occasion, my mother refused to strip away the

happiness of a criminal whose only "misdeed" was to decry the queen and the gods publicly.

At the time, I was upset. The queen doesn't take kindly to dissent, and I feared for my mother. Now, though, I admire her. She was right; it was wrong.

Not that the queen cared. Her response was calm but terrifying: Obey, or she'd have the man *and* his wife executed. My mother unspooled his happiness the next day.

It's a bit difficult, reconciling the queen I met with the one my mother described. She was almost . . . timid that day, always glancing at the walls. Certainly not ruthless. A façade, I imagine, though why bother to put one on for me, of all people? Even so, I trust my mother, and she feared the queen. She wasn't the only one, either, according to the rumors. Competent but cold, people say. Difficult to please. So while I can't be sure of my punishment if I return late, I do know this: I don't want to find out.

I squeeze my eyes shut, trying to focus on my breathing, and it helps when Lukas's voice slips in. Low. Curious.

"What did you say to him?"

A measure of disgust coils inside me. *Him.* The tracker.

I blush, recalling what I whispered in his ear. "I asked him to spare you," I admit. "I told him he could take me, but that if he took you too, I'd fight him every step of the way. That I wouldn't do what he asked or sew what he needed. But if he left you . . ." I shiver, remembering my words just hours ago.

I promise to be docile. To listen. To do whatever you need—just please let him go.

I don't entirely understand what gripped me in those moments. I can only say what I was thinking: That Lukas is good, kind, wonderful. That if I could save him, I had to do it. Because he doesn't deserve this. Because he's my friend, and I care for him.

"I told him I'd follow his directions," I finish, leaving out my motivations. During my explanation I stared at my lap, fiddling with a loose thread, but now I meet his eyes. They're shining. Glossy with unshed tears.

"You did that for me?"

Of course I did that for you.

The answer that rises up is simple, easy, and—above all—painful. Because it comes with a realization.

I like Lukas far more than I should, an ember burning in my chest where there shouldn't even be kindling. Not love, not yet, but a fierce sort of affection.

This new awareness feels like I sucked in a lungful of fresh air only to realize moments later it was poison. Because I can never be with Lukas. Someone as brave as him could never care for someone as fearful as me, and even if he did, if he knew what happened to his father . . .

No. It can never—*will never*—be.

I swallow any remaining hope, but Lukas's question still lingers between us, and I answer him honestly, echoing my initial thought.

"Of course I did that for you."

Lucas clears his throat, coral blotching his cheeks. "Jade, I—"

The door swings open, and a burly man enters, his soul brimming with minty greed and russet loyalty.

"I have orders to fetch you, so come on." He gestures to my wrists. "Put your hands through the bars. I need to bind them."

His vowels are clipped, his accent Fronian, which only makes me more nervous. Fronia's a militaristic nation with a well-documented hatred of thread speakers; no doubt this man could kill me several different ways with nothing more than his bare hands.

Breathe, just breathe.

It's hard, though, when the trembling has already started. My gaze darts to Lukas, his lip still bloody, his eye still bruised, and despite my fear, the sight fills me with determination. I told the tracker I'd fight him every step of the way, and now I have to prove I meant it.

Well then. Fear or no, I'm going to fight.

"No," I answer the man, proud that my voice doesn't waver. "I'm not leaving."

To emphasize my point, I step back from the bars.

The man sighs. "I thought you might say that."

For a brief moment I enjoy my small victory.

It shatters a second later when the man points his gun at Lukas. "Come with me, or I take him to the deck and shoot him."

Oh gods. I really thought I could help things, but now they're so much worse.

"It's fine, Jade." Lukas's voice is urgent, piercing me through the fog of the episode that's begun to close in. "It's okay. Don't listen to him, I'll be fine."

"But you won't!" I barely realize I've spoken until the words have settled, but it's true. I can fight all I want, but all it'll do is hurt Lukas. I'll still be trapped on this boat, the tracker will still make me see him, and the situation will still be hopeless. At least if I listen, Lukas won't be hurt.

Breathe. I force myself to obey my silent command, inhaling slowly through my nose and exhaling through my mouth, exactly the way Lukas instructed me. It helps. The panic still lurks beneath the surface, but it doesn't overpower me yet.

Thank the gods.

I meet Lukas's eyes, begging him without words to understand. "It's okay, Lukas. I'll be okay."

Then I offer the guard my wrists and let him bind them.

CHAPTER EIGHTEEN

JADE

THE TRACKER'S QUARTERS ARE EXTRAVAGANT, DRENCHED IN SUN-light and riches. Gold filigree spirals up the walls, snaking around the paned windows, and my feet sink into the crimson rug. I'm seated at a table set for two, my wrists freed once again and my fingers clenched so hard on my armrests, I'm surprised the wood doesn't snap. Across from me the tracker smirks, while the feather pendant at his throat glitters.

All manner of food spans the space between us: roast chicken glazed in honey and lemon, golden corn cakes, black beans, steaming red snapper sprinkled with cayenne, and, for dessert, one of my favorites—a giant bowl of mamey pudding. If I weren't anxious, my stomach would growl, but it's far too knotted for that.

Say something! my brain screams, but I can't get my tongue to work. We've been sitting in silence for a minute now, and I *know* the tracker is savoring every moment I squirm. My skin crawls, and I open my mouth to speak, fully intending to wipe that smile from his face.

Instead, I make a strange sort of squeak, then promptly break into a coughing fit.

"Oh, come on," the tracker says once I've finished, grin even wider now. "Surely you don't find my company that repulsive?"

"I do." My tongue feels lopsided, and my words lack the intended venom.

He chuckles. "Yes, I suppose you do. Especially after I refused to spare that boy you're so fond of."

My heart speeds dangerously. *Breathe,* I imagine Lukas saying, *just breathe.*

I need to tread carefully—Lukas's life could depend on it—and I force myself to meet the tracker's eyes.

"Why have you been chasing me?"

Okay, that could've been worse. My voice only wobbled a bit, and I turned the attention away from Lukas. I'm doing this.

The tracker tilts his head, taking me in as he answers. "Because you're valuable. A thread speaker soon to be Crown appointed."

My brow furrows. "How do you know that?"

Lukas is the only one I've told about my conversation with the queen. As far as the rest of Mérecal's concerned, my mother's on sabbatical, set to return any day now.

The tracker studies me a second, shrugs, then takes a large bite of corn cake. Around the food, he says, "I'm observant, and I happen to know your mother hasn't been spotted in months. You're Mérecal's only remaining thread speaker, so it stands to reason the Crown is getting antsy."

My grip on the armrests tightens. "And that's why you want me? To prevent the Crown from having me?"

The tracker swallows, and something kindles in his eyes. "I want you because my employer has need of you and your particular skills."

It's not a startling revelation, but I shiver. The tracker and his employer never targeted me until this whole sievech mess, which means they must be tangled in it too. A potent mix of excitement and fear strangles my next words, but they come out clear enough. "Is your employer Johann Schäfer?"

He tsks. "Come now, little dove. You know I can't tell you that." I must visibly deflate, because he chuckles. "What else do you want to ask? I can practically smell the questions oozing from you."

What a . . . vile way to phrase that. Still, I have so many questions and too few answers. This is an opportunity to get some information, even if it makes my stomach squeeze.

I force myself to breathe, to study the table in front of me covered in decadent dishes, almost like the tracker was trying to impress me. Which is odd and gives rise to my next question.

"Why all this?" I take a breath and look up again. "Why meet with me?"

He said his employer has use of me, but the fact he summoned me implies he has use for my skills as well.

The tracker's lips twitch. "Clever dove. I need you to sew something for me."

I'm instantly on edge, imagining all the horrible things he could make me do. Panic rises, choking me, but I recall Lukas's voice and swallow it back down.

"What kind of something?"

The tracker stands, and I flinch, thinking he's coming for me, but instead he approaches a large oak desk pressed against the wall. I watch as he tugs a chain around his throat, revealing a key, and unlocks one of the drawers. Something dark slips between his fingers, and my stomach flips when he sets it directly on my empty plate.

A lock of hair.

It's a midnight black, secured with cerise ribbon, and a soul clings to it, faint enough that it must be at least ten years old. I don't touch the hair, but I do study the colors. Webs of icy determination above all, along with shoots of magenta arrogance and stabs of crimson anger. There's more to it, not all bad, but those are the shades that stand out most.

I lift my gaze to the tracker. "Who does this belong to?"

He waves a hand. "That's irrelevant. What matters is that you can see the soul."

His voice is an octave too high, and his signature grin has faded. The tracker looks, well, *worried,* and I realize—

This *matters* to him. And if it matters, I have some leverage.

Some of my fear fades, giving way to a thin thread of conviction. Because even here, trapped and beaten, I'm not powerless. The tracker can take my freedom, my friend, my safety, but he can't take my magic.

That is mine, and mine alone, to control.

Warmth suffuses me, a heady rush, and slowly a plan begins to form. I glance at the lock of hair, then meet the tracker's gaze. "It's faded," I admit, "but I can still see the soul."

He visibly relaxes, shoulders caving in. *Relieved.*

"What do you want me to sew?" I ask, tone clipped.

His calm assuredness has returned—though now I know it's only a mask.

"It's simple, really." He pauses, brushes his knuckles against the lock of hair, and shivers. "I need you to make her fall in love with me again. Can you do that?"

Her. The woman the hair belongs to.

I scan the tracker's soul, studying those waves of burgundy love choked in vines of jealous chartreuse. Whoever this woman is, she broke the tracker's heart, and he wants her back badly enough that he's willing to force it.

I consider the tracker's request.

Not everyone's aware, but there's a single exception to thread speaking's first rule—that to give, you must take—and that exception is love. Mutual love, to be specific. And even then, I can't give love without taking, but simply bind the souls of those who care deeply for one another, connecting them in a tangible way. It doesn't matter what kind of love they feel. Romantic, platonic, enduring—it all works just the same.

But love, when one-sided, is much the same as the rest. There can be no binding of souls without mutual emotion. So while I can't make the tracker's woman fall in love with him specifically, I *can* add more love to her soul. And who knows? With some more love, especially grafted from his soul, it's quite possible she'll fall for him. But of course, the giving requires taking, and once again, I eye the tainted love of his own soul—more than enough to go around.

"I can," I answer, not quite the truth, but not quite a lie either, and with my words, the last fragments of my plan shift into place. *Please.* I never put much faith in the old gods, but I pray to them now. *Please don't let this hurt Lukas.* Then I add, voice stern, "But I won't."

True rage distorts the tracker's features, my refusal purpling his face.

"You *will*, or I swear to the gods I'll make your friend suffer."

I'm out on a feeble branch, trembling and scared, but Lukas and I are both damned if I don't make this work.

So I don't back down. My mother always believed me strong and capable; it's time for me to act like I deserve that faith.

"No," I say, fingers itching with the desire to clutch my pendant. "I won't. I swore that if you took Lukas, I'd do everything in my power to make your life difficult. Well, you took him, and now I'm making your life difficult. Find someone else to stitch your love."

There's no warning. The tracker backhands me, knuckles scraping my cheek, stars bursting in my vision. Hot blood fills my mouth, and I sputter when he fists my shirt and lifts me from my seat.

"Everything you're feeling now I'll do to him tenfold. This is your last chance, little dove. Agree to sew this for me, or your friend—*Lukas*—suffers."

I'm sorry, Lukas. The whisper echoes inside me, unanswered. My earlier conviction wavers, bruised and afraid.

But if I don't do this, I'll never be free. I'll live controlled by the tracker and his employer, made to do horrible things, and Lukas . . . it won't end well for him either—forced into a life where his pain is a bargaining chip. If I don't gamble now, I'll lose more later.

I'm afraid, but I can't let that fear control me, and I imagine the way I must look as I lift my gaze to the tracker's. Wild eyes. Blood running down my face. Hair a frantic halo.

The moment stretches. Hangs.

Snaps.

I lunge for the tracker, screaming. He grunts when my knee connects with his crotch, and the second he bends, I'm raking my nails through his scalp, blood dampening my fingers. He shrieks, a sound of fury more than pain, and within seconds he has me pinned to the floor, one hand on each wrist.

"How *dare* you," he seethes. "The things I'm going to do to that boy—"

I crack the moment with a sob, the flood of panic finally

breaking through. Once freed, it's a powerful tide, and I tremble. "Please," I gasp. "Please, I'm going to be sick."

The tracker may not be afraid of me, but he's certainly afraid of my vomit, because he scrambles off me seconds before I heave. Even once my stomach is empty, I keep retching, until eventually the peak of my fear is crested and I come down the other side.

The aftereffects of my episode ripple through me in the dense silence, and I force myself to meet the tracker's eyes. "I don't know what came over me. I'm sorry, I was—" I hug myself. "I'm sorry, I'm so sorry. Please don't hurt Lukas. I'll do whatever you want, just don't hurt him."

The tracker must be as desperate as I thought, because after studying me a moment, he agrees. "Next time you disobey, I cut off one of the boy's fingers."

I look at my knuckles, white with the strain of my clenched fists. "I understand. I'll listen."

"Good." His response is curt. "Rest tonight. I'll call you here tomorrow to get started—under my supervision, of course."

"Of course," I say, though my stomach sinks. That will certainly make what I have planned harder.

The tracker calls for the guard after that, and he leads me through the ship, back to the brig. Lukas's eyes widen when he sees me, cheeks heating. "What did you do to her?! I swear to god whoever hurt her—"

"Lukas," I say quietly. "It's okay."

He must hear my weariness, because he quiets, at least until the guard leaves. The second he's gone, though, Lukas is at his cell bars, as close as he can possibly get to me. "Jade, what happened? Are you okay?"

I look at my lap, where my fists are still clenched, and open them. One is empty, but the other . . .

It holds three dark strands of hair, stolen in my assault of the tracker. And despite everything, I grin. Because I did it. I really did it.

"Yes." I meet Lukas's eyes. "I am, actually."

And then, still smiling, I tell him about my plan.

CHAPTER NINETEEN

JADE

FOR FIVE DAYS I'M DOCILE. BENT UNDER MY FEAR FOR LUKAS, OR so the tracker believes. Every morning he sends the same guard to fetch me, and I spend the next few hours sewing in his chambers, the tracker watching me from down the table. I don't fight or argue—I barely even speak—and gradually concessions are made.

My wrists are no longer bound when I'm transported. The tracker doesn't watch me quite as intently, pausing to yawn or eat. A day in, I cause a racket in my cell, begging the guard to bring me ginger tea, and he complies, that night and every one after. Now it's a routine.

I'm on day six now, seated at the head of the tracker's table, laved in midmorning sun. A breakfast buffet is splayed across the wood: mounds of steaming sweet bread, golden jackfruit slices, beans, tortillas, and, of course, heated mugs of champurrado, chocolatey and rich. I interrupt my sewing to sip mine, then look back to my task.

I've been going as slowly as I can, stretching out an assignment that would normally take one day into several. I feel the passage of time acutely—with only thirty days left until the queen's deadline, my time's half up. But if I want to escape, I have to go slowly.

Still, the tracker would notice if I didn't make any progress, and the fruits of my labor blur in front of my eyes, spirals and spikes and eddies of color, a story of souls written in thread. It's beautiful, stark against the black leather I've embroidered it on.

I sigh and settle into a vermillion backstitch, but through it all, I keep my peripheral vision on the tracker. He studies me, persistent, but eventually he cracks and leans forward to grab another roll of sweet bread, his eyes on the food instead of me.

I'm viper quick. My hand darts to the thread kit in my lap, and by the time the tracker sits back in his chair, I've already smuggled a small length of gold thread up my sleeve. The last bit I need.

The only thing left to steal is a bit of leather, a surface on which to stitch my plans, but the tracker's taken all mine from my kit. Fortunately, there's a work-around. Unfortunately, it'll hurt.

Even so, I can't suppress a small curl of satisfaction. I'm actually doing this. *Me.* Defying the tracker.

"Pleased about something?" the tracker asks, and I freeze. He must see it on my face.

Breathe. Just breathe.

I heed the reminder but don't meet the tracker's eyes, my head ducked. "I'm almost finished, is all. A couple more days and I'll be done with your soul portrait. Once it's complete, all I'll have to do is remove some love, then use it for your lover's tattoo patch."

The tracker snorts. "You'd better be nearly done. You must be the worst thread speaker out there."

"Yes," I agree, if only to placate him. "I must be."

Though when you next wake, you won't be so sure about that.

LUKAS

Relief washes through me when the guard returns Jade to her cell.

It's been like this every day. Jade risking herself while I sit down here, useless, praying he doesn't hurt her again. That first morning, when she came back with a split lip—

God of three, the things I wanted to do to him. But I kept myself calm for Jade. Her cell door squeaks now as the guard swings it open. Soon he's gone, leaving me and Jade alone.

Her eyes glitter when she faces me. "I got it, Lukas. The rest of the thread we need."

My heart both leaps and squeezes. Leaps because she did it. Squeezes because our plan is risky, and if something happens to her— No. I don't even want to think about that.

I force myself to smile, hoping she can see my sincerity. "I'm proud of you, Jade. I mean that."

I swear she blushes. "Yes, well, that was the easy part."

I wish she was wrong.

Our scheme requires us to pounce while the sailors are sleeping. That's why despite the itch of anticipation, we sit and wait, reviewing the details of the plan. Eventually the guard comes and goes with Jade's evening tea, the last visitor we'll have for the night. Hours spread before us now, filled with potential.

It's time.

"You ready?" I ask.

She nods. Though she's pale, her shoulders are set, a hard line of determination. She carefully pries away a loose floorboard in her cell, revealing her hiding place. If I crane my neck, I can see the spectrum of threads hidden there, the shades of the tracker's soul.

Jade sits on the floor and spreads them around her, extra careful with the tracker's hairs, nestled inside a fold of fabric.

"Okay," she says, almost like she's talking herself up. "Okay."

She bites her bottom lip, and I grab my cell bars. It's killing me that I can't go to her right now.

"Hey," I say softly. "It's okay—you've got this."

"Do I?" Her eyes are dark and wet. I don't think she even notices when she reaches for her pendant. "I don't know, Lukas. I thought I did, but maybe it's better if—"

"It's not." I cut her spiral off. "We have to try, you know that."

Her voice is so small, I barely hear it. "But if we fail, he won't hurt me. He'll take it out on you."

Honestly, that's the only thing giving me comfort. I'd rather harm come to me than Jade.

"I know." I try to lace my words with meaning, confidence, and warmth. "And I accept that risk, because I know what happens if we stay."

Even though I don't elaborate, the sentiment lingers. If we stay, Jade will be delivered to the tracker's employer. If we stay, they'll control her using me. If we stay, we could lose our souls.

I'd rather die tonight than lose my soul tomorrow.

Jade must feel the same, because she nods, a stiff set to her chin. "You're right," she admits. "Okay."

Then she rolls her pant leg up, revealing a long, slender calf and smooth, tawny skin. My throat bobs beneath the force of my swallow. Even this small piece of her—god. I'm in deeper than I realized. My heated thoughts quickly evaporate, though, as Jade picks up a needle. She reminded me about this, how soul portraits come to life only when stitched into living or once-living materials. In the absence of leather, her skin is the only option.

It's a terrible one—even thread tattoos are first stitched onto specially made plant-based dissolvable cloth so the recipient doesn't have to receive more than a handful of stitches. This time, though? Jade has to sew directly into her flesh.

She prepared me, and yet I still flinch when she pierces her leg with a grimace.

I hate this. I wish I could take those stitches for her, but I can't.

So I wait, attempting to keep my posture relaxed, if only because I don't want to stress her out more. By the time Jade sets the needle down, her brow is beaded in sweat and I'm about ready to snap my cell bars in half.

"Is that it?" I ask her. "Is it done?"

"Not quite," she answers, voice shaky. Her gaze falls to the swatch of fabric folded over the tracker's hairs.

My stomach roils. Jade's taught me a lot about the basic mechanics of thread speaking. To make a thread portrait come alive, it requires a piece of her and a piece of whoever it belongs to. The tracker's hair will be especially important now since the image of his soul isn't complete. Jade could only smuggle so much thread, and when I asked if that would be a problem, she compared a soul to a fingerprint—you don't need the entire thing for it to be distinctive; you just need *enough*.

Now I fight back nausea while Jade stitches the tracker's hair into the portrait. Soon it glimmers, all the threads coming alive with an unnatural glow, fed on his hair and her blood. In that moment it doesn't matter that it's the tracker's soul; I'm amazed by what she can do. Jade, however, is unfazed as she carefully reaches for the gold thread, nearly incandescent now, and delicately unspools it from the portrait.

And just like that, it's finished.

Jade just meets my gaze. "I did it. It's done."

She almost sounds like she doesn't believe it, and I study her. Back straight, cheeks flushed, eyes set on mine. It's hard not to compare this version of her to the way she was the day we met. She cowered then, and I wonder if she notices these subtle changes.

I wonder if she knows how incredible she is.

"What?" she asks, a nervous lilt in her voice. "Did I do something wrong?"

"No, Jade." I hope she can hear the burning intensity in my next words, because I mean them. "You're amazing. You just—you're amazing. Truly."

Lackluster words that fail to communicate what I really mean. How much I admire her growth, her persistence, and, above all, her bravery. A blazing ember, glowing hot and bright, even amid the cool darkness of fear.

The flush of her cheeks burns brighter, and she clears her throat. "We should probably keep going with the plan, you know, if we want to have enough time."

My heart falters at the easy way she brushes off my words. But god, of course she does. Someone like me has no business speaking to her like that, and I remind myself of my place, though it's growing harder.

"You're right," I say, voice scratchy with nerves. "Let's do this."

CHAPTER TWENTY

JADE

IT'S EASY ENOUGH TO DRAW THE GUARD BACK. I LEARNED EARLY on that his room must be positioned beneath mine, so with enough stomping, he arrives, lips carved in a scowl.

"I was *asleep*," he practically hisses. "What's the meaning of this?"

Breathe, in through the nose, out through the mouth. Still, I can't ease the tension in my chest, nor stop the sickly lurch of my heart. For once, though, these vestiges of panic are helpful; it's better that the guard see my fear.

"It's my monthly—it arrived. I need fresh linens."

I lift my hand then, flashing fingers covered in a thin sheen of blood swiped from the stitches on my calf.

He blanches. "God, clean that up. I'll get you linens, just—*god.*"

His expression suggests I flaunted a severed head, not some supposed menstrual blood.

"Could you also get me some more tea?" I wrap my arm around my belly. "With the cramps, I think I might be sick . . ."

And if I'm sick, *someone* will have to clean it up, most likely him—which he well knows.

He glares at me. "I'm not your errand boy."

If anything, his refusal increases my anxiety, and I feel the blood drain from my face. *"Please,"* I whimper. "Please, I don't think I have much longer."

He shakes his head, eyeing my pale complexion. "Fine, but this is the last midnight errand I run for you."

Then he leaves, muttering something under his breath about entitled prisoners.

"That was perfect," Lukas assures me once he's gone. "Honestly. You even looked unwell."

"I *feel* unwell." My stomach sloshes in agreement. Days ago this plan seemed like a good idea, but now that it's here—

"Jade." Lukas interrupts my spiral. "Look at me."

Slowly I meet those viridian eyes, brilliant with a courage matched in his soul.

"Tonight's risky, but I believe in us. I believe in your plan. I believe in *you.*"

My heart breaks, just a little. Because the way Lukas is looking at me, tender and fervent and *blazing,* it makes me want things I can't have.

I took part in your father's death! The words sizzle beneath my skin. *You should hate me!*

And he would, if he knew.

I look down, unable to meet his gaze any longer. "Thank you."

It's barely a murmur, and I practically hear Lukas deflate.

"Jade—"

I snap my head up, equal parts hope and dread gushing inside me. Something about Lukas's tone—I don't know.

It's my turn to deflate when he shakes his head. "Never mind—it's nothing."

"Oh, okay."

I look at my lap, silence festering between us. It feels like we should be talking, sharing memories, *something,* considering the possibility of impending death, but every time I try to find my voice, poisoned thoughts seep in. *He doesn't care what you have to say. You'll just sound foolish. You don't deserve to be his friend, not after what you did, so stop trying.*

In the end I run out of time, because the brig door swings open, revealing the guard with ginger tea in hand, the linens tucked beneath his arm, and a pistol holstered at his hip.

It's time.

Keys jangle as he removes them from the loop at his waist, still muttering about entitled prisoners, and my eyes flick between them and the tea.

"All right," he says as he unlocks my cell door. "Here you go, now can you please—"

I swing my arm up, splattering hot tea all over him. The guard howls, and I use his distraction to my advantage, ripping the keys from his grip and tossing them into Lukas's cell. I reach for the gun next, but the guard recovers quicker than I expected, his hands clenching my throat.

"You *little*—"

I shudder as my back hits the wall, unable to scream against the guard's fingers at my neck. I knee his crotch once, twice, and he grunts but doesn't let go. *No no no no no no.* I try to reach for the pistol, but he shifts, too big and strong and—

Stars flutter in front of my eyes as the guard's grip loosens, then falls away. In the seconds it takes me to regain my composure, Lukas tackles him, scrabbling for his weapon, but it's too close. The guard thrashes, hand inching closer to his hip, and if he gets his pistol— *No.*

I leap into the fray, rip the gun from its holster, and hiss, "Stop or I'll shoot!"

Which is a lie. Our plan hinges on remaining silent until we can't any longer, but the guard doesn't know that, and I'm relieved when he buys the bluff and stills.

Thank the gods.

I don't lower the pistol as Lukas positions himself behind the guard and wraps him in a chokehold. The guard struggles, face purpling, and I have to look away until an unceremonious thud tells me he's out. Unconscious, but not dead, not when we still need him.

"Jade." Lukas is there suddenly, his eyes heavy on me, his fingers whisper soft against my reddening neck. "I'm so sorry. The key was jammed, and— God. I'm sorry. Are you okay?"

"I'm fine." The words scrape my raw throat, boiling with my lie. I'm anything but fine.

Lukas knows it too, because when I meet his eyes, he mouths four simple words. *I believe in you.*

His message sets little fires across my skin, burning away the insecurities. Not everything, not even much, but enough to remind me I have to do this. I have to try.

Thank you, I mouth back.

Then we set about the unpleasant task of dragging the guard's unconscious body to one of the lifeboats, where, if we're lucky, we'll be joining him soon. It's tense, difficult work, and I flinch at every creak of the ship, certain someone's going to catch us. Eventually we make it to a narrow walkway outside, the peeling, eggshell paint of the ship's wall to our left and the gray-black ocean to our right. A slight breeze rolls through, chilling the sweat at my nape, and I shiver.

I never thought we'd get this far.

Lukas grunts as we heave the guard into the nearest lifeboat, a small vessel but one with a sail. I know, because on our fifth day in captivity, I requested some fresh air with the goal of surveilling the space. Like most steamboats, this one is built like a layer cake, with each level growing smaller the higher up you go. Perched atop it all is the pilot's deck, where one of the pirates keeps watch and directs our progress, though fortunately, it faces the other direction.

I glance at it, a beacon of warm light in this cool darkness, then face Lukas with a heavy swallow.

"Right," he whispers. "You ready?"

No. Not at all, because this is where we separate.

"Ready enough." I eye the gun, now tucked into his belt, then add, "Lukas . . . be careful."

He looks at me a long moment, too long perhaps, but even so, I don't break his gaze.

"You too." His words tingle over my skin before the spell breaks and he turns to go. I do the same, my thread tattoo heating as I activate it, ensuring my steps are petal soft. Soon I'm standing inside the tracker's room.

It's different at night, cradled in silver moonlight, shadows creeping over the floorboards. The ocean breathes, a rhythmic slap of water, and the steam engine hums the only sounds.

The space is still. Serene even, an odd discordance from all my earlier trips here, because this time is different. I have the power now, and I'm reminded of that when I tuck back a scarlet curtain, revealing a nook in the wall for a slim bed and the sleeping tracker.

He won't wake for days, maybe even a week. I couldn't smuggle enough thread to do any real damage, but earlier, in my cell, I unspooled about a month of his life. That kind of thing takes a toll, evident in the tracker's slack form, shallow breath, and utter stillness. If I were to lower my head to his chest, no doubt his heartbeat would be sickly slow.

I could kill him if I wanted.

I flinch at the thought, not because it frightens me but because it doesn't, and it should. I don't know why either. What's happening to me?

Maybe I'm losing my sanity. I think something might be wrong with me, creating this bubble of . . . of . . . *euphoria* that's pumping through my veins, scorching my fear in its wake. Is this what everyone else feels like? Is this what it's like to be normal?

Those swirling thoughts force a realization. It's not that I *want* to hurt the tracker. But staring at him, vulnerable by my hand, from my plans, I can't deny the thick curl of satisfaction unfurling inside me. I think . . . I think it might be *pride.* That and relief.

Because all my life I've relied on external sources for protection. My mother. My cabin. Lukas.

But this is all me. I was able to do this for myself.

Of course I don't kill the tracker. I don't want to, not really. I merely enjoy the fact that, for once, I can create my own sense of safety. I *do* remove the key from the chain at his throat, and the locked compartment of his desk clicks as it pops open, revealing Lukas's gun and my thread kit tucked inside.

Thank the gods. Lukas and I are depending on this kit, and I clutch it to my chest, then slide the gun from its holster and check it for bullets.

Loaded. Perfect.

Pleased with my progress, I move to close the drawer when I pause.

Something isn't quite right, and when I inspect the drawer more closely, I realize what it is. The desk is deeper than the drawer is long, almost as if there's hidden space.

I shouldn't waste time prying. Lukas is in the engine room, waiting to wreak havoc once I finish my work here. The second he releases chaos, though, all bets are off.

But what if this is important? What if there's something inside that helps solve these murders?

Someone else must've slipped into my skin when I wasn't looking, because taking a risk like this isn't me. Nevertheless, I fumble around the drawer in the dark, heart skipping when I discover a lip in the wood's base, and when I pull it—*yes*. A plank comes out, revealing a false back, a sheaf of documents, and a familiar lock of hair. Old, dark, and bound in cerise ribbon, it belongs to the tracker's mystery woman. This must be where he keeps it when I'm not around.

I set it aside, then inspect the papers. Most appear to be love letters, written in a woman's loopy script, yellowed and frayed, the parchment soft with age.

My dearest Alejandro, they all begin, and they all contain the same signature too. No name, just a strange marking, a crescent halved by two squiggly lines. Something about the symbol prickles with familiarity, and I flip through the pages, hoping they contain some clue as to why. Nothing stands out, though, and the messages are lovesick more than helpful. *I wish we could be together. I hate this discretion. I miss when we were kids and things were easy. When we'd sneak away from my maid—Corazón, I think her name was?—and spend our afternoons stealing cookies from the kitchen.*

Clearly, the tracker—Alejandro—was engaged in some kind of forbidden affair with this woman, most likely the hair's owner. Sordid, and perhaps interesting, but not what I need, and I'm about to return the papers when I notice one of them, paler than the rest, and sturdier too.

Newer.

This one I read in full.

Dear A,

It's difficult for me to pen these words, especially with the way we left things, but I find myself in need of your assistance. There's a girl, Jade Aguilar, who I require brought to me alive and unharmed. She's Sallenda's upcoming thread speaker, and for obvious reasons this must be handled with discretion. Of course I'll pay the required fee.

Fondly,
CR

CR? My head spins. Just minutes ago I was certain Johann Schäfer employed the tracker, but this letter suggests otherwise. How can that possibly be? I *know* Johann created the sievech—his soul matched—but even so . . .

A lump forms in my throat. I went searching for answers, but all I found was more questions. I can't even tell if CR is the tracker's lover. The handwriting looks feminine, and there are certain similarities—like the way they both dot their *i*'s with more of a slash—but there are differences too. The lover's penmanship is large, loopy, whereas CR's is much more cramped.

I don't have time for this.

Resolved, I tuck CR's note and one of the love letters into my thread kit, then, after a pause, grab the lock of hair too. *If* CR's the lover, having this record of her soul could be useful, and I carefully fit it among the whorls of thread before grabbing my seam ripper.

The tracker doesn't stir as I approach him, doesn't blink or even breathe much as I carefully slide my seam ripper beneath the tattoo on his chest and slice the threads away. He already has some clues as to where we're headed—like the fact that we bartered passage on a steamship to Kabrück, along with my suspicion of Johann Schäfer—but at least I can steal his preternatural ability to locate us. When that's finished, I slice off a dark lock of his hair and tuck it into my kit.

An insurance policy.

This is the part where the old me would scurry from the room, assuming she even had the confidence to get this far, which is unlikely. But I can't. Something glues me to the tracker, a desire to make him experience a fraction of what he did to me. *I'm sorry, Lukas,* I whisper, *just a few more minutes, please.*

Something has come over me, something dark and vicious, and I let it fill me as I steal blank parchment and a quill from the tracker's desk. The note that follows is brief and might as well have been written by a different person.

> *Dear Alejandro,*
> *I stole your hair, I took my thread kit, and I know your soul. Perhaps you'll find me again—if you can manage without your tattoo—but hear this: If you do, I'll be ready.*
>
> *Sincerely,*
> *Not Your Little Dove*

A foolish choice, perhaps, to keep him alive, but it's not without reason. If Johann Schäfer can't give us the answers we seek, we'll need someone who can.

Satisfied, I allow myself a few more seconds with the tracker. A moment to study the cut of his jaw, the now-familiar glint of his pendant, and—in a truly preposterous act—the beat of his heart. As I predicted, it's sluggish, and I grin, my ear still to his chest.

Because *I* did that. Protected myself—and Lukas—from this man who would hurt us.

And as I leave, thread kit in one hand, pistol in the other, I wonder . . .

How can I feel this again?

CHAPTER TWENTY-ONE

LUKAS

I WAS TWELVE THE FIRST TIME I STEPPED ON A FISHING BOAT. IT was our second year in Sallenda, and the family was struggling. *Lukas,* my father had said to me the evening before, *it's time to be a man.*

He roused me the following dawn, and for the next six years, fishing was my life. I never much liked it, but I did learn from it. Where to lay a net. How to spot a storm. And, most important, the general workings of a steam engine.

It's why I'm not lost in the maze of pipes that is the engine room. Why I have a vague sense of what's what, and how to locate the specific pipe responsible for transporting the heated steam, building up pressure, and powering the boat. Of course, once I put a few bullets through it, that function will fail. The crew will be stuck, at least until they patch it. In the meantime Jade and I will get the head start we need.

A perfect plan, minus the fact the waiting's killing me. But Jade needs time to execute her role—even if the thought of her alone in the tracker's room makes my skin crawl.

Ten minutes, she said. *That's all I should need. Count slowly to six hundred once you reach the engine room, then bust the pipe.*

I'm up to 423 when the door swings open, revealing a disheveled sailor with three-day scruff.

Shit.

He recoils when he notices me, then shakes his head. "Sorry, mate. Were you already reloading the coal?"

I blink a second. "Yes. Yeah."

I don't elaborate, terrified of provoking his suspicion. The gun burns at my hip, and I shift slowly, turning my left side away in an effort to hide it.

"Well, all right then. Thanks."

He turns to go. I exhale, relieved, before he looks at me again. "Hey, wait a second, aren't you—"

His eyes widen, mouth a perfect O. My stomach drops. So much for counting to six hundred.

"Shit!" the sailor cries, and there's no time to catch him before he dashes from the room. Not unless I want to shoot him, which I don't particularly want to do. He'll raise the alarm or my gunshot will. Either way, the time for sneaking around has ended. I can only hope Jade's waiting for me in the lifeboat.

Right. Okay. It's time.

Heart pounding, I aim the pistol at the main pipeline and squeeze off three shots.

Steam bursts into the air, impossibly hot. I stumble back, arm thrown across my face. The broken pipe whines dangerously, but I don't stick around to see what happens next, sprinting from the engine room and through the cramped halls of the boat's lowest deck. *Get to Jade, get to Jade, just get to Jade.*

It's all I can focus on. My mantra guides me forward until it's shattered by the pealing of an alarm bell. "The prisoners have escaped!" the muffled cry comes from above. "Secure the ship—the prisoners have escaped!"

Wooden boards fly beneath my feet as I urge myself faster, faster, faster—but not fast enough. That bell means something to these sailors. They know how to move quickly when they hear it. They're out of their cabins in seconds, shouts trailing me as I flash by: *That's him! Get him! Find the girl too!*

I wonder if this is what it feels like for Jade, all that sickly fear. It screams inside my heart. Fogs my head until I'm dizzy with it. I'm terrified for her, for me, for my family if I don't make it back.

I *can't* die here, but I also don't know how to escape. Sailors clog the halls, block the exit I wanted to take, and I'm forced to turn, breath heavy as I hurtle up the stairs and onto the deck—

And promptly regret my decision.

Eight more sailors stand at attention, pistols raised and gleaming. I freeze. Horror steals my voice, and the door hinges shriek as several more spurt out behind me. I'm surrounded. Dead. Done.

There's no way I can outrun this. I can only pray that Jade's in the lifeboat, escaping, and that she'll make sure my family's taken care of.

"Okay," I say slowly, carefully, so many predatory eyes on me. "Hold on. I'm setting my pistol down."

"Don't even think about shooting, boy," one of them says, an older woman with hair streaked gray.

"I won't." I try to keep my words neutral, but heartbreak thunders in.

I'm going to die on this ship. I'll never make Artur giggle again, never be berated by Emma, never get the chance to bring my mother some peace. And Jade. I'll never learn what makes her laugh, or get to see any more of those shy smiles. Will never hold her close or run my fingers through that silky hair.

It's been a long time since I've prayed, but the reflex is familiar, brought on by desperation. *Please,* I beg my triple god, *give me some strength. Help me bear this.*

My throat squeezes as I set the pistol down, eyes burning. When I stand, it's to face my death. Maybe not right this moment, but soon.

"All right." I hold my hands in front of me. "Take me to the—"

A bullet splits the air, and one of the sailors shrieks, collapsing as a dark stain spreads across his leg.

"Lukas, run!" Jade shouts from above. I have just enough time to glance up and see her perched on the upper deck, my father's gun in her hand.

She doesn't have to tell me twice.

I rip away from the sailors, sprinting down the hall and toward the back of the steamship, where the lifeboats are tethered. Shouts ring out behind me, but Jade's voice is louder than them all. "Follow him, and the next bullet goes through someone's skull!"

I swear, sometimes people surprise you in the best ways.

They must listen. There's no thud of feet behind me, no agonizing chase. Wind slaps my cheeks, and my surroundings blur until I skid to a halt and launch myself into the lifeboat. Another bullet cracks the night. I need to hurry. I set the mast and raise the sail, stepping over the unconscious guard in the process. I'm ready—all that's missing is Jade.

As if on cue, she shrieks, a slice right through my bones.

"Lukas!" And then she's there, on the deck above, her face a pale oval in the darkness. "You need to go. I couldn't hold them off any longer!"

Sure enough, the faint thunder of pounding feet reaches me. I can't have more than a minute until they're here, but I refuse to leave without Jade.

"Jump!" I wave my arms at her. "Come on!"

She bites her lip. I can practically hear the gears of her brain grinding, enough to fuel my voice with desperation. "Jade, please! I'll catch you! I promise!"

That does the trick. Jade holsters the gun and launches herself over the railing, hair framing her face like a dark halo. She crashes into my arms, and I collapse onto the boat's floor, my elbow jarring painfully.

God, there are so many things I want to do right now. Sit up, tuck her hair back, meet her eyes, tell her how amazing and inspiring and *beautiful* she is.

But there's no time. Instead of seizing a tender moment, I shift her off my lap and rush to the knots securing us to the ship. My fingers burn as I pull, praying I'll finish before the sailors arrive. Jade sees what I'm doing and follows suit on the second set. In the moments that follow, it's just us, our panting breath, and the coarse rope beneath our hands. My heart surges when my section comes free, and I take over Jade's.

"Stop!" One of the sailors sprints toward us, not far now. "Stop or I'll shoot!"

"Lukas . . ." Jade's voice is edged in fear. I shut her out, focused only on the task at hand—

A gun clicks

A bullet screams.

And the lifeboat falls to the ocean.

CHAPTER TWENTY-TWO

JADE

WE'RE ALIVE. I'M ALIVE. LUKAS IS ALIVE. THE SAILOR WE KIDNAPPED is unconscious but alive.

We did it—we escaped.

Lukas handles the sail with expertise, guiding us through the choppy waters, obsidian dips limned in silver. We've been at sea only a quarter of an hour, and already the steamboat is a speck on the horizon.

I still can't believe we made it. The boat dropped just in time. A second later and Lukas would've had a bullet through his skull. We were lucky, though, twofold. It's breezy tonight, and the winds carried us safely away. I pointed Lukas's pistol firmly at the sailors as we departed, effectively dampening any errant desire they might've had to shoot him. I would've done it, too, if they'd gone after him. Would've shot them.

I *did* shoot them, and a shrieking fills my head from the sailor I wounded protecting Lukas.

I'm fairly certain a healthy person would be racked by guilt, but I'm just...I don't know. Numb? And...*proud*, maybe? I shouldn't be, not over something so violent, but it was like the tracker's room all over again. I protected us, and I don't think I could be ashamed if I tried.

So I don't. I simply sit and allow myself a moment to study Lukas. The slice of his cheekbones, almost cruelly beautiful on skin porcelained by moonlight. The pink stain of his lips, the golden strands of his hair, ashy in this gray-black night. Such painful loveliness, I don't know what aches more—to look toward it or away.

His father, my heart thuds, an agonizing lurch. *Don't forget his father.*

I dip my head, skin heated with shame to be thinking these thoughts after what I did. Even reminded, I can still feel them blazing through me, and I know now it's not the looking toward or away that aches most.

It's the *wanting.*

In an effort to distract myself, I roll up my pant leg, wincing at the tender skin there, still stitched with the tracker's soul. Revulsion churns inside me, acidic, particularly regarding his hair sewn into my flesh. It's safe to remove now that it's served its purpose, and I grab the seam ripper from my kit, overcome with the need to get this off me *now.*

But I can't. My hands shake; fog rolls through my brain—the aftershocks of our ordeal finally juddering through me. I try to cut the threads, each attempt woefully clumsy, and angry tears sting my eyes. I'm halfway tempted to fling my seam ripper into the waves when Lukas is there suddenly, his palm warm on my knee. "Here." He offers his hand. "Let me help."

I'm a hurricane of emotions, bouncing from desire to shame, then shame to anger, and now anger to *this* . . . gratitude and affection, ardor and vulnerability. It's too much, and I burst into tears.

"Hey, *hey*." Lukas's breath flutters on my cheeks. "What's wrong?"

He's so soft, so tender, that I only cry harder.

"I don't know," I admit, aware of how pathetic I sound. "I just—"

I don't know.

Lukas seems to understand, reading me like he always does. "It's okay." His hands lift to my face, thumbs swiping away my tears. "I get it. I feel it too."

"You do?" I hate how childish I sound, but Lukas only smiles, a subtle twist of his lips.

"Why do you think I've been quiet? I've been trying not to cry."

Oh. I hadn't even realized.

"You don't have to," I say, and blush when he cocks his head. "I mean, you can cry, if that helps."

"Jade." My name is a dam breaking, and then *he's* the one crying, crystal tears slipping down his cheeks. "I was terrified. I thought I was going to die, and then you, *you.*" His hands are still on my face, and I become acutely aware of his burning palms on my own fiery skin. "You were amazing, so brave and intelligent and composed tonight, and I— *God.* I don't know how to thank you."

In a different life, this is where I'd kiss him, I think. I bet his lips would taste like salt, and I imagine his roaming hands, featherlight, steel strong. Would his mouth be warm? Would he groan, just a little, like he couldn't get enough?

I don't know, will never know, because in this life I've done terrible things. Have hurt him in ways he'll never guess, rotted secrets festering between us.

I duck my head, forcing Lukas to drop his hands. "I couldn't leave you behind."

This, at least, is the truth.

A moment passes, the breeze cool on my neck, waves lapping

the boat. I wait for Lukas to say something, and after a few tense moments he does.

"All right." The timbre of his voice has changed, a faux lightness there now. "Enough tears. Let me help you."

When I look up, he's extended his hand again, and I remember what started all this in the first place. I offer him the seam ripper, and Lukas takes my calf into his lap, running delicate fingers over the threads there. He looks up at me, viridian eyes shining, and for a moment that earnestness from earlier returns. "Amazing." He whispers it, as if willing me to believe.

And when he says it, I almost do.

Oh so carefully, Lukas severs the threads from my leg, removing the last vestiges of the tracker. Having Lukas this close burns in the best way, and I'm hyperaware of his fingers gliding over my skin, his gentle yet firm touch, and the furrow of his brow as he concentrates, careful not to hurt me. He's only touching my calf, but I react like he's undressing me slowly, my chest tight, breath coming in little gasps; and by the time he finishes, I'm a touch oxygen deprived.

"There." He rolls my pant leg down, then pats my leg. "Good as new."

"Thank you." The words feel disjointed and heavy, but Lukas doesn't seem to notice. He simply returns to the sail, leaving me to my earlier study of him, and oh, how it aches.

The vicious wanting of it all.

CHAPTER TWENTY-THREE

LUKAS

WE ARE, ALL THINGS CONSIDERED, INCREDIBLY LUCKY.

Shortly after the tracker captured us, he changed the crew's orders. In the original plan, they were to bring him to the *Plamara*, then take us all back to Sallenda. Something shifted after we were on board, though. Once they had us, the tracker ordered them to continue to Kabrück, any complaints quickly stifled by his dineda. For a contract crew hired to look the other way when necessary, his money was more than enough incentive to change course.

We learned all this from the sailor shortly after he woke, hours into our escape, a little worse for wear but ultimately uninjured. Able to get us where we need to go, which is why we brought him along.

And now, thanks to the tracker's change in plans, we can still get where we need to go. There's just enough time to travel to Dreiden, question Schäfer, and return to Sallenda before the queen's deadline for Jade. She'll keep her promise, and I'll keep mine to Cora in the process—assuming Cora isn't the killer, that is.

Not long after we made our escape, Jade showed me what she'd found in the tracker's rooms, including the mysterious letter signed by CR. Initials that just happen to match Cora Ramos, a fact Jade and I both noticed. It doesn't confirm anything. Not yet, at least. The letter didn't even mention the murders, just kidnapping Jade; and besides, Cora as the killer doesn't make sense. Why hire me if she's the culprit? Still, it has my suspicions raised, and I'm hoping Johann will give us some answers. If we're lucky, we'll have them soon, and the hope has me turning my face to the coastline. Because after a few days of travel, we're nearly there, finally approaching our destination.

Almost to Kabrück.

There's a chill in the air, crisp and autumnal and fresh. I breathe it in as I sit at the prow of the lifeboat, a cool breeze nipping my cheeks. The sailor sits at the mast, guiding us wordlessly to land, while Jade dozes on the boat's floor, worn-out with seasickness. I watch her a moment, hair an inky spill behind her, lashes dark sickles against her skin, like two black moons. She stirs, a frown pulling her lips. I wonder what she's dreaming. A pleasant fantasy clouds my vision, one where I leave my post, lie beside her, and wake her with a soft kiss to the temple.

Foolish. Every time I inch closer, she creeps away, looks down, shrinks back. It's obvious she doesn't want me, and I shouldn't want her either. I wave the daydream aside and return my gaze to the ocean, until at last it's not just ocean any longer.

Slowly, Kabrück appears. At first, nothing more than a jagged edge against the skyline, but gradually it becomes clearer.

A coastline, a horizon, a strip of verdant pines, rusty oaks, golden aspens. It shouldn't make my throat close up, but it does. Because it's more than a shore, more than the trees, more than a cool breeze and green grass.

It's *home*.

It's the flush of my mother's skin, the sparkle in her eyes as her belly swelled with Emma, Lina, Artur. My father pulling me onto his lap after a long day of work, the scruff of his cheeks beneath the pads of my fingers so rough and familiar. It's summer afternoons spent rolling in the strawberry patch with Emma, seeds in our teeth and juice running down our chins. The sizzle of potato patties frying on the stove, golden and warm and smelling of hot butter. It's swaying meadow grasses, buzzing bees, and Lina sprawled beside me, instructing me how to weave flower crowns because I'd do anything she asked.

It's the last place I was free, and open, and truly happy.

It's *everything*, and my carefully constructed walls crumble to dust.

"Lukas." Jade's voice is low, her hand a soft presence at my elbow. She must have woken when I wasn't looking. "Are you okay?"

I don't realize I'm crying until she says it. I wipe my tears, then face her.

"I don't know," I answer honestly, echoing what she said to me days ago. It's true, though. I don't know which feeling is strongest. Gratitude that I'm here with her, shame that I'm not with my family, or the bone-deep ache of nostalgia. An impossible wish for a happier time.

Jade studies me a moment, her eyes tender, then faces Kabrück with me. "You're home."

So simple, two words, but they resonate. "Sometimes home hurts," she adds, and my eyes burn.

"Yes," I agree. "Sometimes it does."

Roughly twenty-three hours later, we land in Werenberg, one of Kabrück's coastal cities. It bleats and whistles, lively in a way that tugs at my heart. The docks bustle with a horde of people, and I carefully guide us in, seeing as our sailor is currently indisposed. Once we were close enough, Jade unspooled a few hours of his life along with his memories of the past ten days. When he wakes, it'll be with a mess of confusion and a note pinned to his chest, written in Jade's looping script.

> *You were on board the Xiomara, part of the crew paid to kidnap a thread speaker. She bested you and in the process stole your memories of the past ten days. Should you ever be inclined to rejoin your crew and their nefarious ways, know this: I'm the thread speaker in question, and if you ever hurt another person, I'll know, and I'll unravel your life until there's nothing left.*
> *Good luck finding your way home.*

I smiled at that. The day I met Jade, I assumed she was all soft underbelly.

I was wrong.

She has fangs, claws, all of it. I'm not sure what it says about me, but her sharpened edges only make me like her more.

The boat thuds against the dock, interrupting my thoughts. I fasten us to the pier, then jump off and offer Jade my hand. "M'lady."

She blushes furiously but takes my outstretched fingers. "M'lord."

When I was seven, my family traveled to Ausselberg, Kabrück's capital, for their Gebreine festival. The memories have become a blur of apple cake, crisp fall breezes, and the scratchy wool sweater I was forced to wear. One part of that week is crystal clear, though:

the fireworks. Explosions of burning amber lighting up the sky, trails of gold dust and, I was convinced, magic.

The pink of Jade's cheeks, the feel of her hand in mine, that soft twist of her lips—it's like a dozen fireworks exploding inside my chest at once. She shifts, timid, and I realize she's on the pier and I've been staring.

"Sorry." I swallow thickly and drop her hand. When she doesn't say anything, I nod toward the city. "Well, I guess we should go."

I swear Jade pales, but she doesn't disagree. After a quick trip through customs, we march into the fray, every step we take corkscrewing my heart further. The sights, the smells, the *language*—it's all so familiar, I ache with it. The cobblestone walkways, timber-framed houses, men in felt hats and women in apron dresses. My mouth waters as we pass a food cart selling potato dumplings, crisp with butter and thick with memories. Organ notes wash over us, deep and concordant, spilling from a temple for the triple god. The music has my fingers twitching with the familiar urge to sign: a fleeting touch to my lips, my chest, my brow. One tap each for God the pure, God the strong, and God the wise.

I've spent so many years pushing this place away, I forgot how much I love it.

I'm about to turn to Jade, desperate to share my joy, when my eyes snag on a young boy. He's hawking papers, shouting about news from across the sea. A breeze ripples the pages in his hand, but I still catch the article title, stamped in jarring black: "Sallenda's Unseen Death Strikes Again, Killing Queen's Guard."

My happiness sours. I look to Jade, ready to ask her thoughts, only to freeze when I find her trembling. Eyes wide and wet, like in those first moments I met her. A quick glance in the direction she's looking reveals the source of her distress.

Not far off a man's dressed himself as a corpse. White powder cakes his face, while a thick red substance covers his lids and drips from his eyes. A woman's positioned herself with a large, boxy camera in front of him and is charging passersby to take photos with "a victim of Mérecal's Unseen Death."

It's sick, and my stomach twists. Back home, real people—ones I love—are being threatened by this killer. And folks here are making money off it?

"Jade?"

She flinches when a man bursts past us on his bicycle, her eyes welling over.

"L-Lukas." She almost gasps my name. "I can't—I just . . . The p-people. Too many."

Right. A sense of directed focus washes over me. Jade's in trouble, and I offer her my hand. "Come on. I'll get you out of here."

She takes it wordlessly, skin cold as I lead her through Werenberg's streets. Eventually I find a place to stop, a mostly deserted alley between an apothecary and a bakery. A couple stand at one end, locked in a passionate embrace, but they don't pay us any mind.

"Here." I guide Jade into a sitting position, and her back leans against a cool brick wall. "Just take a breath. It'll be okay."

It's like our first moments all over again. I watch as she gradually calms, some of the color returning to her cheeks, the trembling slowing. When it seems like the worst has passed, I ask, "Do you want to talk about it?"

She looks at her lap, shamed, I think. "That just happens sometimes. I mean, you know. You've seen it."

I have. That first day, in the streets. I hadn't thought much about it. Later, when she found the soulless body, her response aligned with the danger.

184

And now today. Earlier, I assumed her fear could be attributed to the garish corpse display, but now I'm recalculating. What did she say when I checked in with her? Something about too many people? A second before that, she flinched when that man flew by her, then grew nervous when we entered the crowd. And in Mugra, the day we met, people were clogging the streets in their rush to escape the body. Slowly, some of the pieces come together.

"You don't like crowds, do you?" I try to say it gently, but Jade winces.

"No. I . . . had a bad experience once."

My mind runs wild with possibilities, but I remain silent. Whatever this is, I sense Jade might need space to share it, so I sit down next to her and offer her my hand. "In case you want it," I say when she looks at me, quizzical.

To my shock, she takes it, fingers winding through mine. Her breath hitches, and the story comes spilling out, her voice shaking.

"I was fifteen, and my mother was transferring some of her duties over to me as part of my training. One of those responsibilities was collecting sentences at the courthouse."

Oh. The thought of thread speaking being used that way has always made me uncomfortable, but it bruises even more now. Imagining Jade at fifteen, forced to hurt people like that—it's painful.

"Those punishments . . ." Jade hesitates. "They require me to strip the qualities people find most dear. It's awful, I know that now. Frightening too, and infuriating to some." She bites her lip, then continues. "On this particular day, I was sent to deal with this man—Fernando. He worked at the bank, and apparently he'd been embezzling for years. I was supposed to take some of his intelligence, his gift with numbers, but . . ." She grimaces. "He didn't want to go easy. He paid the courthouse guards to desert their posts for an hour, then hired some desperate people willing to do seedy work and—"

She shudders. God, it kills me to see her like this, and white-hot fury blazes through me. All I want to do is make Fernando—and those people he hired—pay. But Jade is sitting here, upset, and that won't help her or solve anything.

So I swallow my anger and squeeze her hand. "It's okay if you don't want to tell me. I know this is hard."

"No." She's trembling, but her voice is steel laced. "I want you to understand."

Something inside her shifts when she says it too, because she lifts her chin and meets my gaze.

"They ambushed me on the courthouse steps. Ripped out my hair. Broke my arm. Left me a bloody, bruised pulp. They pushed me down, crowded me, made it feel like I couldn't breathe. There were so many of them, and ever since that day . . ."

She closes her eyes and leans her head back on the brick. "Whenever I'm in a crowd, it feels like I'm living through those moments all over again. Like I can't breathe, can't fight, can't protect myself. Utterly helpless." She shakes her head. "That's why I wanted your help navigating the city. I'm terrified of being out by myself. It didn't matter that my mother hired the captain of the polesa to teach me self-defense, how to fire a gun, throw a punch, all of it. I have the skills, but that doesn't mean the feelings have faded. If anything, all those years spent locked away made them stronger."

She opens her eyes, so dark and endless I forget how to breathe.

I speak without thinking. "You didn't look afraid the other night, shooting at those sailors."

She pauses, contemplative. "I was, but you know, that was the first time in a long time I didn't feel helpless. I thought maybe I was done with the fear, but I guess it's not that simple." She shrugs, looks down, then back at me. "Thank you for helping me."

"Anytime," I say sincerely. "Always, you know that."

Her throat bobs, and she looks around the alley, studying our surroundings. Her gaze lands on the passionate couple, then quickly flits back to me. "So . . . what now?"

I honestly don't know. We have a few dineda Jade tucked into her thread kit, but not every shop will accept foreign currency, and that's ignoring the fact we don't have much. Dreiden is at least four days away, even if we take the train as close as it'll get us, and that's assuming we can afford the tickets. If we're going to make it there, we'll need food, warmer clothes, and shelter.

I blow out a breath. "We need to make some money."

Jade grimaces, as if she knows what I'm thinking. "I don't want to thread-speak for it. In Sallenda we'd at least pay people for their traits, but here . . ."

We don't even have the coin to get started. Jade's fingers are still laced with mine, and I give a reassuring squeeze. "It's okay— I wouldn't expect you to do that."

Though I'm out of ideas. We're quiet a moment, and in the silence my gaze lands on the couple again. "Who knows," I suggest, sarcasm lining my words, "maybe we can rob them. They're so distracted, they probably wouldn't even notice."

Jade cracks a small grin. "I suppose not, and it could be enough—" She pauses, slack-jawed.

"Jade?"

"That's it." Her eyes glitter when she faces me. "That's *it*, Lukas!"

Her energy's infectious. If anyone asks me later, I'll deny it, but I definitely giggle. "What's *it*? You can't think I was serious about robbing them?"

"No." She smacks my arm, playful, and my jaw almost drops. I've never seen her like this before. "We *can* thread-speak for money, and without hurting anyone." Her eyes dart to the couple, then back to me.

My breath hitches. I swear, right now she's so gorgeous it hurts. Pink in her cheeks, hair sliding across her face, glowing with whatever thought has occurred to her.

"Go on," I prod, my voice an octave too high. "Tell me."

She beams, absolutely radiant. "It's easy. All we have to do is bind some souls."

CHAPTER TWENTY-FOUR

LUKAS

AS IT TURNS OUT, BINDING SOULS ISN'T NEARLY AS OMINOUS AS IT sounds. In fact, I'd go so far as to say it's wonderful. I can't deny this as I lift my fingers to the windowpane, watching all the happiness Jade created play out below.

It's been three days since we arrived in Kabrück. Thanks to Jade's gifts, our travels have been a delight. She explained to me in the alley what thread binding was: a process of tethering souls of people who truly love each other. A gift that's in part ceremonial but not without its merits. Apparently, when your soul is bound to someone, you can feel a shadow of their emotions and sense their location, and your connection is intensified in a way that isn't fully describable.

Overall, it's relatively easy to perform, without the steep costs thread speaking usually entails. It's also hard for common folk to come by, seeing as thread speakers are a rarity. Jade, though, makes it accessible to anyone who wants it.

First with that couple in the alley, then to anyone we can find. We develop a pay-what-you-can system. Sometimes that means

Jade operates for free. Other times we part from her customers with pockets full of coin. Most often, though, people pay with the gifts of their trade. Warm coats from the seamstress. Sturdy boots from the cobbler. A night in a ritzy hotel with actual plumbing. Plenty of dumplings, boiled sausages, and rabbit stew, served at taverns, restaurants, and family tables alike. Her gifts even snag us train tickets, which take us as far as Kreipen before the tracks end and we continue on foot.

To my surprise, it's a journey that might be deceptively comfortable if not for the constant chatter about the killer loose in Sallenda. Everywhere we go, people notice Jade's accent and beg us for details. And each time, my heart pinches tighter. It's a grave reminder of the danger my family's in while I gallivant across Kabrück.

Fortunately, no one asked us tonight when Jade secured us shelter at a quaint little lodge. Hours ago, she bound the souls of the innkeeper and her husband, thirty years after they first got married. Now they're outside celebrating with their family. The autumn forest is crisp and colorful around them, everyone's cheeks tinged with a mixture of joy and alcohol.

I can't look away. Jade's in the bathroom, washing up, but I've been glued to the window, entranced by the scene below. Because Jade did this. So much laughter and jubilation, made possible by her and her gifts.

For years I've viewed thread speaking as a cruel, vain thing. A way the wealthy could purchase the qualities they desire at the expense of people like me and my family.

I thought thread speaking was wrong, and the night Lina died only solidified that. Now, though, seeing how happy these people are, I wonder if maybe I was mistaken. Not about all of it—there are definitely issues with the policies around thread speaking—but perhaps the way I viewed it was too black and white.

The bathroom door creaks, breaking me from my thoughts. I turn to face Jade. She's garbed in an apron dress, hair pulled into a damp braid, her feet bare. Soapy steam wafts from the bathroom behind her, dissipating in our room, a small but cozy space. Jade offers me a shy grin, then joins me at the window. "What are you looking at?"

For a moment my mind stops, stuck on her. Always stuck on her. It's been harder to suppress my growing feelings since we landed in Kabrück. Seeing Jade in the clothes of my home, hearing her praise the food, watching her hair ripple in the autumn breeze, cheeks nipped with pink in the cool air . . . it makes me yearn for a life with her. Here. In my home.

God. I need to get myself together, and I nod at the celebration below, answering her question. "Them. How happy they are."

"They are, aren't they?" She looks content, lips quirked in a faint smile. "It's nice using my gifts like this. It feels right."

"It doesn't always feel right?"

A shadow passes over her face, and she looks down. "No. It doesn't. I don't think I realized quite how much until I met you."

She blinks back tears, and my gut churns. "Hey." I bridge the distance between us, raising a gentle hand to her elbow. "I'm sorry, I shouldn't have asked."

She's quiet a long time. Eyes closed, lip trembling, hands clenched into fists. "Lukas . . ." She shakes her head, opens her eyes, her posture stiffening as she takes me in. "Never mind."

A thousand desires rip through me. I want to ask what she almost said, tell her I'm sorry, and confess all these feelings surging inside me. Most of all, I want to make her smile again. To take her hand and lead her down to that celebration. To let her feel all the happiness she created, if only for a little while.

I almost do, too. Almost offer. I'm about to when someone's

voice echoes from below, one of the partygoers. "Hey, Lina! Come look at this!"

It hits me harder than a slap. Everything I've been holding back these past few weeks floods in, reminders of the family I'm neglecting to be here. All I want is to enjoy this evening with Jade, but that suddenly feels unbearably selfish with Lina dead and my family scraping by without me.

I realize, suddenly, how off track I've gotten. I promised my father I'd be there for my family always. While this journey may have begun for them, I can't pretend it hasn't become about something more.

I dip my head, and silence creeps between us. I'm tempted to ask Jade about Lina, to see whether she remembers that night. If she was awake, listening on the stairs while I begged her mother to save Lina's life. I never saw her, but it's not difficult to imagine the possibility.

In the end, I decide against it and simply mumble something about washing up myself and stagger to the bathroom.

As I sink into the still-warm water, I tell myself I was too exhausted to have that conversation right now. In actuality it's something more. The way Jade shut down when I asked about her thread speaking, the fact she couldn't look at me, whatever she almost said—I'm exhausted, yes, but that's not why I didn't ask.

In truth, I'm simply terrified by the answer.

CHAPTER TWENTY-FIVE

JADE

WIND WHISTLES THROUGH THE PINES, SETTING ME FURTHER ON edge. Something is wrong, in the sense that it isn't.

Lukas and I arrived in Dreiden last night, four days after we set out from Werenberg. It's a small village of picturesque log cabins and dirt roads nestled at the forest's edge. We stayed in the town's only inn, and this morning the owner pointed us in the direction of Johann Schäfer.

Which brings us to now. Lukas and I are hidden behind an overexuberant cluster of witch hazel, golden with autumn. The air is fresh, and birds chitter above us, oblivious to my inner turmoil.

As it turns out, Johann Schäfer lives just outside Dreiden in a small forest cabin with a garden out front. The sky blushed pink with daybreak when we arrived, but it's since shifted to a pale cerulean, and there still hasn't been any sign of Schäfer. The innkeeper assured us he was in town purchasing goods just days ago, so he has to be in.

Still, though . . .

I haven't told Lukas, but I don't feel ill. When we found the soulless body, and later when we faced the sievech, I was suddenly and violently sick. I assumed it was caused by the sievech itself, the unadulterated wrongness of it. But now?

This close, Schäfer should be triggering me if he's the killer, and while I'm feeling a bit nauseous, it's nothing that can't be attributed to nerves. Which perhaps should be a relief, but what if there's more to it? I mean, look at where he lives. A cute forest cabin. It makes me wonder—what if Schäfer's *not* the criminal mastermind we envisioned? If he isn't part of some criminal scheme . . .

Then it's unlikely my mother's here. And if my mother's not here— *No.* I can't even bring myself to face the thought. The one that's always lurking, hidden in shadows and biting at edges.

What if she's lost to me for good?

A violent shiver shoots down my spine, and I pull my wool coat tighter around myself, though it's no protection against the chill rising rapidly inside me. This is all terribly wrong, and made worse by the fact that I don't feel like I can tell Lukas. I'm not sure what happened, but he shut down on me after our conversation at the inn two nights ago. One minute he was sweet, kind, himself, and the next . . .

He hasn't been looking at me. When I ask him a question, he gives one-word answers. Something's off, and I've been agonizing over what I could've done wrong—but I can't figure it out. If he discovered what I did to his father, surely he'd be far past grumpy.

"Lukas . . ." I'm not even sure what I'm going to say, other than I miss talking to him.

"Yeah?" His tone isn't mean, just tired, and he doesn't take his gaze off Schäfer's cabin. Like he can't even bear to look at me anymore.

Gods, why did I have to say something? But it's too late to turn back now.

"I'm sorry." My breath is so shaky, I barely get the words out. "I'm sorry for whatever I did. I didn't mean to. I just— I'm sorry. I'm so sorry."

That gets his attention, and I cover my face, wishing he'd just look away. Of course I don't get my wish.

"Hey." The Lukas from before is back. The one who's gentle and sweet and kind. He scoots closer, touches my knee, and lowers his head so we're eye level. "Jade, what's wrong? Why are you apologizing?"

I'm the stupidest person to exist, ever, and my cheeks flame.

"Nothing." I pull back an inch, lower my hands, and look at the ground, anything to make him stop staring at me. "I was being foolish, is all."

"Jade." When I don't say anything, he sighs. "If anyone should apologize, it's me. I've been in a mood lately, but it's not your fault, and I'm sorry I made you believe it was."

I'm not sure what to say. I've been so paranoid I lost his friendship, I forgot I don't deserve it in the first place. The other night, at the inn, I nearly told him about his dad. He asked if my thread speaking didn't always feel right, and all I could think of was standing at the docks, his father's soul in my hands.

In the end I couldn't summon the courage. Typical.

I shake my head. "It's fine. You've been fine; I'm just over-reacting."

Something softens in his gaze. "Jade—"

The cabin door creaks, interrupting him. *Schäfer.* He's coming outside. For a moment we remain frozen, our eyes locked, breath bated. This is it. The person we've traveled to another continent for. A man who could be a serial killer. A soul stealer. The Unseen Death.

Lukas quietly lifts his pistol, and I do the same with mine.

One, he counts soundlessly, and I watch his lips. *Two. Three.*

We both turn and take in this man we've come so far for . . .

I gasp, two truths becoming immediately apparent.

One: That *is* Johann Schäfer.

And two: He is not our murderer.

CHAPTER TWENTY-SIX

JADE

"JADE," LUKAS WHISPERS BESIDE ME, "WHAT IS IT?"

He must sense something's wrong. In front of us, Johann stands on his creaky front porch, his soul clean of rot.

"It's not him," I answer quickly, eyes stupidly burning, my dreams of a reunion with my mother crumbling to ash. And the people of Mérecal . . . we haven't saved them. Not yet, at least. A knot forms in my throat, but I swallow it, then add, "That's Johann. He created the sievech, but he's not the one controlling it."

Lukas's gaze flits to me. "Are you okay?"

Gods, no. Johann's involved somehow, but the longer I study him, the more convinced I become: My mother's not here. I'm heartbroken, but now isn't the time to discuss it. "I'll be fine," I tell Lukas, and when it looks like he might press the matter, I gesture toward Johann. "I can tell he's not the murderer because of his soul," I explain. "It matches the imprint on the sievech we saw, so he definitely made it, but he didn't bind it to himself. If he had, his soul would be rotting, but it's healthy."

And it is. Tranquil swirls of amethyst, kind waves of coffee brown, spurts of merlot passion. If it were rotting, it'd be fading at the edges, whittling away to nothing. It's full, though, healthy too, and I'm forced to confront an unpleasant reality: This isn't the soul of someone who'd involve themselves in a murder plot—not voluntarily, at least.

CR flashes to my mind, the tracker's mysterious employer. When I first read the letter, I was so sure Schäfer was calling the shots that I assumed CR worked for him, but what if I had it wrong? What if Schäfer worked for CR? Or . . .

What if CR forced Schäfer to help them?

It would explain why Johann's here, so far away from Sallenda. Why there's no sievech about, guarding him. He doesn't strike me as a cold-blooded criminal, and as we watch, he approaches his garden, which is bursting with spinach, squash, and green beans. Soft notes weave through the air as he hums a folk tune and harvests the vegetables, his graying hair rustling in the breeze, wire-rimmed spectacles sliding down his nose.

"I think we should talk to him," I suggest at the same time Lukas says, "We were definitely wrong about him."

A beat of silence passes before Lukas nods. "Okay, let's talk to him, but"—he holds up his pistol—"we still don't know how he's involved in all this, so we need to be careful."

I lift my own gun in response, and Lukas whispers, "Behind me."

Then he slowly creeps out from behind the witch hazel. I follow, pistol raised.

Schäfer doesn't notice us right away, but that ends when Lukas steps on a twig. His gaze whips up, and he stumbles back, stammering in Kabrückian. "P-p-please. I don't have much, but whatever you want, it's yours. T-take it."

Some of my fear drains away, heart softening, and I lower my gun. Lukas keeps his raised but doesn't stop me as I approach Schäfer. "We're not here to hurt you, or steal your things," I tell him. "We just have some questions."

Schäfer's still whiter than flour, but his trembling slows. "What kind of questions?"

I glance at Lukas, and when he nods, I explain in Kabrückian, grateful for my mother's lessons. "We came from Sallenda, where a sievech is running loose, and we think you have something to do with it."

Ten minutes later we're seated at Schäfer's kitchen table, mugs of steaming black tea in front of us. The space is homey with log walls, fur rugs, and a cozy stone hearth crackling with a warm fire. Schäfer sits beside me, foot tapping, clutching his mug so tightly, I'm surprised it doesn't shatter.

There's a pinch inside my chest. I know how it feels to be afraid, and I try to make my voice low and soothing. "Really, we're not here to hurt you. We just want to know who's killing innocents and stealing their souls. That's all."

He steadies himself, then nods toward the air around me, where my soul must be visible to him. "To be honest, when you first showed up, I thought you must be involved somehow. I mean, a thread speaker at my doorstep, right in the middle of this mess with the sievech? What were the chances? But now that I can see it's not you . . ." His shoulders slump. "I wish I could tell you who's responsible, but I honestly don't know."

"Don't know?" Lukas sounds incredulous. "But you made it. Bound it."

"I did," he admits, "but not willingly. A few months ago I was abducted from my home and shipped across the sea. I didn't even know I was in Mérecal until I escaped."

I shiver. Just being in a sievech's presence makes me sick, so I can't imagine what the creation did to him.

"But you had to bind it to someone," I nudge him gently. "Surely you at least saw them?"

He shakes his head. "I wish I had. Whoever they were, they remained shrouded and only exposed their arm to me for the binding. And even if I had seen them . . ." He sighs, foot tapping faster now. "They kept me drugged. Not to the point where I couldn't follow orders, but enough to steal everything save for the barest flashes of memory. I can't even remember their soul."

I bite my lip. Lukas and I traveled thousands of miles to get here, hoping to solve this case, but Schäfer doesn't have answers. We're no closer to finding my mother or saving Sallenda's people from terror.

Lukas must sense my frustration, because he leans forward. "Are you sure there isn't anything? Nothing you remember that could help? No detail is too insignificant."

"Well . . ." Schäfer's face contorts in thought. "I was kidnapped by a man, but I *think* the other person was a woman. The one I bound the sievech to. I vaguely remember her speaking once, and the voice sounded feminine."

Okay. I sit back. Somewhere in Sallenda there's a woman with a rotting soul, most likely CR. She'd have to be powerful to pull this off, though the strongest woman I met was the queen, and her soul was intact. Perhaps someone in the Regela? Or maybe Cora? After all, the initials match. Though that wouldn't make sense—why ask Lukas to find the killer if it's her? Then again, several of the rumors *do* speculate the Serpensas are behind the murders. I brushed them aside when I learned Cora was after the killer, but perhaps my assumptions were too quickly made.

Hope rekindled, I prod a little further. "And the man who kidnapped you? Do you remember anything about him?"

Schäfer answers right away, as if relieved to have something useful. "Him I remember. Dark hair. Brown eyes. And his soul . . ." He shudders. "Cruel. Strong. Love choked in jealousy and pain. Not pretty."

The tracker. It has to be. Which means he's been here before and knows how to find us even without his tattoo, though I don't let myself dwell on that fact now.

"And do you know why they sought you out specifically?" I ask. Now that we know Schäfer didn't go willingly, it doesn't quite add up. Why *him*? There aren't many thread speakers, but at least a few live closer to Sallenda.

"I think it's because they knew I could do it," he answers. "Most thread speakers haven't even heard of sieveche, and the ones who have usually don't know how to make them."

Well, that explains why the tracker turned around once he had us. After I mentioned Johann, he must've figured we were already halfway to Kabrück, so he might as well finish the journey and retrieve Schäfer again.

"If that's the case, how do you know how to make a sievech?" Lukas asks, jarring me from my thoughts. "And more important, how did your kidnappers know you could?"

Schäfer sighs and sits back. "This might be easier if I start at the beginning."

When Lukas and I don't object, he continues.

"There used to be a thread speaker located in Ausselberg," he explains, "Tobias Braun, who was known to take on apprentices. I studied with him when I was sixteen."

I'm instantly alert. *Tobias Braun.* Why is that name familiar?

Schäfer continues, oblivious to my confusion. "There were a few others under his tutelage at the time, and I made some friends, but over the years we went our separate ways, and I was the only one who stayed in Kabrück." He gestures to the cabin around us. "I settled down here, preferring a quieter life."

That makes sense. Most countries have strict regulations when it comes to thread speakers, but not Kabrück. Here thread speakers are free to do as they please, provided they don't use their gifts on others without consent.

Lukas eyes him. "I'm guessing it didn't stay quiet?"

"No." Schäfer traces the wood grain of the table. "It didn't. When I was in my early twenties, I was in Ausselberg for a visit, and I stopped to see Tobias. He'd . . . changed." He visibly tenses. "I'm not sure what did it, but he wanted *more.* More wealth, power, land; felt that he deserved it. I felt ill just standing near him, which in hindsight was a sign he must've already created a sievech." He releases a sad huff. "When I saw Tobias, he dropped hints regarding his plan to create an army of sieveche and asked if I wanted to help him. I declined, of course. But I was concerned. I should've alerted the authorities, but Tobias . . ."

Schäfer wipes his eyes. "He'd been my mentor. I didn't want to hurt him, and I didn't think he'd actually figure it out. So I decided to stay in Ausselberg and monitor him. It was a poor decision."

Dread brews, bitter acid churning inside my stomach.

"He did it, didn't he?" I whisper. "He made his army."

"He tried." Schäfer's words come out resigned. "In the end he only succeeded in making three, but it was enough. People died. First the poor and vagrants, then anyone Tobias felt had slighted him. By that time I'd visited the morgue and seen one of the bodies, the absence of their soul . . ."

He shudders, then meets my eyes. "To kill a sievech, first you must kill its master, and to do that, you need to unspool their life thread. I didn't know this at the time, so I wrote to one of my friends overseas, someone who'd trained under Tobias with me. She came right away, and together we found his research, then used the information to kill him. Afterward she destroyed his journal and went home."

A prickle of hope? Unease? Excitement? *Something* ripples through me, an electric current beneath my skin, because what if his friend didn't destroy the notes? What if she stored them away in her attic to collect dust?

Schäfer continues. "Of course, the murders stopped after Tobias died, but no one knew what he'd done. They even had a funeral for him; it was a huge affair. He'd trained most of the practicing speakers alive at the time, and there were dignitaries from all over." He looks at me. "I even met your queen. Fierce woman—beautiful too—with a soul more determined than I've ever seen."

I blink. The image Johann painted doesn't exactly line up with my memory of the queen, who struck me as more hesitant than fierce, and more plain than beautiful. To be fair, there *was* some determination in her soul, but it wasn't enough for me to note it as one of her dominant qualities. Then again, it's perfectly reasonable that her soul might have changed with time—this was years ago, after all, and as people grow and adapt, so do their souls. It's a reasonable enough explanation, and I brush my questions aside as Johann continues.

"After the funeral, the paper featured an article about Tobias's passing that quoted me. I suspect my kidnappers came across it and realized I was connected to it all, because twenty-two years later, I was ripped from my home, and they demanded—"

He cuts off abruptly, unable to continue. I have about a dozen questions, but Lukas speaks before I can voice them.

"And what about your escape? How did you make it home?"

Schäfer's so still, at first I don't think he's going to answer. I bite my lip. Something is *wrong*, and when he opens his mouth, I nearly ask him not to tell us before I swallow the urge.

"My friend saved me." His words are quiet. Defeated. "The one who helped me all those years ago. I don't know how, but she figured out I was in trouble, learned where I was, and broke in to free me. But"—his voice cracks—"someone—a guard, I'm not sure—arrived before we could get away. There was a fight, she told me to run, but then I heard a gun go off and—and—" He grabs his chest, tears slipping down his cheeks. "When I looked back, she was on the floor in a puddle of blood, not moving, and I—I *left* her. I'm a coward who left her, and now she's dead and—"

Any coherent words give way to sobs, but I barely hear them, can hardly see. The first spikes of an episode pound through me, a wash of icy cold filling my limbs. It's like I'm outside myself, a ghost watching a memory of her past life, and I don't even feel my lips move as I face Schäfer and somehow manage to ask, "Your friend, please. What was her name? I need to know her name."

Schäfer doesn't meet my eyes when he mumbles it into the air, but it's enough. The words slice me open.

"Zamora Aguilar," he says, tone heavy. "Her name was Zamora."

Zamora. Zamora. Zamora.

Her name screams through me, and in its wake a venomous truth:

My mother isn't missing.

She's dead.

CHAPTER TWENTY-SEVEN

JADE

I'M DROWNING. INKY WAVES CRASH OVER ME, DRAGGING ME deeper into the abyss. I can't think, can't breathe, can't *be*.

Crushed in an ebony ocean.

A flash of awareness. A distant rush of sensation. Palms scraping, bleeding, as this body crashes into a tree. A cradle of soft, damp soil. Midmorning sun filtering down, starbursts between the trees, and then viridian eyes. Deep. Concerned. Courageous.

Breathe, a gentle voice says. *Jade, just breathe.*

I swim toward the surface. Lungs bursting. Fingers clawing at those sooty waves.

I come to slowly. Splintered pieces of my surroundings gradually slide together to form a picture. A canopy of trees above me. The fragrance of pine in the air. My clothes damp, covered in soil. Stinging cuts on my palms, my knees. And my head nestled in a lap, soothing fingers running through my hair, tucking it back from my face.

Lukas.

I don't realize I've said his name aloud until he stills. "Jade?" Worry lines his voice, and when he looks down, his eyes are wet. "I was terrified. I thought . . . I don't know. I don't know what I thought, I was just scared."

"What happened?"

The words scrape, and Lukas sucks in a breath. "We found Schäfer. He told us what happened, about how your mother . . ."

He doesn't finish. He doesn't have to, not when I shut my eyes against the burn of tears, though they still leak out.

My mother is dead. I force myself to think it again and again. To brand that truth inside my skull, because if I don't, I won't believe it, and if I don't believe it, I'll have to relive this moment on repeat.

I don't think I could survive that; I'm barely surviving *this.* A tsunami of memories roars through me. The first day I met my mother, at the orphanage. How kind she was as she asked about the souls I could see. The way she held my grubby little hand as she led me out those doors, and the sense of absolute safety I felt in her presence, like finally this was someone who could care for me. Late nights of shortbread and hot milk when I couldn't sleep, her patience as she helped me compile my first thread kit, and her beaming smile when I stitched my first soul.

And every night—every single night—she would wrap her arms around me, pull me close, and whisper, *You are strong, capable, and wonderful. Don't ever forget it.* Then she'd kiss my brow and murmur into the fringes of my hair that she loved me. I never failed to whisper it back either. *I love you, Mom.*

I'll never get to tell her again.

Every memory slices into me, another cut of my battered heart, but I don't tip into that ocean, not a second time. Lukas pulls me to his chest as I sob, rocking me slowly. *I'm sorry, I'm sorry, I'm so sorry,* he whispers until I calm some.

My face is sticky when I eventually pull away, and I ask, words shaky, "And after Schäfer told me, what happened?"

It's all black. A pit of terror like I've never experienced before.

Lukas swallows. "You went really quiet before you—I don't know—you made this *sound,* and then you ran out the door and kept going until you collapsed here. It was like you weren't in control, like someone else was in there, pulling your strings."

I didn't *feel* in control, and I shake my head. "Thank you, Lukas, for taking care of me, really."

He looks at me so hard then, it almost hurts, like he's the one who can read souls. "Jade. I—" He takes a sharp breath. Runs a hand through his hair. "I know this started as a sort of business arrangement, but it's more to me now. *You* are more to me now, and you have to know, I'm here for you if you need me."

I'm weary to my bones, but I summon the strength to lift my head and study Lukas. *Gods,* maybe it's not the time to think it, but he's so beautiful it takes my breath away. Golden hair, fine skin, eyes like, well, *jade.* And his *soul.*

From those first moments in the alley, I knew Lukas was good. It was written in his soul, but more than that, it was a presence in the air. Something both intangible and undeniable. I'd been afraid, but then he was there and I just . . . wasn't anymore. Similar to the day I met my mother, took her hand, and felt safe.

But where my feelings for my mother were always affectionate, warm, and familial, with Lukas it's something different. There's heat beneath my emotions, a boiling in my veins.

And now my mother is gone. I'm alone and have no one—

Except this boy who makes me burn.

Grief is a strange thing. I know I'm supposed to wallow and ache and float through my days, a numb husk. But there's a gaping hole inside my chest, not just where my mother was but where all that feeling was stored, and I—

I can't take it. Which is perhaps why, instead of grieving like a normal person, I whisper, "Can you kiss me?"

"What?" Surprise blazes in Lukas's eyes.

Any other day I'd shrink back. Gods, any other day I wouldn't have even asked. But I'm feeling small, alone, *scared*. If Lukas kisses me, I won't feel that way anymore.

"I want to kiss you," I tell him. "And I'm hoping you want to kiss me too. So if you do, just please do it. Kiss me."

Later, I'll be mortified I begged like this. Right now all I can focus on is the way Lukas's nostrils flare, how his pupils dilate, the flush crawling up his skin. His throat bobs, a heavy thing. "Jade, I'm not sure. You just—"

"I know what just happened." I cut him off, not cruel but firm. "I know I'm emotional right now. But even if I hadn't just learned about my mother . . ." I falter, the air growing thin, but when I focus on Lukas's eyes, I can breathe again. "I've wanted to kiss you for a while," I admit. "The only thing that's changed is now I'm brave enough to ask."

"Jade." My name is almost a whimper, and emotions cascade across his face so fast I barely catch it. Affection, tenderness, and then, *yes*. Longing. The first crack in his already fragile composure. "You've really wanted this?"

I nod.

"And you're sure?" His voice is a shade too high. Breathless. "I don't want to hurt you."

"You won't," I say, because it's true. "You couldn't."

I see it, the moment the dam breaks. The ripple of longing bursts, giving way to steely determination. Lukas shifts, faces me, and leans closer. His fingers curl in the grass before he lifts his hand to my cheek. He traces the bone there, then cups it, warmth flowing into me where our skin meets. He uses his other hand to grip my waist and gently tugs me into his lap, the fire in my veins roaring.

"Jade." My name on his lips is a reverent thing, and he leans his forehead against mine. I'm dizzy with his nearness, my heart pounding, not with fear but with excitement, affection, and longing of my own.

"Lukas," I whisper back, and his breath hitches.

The world is black, my eyes closed, but I can hear the desire as it drips from his words. "I've wanted to kiss you for a while too," he says.

And then he does.

The first brush of his lips is soft, tender, hesitant, almost like he's waiting for me to pull back. What he doesn't know is that right now, he's the only tether keeping me grounded, and I push into him, tangling my hands in his hair. He moans, and I shiver with it, this heady effect of him rippling over my skin, scorching me every place his body meets mine.

"Lukas." His name is an exhale, a flit between one kiss and the next. I've wondered for years what this moment would be like, for weeks what it would be like with him, and now I know.

It's the pleasant fluttering of my heart. The smell of spring's first rain. It's a deep wine red flecked with amber. It's Lukas's arm wrapped around my hips, his hand fisted in my hair, our chests pressed together, hearts beating in tandem.

I never want to let him go, and I wonder absently, *Why didn't I do this sooner?*

Slowly, through my kiss-drunk haze, the answer surfaces: his father.

I freeze, horror clawing my insides. If Lukas knew—if he had any idea— *Oh gods.*

I rip away, trembling, tears already flowing. An episode threatens anew, those foamy waves beckoning—*no. No no no.*

"Jade?" Lukas's voice is quiet. Strained. "Are you okay? What's wrong?"

"I—"

But what do I say? *I helped kill your father, but I've been too scared to tell you, and now I've kissed you when I knew it was wrong.*

Which is exactly what I should tell him, but I can't. I don't think I could survive Lukas hating me, especially with my mother's death this fresh.

I hang my head, focus on taking deep breaths, and, once I'm composed enough, say, "I'm sorry. This was a mistake." My voice cracks. "I'm sorry. I shouldn't have done that, and it can't happen again."

It's only a flash of emotion, but I catch it. The way Lukas's face crumples, caving in on itself. Confusion and hurt rip across his features, and in that moment I hate myself more than I've ever hated anything.

I'm a selfish, horrible person, and in an effort to protect some of Lukas's feelings and save myself, I add, "Can we still be friends, though? I don't think I could survive it, losing you."

LUKAS

I don't think I could survive it, losing you.

Emotional whiplash. That's the only way I can describe it. The panic when Jade ran out, of seeing her like that, bleeding into relief when she sat up, and then—god, when she asked me to kiss her? I don't think there are words for the way I felt with Jade in my arms, her lips on mine, hair sliding beneath my fingers. The sound she made—I don't even think she noticed it—a contented little hum.

I could've kissed Jade forever. But now she's looking at me, heartbreak in her eyes, reflecting the cracking inside my own chest.

This was a mistake. I'm sorry. I shouldn't have done that.

I don't think Jade was lying when she said she's wanted to kiss me for a while, but her rejection was honest too. She didn't have to say what I've known from our first moments together: I'm not good enough for her. She may want me, true, may even care for me, but she'll never let herself have me, knowing what I am.

Just a dirty boy from Mugra.

I don't care about that.

Jade's words, spoken the night she stitched me up.

And maybe I should give her more credit, should give *myself* more credit. But whatever her reasons, nothing's changed. This was still a mistake—her words, not mine.

"Lukas?" Jade's voice wobbles. I realize I've been sitting in stunned silence for some time.

"It's okay," I reassure her, voice cracking. "I understand. You're right, this was a mistake." When her face falls, I'm quick to add, "But of course we can still be friends."

It'll burn when I want so much more, but in this Jade and I are aligned. I couldn't survive losing her either.

She closes her eyes, a few tears slipping out. I resist the urge to wipe them away. A few moments ago that was natural, but now it feels like crossing a line. So I remain still, fingers itching, until she opens her eyes, meets my gaze, and says, "I think maybe you should go home now."

What? I flinch. Just seconds ago she begged me to be her friend, and now she's sending me away?

Jade must see the hurt on my face, because she pales and quickly adds, "I don't want you to leave, but your family. They're still in Mérecal with a sievech running about. We don't know who's controlling it, but we do know they aren't here. And if CR is Cora, is the murderer, you should get your family away from her, just to be safe."

Jade's words hit me like a punch to the gut. It's more difficult to dismiss Cora as a suspect now that we know the killer's a woman. Plus, the initials match, she's known to be duplicitous, and several rumors claim the Serpensas are behind the deaths.

I don't know. Nothing makes sense anymore—I still don't understand why Cora would send me after the murderer if she's the culprit. And *is* CR even the killer?

My head spins, but amid it all I know one thing to be true: I don't *want* Cora to be responsible. If she is, I may have put my family in more danger.

Perhaps that's why I object. Or maybe it's because I sense Jade is about to push me away further, and I'm not ready for it. "And how do I get my family away from her? We don't have the money to start over somewhere new."

Jade's eyes soften as she spots my words for what they are: a paltry attempt to stay by her side.

"I could write a letter to transfer the remainder of my funds into Emma's account," she offers. "We could have it notarized. It would give you more than enough to settle down somewhere else. Somewhere you could be free."

Except I wouldn't, not without her. My heart squeezes painfully. "And what about you?" I ask. "You wouldn't come with me?"

She shakes her head, a sad, brittle movement. "Someone has to interrogate the tracker, and it might as well be me. You have a family to protect back home, but me . . ." She swallows, her eyes glossy. "I don't have anyone anymore."

I nearly flinch. My next words tremble, a current of barely repressed emotions raging behind them. "That's not true. You have me."

She's silent a moment, blinking back tears, her breath shallow. It takes her a minute to compose herself enough to reply. "I know I do. But I don't want to steal you away from your family."

She's right. I hate it, but it's true. I need to get back to them, but the prospect of leaving her grates on me like coarse sandpaper over soft skin. Which is why I say the only thing that might convince her to leave with me.

"And the queen's deadline? You'll miss it."

We're already cutting it close. If Jade doesn't leave in seven days, she won't make it back in time, and the wrong side of a queen is a dangerous place to be.

She absently fiddles with her pendant, unable to meet my eyes.

"I have a little time, and the tracker will be here soon. When he arrives, I'll just . . . I guess I'll . . . well, I'll have to find a way to capture and question him. Then I can turn him in to the authorities and leave."

I hate that I consider it.

If this had all happened six weeks ago, before Cora, I would've immediately agreed. I might not have liked it, but I know my purpose: to care for my family always. They come first, before my own wants and happiness and hopes. I wouldn't hesitate to take a bullet for them.

But this isn't six weeks ago. Things are different now. *I'm* different with Jade in my life. She gave me a taste of freedom, and now I'm drunk on the nectar. I want to stay, even if she never cares for me the same way I do her. I want to help her through her grief, and just the thought of leaving—

No.

The word clangs inside my skull, awkward and foreign in this context. Thanks to Jade, my family is housed and provided for. They'll need me soon, but they're okay right now and Jade isn't. I don't want to leave her.

And I won't, I decide, not yet.

Selfish. My father never called me as much in life, but surely he would now.

Shame burns my throat, but I swallow it, then face Jade and say, "No. I'm not leaving you."

"But—" she protests.

I cut her off. "I'm sorry, but it's not happening. The tracker's on his way here, and what do you think will happen when he arrives?" She flinches, and I soften the barbs in my voice. "I'd bet on you, but I also don't want to risk you."

The day I met Jade, I thought she was a girl of lace, chiffon, silk—I was wrong. All those gauzy fabrics hide a steel backbone, and she reveals it now.

"No," she says, voice firm. "Whether or not I risk myself is *my* choice, not yours, and I refuse to let you be collateral damage in my mess."

My answer is equally firm. "You're right, but it's *my* choice to stay."

And it's true. If this were any other scenario, I'd honor her wishes, but now I've finally found a backbone of my own.

"Lukas." She looks down, takes a steadying breath, then meets my eyes. "You shouldn't risk yourself—risk your family—for me. I don't deserve it."

My mind flashes back to the evening spent in that quaint lodge, shadows in Jade's eyes as she hinted at the darker side of her gifts. The way she nearly told me something before she backed off.

Another memory surfaces of a black night, my skin damp with rain before Zamora slammed the door in my face. I've relived those moments so many times, they're branded inside my skull. Now I imagine a slight quirk, a different angle. It's a vision I've entertained before, but it suddenly feels all too real. In it Jade's sitting at the top of the stairs, younger and leaner, fingers clutching the railing. Listening to me sob. Watching her mother turn me away.

Just because I didn't see her doesn't mean she wasn't there.

Two days ago that possibility infuriated me, but now? Jade was just a kid. And whether it's true or not, I decide I don't care. Not anymore.

"You do deserve it," I insist, "and I'm not leaving you."

Her lip trembles, and she moves so quickly I don't have time to react. She darts into my chest and wraps her arms around my middle, her next words muffled in my shirt. "Thank you." And then, quieter: "I don't want you to leave either."

I sigh and pull her closer. "Good, because I'm not going anywhere."

PART THREE

CHAPTER TWENTY-EIGHT

JADE

I CLUTCH MY PENDANT AS I WIND THROUGH DREIDEN'S SMALL market, past stalls selling furs, dumplings, or little wooden totems of their triple god, the trinkets preparations for their upcoming holiday, Gebreine. It's difficult to keep the panic down, but I manage it, because for the past two days Lukas and I have practiced walking through this market.

When the tracker comes, it's best he finds you in a public place, Lukas said once we realized we had to prepare. *Perhaps the market—it goes right by the inn.* From there we carefully pieced together a plan, told Johann who we were, then explained what we wanted to do. And though he was nervous, he offered to help. He's kept his word, too. We've been staying in the little barn behind his home, and late yesterday evening we woke to his knock on our door. A note from the innkeeper, a friend of his, was gripped in his hands. It was two words. Simple.

He's here.

Breathe, Lukas told me as I held the paper in trembling fingers. *You've got this.*

And I do. A wind chime tinkles, one of several in a nearby stall, a soothing ring as I recall those moments aboard the *Xiomara*. How I watched the tracker sleep, rendered vulnerable by my hand. I stitched his thread portrait the day after that, and some nights I contemplate all the traits I could steal away.

I don't, of course. My mother taught me not to meddle. *You must remember, Jade,* she liked to say, *our power is a dangerous thing. To wield it as a god is to become a monster.* My eyes burn, and I lurch to a stop in the middle of the market. These past two days . . . thinking of my mother is too painful, so I've simply avoided it the best I could, but now I'm flooded with an image of her in a pool of blood. Dying. Scared.

Dead.

The episode rushes up, a vicious tide, the air suddenly too thin, my clothes suddenly too tight. I want to cry, scream, crumple, but I force myself to remember Lukas and his courageous eyes. *Breathe,* I imagine his voice, *just breathe, Jade.*

Slowly the wave crests, though I'm left pale and trembling. I reach for my pocket, where I've kept the tracker's thread portrait— a demented sort of security blanket—before I remember it's not there.

Gods. I need to get it together, and I shake my shoulders as I pass another stall. This one is busier, a cluster of people around it, whispers hot on their lips and a newspaper spread among them. When I crane my neck, I can just make out the article they're reading:

"Polesa Scramble as Unseen Death Strikes Again, Leaving Two Bodies in One Night."

"See, what did I say?" a stout woman announces, tapping the headline as she faces the burly man at her side. "I told you it would get worse. Two bodies in one night, and you said it would never surpass one." She holds out her palm. "Pay up. You lost the bet."

The man grumbles but hands over a few coins while I gape at them.

People are *dying,* and they're making bets?

I'd scold them if I wasn't so terrified, and my cheeks burn as I stomp away, not stopping until I reach a familiar stall.

"Good morning, Clara," I greet the older woman, her cart filled with bolts of fabric, from pale linen to inky wool.

"Jade." She smiles at me. "Lukas isn't with you today?"

I fight off a wince. I tried to do the right thing, to make Lukas go home to his family. It's the least I could do after hurting him, but stubborn as he is, he refused. And because I'm horrible, I let him stay.

Now his family might die for my selfishness. And with the killer accelerating her attacks . . .

My lips twitch in an unenthused smile, the best I can muster under the current circumstances. "He stayed home today," I lie. "He wasn't feeling well."

But it's not Clara who replies.

"How fortunate for me."

I freeze at the cold, deep voice in my ear. The fingers twining around my wrist.

The tracker.

I don't move, but Clara frowns. "Are you okay? Is this man bothering you?"

I want to say yes, activate my tattoo, and run away, but I force myself to lift my chin and meet those dark eyes. "No," I tell Clara, tell *him.* "I'm perfectly fine. We know each other." And because apparently I've lost all sense of self, I add, "This is Alejandro."

The tracker's grip on me tightens, and Clara's gaze travels between the two of us, assessing. "All right then," she finally says. "But if you need anything, you know where to find me." She pins the tracker with a pointed glare, and I make a mental note to return and thank Clara later.

"I will," I assure her, then yank my wrist from the tracker's grasp and march into the market's throng. It's not nearly as busy as Sallenda's streets, but it's still nice and well maintained. Unlike Mérecal, Kabrück is made up of dozens of estates, each run by a different family, and the quality of life can differ vastly among them.

Dreiden is run nicely, though; the family that manages it is kindhearted, and it shows in this small but vibrant market. Weeks ago I never would've dreamed of navigating it by myself, but with Lukas's help, the task has become manageable. Still, it's not easy, and I swallow.

The tracker notices, his step even with mine. "Nervous, little dove?"

"No," I say, and he laughs.

"Oh, you're a liar. And a feisty one. I'll confess, on the ship I didn't see you coming, but now . . ." He studies me, and my skin crawls. "I'm willing to admit I underestimated you."

I force myself to sneer. "Like I could ever care what you think."

In truth, while I'd never admit it, his confession pleases me. Not because I want to impress him, but because if *he* sees me as a threat, maybe there's something there. Maybe I have fangs after all.

The tracker merely grins. "Oh, I think you do care what I think. I think you care a great deal."

"I don't." We're reaching the end of the market, the stalls emptying into Dreiden's "downtown"—if it can even be called that. There are only a few buildings here: the inn, a general store, and of course a tavern, its crooked sign out front reading *The Fat Dog* in peeling white paint.

"You do, though." An undercurrent of fury has entered the tracker's voice, and he grabs my arm, then yanks me back. "You took one of my letters."

That's what he's mad about? Not long ago I would've cowered, but we're still in a public place, and for once I don't have to worry. These people won't hurt me, but they *will* protect me. Which is perhaps why I have the confidence to say, "I also ruined your tattoo and stole time from your life—I'd assume you'd be more upset about that."

His next words are a hiss. "How dare you—"

"How dare I what?" He's kindled my own fire. This man violated my home, kidnapped me, and threatened Lukas. It's past time I put him in his place. "How dare I talk to you like that? How dare I read your letters or ruin your tattoo? I'm done letting you push me around, *Alejandro*. Just because I left you alive last time doesn't mean I'll do so again."

Oh gods. Oh gods oh gods oh gods. Did I actually just say that? My dress is tacky with sweat, and I have to clench my hands to keep them from shaking.

The tracker, however, seems to get ahold of himself. "And why is that, hmm? Why am I alive, little dove? You could've killed me a hundred times over, and yet here I stand."

I huff and pull away from him, marching for the alley between the bar and general store. The tracker follows, his voice at my back. "You want something from me," he says. "I know it. You want answers. You couldn't get them from Schäfer, so now you need them from me."

My heart kicks up, but I keep my voice steady as I brush into the alley, rapping my knuckles against the tavern window as I go. "Is there a question in there?" I say, hoping to distract the tracker. "Or are you just going to tell me what I want?"

"No question." The click of a gun punctuates his words, and when I cast my gaze behind me, it's pointed right at my back. The tracker grins. "Tell your pup to come out."

Breathe. Just breathe. It's going to be okay.

My fear swells, but I manage to choke some down, enough so the rest doesn't overwhelm me.

Yet.

I stare at the tracker, unwavering. "You're not going to shoot me."

I saw the letter. Whoever CR is, they want me alive and unharmed.

"Perhaps," the tracker agrees, "but him I have no such qualms about."

My stomach plummets when he swivels his pistol toward Lukas, who's emerged from the shadows behind the general store. He has his own gun raised, pointed straight at the tracker, and his next words are made of burnished iron. "Put it down or I'll shoot."

The tracker clicks his tongue. "Awfully bold, when I could say the same."

Lukas's eyes flick to me. Just a second, but I hear what he doesn't say and nod. It's time.

I pray for a fraction of Lukas's bravery, then step in front of the tracker, the cold barrel of his gun pressing into my chest.

"Jade—" Lukas sounds strained. This wasn't part of the plan, but after all the ways I've wronged him, I'm not risking his life.

"Move." The tracker's voice is edged in irritation. A rare moment when he and Lukas agree, but I don't listen to either. It's my mother I hear, a memory of her words ringing inside my head. *You are strong, capable, and wonderful. Don't ever forget it.*

My lip trembles, but I push the memory down along with the panic. Later I'll break and burn, but I can't afford to now.

"I'm fine," I say softly for Lukas's benefit, then meet the tracker's eyes. "You're not going to shoot Lukas either, because if you do, you'll lose your memories."

"What—" the tracker begins before I cut him off.

"You saw my note. You know the power I have over you. You also know who lives here, in Dreiden. You kidnapped him last time you visited."

The tracker blanches. Lukas he expected to fight back, but Johann?

"That's right." I confirm the understanding dawning on his face. "Johann's waiting in that tavern, his needle poised at your thread portrait. The second he hears a gunshot, he's been instructed to decimate your earliest memories, and after what you put him through, he won't hesitate."

A curl of satisfaction rises inside me at the horror on the tracker's face, the way his eyes widen, jaw going slack before anger bursts through. "You—how *dare* you—you need my memories, you need answers!"

"True," I say, gaze unwavering despite the fact that my body is humming with a barely repressed episode. I'm definitely going to vomit after this. "But really, I only need one: to know who CR is. The rest, the older ones?" I shrug, false bravado. "Those can go."

It was difficult, guessing what the tracker would value more than his life. Because if he risked stepping into this alley, where he surely knew Lukas was waiting, that was something he was willing to gamble. His memories, though?

It's our experiences that make us who we are, the building

blocks of who we become. It's why they're part of our souls, integral to our identities. People are willing to give up a lot before they let go of a single memory.

Now the tracker's are on the line, and a muscle twitches in his jaw as he processes this and perhaps considers unloading his pistol toward the bar—though it would be useless against the brick walls. A single gunshot, and Johann will act.

"Fine," the tracker agrees.

I blink in surprise. Even with our plan carefully laid out, I hadn't expected it to go this well.

The tracker makes a show of slowly unloading his pistol, setting it on the ground, and offering up his wrists. "Do your worst," he says, sneering like we haven't just gotten the best of him.

I can only stare, numb, studying his face. He didn't even fight, didn't even try—

"Jade." Lukas is at my side, hand on my shoulder. "It's okay— we did it."

But as Lukas kicks the pistol aside and binds the tracker's wrists, I can't help but wonder.

Did we?

CHAPTER TWENTY-NINE

LUKAS

JADE DOESN'T STOP TREMBLING ALL THE WAY BACK TO JOHANN'S house. I'm desperate to wrap her in a hug, but my hands are occupied with the tracker, my gun at his back while I guide him forward. Fortunately, no one seems to notice we've taken a captive, and it's easy enough to sneak into the nearby forest cover. Twigs snap beneath my boots as we go, and the air is crisp with autumn, a small joy I've missed in Mérecal.

Jade and I discussed at length what to do when we captured the tracker. Soon the decision rests at my feet. A trapdoor, not far from Johann's property, leading to a root cellar we emptied just for this. It'll do as a holding cell until we can send a letter off to Kreipen, detailing the tracker's crimes and requesting that the enforcers there come and take him away. It'll likely be a while, since they'll be busy with Gebreine approaching, but we can't do anything about that.

So for now he's ours to question.

"Go on," I tell him, none too gently. "Open it. Get down there."

The tracker looks between me and Jade. Johann left, electing to go back home after one glimpse of Alejandro. I can't blame him, with his ordeal still fresh. Now the tracker sneers. "You're really going to store me in some pit?"

He directs the words at Jade, and I feel myself flush. "Don't talk to her like that."

His eyes snap to mine. "It was a simple question."

"There was a tone," I insist, then realize it's pointless to argue. Jade's so pale, she almost looks translucent. I need to move this along. "Just open the door and get down there without a fuss, or a bullet might find its way into your foot."

He looks between the two of us again before his gaze settles on me. "You know, there's something familiar about you. Your eyes—"

"Go. *Now.* I don't want to ask again." My voice is authoritative. Clear. But beneath it there's a tremble.

I have my father's eyes. The tracker should have no reason to find them familiar, and yet—

No. I'm not going there.

The tracker smirks, aware he's hit a nerve, but doesn't push the matter further. With a click of his tongue, he slides open the bolt and lowers himself into the dank space.

The moment his head disappears from the opening, I shut the door, lock it, then turn to Jade. "Are you okay?"

"I'm going to be sick."

I have just enough time to pull her hair back before she vomits all over the forest floor. A heaviness settles inside me as I watch her, whispering comforts until she finishes, wipes her mouth, and straightens.

"I'm sorry." Her words are wobbly, her eyes wet. "I didn't mean for you to see that."

"Jade." A tender, protective urge tugs at my heartstrings. "I'm glad I was here for it. I never want you to suffer alone when I'm around."

I'm not sure how to label the emotion that flits across her face. In a blink, she shifts and it's gone, hidden by the curtain of hair when she looks at her shoes. "Thank you."

Her voice is small, and god, I hate seeing her this miserable. She was so brave in that alley. I swear every breath of air was sucked from the world when she stepped in front of the tracker's gun.

All to save me. No one's ever cared for me like that before. Honestly, I don't know what I did to get Jade as my friend—I'm just glad I did it.

"You're welcome," I tell her, voice rough. "Are you okay?"

"I will be." She shakes her head. "It's just one of my episodes. I held it back in the alley, but it had to come out somehow. They're not usually this intense, but with everything . . ."

She drifts off, but I get it. It's a lot of emotion.

I wish I could tuck her into me, kiss her brow, and breathe in her rosy scent, but I refuse to cross the line she drew between us. So I remain where I am but still offer what I can. "Do you want me to take you back to Johann's? I can question the tracker alone, or we can wait until you're feeling up to it."

This time she's quick to answer, gaze flashing to mine. "No! I want to do this together, and I want to do it now." Her throat bobs. "I'd rather get it over with."

"Okay." I've watched Jade gun down a sievech, hold off a crowd of angry sailors, and sew into her own flesh. If she says she can handle this, I trust her. "Let's do it."

The tracker has been in the root cellar for only a few minutes, but by the time we join him, he's sprawled out like he owns the place. He's sitting, back leaned casually against the wall, legs spread wide, and wrists bound in his lap. It's a damp space, dark with the single lantern, scented of earth and mildew. The tracker seems to have recovered in the minutes we were aboveground. He grins when he sees us, his eyes going to Jade. "Here for your answers, little dove?"

I itch to snap at him, but Jade said she could do this. I need to let her.

And I do. Pride swells inside me when Jade faces the tracker and says, not a tremble in her voice, "Yes. Starting with CR." She removes CR's letter from her pocket. "Who is she, and is she the same person who wrote all those love letters I found in your desk?"

The change is instant. The tracker flushes, his words a barely contained hiss. "You had absolutely no business—"

"Shut up," Jade orders, and my mouth nearly drops to the floor. "If you didn't want me in your business, you shouldn't have kidnapped me. So I'll ask again. Are CR and your lover the same person?"

The tracker's jaw is rigid, a muscle ticking there. Then: "No."

Jade stares him down. The tracker meets her glare. A few moments pass in silence before Jade straightens and fires off her next question. "And CR? Who is she?"

"She?" The tracker's eyes glint. "How do you know she's a woman?"

Jade doesn't budge. "Just tell me who she is. Or have you forgotten I could take your memories?" She pats her satchel for emphasis, where the tracker's thread portrait now rests, returned by Johann.

The tracker grimaces. "You're no fun, but fine. CR is Cora Ramos. She wanted me to bring you in."

No!

I don't realize I've spoken until both sets of eyes turn to me. My head is spinning. I knew it could be Cora—the initials match—but to hear it confirmed is something else entirely.

"Surprised?" The tracker cuts through my haze, somehow managing to look down on me despite the fact that I'm standing over him. "Didn't expect the underqueen, did you?"

That's the problem, though. I did, and I tried to ignore it, desperate for it to be anyone but her. That she's after Jade makes this entire mess even more convoluted.

"Why would Cora want Jade?" I ask, in an effort to fit all the pieces into place.

The tracker makes a condescending tutting sound. "For the same reason she wanted you dead. You were getting too close to the truth. You"—he nods in my direction—"were useless to her. Just a potential leak. But you . . ." He looks at Jade, eyes practically glowing. "Your gifts she could use. Enough to risk bringing you in."

I'm not following. Cora wanted me dead for pursuing the same investigation she put me on?

Jade must be thinking the same thing, because her next words are sharp. "But Cora asked Lukas to bring in the killer. Why would she want him dead for finding answers?"

The tracker sighs. "I expected better of you. Come on, think. There's a logical explanation."

My stomach sinks. Jade and I never knew for sure whether CR and the killer were one and the same, but the more the tracker shares, the more it appears they are. And if CR is Cora—

"Cora's the killer," I breathe, understanding dawning. "She's controlling the sievech, and she had me investigate because . . ." *Why?*

The tracker leans forward, invested now. "Because . . . Come on, boy, don't make me spell it out for you."

And just like that, the answer surfaces.

"Because she wanted to look innocent." My throat tightens on the words. "Serpensas have been dying too, and she wanted to make sure none of her followers suspected her."

And what better way to do that than make a show of searching for the murderer herself?

"Very good." The tracker smirks and raises his bound wrists. "I'd clap, but, well. You understand."

It's starting to come together. I never understood why Cora would ask for my help. I have no resources, no special abilities, nothing at all but determination. Asking me to find the killer was a waste of time. Unless of course, Cora never wanted me to catch them—catch *her*. I was just a diversion, a piece on a board meant to make her appear innocent, but never intended to actually succeed.

Still, there are fragments missing, and Jade voices exactly what I've begun to wonder. "But some of the victims were Serpensas. Why would Cora murder her own people? Why kill anyone at all?"

The tracker shakes his head as if disappointed. "Have you ever seen Cora's lair, little dove?"

"No, but I hardly see—"

He cuts her off. "She's built herself a throne. A court made of criminals and scum, an underworld to rule over, but Cora Ramos was never going to be satisfied with scraps beneath the surface. The underqueen decided it was time to leave her sewers and pursue some real power."

God, didn't I know that? Rage burns through me, fed on all those clues I didn't see. I heard the rumors she wanted the throne—*knew* she was the kind of person who would do this. Sadistic and power hungry, that's how she described the killer. Traits that fit her perfectly. It's why most people thought she was responsible, why they whispered she and her Serpensas were behind the murders. I dismissed the rumors, though. Foolishly assumed they were nothing more than wild speculation.

And that's not even the worst of it. I saw that pin in a puddle of blood. I knew she murdered a queen's guard, and weeks later, when I learned the killer had struck down a queen's guard, I didn't make the connection.

I've been foolish, and Cora used that. "Be that as it may," I say, voice stained with anger, "it still doesn't explain why Cora killed her own."

"Sure it does." The tracker's gaze swivels to mine. "To anyone smart enough to understand. But fine—I'll spell it out for you. Cora may look like she rules the Serpensas with an iron fist, but there are whispers about her rule. Apparently there are some cracks in the foundation, dissent creeping in. Now, I'm not an official member of her gang, only contracted out, so I haven't seen all those cracks, but my guess is she wanted to patch them up before making her play for the Crown. Or, in case you're too thick to understand the metaphor, to kill the dissenting members before they made more problems for her."

It's not hard to believe. I remember the way I felt standing in front of Cora Ramos. The icy gaze from those amber eyes. Her nails pricking my chin, my blood sliding down her fingertip. If anyone has the guts to murder her own, it's Cora.

And of course, I had to go and make myself one of her own. Had to put my family in her sights. They could be a target now, and it's all my fault.

"And the others?" Jade's voice is thin, mirroring some of my own fears. "All the innocent people she killed?"

The tracker sounds bored when he answers. "Again, I'm not privy to her plans, but I'd assume the murders are intended to stir up panic. To weaken the throne before Cora makes her play."

It's working, or at least the panic is. People are terrified, though many are flocking to their faith, and to the throne by extension. A misstep on Cora's part, perhaps.

"So that's it." Jade's words are heated, her cheeks flushed in the lantern glow. "Cora's the answer to this. Her need for power, her greed, it—it—"

Her chest heaves, breath becoming strangled gasps. I reach for her. "Jade."

The tracker's voice is harsh. "It what, little dove? Say what's on your mind."

"It killed my mother! *She* killed my mother! And you helped her!"

The words rip from Jade's chest, thud against the dirt walls, and fall to the floor. Tears jewel at the corners of her eyes. "You're the one who took Johann to Cora. If it weren't for you, my mother never would've tried to save him! Never would have—have—"

She hiccups. Sobs.

"Jade." My voice is soft, but when I approach her, she moves back.

I nearly flinch, and it doesn't help when the tracker speaks up. "I had no idea she killed your mother. My job was to bring Johann in, then you. Anything beyond that wasn't my responsibility."

His words are cold. I think that more than anything sets Jade off. She lunges for him, screaming, nails raking across his face. "My mother is dead because of you! What you did!"

I'm not sure what to do, and I watch, numb, as Jade pummels the tracker. Kicks and scrapes and punches, a whirlwind of furious grief. My first instinct is to stop her, but why should I? The tracker has caused so much pain, it doesn't seem fair to prevent Jade from inflicting a bit of her own. However, as the seconds pass by, my lump of discomfort grows. I begin to wonder who Jade's hurting more—the tracker or herself.

Reluctantly, I step forward. "Jade."

It's barely a whisper, but it does something to her. She freezes, her eyes going wide as she surveys what she's done. The blood streaming from the tracker's nose. The scrapes marring his skin. Her gaze flashes to me, and my heart breaks at the horror on her face. "I—I'm sorry, I just— I need to go."

Before I can stop her, she backs away and scrambles up the ladder, fleeing from these horrible truths.

CHAPTER THIRTY

JADE

VERMILLION CRUELTY. CHARCOAL STRENGTH. MINTY GREED. THE tracker's soul stares back at me, my needle poised, ready to wreak havoc. I could decimate his intelligence, unspool his life, sap his potency, destroy his memories.

Such violent desires, contrasted by the cool autumn breeze rippling through the trees. The grass, soft beneath my knees. The smell of earth and dead leaves, cerulean sky bursting above the foliage.

Oh, such horrible things I could do, wrapped in this beautiful forest. The villain I could become.

I'm still considering the possibility when I hear him, whisper soft behind me. Lukas.

"I'm sorry I keep doing this." I don't turn to look at him but gesture at our surroundings. "Having emotional episodes in the woods. You must think I'm a wreck."

He doesn't say anything, but I hear him come closer, until he's crouched in front of me, his viridian eyes warm and kind. "You're allowed to be a wreck," he tells me. "It's not a weakness to feel, and quite frankly, I don't think you're a wreck. Vulnerable maybe, and human, but all the stronger for it."

I blink, taken aback. "Did you not see me in there? The way I attacked him?"

I was . . . I don't even know what I was, but it scared me. Feeling so out of control.

"I did, but that wasn't everything I saw today." Lukas sounds calm. "You're forgetting all these other moments. Braving the market. Outsmarting the tracker. *Stepping in front of his gun for me.*"

My heart squeezes, and Lukas pauses, an expression I can't name on his face.

"You have to understand: I was terrified. I *hated* that you put yourself in danger. But at the same time, it was just another reminder of how incredible you are. How good and fierce and *brave,* and—I don't know." He runs a hand through his hair. "It's just, sometimes . . ."

"What?" Maybe it's shallow, but I'm desperate for more insights into how Lukas views me, so different from the way I see myself.

Lukas blows out a sigh. "Sometimes I feel like I don't deserve you. To be your friend, be around you, talk to you. It's hard when you're you, and I'm . . . well, you know."

My indignation prickles. This isn't the first time Lukas has talked about himself like this, but the more I hear it, the more it grates on me, and Lukas deserves to know why. Suddenly the weepy mess is gone, that firmer version of myself back.

"No," I tell him, prim. "I don't know, actually."

He rubs the back of his neck. Looks down. Mutters, "You're incredible, Jade. Intelligent. Kind. Compassionate. A fucking thread speaker. And I'm . . . I worked on a fishing boat. I sleep on a pile of dirty blankets. I've made selfish choices, and . . ." He shakes his head. "You deserve better than me."

Lukas's words are fresh needles pricking my tender heart. It hurts, knowing he sees himself this way, and my eyes heat as I clear my throat, then bring my fingers to his chin and tilt his face so he's forced to look at me.

"Lukas Keller." I try to keep my voice firm, but it wobbles, though I don't let that stop me. "You may only be able to see your surface, but don't forget for one second that I see your soul. Which is how I know, perhaps better than most, that you are kind, strong, and fiercely protective. You love harder than anyone I've ever met, and it doesn't matter where you work or where you sleep, or the number in your bank account—you are *special,* plain and simple, and it breaks my heart that you can't see what I do."

His eyes bore into mine, green and heated and intense. My fingers are still on his chin, a gentle pressure, an aching touch, and the kiss-that-shouldn't-have-been burns between us—a reminder of everything I can't have. Because last time we sat in the forest, I had no idea what it meant to kiss Lukas.

Now, though, I'm seared by the memories of Lukas's hands on my body, his fingers wrapped in my hair, lips brushing mine. Scorched by the knowledge of exactly what I'm missing out on. Because I can't kiss him, not with our history, nor can I confess, not if I don't want to lose him.

So the moment heats, blisters, and passes with a dip of my chin, a lowering of my hand. Lukas sighs, then leans back, and his next words are rough. "So the tracker." He nods to Alejandro's soul portrait, still next to me on the grass. "Are you going to kill him?"

I startle at his cavalier tone. "You wouldn't try to stop me if I was?"

He relaxes against a nearby tree, studies the portrait at my feet, and, after a moment, shakes his head. "No. I wouldn't."

Somehow, Lukas giving me the space to commit murder is nearly as meaningful as everything he just said to me. Which is horrid on a multitude of levels, but that doesn't change how it makes me feel.

Emotion balls in my throat, but I push through it and consider his question. *Am* I going to kill the tracker? But the idea, so tempting just moments ago, has soured, and I remember my mother's words. *Our power is a dangerous thing. To wield it as a god is to become a monster.*

She wouldn't want me to destroy a life simply because I can, and I sigh. "I'm not going to kill him, at least not yet. We'll send the letter to the enforcers. They can deal with him."

That'll give us more time to question the tracker further, and as a measure of calm settles over me, I think back on everything we just learned. About Cora Ramos, the tracker's role, the truth of it all—assuming it wasn't false. But as I mull it over, some of my apprehension returns, and I release a shaky sigh as I face Lukas. "Do you think he was being honest back there?"

He appears to reflect on it. "I can't be sure, but I think so. It adds up, doesn't it?"

"I guess. I just . . ." I shake my head. What the tracker said about CR—*Cora*—and his lover being different people . . . I'm not sure. Something about it is bothering me, especially his lover's signature. That crescent with the squiggles is *so* familiar, but I can't place it, the answer a shade out of reach.

And it was all so easy, too, first capturing the tracker, then questioning him. I'd expected more resistance, but he didn't hesitate to give us answers. "I don't know," I eventually say. "I didn't think he'd admit everything that freely."

Lukas's eyes dart to the thread portrait. "You did threaten to eviscerate his memories if he didn't talk."

"You're right," I admit. I'm being irrational, and I release some of the worry with my next breath, letting the breeze sweep it away. It helps a little, until I realize what this development means.

"We did it." My voice squeaks. "What we set out to do. It's done."

Lukas sits up straighter. "You don't sound happy about it."

No. He's right, I don't, though I *should*. But gods, something is definitely wrong with me. I should be celebrating—we have the information we need to stop a soul-thieving murderer! And I *am* glad about that, truly and deeply. Even so . . .

"It's just . . . now what?" My words are small. "Your deal with Cora is void. You can turn her in to the authorities and be done with this whole mess. You can go home, and I . . ."

I'm not sure if I want to go back. My mother is dead. My house is burned. In twenty days I'll be forced to become thread speaker to the Crown, and while I've never wanted my mother's role, after this journey it feels especially abhorrent.

In Sallenda, I would only have Lukas, but I can't truly have him either.

Lukas is looking at me, expectant. "You don't want to go back?"

His voice is tight, and I close my eyes against the sting of tears. The sad truth is I would return in a heartbeat just to have more time with him. But I can't, not with this lie between us, and telling the truth won't change that. He'd never talk to me again.

"Yesterday evening Johann invited me to stay here with him if I want."

My words are heavy, a weight I've felt since Johann approached me. I'd been tending my thread kit, and he seemed nervous. My mother was important to him, he explained, and while he didn't save her, he wanted to do right by me.

In Kabrück, thread speakers are permitted to live as we wish, provided we don't use our gifts without proper consent. Here, with Johann, I could be free in a way my mother never was, always required to serve the Crown.

Lukas must sense something in my tone, and his voice trembles. "Jade? What are you saying?"

I close my eyes, unable to face him.

"I'm saying that maybe it would be better if I stayed here."

There's a long pause. I still can't look at Lukas, but his breathing is fast, labored. When he finally speaks, he sounds small, and I hate that I'm the one doing this to him.

"What if I'm not ready to lose you?" he whispers.

I've always thought fear was the most painful emotion, and that someday it would kill me.

I was wrong. Heartbreak is far worse, and it takes everything I have not to break down. When I open my eyes, Lukas looks just as miserable, and I remind myself that I'm doing this for him. Because if he knew the truth, he'd want nothing to do with me.

"I need to stay here," I tell him. And though it kills me, I add the only thing that I know will make him listen. "But you have to go back. Your family is waiting, and they need you. Mérecal needs you."

Lukas gapes at me, a spot of coral in each cheek. I sense that he's close to the brink, so I give him that final shove. "You could leave today if you wanted. I can handle things here. There's nothing stopping you."

"I . . . you . . . *you're* stopping me, Jade!" A spark of anger glints in his eye. "How can you expect me to leave without you? After everything we've been through together, I thought—" He stops abruptly and slices a hand through his hair, rumpling the blond locks.

You thought what? I'm desperate to ask, but I'm also wise enough to know that's a dangerous path. So I wait, and a few seconds later Lukas continues, quieter now. Colder.

"What about the queen? She'll be furious when you don't return."

He's right. I'm oathed to the Crown, forbidden to reside anywhere save for where the queen has permitted. Staying here is a clear violation of her rules, and if she finds me, she'll be furious. Not enough to kill me—my skills are too valuable for that—but enough to steal my freedom, perhaps. To imprison me inside her palace.

But she has to find me first.

And I've been thinking lately about the tracker's tattoo. About all those traits stitched into his skin, stripped from animals, an uncommon practice but perhaps a useful one. If only I'd considered it earlier, but at least it's occurred to me now, and I tuck the thought away in case I need it.

Now, though, I need to be focused on Lukas.

"And she's exactly why I can't go back." I meet his eyes, begging him to understand. "You hated thread speakers before we met, and for good reason. The way we use our gifts is rarely ethical, and if I return, the queen will expect me to continue that pattern. You saw what I did here, though, how happy the soul bindings made people. Perhaps in Kabrück I can actually do some good."

"Damn it." Lukas rubs the back of his neck. "That's a really good reason."

"I know."

Silence settles between us like a goodbye. And in a way, I suppose, it is. Lukas has to go, and I need to stay, a truth made no less painful for its simplicity. We sit for a minute, soaking it in, until Lukas clears his throat.

"Five days."

Hope kindles inside me. "What do you mean, five days?"

Heartbreak is still written in Lukas's glossy eyes, but something else has since joined it. His chin has a determined tilt, and his shoulders have gone from slumped to steady.

"A decision like this deserves proper time to think it through," he explains. "I know Kabrück seems like the better option—I mean, damn, it probably *is* the better option—but the queen. If she finds you, well, you're taking a risk. You could get hurt, and I—" He pauses, fingers shifting with something akin to agitation. "I just think it might be smart to take some time to think it over. Once five days have passed, if you still want to stay, I won't fight you on it. But if you're inclined to come with me . . ."

"I can still make the queen's deadline."

"Exactly." He nods.

Somewhere inside me a blossom has unfurled its petals and faced the sun. I shouldn't be relieved, and I know this is where I should confess my sins. *Lukas,* I imagine myself saying, *we need to talk about your father.*

But then he would hate me. Our time together would be tainted, and he'd leave feeling a fool. Earlier, I told him I couldn't survive losing him, and that's true. But that's not what stays my tongue. I can tell Lukas the truth and give us both this pain.

Or I can keep my secret and he can leave happy. I'll never see him again, but at least he won't hate himself for letting me in.

Hurt Lukas or not. The choice is easy, but I still try to dissuade him.

"And what about you? You could leave now; you don't have to wait."

He leans in closer, and his gaze drops to my mouth before flicking back up to my eyes.

"You're right. I should probably leave now, but I just . . ." He shakes his head, and I sense the floodgates cracking open inside him. "I know it's selfish to stay, but for so long, I've made everyone in my life a priority except myself. I'm exhausted, but ever since I set off with you—I don't know. I've felt free again. *You* make me feel that way, and right now I *want* to stay. To have this time with you—to celebrate Gebreine again. When I return, it'll be to a life where I live only for others, so let me have this, Jade. Give me these final days with you. These final days of freedom."

It's tempting, a decadent slice of cake just within reach, my mouth watering. But if Lukas truly wishes to stay, he deserves to have all the information, and I feel my shoulders slump as I recall the paper at the market this morning. With everything that happened, I'd forgotten about it until now.

"I'd love that Lukas, truly," I tell him, "but you should know the killer—Cora—is accelerating her pace. There was an article in the paper this morning. Two bodies were found in one night. Your family . . . the danger is getting worse."

He stiffens, his fists clenching, eyes going distant. Time seems to stretch before he finally responds.

"I hate this," he admits. "That they're in danger. That I feel like I have to choose between . . . fuck, between happiness and duty, but I'm still staying. With Gebreine, there won't be any ships leaving anyway, and the trains will all be booked or not running. I won't get home much earlier than if I wait. And even if I did, it's not like my presence will make much difference. They have your money and Emma's efforts. If anything, my return might mean they're worse off. It could bring Cora to their door." He shifts, something resolute in the lines of his posture. "There's a risk, yes, but for once I'm willing to pay that price. Take that chance. I still want this time, if you do too."

I think I might just burst—with all of it. Relief Lukas is staying, guilt because I don't deserve it, and this terrible, ripping *want*. To bring my lips to his, taste him again, and steal a few more moments.

Perhaps in another life. In this one, though, I've been given a gift. It may not be everything I desire, but it's more time with Lukas, a small slice of the life we could've had together. Not nearly enough, *never* enough, but even so, I clench it tight in feral fingers.

"Okay," I whisper. I should fight more, but I won't. "So then, five days?"

Lukas's lips twitch, almost in relief. "No more, no less."

And that's that.

CHAPTER THIRTY-ONE

JADE

I GRIN, CHEEKS WARM AS I TAKE IN MY NEWEST CREATION, THOUGH it's a bittersweet kind of happiness.

Bitter because four days have passed, and tomorrow morning Lukas will leave while I stay behind. Sweet because of the thread portrait in my hands, brimming with coffee brown, shimmery violet, and waves of burgundy.

Perfect—just like its owner.

It's the eve of Gebreine, one of Kabrück's largest holidays, meant to honor the birth of their triple god. It's a time of celebration, and I spent all afternoon cooking a veritable feast with Johann, from soft pretzels and rabbit stew to apple cake and gingerbread.

Now I sit in the hayloft above Johann's barn, where Lukas and I have been spending our nights. Golden rays slide through the windows, a final gift from the setting sun as I pocket the thread portrait. I'm not sure where Lukas is—he disappeared after dinner, most likely to finish setting up the small festival Dreiden puts on every year.

So I sit back and wait, cushioned on a mound of scratchy hay, and my thoughts turn, as they have been lately, to the tracker. We've sent word to Kreipen, the nearest city equipped to aid us, asking them to dispatch enforcers to pick him up. Our trouble with him is almost over, but I still can't shake the feeling we missed something. Like those letters from his lover. They should be irrelevant, but what if they're not? What if Lukas and I overlooked an important piece? Maybe if I talk to the tracker again, I can—

"Jade?" Lukas interrupts my thoughts, head poking over the edge of the hayloft, one hand gripping the ladder. I've been so preoccupied, I didn't even hear him come up, and I swallow a lump at the sight of him, blond waves gilded in the setting sun, lips quirked in a half grin. "What are you doing all alone up here?"

"Waiting for you," I say, then realize that probably sounds creepy, but it's too late. Thankfully, it just makes Lukas smile wider.

"That's good, because I was looking for you."

A flutter takes off in my chest, the beating of a hummingbird's wings. I know better than to let these feelings, this hope, take flight, but I can't quite stop it either. "What for?"

He doesn't move, just keeps staring at me from his position on the ladder. "Well, as I'm sure you're aware, it's the eve of Gebreine."

"Yes," I say slowly, then add, "I may have noticed that while cooking a giant Gebreine feast with Johann."

Lukas's eyes sparkle, but he doesn't comment on my sarcasm. "So then you also know it's a night for giving gifts."

The air has grown thin, though for once it's not from fear but something anticipatory. "I do."

The portrait in my pocket burns, but I don't take it out. Lukas, however, lifts his other hand, revealing a gorgeous crown of burgundy dahlias, ivory snapdragons, and ruby roses, all braided with a verdant array of leaves.

I gasp while Lukas blushes. "I know it's not much, but it's a tradition I thought you might enjoy. All the women wear them on Gebreine, a way to honor the divine mother who birthed our god. And, well, red is your favorite color, and you love the smell of roses, so I thought—"

"It's perfect." I breathe the words, and before I know it, I've crossed the hayloft and crouched down, close enough that I can see the flecks of bronze in his eyes. Roses perfume the air between us, and I caress a soft petal, even though I'd rather run my fingers through his hair. It kills me that in a matter of hours Lukas will wake up, walk out of this barn, and leave me behind forever. Perhaps that's why my voice wavers. "Did you make this yourself?"

He gives a noncommittal grunt and sets it on the floor between us.

"Lukas?"

"I did," he admits, sheepish. "I used to make them when I was a kid." He pauses, his eyes welling over. "With Lina, actually. She loved them, but Emma could never be bothered with girly activities, so I'd make them with her."

Imagining Lukas as a child, braiding crowns with his little sister simply because she loved it . . .

Maybe it's foolish, but I cup Lukas's cheek, then swipe away his tears with my thumb. His skin burns beneath mine. "You don't talk about her much. About Lina."

It's true. In the weeks I've spent with Lukas, he's slowly opened up, sharing bits about his family, little pieces of Emma, Artur, his mother.

But not Lina. Never Lina, save for once, when he shared that his family moved to Sallenda for her, because she was too sick to survive another Kabrückian winter.

Lukas shudders and looks down a long moment, his knuckles

white from the strain of gripping the ladder, and my hand slips from his face. Though I know what's coming, bile churns in my gut.

Finally he says it.

"She died two years after my father. Got sick enough I couldn't save her. She was only ten."

His words are cold, deadened things, and I shiver. My heart breaks for Lukas, and suddenly all the blackened grief in his soul makes sense—not just for his father, but for his sister too.

"I'm sorry, Lukas," I say, because there's nothing else *to* say. "I am so, so sorry." And then, because I know how he views himself, I add, "But it's not your fault. You know that, right? Nobody could've saved her."

He wipes his tears, gaze full of something I can't name, and the hairs at my nape prickle. "You could've, though," he whispers. "A thread speaker could've."

I search his face, looking for whatever it is he wants me to say. When I come up empty, I settle on the truth. "You're right, I could've."

I don't add the rest. That I wouldn't have, even if I'd had the opportunity. That healing someone so sick requires stealing someone else's life, and for Lina, I'm sure Lukas would've been the only volunteer.

The admission won't make anything better, so I let it lie. Lukas takes a deep breath, holds it, then blows it out. "You would've been fourteen," he says, "when she died."

I don't dispute it. It's a strange thing to say, but I'm sure Lukas is right, so I repeat the only thing I can think of to add. "I'm sorry I didn't save her."

It doesn't matter that I didn't know Lukas then, or Lina. It's still an awful situation, and I'm sorry it happened at all.

Lukas stares at me a long moment, shoulders stiff. Sweat breaks out on my skin, and I wonder what he's thinking, if he hates me for what I couldn't change. But then a muscle ticks in his jaw once, twice, and he lowers his gaze and lets out a breath.

"It's okay," he says. "You were only a kid."

Which, again, feels like a strange thing to say—there were several reasons I couldn't save her—but I don't argue. He needs to process this in the way that makes sense to him, but all the same, I can't resist adding, "So were you."

A ripple goes through him. He trembles, shakes, stills, his face flushed with emotion. "I guess I was."

We sit like that awhile. My breath bated, Lukas frozen save for the tears slipping over his cheeks. I itch to pull him fully into the loft, wrap him in my arms, rock him and comfort him and brush the hair back from his face, but I don't; I can't. I'm not sure if the touch would be welcome or if he needs space. So I wait until Lukas coughs and looks up at me, his gaze a shade lighter than before.

"She would've liked you, I think. Lina."

Warmth blossoms inside me. "You think?"

"I do." He picks up the crown and offers it to me. "Consider it a gift from Lina too. I never would've learned to make them if not for her."

There's a deep, splintering ache taking root inside me, and my throat is tight when I respond. "Then it's even more perfect than I realized."

He is even more perfect than I realized.

Carefully, I take the crown and set it atop my head. It fits perfectly, the rosy fragrance light and fresh, and a shy grin tugs my lips as I face him. "How do I look?"

Lukas doesn't answer right away. An odd expression has eclipsed his features, almost like he's in pain.

"Lukas?"

"Beautiful." He sounds a little breathless when he says it. "You're absolutely beautiful, Jade. You have to know that."

A kaleidoscope of butterflies erupts inside my chest. It shouldn't matter much—looks are only physical, after all—but I sense Lukas means more by it, and though it takes all my bravery, I meet his eyes when I reply. "So are you."

And I don't simply mean his sharp jawline, feathered hair, or courageous eyes. I mean down to his marrow, his soul—and I would know. It's sitting right inside my pocket.

Lukas swallows, heavy, but doesn't break my gaze. "Will you go with me to the festival tonight?"

Six weeks ago, I would've said no. I wouldn't have hesitated, or even considered it. All those people, pressed in close quarters. Music and dancing and fun for everyone else, but fear and chaos and *danger* for me. But I've come a long way since then. I've fought off a soul-eating monster, escaped the tracker, and learned to navigate Dreiden's market. Have solved murders and hopped continents.

The only thing that's remained the same, really, is that I don't hesitate.

"Yes," I tell Lukas, grinning. "I'd love to go with you."

CHAPTER THIRTY-TWO

LUKAS

DREIDEN DOESN'T HAVE A TOWN SQUARE, SO THE GEBREINE festival is held in the forest, which is even more perfect. I spent most of my day here, helping to set up. It was worth it for the look on Jade's face as we approach.

Pines surround the clearing, tall and looming, the lanterns strung between them twinkling in the darkness. Several wooden tables have been brought out, brimming with bouquets of autumn flowers, from sage and pansies to goldenrod and heather. Their light floral scent mingles with the fresh earth tones. Somewhere in the distance thunder rumbles, though no drops fall from the heavy clouds, and the crowd's too ensnared in the celebration to care. The sharp notes of a mandolin cleave the night, a joyous tune, while revelers dance, all dressed in white to signify the purity of our god, coronets of flowers snug atop the women's heads.

The scene settles over me, more comforting than a familiar quilt. *Home.* The word sets off a pang in my chest. It's been ages since I could celebrate Gebreine like this, and now I get to enjoy it with Jade. The only way it could possibly be better was if my family were here too.

At some point on the walk over, I reached for Jade's hand, and she let me take it. Now she squeezes my fingers in a nearly bone-crushing grip while her free hand brushes the shell hidden beneath the neckline of her dress.

"It's okay if you want to go back," I tell her, even though I really hope she says no. Last time we had an opportunity like this, I turned away from it, convinced seeking happiness with Jade was selfish.

Now, though, I'm not sure. I don't know why I asked Jade to the festival. Perhaps it was that conversation about Lina. The unspoken acknowledgment that Jade was there that night, and my decision to forgive her. Or maybe it was simply the sight of her in that crown, so gorgeous I was desperate to show her off, even if she isn't truly mine.

Really, though, I think it was what Jade said. That I was a kid too when Lina died and—god. That hit me hard. Because if I was willing to recognize she was only a child and forgive her, why couldn't I do the same for myself? Why can't I?

I'm not sure. The weight is still there, but tonight seems like a small step in the right direction. Choosing to be happy, even if it's only for an evening.

So I'm relieved when Jade replies, "No, no. Let's go in, I *want* to go in, just . . ." She squeezes my hand again. "Don't let go of me?"

I clutch her fingers right back and meet those dark eyes, my own earnest. "Never."

Time freezes, our gazes locked, and my own dips to Jade's full lips. A beast of memories stirs inside my chest. I recall the way

253

Jade tasted, so sweet, her mouth soft beneath mine. That little gasp she made, the shiver as I pulled her in close—

"Okay, then." Jade brings me back to the present. "Let's do this."

I give her a moment to take a deep, slow breath, and together we wade into the celebration.

JADE

I can stitch souls, but never have I experienced magic like tonight.

True to his promise, Lukas doesn't leave my side, doesn't even drop my hand. He's with me through it all, and while fear creeps along the edges, it slowly gives way to something different. Excitement. Happiness. Wonder.

The night begins with prayer, everyone's voice low and pious as they honor their triple god, hands joined. I'm acutely aware of Lukas's palm in my own, the way his calluses scrape over my skin, sending shivers down my spine. Afterward the celebration begins in earnest, and my heart thrums through each new discovery: the bite of apple cider, burning as I swallow it, or the steps of the gazende, a traditional Kabrückian dance. I make a fool of myself stumbling through the choreography, skin heated everywhere Lukas's hands brush me. My hips, my shoulders, my cheek at one point.

I am . . . deliriously happy, my world warm and sparkling—which may be in part due to the alcohol. I giggle as Lukas offers me an iced gingerbread, and he beams back at me.

"I think maybe that's enough cider for you tonight."

"I don't care," I say, then take a bite, adding once I swallow, "As long as I can eat as many cookies as I want, I really don't care."

Mirth glows in Lukas's gaze. "Jade Maríana Aguilar, I solemnly swear on the little honor I have that I will never, ever stop you from eating cookies."

My tone drops, taking on a serious edge. "You know, you really are perfect."

I study the space around him, that gorgeous soul, and Lukas swallows. "If that's your definition of perfect, then I'd say you set the bar woefully low."

"Lukas." I shouldn't be reeling him in when I need to push him away, but come morning, Lukas will be gone from my life, which is perhaps why I add, "My bar isn't the issue here."

His cheeks color right as the music changes, going from a heady rush to something softer, sweeter. Slower. Lukas's nostrils flare, his eyes never leaving mine, and he asks, voice strained, "Dance with me?"

There's no hesitation in my answer, and I take his hand. "Of course."

He sweeps me into the space cleared for dancing, grass plush beneath our boots. One of his hands remains locked with mine, while the other goes to my waist and tucks me into his chest. I breathe him in, scented of the pine he worked with all day, and rest my head on his shoulder. Lukas sighs, the breaking of a small dam, lowers his chin to my head, and pulls me even closer.

For a while we simply sway, exist, and savor one another. I can hear the beat of Lukas's heart, feel the flush in his skin, and I wonder what he senses of me. If he knows all the ways I've let him in.

It's a perfect moment, and my eyes heat when I realize my mother will never witness it. She always hoped I'd be able to face the world someday, and now that I finally have, she isn't around to see it. A tear slides down my cheek, then another, and soon I'm shaking in an effort to suppress my sobs.

"Jade, hey." Lukas pulls back, brow furrowed. "What's wrong?"

If he were anyone else, I'd run from the truth, but this is Lukas. I'm safe with him.

"It's my mom," I whisper. "I miss her. I wish she could see how far I've come."

His arms stiffen around me before he kisses my brow, and my blood thrums as he releases a heavy breath. "I may not have known her, but I'm sure she would've been proud."

He's right. She would've. I squeeze him tighter, a silent thank-you, then say, "I don't want tonight to end. Ever."

"Me neither." He sighs, and I swear I feel the ghost of his lips on my hair. "I wish—"

Lightning splits the sky, a violent crack, and I jolt at the sudden boom of thunder. Lukas's grip tightens at my waist, but even he can't save me from the icy rain that falls a second later.

"Shit." Lukas tries to shelter me beneath him, but it's useless, and we're drenched in seconds.

The townspeople bustle around us, irritated exclamations filling the air as everyone rushes to escape the damp. I yelp when one of them brushes my shoulder, panic edging in. There're too many bodies, too many people, too much noise and sensation and—

"Shh," Lukas whispers, soothing. "It's okay. I'm going to get us out of here."

And to his credit, he starts to. He wraps his arm around my shoulders, keeps the other hand clasped in mine, but when he tries to take a step, I don't move with him.

"Jade?" he asks, but still I don't move.

Water slides down my neck, drips from my chin. Lanterns wink out around us, the clearing growing darker by the second, the chaos reaching its pitch. But no one pays attention to us or comes for me, and I remind myself that this is *not* two years ago. I'm no longer helpless on the courthouse steps.

The truth is I've lived my entire life either in fear or protected by someone who made me feel safe. First my mother, now Lukas. I've been content that way too, but starting this investigation, seeing what I can do . . . it makes me *want* to be brave.

Perhaps I'm not quite ready yet, but tonight I can at least take a small step. So I straighten my spine, lift my chin, and gently remove Lukas's arm from around my shoulders. My heart pounds, but I'm determined. "Together," I say.

Not him shouldering the burden. Not me crumbling beneath its weight. But both of us, as one.

Lukas understands. "Okay."

And that's exactly how we do it. Hands clasped, we sprint through the downpour all the way home.

Together.

CHAPTER THIRTY-THREE

LUKAS

JADE'S SHIVERING VIOLENTLY BY THE TIME WE REACH JOHANN'S barn—we both are. I quickly light a few lanterns, and we scramble up to the hayloft, rain pounding the roof above us.

"Come on." I wrap an arm around her shoulders, and this time she lets me. "We need to get you warm. Let's change into something dry."

Jade, though, shakes her head. "My clothes—I did the washing today. They were still hanging on the line when we left."

Shit. They'll be just as soaked as she is. "Were mine drying too?"

She answers through chattering teeth. "N-no. I did yours earlier in the day."

A little spark of warmth lights inside me. I imagine myself pulling Jade closer and kissing her deeply. It's what I *want* to do, but instead I say, "Thank you. You didn't have to do that, but I'm grateful all the same."

Grateful for you, I don't add.

"You're welcome," Jade mumbles, adorable. It takes everything in me to leave her side and cross the loft, to where she's neatly folded my clothes near my designated lump of hay and blankets.

I grab two sets, then offer her one. "Here. It'll be large, but at least it'll be dry."

"Are you sure?"

"Jade." I groan. "I'm not going to let you freeze."

That does it. She takes my offering. I turn around, affording her a measure of privacy, and imagine she does the same. My wet clothes smack against the wooden floor. I kick them into the corner before pulling on the drier items, which—unsurprisingly—smell like roses. Jade must have used her favorite soap. I grin, then ask, "Are you decent?"

"Well, I mean . . ." She sighs. "You can turn around."

My jaw nearly drops when I do. Because standing there in only my shirt and her crown, smooth legs on full display, is Jade. Which, I mean, of course it's Jade. It couldn't be anyone else, but it appears I've lost the ability to rationally process information. Seeing her like that, flowers at her brow, jeweled in raindrops—I *love* seeing her dressed like my people. And those *legs.*

Every useful thought I might've had is temporarily eclipsed by an image of me kissing those legs, working my way steadily up, lifting the hem above her thighs—

I'm being indecent and disrespectful. I rip my gaze to Jade's face to find her blushing. Shit. "I'm sorry," I apologize. "I shouldn't have— I mean . . ."

It appears I've also forgotten how to speak. Fortunately, Jade saves me from saying anything too foolish. "It's okay. I should've warned you. The pants kept slipping, and I figured this would cover enough."

It does. It hits her mid-thigh, and yet it does nothing to temper my thoughts, growing more heated by the second.

"Right, then." I clear my throat, my gaze still adamantly on her face. "I guess we should go to bed."

But neither of us moves. A beat of silence passes before Jade breaks it. "Actually, I have something for you. A Gebreine gift. I meant to give it to you earlier, but I got swept up, though now it's wet, but it'll still do and— Oh gods. I'm babbling now, aren't I? I'm sorry, I'm just nervous."

"It's okay," I reassure her. In seconds I'm across the space, unable to resist placing a comforting hand on her elbow. "I like it when you babble. It's cute."

"It is?"

"It is."

She releases a slow breath, her gaze focused firmly on my chest. "Well, that's . . . okay. I mean, not okay, that's good, I guess, and—" Her hand juts out, and for the first time I notice something's clasped in it. "Here. Your present. Take it before I keep talking."

I let out a chuckle, but it's cut short the moment I take the gift and unfold it, my breath temporarily stolen by the image staring back at me. Because I know what this is, carefully stitched into worn leather. I've seen enough souls these past weeks to recognize one when I see it. What I don't know is who it belongs to, and it crosses my mind that maybe it's Jade's.

"Whose is it?" I ask, voice rasping.

But Jade ignores my question and lifts her hand to the portrait, brushing a vein of purple. "See that? It's intelligence. And this?" She lowers her fingers to several green swirls. "This is nurturance, which pairs well with this." She points to a swell of brown. "Which is kindness. So much kindness. There's anger too, and strength. Passion and spirituality, beauty and sensitivity, and

260

of course courage." She taps a spike of pine-needle green, briefly meets my gaze, and blushes. "I've always thought your eyes looked like courage. The shades are nearly identical."

Before I can respond, she's focused back on the portrait, lips grim as she traces a river of black. "This is grief, running through all of it, but it's only made possible by my favorite part. This." Her touch skims a red well. Dark and deep, its roots overflow into every aspect of the portrait, twined with several other colors. "This is love. Pure, enduring love. It fuels the grief, but it also makes other aspects possible. Happiness. Hope. Compassion. All of it born of love."

She lifts her head and faces me, radiant. "It's beautiful, isn't it?"

I can't help but agree as I imagine that soul hovering around her. "It is," I say.

She positively beams at me. "Of course it is, because it's yours."

My mind goes quiet, a blanket of shock settling over it.

"What?" I've been so wrapped up in the idea this was Jade's soul, I never paused to consider she might've gifted me something just as powerful.

Jade takes my free hand and whispers, "You're always down on yourself, talking about your work and your home as if they reflect badly on you. But from the day we met, *this* is what I've seen. This beautiful, glorious, incredible soul. From those first moments in that alley, I trusted you, because I knew the truth of you. You are *wonderful,* and words don't do you justice, so I stopped using them." Her gaze shifts to the present in my grasp. "You're everything in that portrait and more. Love and courage and kindness, and I hope now you can see it too."

Jade told me I had a beautiful soul once, but I didn't quite believe her. I assumed then she was being nice; now, though—I don't know. I thought the soul was stunning when I believed it to be hers. Why should her revelation change that? For months now Jade's insisted I'm better than the way I see myself.

Maybe . . . maybe she's right. I'm not wholly convinced, but the possibility is enough to have my fingers clenching the portrait.

"Thank you." The words scrape. "This is . . . No one's ever done anything so kind for me."

"Well, that's a shame," she says, a little breathless, "because you deserve kindness like this every day of your life."

Desire ignites inside me, so robust it's a miracle I don't turn to cinders. I meet Jade's eyes, those dark, gorgeous depths. It takes everything in me not to cup her jaw, lower my mouth to hers, and kiss her within an inch of her life. But she pulled away last time. I don't want to make her feel pressured or uncomfortable. It's nearly impossible, though, when she looks at me like *that,* such blatant adoration in her gaze. Enough that I can't resist a question.

"Why did you push me away that day in the woods? Why didn't you want me?"

The second part slides out, unplanned and unwelcome, but now that it's between us, I can't take it back.

Jade pales and looks down. *I'm sorry,* I should say. *You don't need to tell me.* But I can't make myself do it. Not when I'm desperate for an answer.

"I didn't want to tell you," she admits, so quiet her words become creations of spun glass. "But it's wrong, keeping this secret. You deserve to know the truth."

I can't breathe all of a sudden, my mind running to the worst-case scenarios. "What is it?"

Jade's eyes glisten, and a tear runs down her face. "When I was a kid, I did something bad. Something that hurt your family."

The second stretches, grows, expands, and suddenly I'm not here, in this moment, any longer. I'm fifteen years old, soaked to the bone, begging Zamora to save my sister. I'm standing at a window, festivities muted outside, while Jade confesses that her thread speaking doesn't always feel right. I'm living six paces to the left, three hours back, while I told Jade about Lina. *I'm sorry I didn't save her,* she whispered, and I heard everything she didn't say. The admission. She was there that night, watching, but chose to remain silent. She didn't have to tell me. It was written in all the words left unsaid.

Now, though, she means to say it. She must be worried I didn't understand earlier.

But I did, and I stop her before she can say anything else. "It's okay, Jade. Really. I already know, and I've forgiven you for it. You were young and scared, and probably didn't know what to do, but it's in the past now, and . . ." My breath hitches as I scan her face, her eyes wet and skin flushed. "I'd rather live in the present. With you, if you'll let me."

She opens her mouth. Closes it. Cries openly now, and her voice squeaks. "Are you sure? That's a big thing to forgive. You lost someone you love because of me."

Perhaps I did, but Jade was only a child. We both were.

"Positive."

I'm leaning in now, but Jade pulls back. "You really don't care?"

"At first I did a great deal," I admit, and it's true. "But that time has passed. I've forgiven you. Truly."

And I mean it with my entire soul. Jade must see that I do, because she gives me a watery smile. "That is . . . I don't have words. Just thank you, so much, Lukas. For understanding, and for seeing that I never meant any harm."

And with that, the wall between us crumbles.

Slowly, I fold the thread portrait and place it in my pocket, then face Jade fully. Her breath hitches at the blatant desire in my gaze. I grab her wrist. A gentle tug, and she's flush against my chest. I wrap my arm around her waist, gripping the curve of her hip, and look down at her. The light's dim, but there's enough for me to see her pupils dilate. Her heart races beneath mine.

I swallow. "Now that you know I've forgiven you, are there any other reasons you don't want this?"

"None," she breathes out. "I want this."

"Thank god."

Our last kiss was a slow build. A soft brush of lips, a mingling of breath that gave way to something headier. But now I know what it's like to have Jade pressed against me, know the taste and sound and smell of her, and I can't bring myself to be patient any longer. So when I kiss Jade, it's not a soft thing but a crush of lips, a clash of teeth. She moans into my mouth, heating my blood. I grip her even tighter, wanting more, more, *more.*

"Lukas," she breathes, her hands winding through my hair.

"Gods," she sighs, my lips at her throat.

"Please," she whimpers, her back arching, pressing her into me more.

And each word, every breathy little gasp, only has my hunger growing hotter, wilder. I dip one of my hands and trace the skin of her bare leg, moving steadily higher until I hit the hem of my shirt. I pause there, waiting for permission.

"Don't stop." Jade's words are an intoxicating rush, as desperate as I am. "Please, I want this."

I'm powerless to disobey her request. My palms skim the hot flesh of her thigh, everything inside me burning when I realize she's not wearing anything beneath my shirt. Jade shivers at my touch, and I nearly explode with the desire and euphoria coursing through me.

This, I realize. This is what I want, for the rest of my life. Jade.

But we have only a handful of hours, and I decide to savor them, savor *her.* It starts with trailing my fingers higher, the stutter of her breath fueling this feral beast inside my chest. Everything inside me screams to go faster. I don't let that base instinct take over, though. This isn't my first tumble, but it's my most meaningful. And for Jade, I sense it might be new.

So I slow down.

Outside, thunder booms, in sync with the beat of my heart but much less powerful. Every pounding of blood through my veins whispers the same thing. *Jade, Jade, Jade.* As rain lashes the barn, fervor building as Jade and I slide closer to that peak, I know something to be true:

Nothing will ever be as perfect as this moment.

CHAPTER THIRTY-FOUR

JADE

I'M IN LOVE WITH LUKAS.

That particular truth has become undeniable, and I nuzzle his throat, wrapped up in him, no clothes left between us. I still can't believe he forgave me after what I did to his father, and tomorrow I'll ask him how he found out—but not tonight. These hours before the dawn are just for us, and I snuggle deeper into the blankets.

"Thank you," I whisper into his neck. "For making me feel brave, and loved, and beautiful."

He pulls me closer and kisses my brow. "You were all those things before I came around, but I'm glad you can see it now. I'm glad I got to help you see it."

I wonder if love is always like this, if it brings out the best in people, like Lukas does with me and, I hope, I do with him.

"You know," Lukas interrupts my thoughts, "I've been thinking."

"What about?" I raise an eyebrow. Whatever he's going to say, judging by his tone, it's something serious.

He carefully slides out from under me and flips onto his side so we're facing each other. "I know this is going to sound ridiculous, but I want you to promise to hear me out."

He's nervous, but there's something else there too—excitement maybe? His cheeks are flushed, and his eyes shine in the dim light.

I cup his cheek, a bubble of happiness filling me that I can touch him like this whenever I want, because he wants it too. "Lukas," I tell him, "I'll always hear you out. What is it?"

He lifts his hand to my wrist, my spine tingling as he traces delicate circles there. "I was thinking," he says slowly, carefully, "that maybe we should bind our souls."

My mind goes completely blank. I must have a visible reaction, though, because Lukas rushes on, face flaming. "I know, I *know*, it probably sounds foolish—I mean, we've only known each other for six weeks—but, Jade . . ." He squeezes my wrists. "The things I feel for you, everything we've been through together—I want to be even more connected to you. And we don't have to, of course, we won't if you don't want to, but—"

"Lukas." My voice is soft, but it cuts through his chatter, and he immediately quiets. "I would love nothing more than to bind my soul with yours. I *want* to, really—but I can't."

It's true. Thread bindings can be done and undone with relative ease, though the undoing is temporarily painful, like a fist squeezing your heart. With Lukas I doubt I'd ever want to unravel our bond, but we're young, and having the option makes me sure I want this too.

Unfortunately, what I want and what's possible are two different things.

Lukas's face crumples. "Why not?"

I swipe my thumb over his cheek, tracing the delicate bone. "Because I can't see my own soul. It's part of being a thread speaker—we can see everyone's soul except our own."

Which makes binding myself to Lukas impossible. The ritual requires that each person have the core elements of their partner's soul stitched onto them, so without the knowledge of mine, it won't take.

"You can't?" His eyes widen. "I guess I always assumed you could."

I shake my head. "I can't. If I could, I'd bind us in a heartbeat. And, well . . ." I take a deep breath, steadying myself. When Lukas forgave me earlier, it got me thinking. Returning to Sallenda won't be easy, but with him by my side, I think it's worth it. Before, that wasn't possible, but now?

Now that future—one where we're together—is within reach, I just have to be brave enough to grasp it.

So I do.

"We could ask Johann, but I don't want to wake him in the middle of the night. There's always morning, but we'll have to rush so we can leave afterward and make it back to Sallenda by the queen's deadline."

I've never seen Lukas go quite this still. I'm not even sure he's breathing, and my heart's racing by the time he responds, voice high and slow.

"Jade . . . are you saying what I think you're saying?"

Ever since I realized my history with Lukas's father, I've been tortured with want. The desire to pull him close, the need to push him away. But the latter always hurt, for both of us, I think, and I'm relieved it's no longer necessary.

"Yes." My eyes water. "Let's go back together."

The quiet's so thick, a single exhalation could shatter it. Lukas swallows, heavy in the silence, then whispers, "But the queen . . . your thread speaking. I know I told you to think things over, but I hate the thought of you being imprisoned by her whims."

In truth, so do I. But I've accomplished a lot since meeting Lukas, and perhaps this is simply one more obstacle for us to navigate together.

"I know," I tell him. "I don't like it either, but I'm the queen's only remaining thread speaker. Perhaps she and I can strike a bargain, and if not?" I shrug. "The world isn't as frightening anymore. I could escape back into it, with your help. For now, though, I'd like to return with you and finish what we started—assuming you'd like that too, of course."

A beat of stillness passes, and then Lukas is peppering me with kisses, his lips imprinting my throat, my shoulders, my cheeks. My giggles fracture the silence until it's shattered completely, and Lukas and I collapse beside each other into a delirious, happy puddle.

"So." Lukas turns on his side to face me. "I have an idea."

"Oh?" I pull back for a better view of him. "About what?"

He glances down, almost shy, even after everything we've just done.

"About binding our souls. We could wait until morning, but if you'd rather not, there's something else we could try, if you wanted."

"Oh?" I feel my eyebrows rise. "What's your idea?"

"Well, I was thinking . . ." He releases a sharp breath, and his next words follow in a rush. "I know you can't see your own soul, but what if I help you?"

"Help me?"

"Yeah, I mean—" He runs a hand through his hair. "It's probably stupid, but the contents of a soul, it's kind of like what you shared with mine, isn't it? Things like love and kindness. I don't know the colors, but I do know *you*." He meets my eyes. "I could tell you what I see, and you could translate that into soul speak."

"I . . ." I'm not sure what to say. The fact that he wants to do that for me makes me ache with tenderness. But actually facing my soul . . .

My mother offered to stitch my soul for me just once. I was only fourteen at the time, and I turned her down. I didn't want to see it, convinced I'd hate it.

Even now I can't imagine that I'll like what I see. Already I can picture the colors in it. The sour yellow fear, the chartreuse jealousy. I'd rather not know. But Lukas sharing what he sees, *that* might not be bad. That might actually be nice.

I steady myself and meet his patient gaze. "Okay, we can try. Though I can't promise it'll work."

Lukas's response is a sudden kiss, deep and warm. He still tastes like cider, and by the time he finishes, I'm dizzy with want. He must see that too, because he chuckles. "Later," he promises, "after."

My skin heats just thinking about it. Honestly, I don't even recognize myself anymore, especially when I admire Lukas's lithe form as he retrieves my thread kit. I sit up when he places it in front of me, then select a burgundy spool and a short length of dissolvable fabric. "Let's start with your soul."

I thread my needle and begin the process of stitching the core elements of Lukas's soul into the fabric. My fingers are quick, nimble, honed by instinct and magic, and thirty minutes later I have a respectable patch, the core elements of Lukas's soul proudly displayed.

Next comes the difficult part, and I pick a spot near my heart, then begin stitching into my skin, just enough so the patch is secure. Blood beads, and I grit my teeth. It hurts, but the pain is almost refreshing. Revitalizing. Because it's the ache of letting someone in, the burn of expanding my life to include him.

It's a beautiful thing, and I admire my work once it's finished.

The key pieces of Lukas's soul are stitched onto my chest, right above my heart, a clear spot left in the center. In a few months, the fabric will dissolve with wear and time, the thread sinking more fully into my skin, as only a tattoo given by a speaker can.

"Do you like it?" I ask.

Lukas's nostrils flare. "To be honest, I didn't expect to like it this much. Seeing my soul on you, though . . . it *does* something to me, Jade."

I can't help it—I giggle. Watching Lukas get all crazed fills me with a heady rush, though it dampens when I remember what's next.

"Okay, your turn." I gesture to the thread kit. "Tell me what traits you see in me, and I'll pick the corresponding color."

Lukas stares at me a moment, eyes narrowed, and my stomach churns. I'm just about to suggest we try this another time when he says, "Let's start with the obvious, what anyone could see. You're beautiful."

It shouldn't affect me—he's said it before—but I'm powerless against the flush crawling up my neck as I select a spool of shimmery emerald thread. Lukas's gaze never leaves me as I prepare the needle, and my breath is shallow as I create a series of stitches that come together to form a few starbursts. Lukas is calm as I work, still looking at me.

I pull back once I'm finished. "What next?"

He's had time to think now, and he answers right away. "Generosity. You're the most giving person I've ever met."

It goes on like that for a while, and every trait Lukas suggests warms a cold place inside me. Kindness. Sensitivity. Love. Compassion. Grief.

Soon a soul is forming that's, well, beautiful. Is this really how he sees me?

Even so, it can't last. There's a key shade missing, and I pause after I return violet intelligence to my kit and face him. My heart races, but I force myself to say what's on my mind. "There's a trait you're leaving out."

Lukas studies me a minute, thoughtful, then says, "Fear, right?"

My heart clenches—with what I'm not exactly sure. Horror that he's read this part of me so clearly, or perhaps relief that he does see it but still wants me.

"Yes." My throat is tight, and my fingers tremble as I reach for that sour yellow thread. "Fear. It's always been a part of me."

Lukas's gaze doesn't waver, but when I lift my hand, he grabs my wrist. "Wait one second."

He pulls my thread kit to him and riffles through the colors—careful not to disrupt the organization—until he removes a spool of viridian. He turns it over, studying it, then holds it up. "Courage, right?"

I swallow. He must have known from his own portrait. "It is, but I hardly see how it could have a place in my soul."

Lukas doesn't miss a beat. "In the weeks we've known each other, you've taken on a sievech, the tracker, and a horde of furious sailors." He presses the spool into my open palm. "True bravery isn't the absence of fear but standing up despite the weight of it pushing you down. Maybe it bent you once, bends you still, but every day I see you fighting against it, and *that* is why this belongs in your portrait. You're the most courageous person I've ever met."

Even if I could speak right now, I don't know what I'd say. There's too much raging emotion coursing through me—love and gratitude, and still that tang of fear. I'm terrified Lukas is wrong, that he'll discover the truth and leave me when he realizes I'm not this person.

But there's also a bud of hope that maybe, just maybe, he's right. That I'm exactly as brave as he says I am. A few tears leak out, and Lukas brushes them away. "I see you," he whispers, "all of you."

Six words, and they almost break me. "Okay," I whisper. "I trust you."

He tucks my hair behind my ear. "Good. Now finish your portrait."

There's a slight grin on his lips, and I match it as I bring the yellow thread to the delicate fabric and carefully wind it through everything already there. When it's finished, I don't hesitate to add viridian right alongside it. Everywhere fear goes, the courage follows, a spiral of parallel emotions.

I pull back once it's done, throat tight. I don't know yet if this portrait is accurate, but if it is . . . it's lovely. Nothing worth all the fear I spent on it.

And now it's ready to be placed. Stitched over the heart of the boy I love.

Gently, I place it on his chest and lift my needle, though I don't lower it yet. "Are you ready?"

"Of course." His voice remains steady. "I've been waiting for this a long time. Waiting for you."

That does strange things to my heart, but rather than focus on it, I carefully pierce Lukas's flesh, binding the tattoo to his skin with a series of deft stitches. When I finish, Lukas brushes his fingers over it, then faces me. "It's perfect. *You're* perfect."

I grin, almost giddy. "If I am, then you are too."

His lips twitch, but he doesn't acknowledge my words, just nods to the thread kit. "Come on. Time for the next part."

I grab a spool of pure white thread and trim a length of it.

Lukas waits patiently as I prick my thumb with the needle and, with the blood that wells up, dye the thread a deep ruby. I pass it to him once I'm finished, and he does the same.

Lukas scoots closer as I stitch into my skin once again, filling the center of his portrait with a small circle. His hand is warm on my knee, and he squeezes as I trim the strand, then lift my eyes to his.

"Are you sure you want this?" I ask. "It's not like there's no going back once I finish, but it would hurt."

Lukas doesn't hesitate. "I'm sure, Jade."

A shiver ripples down my spine, and I lift my needle to his chest. I've just pierced the skin when Lukas voices a question.

"Why is it that everything else you do has a cost, but this is free?"

I've wondered the same thing myself, so I'm ready with an answer.

"Because everything else involves taking," I tell him, still sewing into his chest, right above his heart. "I can't create traits, only redistribute them, but *this*, tethering souls . . ." I pause. Swallow. "The threads that bind us don't have a cost because they're selfless. When people agree to be bound, it's because they want to give. Love. Affection. Kindness. It's not about taking but generosity, so it's not free so much as a gift freely given."

I'm nearly done, but when I feel Lukas staring at me, I pause to meet his gaze. "What?"

"Nothing," he says, but he's smiling. "I just really liked that sentiment."

I didn't think it possible, but a little more warmth trickles in. "Me too," I admit, then nod to his chest. "I'm almost done. Are you ready?"

"Of course," he says. "Always."

And because he's Lukas, and he makes me feel beautiful and brave, I rise onto my knees and bring my lips to his. The kiss is meant to be fleeting, but Lukas winds his fingers through my hair and pulls me to him, and by the time we break apart, my skin's on fire. "Do it now," he whispers, face still a hairsbreadth from mine. "Bind our souls."

And I do. My movements are steady as I finish the last of the satin stitch, creating a perfect ruby dot in the middle of the portrait.

A moment passes, weighted and drenched in hope. I don't think I breathe, don't hear Lukas draw in a breath either as we wait for a sign that it worked. But as the seconds slide by and nothing happens, I realize Lukas must've been wrong. He doesn't see me as I truly am—

I gasp when it hits me. A rush of so many feelings, I can't decipher them all at once, I just know they're warm and loving. And for a moment it's like I'm no longer myself, like I'm living in Lukas's skin, his heart beating inside my chest, my blood running through his veins. The world splits, fractures, melts, before in a snap I'm back inside my own body.

But it's different now, a fraction off from what it was before. I can feel Lukas's emotions, not as if they're my own, but like an undercurrent in a deep ocean. And somewhere inside my chest, a compass lights up, pointing me to him.

My true north.

"Jade." Lukas sounds winded. "Do you feel it, feel *that*? It's like . . . like . . ."

But he doesn't find the words, because there aren't any, not to describe this. Never before have I felt so connected to another person, and when I run my palm across Lukas's cheek, my eyes are wet.

"Thank you," I whisper. "For seeing me."

His breath hitches, and he catches my hand, then pulls it to his lips for a shiver-inducing kiss. "Thank you for letting me."

And then we're tangled again, skin on skin, his mouth on mine, and I'm sure of it, even more than I was before, so sure I could burst. I'm in love with Lukas.

And I think that maybe, just maybe, he might be in love with me too.

CHAPTER THIRTY-FIVE

LUKAS

I'M IN LOVE WITH JADE.

There's no denying it after what we just shared, and I watch her in the dim light. She's passed out, all curled up in the blankets, her arm thrown across my chest, hair an inky spill speckled with stray bits of hay. I carefully pull a few out before my gaze dips lower, to my soul embroidered above her heart. Seeing it there does something to me. I brush the thread on my own chest, almost in wonder.

Six weeks ago I wouldn't have understood how someone like Jade could care for someone like me. I'm beginning to find some clarity now, though. The way our souls look together—we just fit.

And we could keep fitting together, if we wanted. As I watch her sleep, it's hard not to imagine what our life could be like here. Purchasing a small timber-framed house. Warming ourselves by the hearth in the winter, a fire crackling between us. Cooking some of my favorite dishes, rabbit stew and pork sausage, dumplings and pretzels and too many potato patties. She'd earn a living binding souls, and I'd help too. Find a job in the timber industry like my dad, perhaps. Make enough to bring my family back home.

An entire life we could have together. Right now it's so easy to see it. To taste and feel and believe in it. Maybe, if I'm lucky, I'll get to make it a reality soon.

"I love you, Jade." I whisper it, because if I don't, I might erupt. She doesn't stir, but that's okay—this one was just for me. I'll make sure she knows in the morning. Now, though, I carefully extricate myself from her grasp, brushing a kiss over her knuckles when she reaches for me. "I'll be back soon," I murmur. While she's not quite awake, she does relax at my reassurance.

A few minutes later I'm dressed and slipping from the barn, a loaf of bread slung under one arm, a carafe of fresh water cradled in the other.

It's dark outside, the smell of damp heavy in the air. Raindrops gleam like tiny diamonds in the moonlight, bejeweling the forest. Fortunately, the downpour has ended, and fog rolls around my ankles as I make my way between the trees, walking a few minutes before I reach it.

The cellar.

In the chaos of the day, we forgot to bring the tracker fresh food and water. I know I should've woken Jade—we promised never to visit him alone—but watching her rest, I couldn't bring myself to disturb her.

It should be fine, anyway. The tracker's always restrained, and I'll only be a few minutes. Or at least that's how I reassure myself as I slip down the rungs and into the humid dark, wrinkling my nose at the smell of stale piss. Seconds later I'm on the cellar floor, the tracker seated in front of me, his wrists bound and back pressed against the wall. He must've heard me open the latch, because he's awake and grinning in that almost serpentine way, his features mapped in shadow, a lantern flickering to his right.

"Lukas." His gaze flits over my shoulder. "You're alone. How . . . unusual."

"Jade's asleep," I offer in explanation, then hold up the loaf of bread. "I brought you this, though god knows you don't deserve it."

"Perhaps not." That grin of his twitches in clear amusement as I place the paltry meal near his feet. "Though I'm not too concerned about the afterlife."

A lick of fire blazes up my spine, over my skin, across my throat. "Maybe you should be, considering you'll be spending the rest of this life in a Kabrückian prison. Miserable and cold and hungry, wasting away until they decide to hang you for your crimes."

I think I wanted to see the look on his face when I told him of his fate, but his expression is immensely unsatisfying. If anything, he looks uninterested.

"Is that so?" he asks. "Thank you for telling me—I was curious."

I have to shove my hands into my pockets to keep from clenching my fists. The tracker's done so much to hurt us, hurt *Jade,* and now that we've struck back, he simply doesn't care? "You're going to stay away from Jade," I seethe. "You're not going to look at her, talk to her, so much as touch her, or I swear to god I'll kill you."

The tracker sighs. He doesn't even have the decency to appear startled. "I'd assume my impending imprisonment would make that impossible, but if you're here making threats anyway . . ." He looks me over, from my wrinkled clothing to my disheveled hair. I step back, disgusted, when his lips form a self-assured grin. "Well then. It would appear you're quite enamored with her, and apparently she is with you as well. I must say I'm surprised, given what she did to your father, but then I suppose true love conquers all."

It's like I've been dunked in a vat of ice water. Did Jade do something to my father?

No. I'm being ridiculous. He's probably just trying to turn me against Jade.

But deep inside me a crumb of doubt lingers. In truth, it's been festering since we captured the tracker, when he said I reminded him of someone. He mentioned my eyes, similar to my father's.

Perhaps that's why I find myself saying, voice faint, "Jade never did anything to my father."

A question cloaked in a statement. The tracker must know this, because his eyes sparkle. "So she never told you. Interesting."

I *want* to ram my fists into his face. I *should* leave right now and ask Jade what the tracker's referring to.

I do neither and settle on a third option, trembling as I stare the tracker down. "Tell me what you know and how you know it. Now."

He tsks. "I'm not sure it's my place, but if I'm about to spend the rest of my days in a Kabrückian prison, perhaps I deserve one final bit of entertainment." He licks his lips, clearly enjoying this, even as I debate throttling him. "I'm sure Jade has informed you of my particular set of skills and the tattoo that fueled them. I had it a long time, and it secured me lots of jobs for many different people. One of my most frequent clients was Zamora Aguilar."

I reel back. Jade's mother hired the tracker? My head's spinning, but the tracker chuckles and continues.

"I can see you're surprised, but yes. Zamora did her fair share of official work for the Crown, but on the side she took on more . . . unsavory jobs. And as you're certainly aware, any kind of thread speaking requires a little bit of whoever's soul is being used. She couldn't always secure those pieces, and when that happened, she'd come to me. For a small fee, I'd locate whoever she needed and bring back a few strands of their hair."

I'm not sure what I was expecting him to reveal. This, though . . .

Wherever it's going, I can already feel the dark, poisonous nature of it. I should leave. Even so, I remain rooted to the spot.

The tracker grins. He's ensnared me, and he knows it. "Years ago she gave me a target. As always, I found him with ease. He was a fisherman working at the docks, and I'm not sure why, but in this particular instance, when I delivered his hair, I asked Zamora what fate she had in store for him. She refused to tell me her plans, but she did confess one thing—that *she* wasn't going to do anything. Apparently, she'd decided to introduce her daughter to the darker nature of their trade, and her first assignment was this man." The tracker leans closer, and I fight the urge to step back as he whispers, words dripping in smug arrogance, "Would you care to guess his name?"

I swallow. I wish I'd stayed tucked beside Jade, happy and warm and in love. But I didn't, and I can't go back now. I won't.

"Egon," I whisper. "His name was Egon."

My father.

The tracker's entire face lights up. "You look just like him, especially your eyes. I couldn't figure it out at first, why you were so familiar, but I never forget a mark. Then I remembered your gun, and it clicked. Such a distinctive weapon, one your father carried around when I tailed him. You're Lukas Keller, Egon's son, and apparently quite devoted to the girl who killed your father."

I wonder if this is what Jade's episodes feel like. I can't breathe, can barely think straight, and my blood's turned to ice in my veins. Denial shrieks inside me. Jade couldn't—would never—do something like that. But my doubts are doused by another memory, just hours ago now.

When I was a kid, I did something bad, she said. *Something that hurt your family.*

Of course, in that moment I assumed she was referring to Lina, but what if I was wrong? What if it was this?

I'm going to be sick, but I force myself to prod deeper because I need the truth. "How do you know she killed him?"

And why was he a target in the first place? The question burns beneath my skin, too hot to touch. Emma always thought he was involved in something, but she couldn't be right; he wouldn't—what? I don't even know where to start guessing.

"Because," the tracker answers simply, "a week later he was dead. I read the obituary in the paper."

I can't be here anymore. My brain is fuzzy, and everything feels strangely dimmed, but somehow that thought breaks through. I faintly register my own movement. Wood scraping my hands as I climb the ladder out. The cold metal of the hatch as I slide it closed and pull the bolt through. Twigs snap beneath my feet and cool air brushes my skin as I walk through the moonlit forest, headed where, I'm not sure. Eventually I crumple to the ground, crushed beneath the weight of it all. Wet soaks the knees of my pants, chilling me, but I don't shiver.

For a while I simply sit. Numb. Trying to process this new information, because it doesn't make sense. Jade couldn't do something like this. She's warm and kind, generous and wonderful. I know this for a fact, it's stitched onto my fucking chest, and yet—

I can't brush the tracker's story aside. He knew too many details he wouldn't otherwise know, like my last name, or the fact I inherited my father's pistol as well as his eyes. He could've been lying about Jade's involvement, but Jade herself admitted she'd been keeping something from me. That she'd hurt my family. And when I told her I forgave her, she was shocked.

Now I know why.

I squeeze my eyes shut, but that doesn't stop the burn of tears, my grief and rage mixing together. Fury toward not only Jade but myself. Because I did this.

I stayed when I should've gone back.

Fell in love when I should've maintained my resentment.

Bound our souls when I should've kept my distance.

All for my father's killer.

He trusted me to take care of my family, but for Jade I ignored his advice. I chose my own happiness over Emma, Artur, and my mom. Now they're alone in a city with a soul-eating monster because of my poor choices.

No. Not just poor—*selfish*. There's no other way to spin my actions.

I'm not sure how long I sit out there, shrouded in fog and sorrow. All I know is that when I stand, I've made a decision.

Dawn isn't far off when I slink back inside the barn. Fortunately, Jade's still fast asleep, but I don't allow myself more than a passing glance her way. Anything extra would be too painful. I pack my belongings in silence but freeze when I get to the thread portrait Jade made for me. Tears sting my eyes. *It's beautiful, isn't it?* she'd said, and I had agreed. Because it was. Because she made me believe that about myself for the first time.

What a waste.

What a lie.

I toss the portrait to the floor and finish packing my things.

When I'm done, I quietly open Jade's thread kit and remove the seam ripper, swallowing as I lift it to my chest. Right above my heart. Every time Jade bound two souls, she made sure the owners knew how to sever the bond. It's as easy as snipping the center thread. Just hours ago I thought I'd be bound to Jade forever. Now the blade trembles in my grip, poised to destroy the bond.

But then I remember Jade standing in front of the tracker's gun for me. Rescuing me from those sailors. Kissing me in the forest. All of it sloshes around my brain, and I just—I can't. I truly am selfish, because I can't separate myself from this girl who murdered my father. I think I'm still in love with her, and I hate myself for it, even as I return the seam ripper.

Still, when Jade wakes up, she needs to know that whatever we have—had—is over. Fortunately, there are a few clean sheets of parchment in her kit, along with a pencil, and I scrawl a quick note, my handwriting sharp and angry. I fold it carefully, then force myself to turn and face her.

The blow is swift, like a bullet to the heart. She's so peaceful, her breath deep, her lashes twin crescents, one on each cheek. And it splits me in two, the burning desire to kiss her forehead, lift the blankets, and slide in next to her. To pretend the past hour never happened and nothing changed.

Selfish. The word thuds inside me, a solemn chant. *Selfish, selfish, selfish.*

I shouldn't feel this way after learning what she did. It's shameful, and my lip curls as I leave the note next to Jade. She frowns as I do, almost as if she can sense this war raging inside me, which I suppose she can. We're bound now. She murmurs my name in her sleep, and I swear my heart bursts into flames. I have to get out of here.

And I do. My note delivered, I heft my bag over my shoulder, then turn from Jade. I don't spare a single glance backward. Not as I descend the ladder and leave the barn, or even as I depart Dreiden, the sun just cresting the horizon. It promises a beautiful day, but not for me or for Jade.

Never for us again.

CHAPTER THIRTY-SIX

JADE

SOMETHING'S WRONG. I FEEL IT THE MOMENT I WAKE UP, LIKE A ball of writhing snakes has lodged itself beneath my rib cage. It takes me a moment to process what I'm feeling, the morning sun streaming through the barn windows contrasting with the mess of emotions inside me.

Lukas, I realize. *Something happened to Lukas.*

Because what I'm feeling . . . it's not mine. It's anger and betrayal and deep, dark shame. He's hurting, and I lurch to my feet only to realize he's not here. Not beside me, not with Johann, not even in Dreiden. I can sense it through the bond—he's left.

The panic is swift, and I drop to my knees, flooded with it. Its tide has nearly pulled me under when I spot a wrinkled piece of parchment folded in half, my name scrawled across it in Lukas's script, the letters uneven, their appearance rushed.

I swallow, an attempt to dislodge the sudden lump in my throat as I reach for the paper with trembling hands. Whatever's inside, it's going to change my world in the worst way possible—I can feel it.

For a moment I consider dropping the paper and going to Lukas. He's not *that* far yet—I'll find him if I'm quick. But he left this message for a reason, so I force myself to take a breath, then slowly unfold it.

> *This was a mistake. I wanted to love you, but I'm sorry, I can't move past what you did to my father. I'm leaving. Don't try to follow me. I'll make sure the queen knows about Cora Ramos and the sievech.*

A sob rips from my throat, and an episode sweeps me away. I'm not sure how long I lie on those blankets, trembling and racked by shivers, my thoughts a knot of tangled yarn. *What changed? Did I say something wrong? I've ruined everything—of course I have.*

And then, louder than the rest, a familiar sting. *I can't do this. I can't do this. I can't do this.*

Can't find Lukas. Can't face my fears. Can't let anyone in. No matter what I do, where I go, whom I love, I'm going to get hurt. Nothing and nowhere and no one is safe.

Johann finds me eventually. By then the light has turned afternoon-bright, but still I shiver. I don't think I'll ever be warm again.

"Jade?" Johann says from the ladder, peering at me. "Are you okay?"

I don't answer. I can't find my voice, and the wood creaks as Johann climbs the rest of the way up. He glances around, taking in my disheveled state, the note open beside me, and the absence of Lukas's belongings. Quietly, he sighs. "Come on," he says. "Let's get you cleaned up."

I have everything I ever wanted.

The thought is hollow. Dead. But it's true.

It's been five days since Lukas left, and there's no way I'll be making the queen's deadline now—not that I intend to try. I've spent all my time at Johann's, and I'm currently seated in his living room, absently organizing my thread kit. He's been so kind these past few days, clearing a space for me on his sofa, insisting that he didn't want me in the hayloft all by myself. He's even taken over the tracker's care, and while the tracker's been asking for me, I haven't bothered to visit. I don't have it in me. Any day now, the soldiers from Kreipen will arrive to take him away, and he won't be my problem any longer. My troubles will be gone.

Not all that long ago this existence was everything I always wanted. A kind, compassionate caregiver. A secluded home. Relief from my thread-speaking duties. Safety.

So then why does it feel rotten?

I try to force the poison thoughts from my mind, but they crescendo as I select another spool, this one a bright viridian. The color of courage. Of Lukas's eyes.

Damn it. I blink away tears and shove the spool back inside my kit, but something clinks when I do. After a moment of inspection, I pull out a dineda, winking in the afternoon light. I study it for a moment, the magnificent eagle on one side, before I flip it over to the image of the queen.

Even rendered in silver, her image no larger than my thumbnail, she's striking. High cheekbones, full lips, thick eyebrows. Long, straight hair frames her face, and I wonder absently at the liberties the artist must have taken, because when I met with the queen, she was pretty, but not gorgeous like this. Almost as if—

I gasp and drop the coin, heart pounding. It can't be. *It can't.*

But when I pick up the dineda, it's there, etched in silver. Either the artist took some dramatic freedoms or—oh my *gods.*

The coin slips from my fingers and clinks against the floor, but I barely hear it as I rummage through my bags and rip out the tracker's letters. I knew it—*knew* something was wrong with his confession, that there was more to his lover than he ever let on—and a knot forms in my throat as my eyes sink to the bottom of her letter. The lover's signature glares back at me, and finally the answer appears like a hazy vision on a foggy day, gaining clarity the closer I draw. Not just a crescent, but a moon. Not merely curved lines, but a river.

A rudimentary version of a symbol I've seen many times, usually stamped in wax, but most recently on a ring.

Oh gods.

I need to speak with the tracker.

It all comes together in the minutes it takes me to reach the cellar. I doubted what the tracker told us about Cora Ramos, then later waved off my suspicions as paranoia. Now, though, I realize I might've been onto something, and my gut churns as I open the hatch and climb downward, praying I'm wrong, because if I'm not . . .

Lukas is in more danger than he realizes.

The tracker grins when he sees me, all charm despite the patchy beard shading his jaw and the greasy strands of his hair. He's pale and gaunt in the flickering lantern light, dark rings beneath his eyes.

"Jade," he says, that single word loaded with sneering condescension. "It's about time. I've been asking for you."

I should get right to the murders, but somehow that's not what comes out of my mouth. "Lukas came to visit you, didn't he?"

My hands tremble, but I ball them into fists and focus on my breathing. I can't succumb to an episode now.

The tracker's gaze flits to my hands before rising back to my face. "He did. I would've told you as much if you'd deigned to visit."

Blood thunders in my ears. Ever since Lukas left, I've been wondering what could've changed his feelings for me in a matter of hours. I'm still not sure, but I keep coming back to the tracker. That he must've meddled in some way.

It's an effort to speak through my clenched teeth. "And what did you say to him?"

The tracker clicks his tongue. "Something you should've told him a long time ago. The truth about his father, and how you killed him."

But that shouldn't have changed anything. I *told* Lukas about his father—

Except I didn't. Not really. I started to discuss it, but Lukas cut me off before I could finish, told me he forgave me. Then, I assumed we were referring to the same thing, but—

Oh.

Oh gods.

Lukas didn't know about my role in his father's death. We must've been unknowingly discussing different events, so when the tracker told him . . .

I think I'm going to be sick, and I have to force my next words past a raw throat. "How did you know about that?"

I feel like I'm suffocating. The tracker, however, merely raises an eyebrow and says, "You tell me. I can see you working it out."

The gears of my brain are grinding, all the possibilities whirring, but there's one explanation simpler than the rest. "You brought my mom the lock of hair," I say. She wouldn't have been able to secure that herself, but the tracker could've done so easily.

That said, my mother never would've killed anyone, not unless she was ordered to by one particular person. Which, of course, begs another question, and I step closer to the tracker. "You work for the queen. She had you bring Egon's hair to my mother."

The tracker blows out a low whistle. "I have to say I'm impressed. Tell me, what else have you worked out, little dove?"

Quite a lot. But I'm still praying I'm wrong when I level my next accusation. "That you're in love with her. The queen. Those letters I found were from her."

The tracker's barely perceptible flinch tells me I'm right. Because as soon as I factored the queen into all this, everything fell into place. The signature on those letters was an earlier version of her crest, minus the feathers and a bit of refinement. If she was in love with someone like the tracker, she'd need a way to keep her signature discreet in case her letters fell into the wrong hands.

"Well done." The tracker's tone is his usual bored drawl, but his eyes are tight. "You're learning all my secrets now. What else have you uncovered? I know you're not done."

I'm not. There's one more—the biggest, worst one. I almost don't want to say it, as if by whispering it now, I speak it into existence. But if I don't say anything and I'm right, I'll never get the chance to fix things, so I meet the tracker's eyes as I say, "Cora isn't the killer. The queen is, isn't she?"

A buzzing fills my ears, and time seems to freeze.

The queen I met didn't look like her portrait because she *wasn't* the queen. Tethering yourself to a sievech rots your soul, and the queen knew if I saw her, I'd discover the truth. So she hired an imposter, but she was there, likely watching from some secret compartment. *That's* why I was ill that day, not with fear, but sick with proximity to a rotting soul.

I should've figured it out the day I met Johann. His description of her didn't match mine, but I brushed it aside. Not to mention the queen's behavior the day I met her—she seemed unsure of herself because she was acting a role. And when the imposter asked if I could track down the killer, that wasn't because the queen needed my help—quite the opposite. She wanted to be sure I'd never learn the truth.

And *gods,* those initials, CR, not for Cora Ramos but for Celese Ríos. She must have dropped the María, the way the imposter did when she had me call her Celese, probably under the queen's instructions, and it doesn't seem far-fetched that she'd do the same in her personal life as well. Her crest was too recognizable to leave on a letter like that, so she went with her initials, knowing her past lover would understand.

It even explains the tracker's comment about my upcoming role as the Crown's official thread speaker. He passed it off as speculation, but really he knew because the queen had told him.

Every avenue, every clue, all leading back to her. But all my evidence is circumstantial, which is why I need the tracker to confirm what I'm barely brave enough to suspect.

The tracker studies me a moment, watching all this cross my face, and chuckles. "Oh, little dove, you are a clever one."

My stomach shrivels, and my next words rasp. "So I'm right. It really is the queen."

"Yes." The tracker's grinning, enjoying this far too much. "You look distressed. Why is that? I wonder."

Lukas.

He still believes Cora's the killer, is going to tell the queen that—

Oh gods.

He's going to get himself killed. And Mérecal, all those people, unaware of the true beast in their midst. More people will die.

I stumble backward until my spine bumps the wall. I knew when I came here this was a possibility, but to have it confirmed . . .

I'm so distracted, too blinded by the panic creeping in to notice the tracker stand, which is why I'm not ready when he shakes off his bonds and lunges for me suddenly.

"Ah—"

I can't even get out a scream before his hand covers my mouth, stifling me. Tears burn my eyes, my heart pounding as my training kicks in and I yank my knee up, but the tracker idly steps aside before I can make contact. In one fluid movement his arm is wrapped around my throat.

No.

An icy cold wave of terror rips through me. I'm no better than a javelina in the jaws of a jaguar, and though I hate myself for it, I whimper.

"Shh," the tracker croons, "it's okay. Just breathe."

My stomach flips. It's so close to what Lukas says, but it's wrong, twisted in such a dark way. And while it shouldn't matter, I still ask, "How did you get free?"

I don't have to see the tracker to hear the pleasure radiating from his voice. "A needle has more uses than sewing, and it's not all that difficult to hide. Small, but sharp, a few used well and with patience can fray a rope enough to snap."

Oh gods. Realization settles in, and my next words croak. "You planned this."

I knew his capture was too easy. But again, I dismissed my doubts as paranoia.

I was wrong, and the tracker confirms as much. "I never could've gotten all three of you back to the queen by myself. But with a little patience . . ." I feel him shrug. "I knew I could motivate two of you to return on your own. Or at least I *thought* I could, but as time passed and you still didn't leave, I was forced to get creative."

Cold prickles my veins. That's why he lied about Cora. He knew Lukas and I would go straight to the queen to warn her and, in the process, fall into his trap. But then we stayed, and he grew desperate. He didn't know we'd simply delayed our departure, not canceled it, so when Lukas came down here all by himself . . .

He saw his chance and he took it. He sent Lukas into the trap alone, knowing I'd follow.

I'm going to be sick. I played right into the tracker's hand, a moth fluttering straight into an open flame, entranced by the glow.

"And the third person?" I ask, unsure I want to know. But the tracker said he could motivate only *two* of us.

"Johann was easy enough to manage the first time around," he says, smug. "I doubt this time will be much different, and I'm quite looking forward to having him restore the tattoo you destroyed."

My limbs feel as if they've turned to liquid. Johann's been nothing but kind, and now he's going to suffer again because I led the tracker here.

"You're disgusting." If only words were lethal, mine would slice straight through bone. "You're a vile, disgusting, horrible man, and I hope you rot without a soul. You and the queen both."

"Perhaps we will," the tracker agrees, "but I don't much care."

And before I can react, he shoves me suddenly, straight into the opposite wall. I skitter along the dirt floor, pivoting as fast as I can. The tracker is already scrambling toward the ladder, and I lunge for him, grab his ankle, and pull.

"Get back—"

The tracker kicks, nailing my temple, and stars explode across my vision. I go down hard, teeth clanking together, and in the seconds it takes me to stand, the tracker has clambered up the ladder and reached the hatch.

He peers down at me. "Sorry, little dove," he says, mocking. "I promise someone will be by to free you soon. In the meantime, ration that water."

Then he slams the door shut and slides the bolt through, imprisoning me alone, no company save for my fear.

CHAPTER THIRTY-SEVEN

LUKAS

SIXTY DAYS.

A deadline given before Jade hurtled into my life and wrapped me up in it, wrapped me up in *her*. We packed so much terror, bravery, and heartbreak into that time.

Now it's over.

Today is day sixty. The queen's deadline. She'll be expecting Jade to present herself as thread speaker, but what she'll get is me, warning her of a murderer.

The thought is somehow bleak and terrifying all at once, and I try to shake it as I step off the boat and back into Sallenda. Gulls shriek, flapping about as my steps creak on the rickety pier, sailors bustling around me. There's a sharp pang in my chest, a slice beneath my heart, homesickness for Kabrück carving itself anew. A wound I had thought healed, reopened once again.

God. Not that long ago, these docks, boats, and sailors were my world.

It feels like a lifetime ago now.

The thought numbs me, and in what seems like a blink, I've

arrived at the palace. I ascend the steps and approach one of the guards. His uniform's a deep blue lined with gold thread, and a familiar pin is affixed to his chest. It's a wreath of gold feathers surrounding a pair of crossed swords—the symbol of the queen's guard.

Last time I saw one, it was drenched in a puddle of blood at Cora Ramos's feet.

My heart thunders, but I steady my breath. "I'd like to request an audience with the queen," I tell him. "I know who the murderer is, the one gouging out eyes, and I believe the information is sensitive enough that it should go straight to her."

The guard is shaking his head before I even finish. "Sensitive or not, something like that has to go to the polesa first. If they decide it's worth it, they'll go through the usual channels."

Perhaps. Or maybe they are already in Cora Ramos's pocket.

"Please," I insist, "just tell her I came by. My name is Lukas Keller."

For whatever reason, *that* gets a reaction from him. He stiffens and looks me over with a newly assessing gaze. "Lukas Keller? The queen's expecting you."

"She is?"

I wasn't even aware the queen knew I existed. I frown, puzzled, but the guard ignores my discomfort and waves me along. "She is. Please follow me."

I brush aside my worry—she's the queen, she has ways of knowing things—and follow him inside.

The queen's receiving chambers are ridiculously fine. I expected to be led to a throne room, but the guard delivers me to a verdant parlor, the walls painted to look like Mérecal's vibrant jungles. Blue tiles shimmer beneath my feet as I sink into a thick leather sofa and settle in.

I assume I'll be waiting hours, so I startle when just minutes later the door creaks open, revealing the queen, almost identical to her image on the dineda. She's garbed in a bright red dress, and a golden crown sits primly atop her shining black hair, crafted to appear like a series of interlocking feathers. While I'm no expert on Mérecal's old gods, even I know the diadem is meant to be a symbol of Oro. King of the gods and supposedly the queen's ancestor.

She smiles when she sees me, and I shiver involuntarily. Something about that crooked quirk of her lips feels familiar. Which is preposterous—I've never met her before.

"Lukas." She glides over to me. I begin to stand before she waves a dismissive hand, then holds it out to me. "Please, there's no need for that. It's a pleasure to make your acquaintance."

That seems doubtful—not that I say as much. Unsure what to do, I awkwardly remain seated and take her outstretched fingers. "I could say the same, Your Majesty."

"Oh, please." Her eyes flash, and her grip on my hand tightens, a shade past discomfort. "Call me Celese. I suspect this meeting will grow personal, so we may as well be on a first-name basis, don't you agree?"

A shiver rolls down my spine. I ignore it and force myself to smile politely. "Of course, Celese."

It feels like the safe thing to say, and the queen's lips twitch as she sits on the couch across from mine. It's almost as if she knows I'm holding back. Her skirts shift as she crosses her ankles, a picture of elegance, then fixes her eyes on me. "I hear you have information on the murders?"

Right—yes. I shake off my unease. I'm here for a reason. "Yes," I tell her, then rush to get the rest out. "Cora Ramos is responsible. She kidnapped a foreign thread speaker and forced him to create a soul-eating monster for her to control, and she's been using it to kill people in the city."

The queen looks at me a long time, her gaze assessing in a manner that reminds me of Cora. And in an odd way they're almost similar. Cora is lethal seduction, and the queen is all deadly elegance.

Her next words are a frosty chill icing over my skin. "Interesting. It would appear Alejandro's plan worked—at least by half. I had doubts whether or not you'd fall for it."

My world tilts, drops, shatters.

For a second I'm a bumbling, confused mess, baffled by the queen's response. It doesn't fit with what I know to be true. Though it's pathetic, my next words are rough. "What are you saying?"

She cocks her head, but her expression remains smooth as marble. "Come on, Lukas. Think it through. You have the answers."

When I was a boy, my father took me hunting once. We spent weeks preparing for the trip. My dad carefully trained me how to load a rifle, aim, and shoot. That day we went into the forest and waited for hours, until eventually a deer wandered our way. *This is it, Lukas,* he whispered. *She's yours. Get her.* I stood then, all wobbly and nervous, and the doe's gaze snapped toward mine.

I'm not sure how to explain it, but in that moment we were connected, like I could feel the fear in those wide doe eyes. She stood, frozen, almost as if she knew her death was near and accepted it.

In the end, I didn't take the shot. I couldn't bring myself to kill another creature, but now I know how that deer must've felt looking down the barrel of my gun.

I swallow. The queen doesn't seem like the sort to hold back her shot.

"Alejandro," I say, recognizing the familiar name. The tracker. "He wasn't working for Cora. You hired him."

That crooked grin returns, but a shade more devious this time. "Finally catching on, I see. Now tell me, what does that mean?"

Oh god. I shove my hands into my pockets to keep them from shaking. I was a fool to come here, to listen to the tracker. Jade said it didn't feel right, but I wanted to believe Cora was responsible, so I did.

But Cora Ramos was never the killer.

"You." My voice rasps, but I force myself to say it. "You're the murderer."

"Excellent." The queen's eyes flash. "I have to admit I was beginning to doubt you."

Her cavalier tone—all of this—makes me sick. I'm dead. Given what I know, the queen won't let me live. It's that simple. She could have her sievech tear my soul apart. And my family—

Oh holy three. I feel the blood drain from my face. Emma, Artur, my mom. I did all this to protect them, when really I was damning them.

I force myself to breathe, remembering my advice to Jade. There's no way I'll walk out of this alive, but if I steer the conversation away from my family, maybe the queen won't think to hurt them. In an effort to distract her, I meet her eyes and ask simply, "Why?"

She's the queen. She could order anyone's death, so why all the secrecy and deceit?

Her expression turns contemplative. "Did you know that my parents never wanted me to be queen? My mother especially. She always favored my sister, when I was the obvious choice."

It's not the answer I was expecting, but I'm grateful for the diversion. Anything to keep the queen focused on something other than my family. With that in mind, I prod more. "Why didn't they want you to be queen?"

She rolls her eyes. "Because I had the great misfortune of being born second. My sister was the heir, and I was the spare. They raised her to be a queen, while they raised me to be nothing more than a piece in their games, a wife to some distant prince or politician." She leans forward, honeyed eyes practically glowing with intensity. "I was better suited, though. My foolish sister never wanted the crown, but me? I studied in secret, planted spies, and forged alliances. Over and over again I proved to them I was more fit to rule. Shaped in Oro's image in a way my sister never was. Did my parents listen, though? No. They didn't. Of course they didn't."

I rub my sweaty palms against my trousers. Everyone knows the queen's family died in a fire. Tragedy is the official story, assassination the well-known rumor. But even though most agree the royal family was murdered, no one's ever been able to identify who did it.

I wonder now. Could it have been the woman seated in front of me?

I don't dare ask. Instead, I venture a question. "So you're killing citizens to spite your parents?"

She lets out a chuckle, but it's a dark, poisoned thing. "Gods, no. My parents are dead and buried. This I did to spite the living." Her fingers brush the gold of her crown, almost subconsciously. "My citizens lost faith in the old gods, lost faith in *me*, their queen, descendant of our greatest god. There was even talk in the Regela of eliminating my position altogether, those traitorous snakes. So I took matters into my own hands."

I swallow, too afraid to interrupt her as she leans back. She looks smug, self-satisfied, like a cat luxuriating in a sunbeam. Only in this case her satisfaction stems from her own misdeeds.

"I started with the laws," she explains. "If my people couldn't respect their god-deemed queen, then they could suffer. Lower wages, fewer jobs, limited medicine. Still, though, they didn't return to me, which meant I had to get creative. Had to *make* them see reason."

My stomach churns, but I force myself not to break her gaze. "And that's why you killed them. Why you made them believe the gods were responsible. So they'd come flooding back to you."

She didn't need a sievech for that, though. Didn't need to steal people's souls. That part was purely vindictive, a punishment, I can see now. Vengeance and cruelty born from a bruised ego.

The queen grins, the gesture honed to a blade. "And flood back they did."

I think of all the once-empty temples, bursting ever since the murders started. It makes sense that as people's faith returns, so too does their devotion to the queen, Oro's supposed heir. Jade and I hypothesized the killer was a religious fanatic, but we never considered they might be a religious descendant.

It doesn't escape my notice that the queen wouldn't tell me this, not unless there's no way I can spread it. I dig my nails into my palms, hard enough that I feel blood, hoping the pain lends me some clarity of mind. "How do you plan to kill me?"

The queen appraises me, her head tilted, her jaw knife sharp. "The people need a scapegoat, and I need Jade Aguilar. I think you can help me with both."

I should be relieved by her admission. A scapegoat implies a public execution, which means I just might escape this with my soul intact. But any relief I might feel is stolen by the queen's mention of Jade. "What do you mean, I can help you with Jade?"

She doesn't answer me, not right away. Instead, she kneels in front of me, her gaze never leaving mine.

"Alejandro sent me a letter," she says, so cool and steady my skin crawls. "In it, he told me about you and Jade. The way you were together and the sacrifices you made for each other. He wrote of a devotion that suggested if one of you was in trouble, the other would follow."

My stomach plummets right through the floor. *Oh god.* When I left, I experienced not just my own heartbreak but Jade's too. I tried to tune her emotions out, but I couldn't ignore the sudden spike of fear. It left me curled on my cabin bed, shaking and terrified for a girl I have no business caring for. And then, seven days ago, another shift occurred and I was flooded with this deep sense of knowing. Jade left Dreiden to return to Sallenda. At the time I assumed she intended to repair things between us, but what if I was wrong? What if she knows I'm in trouble and is returning to save me?

I open my mouth to say something—what, I don't know— but all coherent thought leaves my mind when the queen lifts her hands and slowly undoes the top three buttons of my shirt. Everything inside me goes clammy, and I'm nearly overcome by the urge to rip her hands off me. I would too, if my family wasn't on the line. But I have to think of them, so I'm forced to remain still as she peels back my shirt, revealing Jade's soul embroidered above my heart.

"Oh, this is perfect," she whispers. "Alejandro was right."

I can't take it anymore. I flinch backward, then scramble to the side. Perhaps not dignified, but I'll do anything to have her hands off me. I stand, fury roaring through my veins as I look down at her. "You're going to leave Jade alone, or I swear you'll regret it."

My reaction isn't rational, but I can't quite stop myself either.

The queen tuts. "Such confidence for someone in your position. Predictable, but even so, I'd like to remind you where you stand, Lukas Keller." Her eyes narrow, and though she's the one kneeling, there's no mistaking who has the upper hand. "You're powerless here, and you *will* do what I say. Right now your family is free to go about their lives, but if you disobey me, I'll have my sievech rip them limb from limb. Do you understand?"

I can't speak. I have no words, no air, nothing left, and my surroundings dissolve until all I can picture is little Artur crying as a sievech prowls closer.

The queen slices through my horrid vision. "Good. I can see from your expression that you do." She faces the door and calls for her guards. Two of them arrive in seconds, all liveried obedience. "I need him taken quietly to the pit," she tells them. "Understood?"

They nod, and I don't fight as they grab me. I can't. Even as I tremble, rage and terror coursing through me, I don't say a word, because the queen was right.

I'm powerless.

PART FOUR

CHAPTER THIRTY-EIGHT

JADE

THE NEW THREAD TATTOO ON MY HIP ACHES, A CONTRAST WITH the cool breeze on my cheeks, scented of Mérecal's jungles. It's been two weeks since I departed Dreiden, seven days since I missed the queen's deadline, and I'm finally mere hours from Sallenda, standing at the prow of the steamboat I bartered passage on. Almost back to Lukas.

So much has changed since he left.

I spent two days in that pit, scratching my arms raw with terror when the lantern sputtered out. That time . . . it left its marks, and not just the physical ones. I could hardly stand to be in my cabin, uncomfortable in the cramped space. Every night I reminded myself that I was safe—that I could escape my room at any time, just like I escaped that cellar. Though of course, my liberation was another part of the tracker's plans.

He mailed a letter to Clara, the kind woman who witnessed our interaction in Dreiden's market, and signed it as Johann. In it he asked her to retrieve some old potatoes from Johann's cellar before they spoiled. She screamed when she opened the hatch and, instead of old potatoes, I rushed out, barely capable of words.

I wanted to crumble, cry, break. *I can't,* I nearly sobbed, the belief pounding through me. But neither did I have a choice—which is why my mantra has changed. No longer *I can't,* but now *I have to,* because Lukas and Johann are in danger, and they're not the only ones. Mérecal's people have been terrified, been murdered, had their souls ripped from their bodies long enough. If I don't do something, no one else will.

So I'm determined to try.

That morning I packed my things. Fortunately, the tracker left my thread kit—he probably didn't want to lug it around, or perhaps he suspected I'd delay my return to Mérecal if I needed time to reassemble it. Unfortunately, he stole the thread portraits of him and his past lover, the queen, along with both their locks of hair. A difficult blow, considering I can't alter their souls or unspool their lives without pieces of their persons. Thankfully, I was at least able to re-create the lost portraits from memory, and now they sit, alongside Lukas's, secure in my pocket.

I'm ready, and when my ship docks in Sallenda, I don't hesitate. I'm the first to step onto the pier, my chin held high even as my heart races. It's difficult to shake the vulnerability of walking out in the open like this, along with the fear that I'll turn the corner and find the tracker there. By now he's probably had Johann redo his tattoo. But even if he's waiting on the docks, I doubt he'll notice me—not with my new tattoo.

I had the idea back in Dreiden, when I first considered remaining there. Sooner or later the queen would come calling, so I concocted a way to ensure that when she did, I'd remain hidden. Searched for but never found.

Inspired by the tracker's own tattoo.

Because while his conferred the qualities of a predator, I now have those of his prey. And though it may sound weak, there's power in it, all embroidered onto my hip. Navy silence, taken from a deer. Flaxen speed, stolen from a jackrabbit. Mossy camouflage from a moth, so when eyes land on me, they have a tendency to slide away. And from a spider an earthy brown to mask my scent.

The tracker spun a trap in which I came to him, weak and afraid, but he never considered that in becoming prey, I gave myself strength. So despite everything, I smile as I slip down the pier, my new tattoo heating as it activates. I want nothing more than to run to Lukas, but I'm not a complete fool—I'm sure the queen has him heavily guarded. For that reason I don't follow the tug in my chest but make my way to the Eastern District, where Lukas's family is holed up in my mother's secret apartment.

It's not long before I'm standing on the threshold, and I force myself to take a breath and slow my tumbling heart before I knock.

Seconds slide by, and when the door creaks open, my face must be redder than a pomegranate. A girl answers—Emma, I assume. Her coloring is different from Lukas's. Where Lukas is fair, Emma has coppery hair and warm brown eyes, but her cheekbones are equally sharp, her lips full in just the same way as his.

Her eyes narrow. "Who are you, and what do you want?"

I'm immediately grateful I practiced what I was going to say. "My name is Jade, and I'm a friend of Lukas's. Can we talk?"

"Jade?" She opens the door wider, her gaze softening. "Jade Aguilar. The one who transferred me all the money?"

She looked at the bank slips, then. Lukas's letter didn't name me, but it would've been easy enough for her to figure out where the funds came from.

I nod. "Yes. That's me."

My head buzzes as Emma unleashes a barrage of questions. "How do you know Lukas? What's going on? Do you know what he did? They won't let me see—" She pauses, perhaps noticing my dumbfounded expression, and steps back. "Why don't we talk more inside?"

I fight down a prickle of unease, not from Emma's invitation but from her questions about Lukas. As I suspected, something's wrong.

"Thank you." I gently brush past her, and there's a pinch in my chest as I step inside the apartment. I haven't spent much time here, but my mother did, and her touch is heavy in the décor. The walls are painted a soft lilac—the shade of compassion—and hung with several thread works of the gods she most revered. Sunlight speckles the room, filtered through the white lacy curtains, and the entire space smells like her favorite vanilla soap.

My eyes burn. Because for a moment it feels like such a simple thing for her to walk through that door, sweep me into her arms, and kiss my brow. Here a little piece of her lives, and it hurts me as much as it heals me.

I blink, willing myself not to cry, and face Emma when the door clicks shut.

She looks at me, expression severe. "How do you know Lukas?"

My throat bobs, but I don't break her gaze. "Lukas came to me for help nine weeks ago. He was trying to catch a murderer, and he wanted my assistance."

The rest spills out from there. I don't share the romance, but neither do I hide any of the other details—Cora, the tracker, queen, all of it—and by the time I stop speaking, my throat is dry.

For her part, Emma doesn't interrupt once, doesn't even break eye contact, unnervingly intense. She's silent after I finish, then asks, voice level, "So you believe Lukas went straight to the

310

queen when he arrived, and delivered himself into the true killer's hands?"

It's an effort not to reach for my chest, where Lukas's soul is stitched beneath my shirt. His emotions have been a steady undercurrent, but they spiked seven days ago, and I almost spiraled into an episode, his fear was so intense. "Yes," I tell Emma. "I'm almost positive that's what happened."

She swears and breaks my gaze for the first time. I give her a few moments to process. She brings a fist to her mouth, and her eyes are glassy when she looks at me again. "I suppose that would explain this."

She reaches into her pocket and removes a piece of parchment, frayed from heavy use. A wave of cold hits me as she holds it out, and I already know that whatever's written there, I don't want to see it. *I can't* rises up, a familiar echo, and my old instincts scream at me to get far away from Sallenda, from Emma and Lukas and my problems. It would be easy, and with this tattoo on my hip, I could live a life in the shadows, unknown and unfound. Safe.

But I nearly had that with Johann, and I was miserable. So while the *I can't* is still there, it's no longer alone. *I won't* leave Lukas. *I have to* try. *I will* save him.

All those messages beat inside me as I take the paper from Emma. Though I was expecting the worst, I practically faint when I see what's written there. An announcement for an execution.

Lukas's execution.

My eyes burn as I scan the words once, twice, three times, taking in more fragments with each pass.

Responsible for the recent string of murders.

Summoned Vada's dog.

Sentence: Death by hanging.

The queen is going to kill Lukas for the murders she committed.

The realization hits me like a poison, slow to spread but no less deadly for it. I should've expected this; her cruelty is boundless, after all, and I absently wonder what made her this way. If it was the death of her family, perhaps, swallowed whole in that vicious fire.

I'm trembling by the time I offer Emma the flyer, and her voice shakes too. "I'm not sure what to do," she admits. "They went up all over the city a few days ago, and I just— Lukas was my rock, *our* rock." She nods toward a closed door. "My mom and Artur are in there. She hasn't left since she heard the news, and I can't let this happen—I *can't*—but I don't know how to stop it either."

All my life I've been sheltered. Protected. First at the orphanage, then by my mother, and later by Lukas. I'm used to others looking out for me, so it feels a bit odd when I put a reassuring hand on Emma's shoulder and try to make my voice calm and soothing, the way Lukas would with me. "It's okay," I tell her. "I do."

And by the gods, I really hope I'm right.

CHAPTER THIRTY-NINE

LUKAS

THE PIT IS APTLY NAMED.

When they first brought me here, the guards blindfolded me, so I don't know where I am, but I do know this: It's somewhere deep in the earth. The walls are made of blunted stone, dark save for the few oil lamps mounted between the cells. It smells of must, mold, rot, and other things I'd rather not consider.

On my fifth day here the tracker visited. He boasted of his escape and capture of Johann, though he refused to tell me where the queen's keeping him. I sat there, seething through it all, until he told me what he did to Jade. How he left her, terrified and alone, in that cellar. At that point I couldn't hide my fury any longer. I lunged at the bars, screaming. Even now I can still hear the tracker's cold chuckle as he walked away.

I spent another day after that in quiet misery, no visitors save for the guards who bring my meals—until now. Day seven. My heart jackrabbits when the door creaks above, because this time it's not simply a guard delivering my meal. There's the telltale jangle of chains that suggests another prisoner. I can't breathe as I imagine Jade, bent and scared as the tracker leads her to a cell.

I brace myself, taut as I watch the stairs and wait for her to appear. But when the prisoner rounds the corner, it's not Jade. Nor is it someone I thought I'd ever see again, or wished to. A wave of frosty surprise hits me, followed by a tsunami of rage and a trickle of . . . relief?

Because while it's not Jade, it is someone I'm familiar with.

Her mother.

Not dead as Johann believed, but here, alive. The queen's prisoner.

She's different from the last time I saw her: no longer tall and proud, but hunched, with an ashy hue to her dark skin. I'm not sure where they've been keeping her, but it's clear she's been captive for a long time. Her hair's become matted, and her gray eyes are tired. I watch, barely able to process what's happening as the queen's guard leads her to the cell across from mine, locks her in, then departs.

Leaving me alone with her. This woman who let Lina die. Who had Jade murder my father. She must've noticed me, but she hardly spares me a glance. My rage boils over, my skin burning as I stand and approach my cell bars.

Zamora doesn't look up, not until I clear my throat. "Zamora."

Her gaze darts to mine. I don't expect her to remember me, but recognition flickers across her features. "You."

Her voice is rough, but there's depth to it. Surprise.

"You remember me?" I hate how breathless I sound. Hate the fact that she knows me too. It was easier to despise her when she was heartless, and the tenderness in her gaze has my walls going up.

"Of course." She shifts closer to her own cell bars. "Your sister was ill, but I turned you away. I agonized over that decision for months afterward."

Only months? For me that agony has never stopped. "Oh yes, I'm sure that was horrible for you. Letting a young girl die all because we couldn't pay."

She recoils but doesn't respond immediately. When she does, her voice is solemn. "For what it's worth, I am sorry. Truly."

I sit down, suddenly dizzy. This is all too much, everything I thought I knew tilting. I've imagined this moment hundreds of times, and in it Zamora always responded with anger and condescension. *Of course I let her die,* she'd say in my head. *She wasn't worth saving.*

In a strange way that fantasy was preferable to this reality. At least then I had a release for my anger, but *this,* her sorrow—I don't know. I don't want to accept the fact that she's conducting herself outside the role I set for her, so I pivot the conversation to something safer. "How are you alive?"

Her eyes narrow. "Why wouldn't I be alive?"

Shit. I walked right into that one. I settle on a lie, since I'm not ready to tell her about Jade. "It's not a secret you've been missing for months. Everyone assumed you were dead."

She sniffs, pieces of the regal woman I met that night returning. "They assumed wrong."

Some of my earlier rage rekindles at her tone, and it's almost a relief. "Yes, well, you're *here,*" I point out, then gesture to a puckered scar beneath her collarbone. "And it looks like you were injured, so maybe the assumptions weren't entirely unfounded."

I know you were shot, I want to say. *Johann told me, so you can give up the act.* But if I admit that, I'll have to reveal the rest, so I'm thankful when she caves with a sigh.

"My friend was captured by the queen. I knew of this place, because I'd meet her here whenever she had secret or unsavory jobs for me. I came here to rescue him but was shot in the process. Johann—my friend . . . I didn't think he'd leave me. So I held in my screams, hoping he'd think me dead and run, and it worked. I woke up to the queen's private medic tending to me, and I've been here ever since."

"You weren't here when I arrived."

Her expression darkens. "No. I haven't done as the queen's asked, and she punished me by putting me in a cell even deeper. One they keep pitch black."

Zamora let Lina die. Made Jade kill my father. I shouldn't feel any sympathy for her, and yet there's a small twinge of it inside my chest, because I arrived seven days ago. To be kept in the dark that long—

No.

She nearly fooled me earlier, but I need to remember what she is. I scoff. "You speak like you've done something honorable, but you're forgetting the fact that you abandoned your daughter."

Talking with Zamora, I'm not sure how to feel about Jade, all my fury with her bleeding into confusion. Above it all, though, I remember the way she looked the day we met. So terrified and alone. Zamora would've known the risks when she rescued Johann, but she still left Jade to fend for herself.

Zamora's eyes flash. "You don't know what you speak of—I would *never* do anything to hurt my daughter."

"Really?" I stand again, my own fire igniting. "Then why'd you make her kill my father? She was only twelve years old, and you made her do it."

I realize my mistake when Zamora's mouth falls open. She'll have questions now, but I'm past the point of caring. So I wait, burning, as she collects herself. Slowly, she straightens her spine, then asks, "How do you know about that?"

She doesn't even try to deny it. I shake my head, too angry to look at her. "The queen's tracker told me."

It's better than admitting my relationship with Jade, but Zamora's perceptive. She hears what I don't say. "And why would he tell you that?" A pause while I study my shoes before she adds, "You know her, don't you? You know Jade."

I don't answer, but I can't stop the involuntary jerk of my hand toward the thread tattoo on my chest. I should've severed the bond, but I couldn't—can't. I'm too weak, and suddenly all the anger drains out of me, leaving nothing but exhaustion in its wake.

Zamora doesn't miss the gesture, and her next words are sharp. "What is that?"

I glance at my chest, where the edges of Jade's soul peek out, and sigh. "You know what it is."

I tug my collar to the side, and she gasps. Her eyes water, revealing the caring mother Jade has such adoration for. "You don't just know her, you love her."

"Yes." There's no point in denying it, no matter how shameful it is. I'm in love with the girl who killed my father.

I'm pathetic.

"And she loves you too?"

I consider her question, all my memories of Jade whipping together, a frenzied collage inside my mind. When it fades, I know the answer to her question.

My eyes sting, and I wipe away a tear as I meet Zamora's gaze. "She does."

She never said it, but she didn't have to.

Zamora's inhale is jagged. "You should know the truth, then, about what happened. About your father."

Hope is a strange, fragile thing, because somehow once it's broken, the shards of it rip you up inside, worse than if you'd never hoped at all. Perhaps that's why I tense up. "I already know the truth. Jade killed him. You made her."

But Zamora's shaking her head before I even finish speaking. "You're wrong. Alejandro told you that, but he doesn't know the whole story. I do."

I can barely breathe, and I definitely can't find the words to say anything, which Zamora must sense, because she continues.

"As thread speaker to the Crown, my duties go beyond what the public knows. I collect punishments at the courthouse and do tattoos for the wealthy, as is expected of me. Sometimes, though, when the queen needs someone dead and it has to look natural, she brings me in. It's only happened a few times over the years, and I've never had a choice in the matter. Denying the queen would've put Jade in danger, so I always obeyed."

My stomach churns. The tracker made it sound like Zamora was willing to kill for the right price. If she's telling the truth, this is a different matter altogether. She seems genuine, too, her eyes misting as she speaks.

"When Jade was twelve, I received a message from the queen. She wanted your father dead, and she wanted Jade to be the one to kill him. Training, she said, for when Jade would become thread speaker to the Crown. I begged her to reconsider, but she refused. Alejandro was there with your father's hair and saw the interaction unfold. All these years later, he must still remember it."

She shudders. "The queen is a dangerous woman, so I tried to obey her. I gave Jade the hair and had her stitch your father's portrait without telling her what it was for. When she finished, I took her down to the docks. I thought . . . I don't know. I wanted her to see him, to know that taking a life was a serious thing. But it was a mistake. I'll always regret making her face the realities of our situation so young. She deserved better."

I imagine a young Jade, trembling on the pier, my father's soul in her hands. Neither of us knew it then, but in that moment a tether was spun between us. One of horrible, unbreakable connection. "She did," I agree.

Zamora's gaze is solemn, and she takes a slow, steadying breath.

"I didn't tell her what she was meant to do until we saw your father. She cried, begged me not to make her, and I just . . . I couldn't do it. I swore her to secrecy, then had her look away while I unspooled your father's life thread. Jade may have stitched the portrait that killed him, but she didn't strike the final blow. That was me and me alone."

I wonder if Jade can feel all these emotions surging inside me. Renewed grief, because while Jade was just down the pier, in the shadow of her mother's protection, I wasn't far away, sobbing over my father's corpse. We both lost something that day, and it cracks anew, but there's more there too. Relief that Jade wasn't the one to kill him. Confusion regarding her mother. Not who I suspected, but not quite different either. Hardened, but perhaps not cruel.

"Why did you stay in Sallenda?" I manage to ask, still thinking of a young Jade. "Why didn't you run, or fight?"

Surely with her skills she could've done *something*.

I must be wrong, though, because she's already shaking her head.

"Harming the queen wasn't an option—she was always careful to ensure I never got a piece of her. Without it, any soul portrait was useless. My only way to fight back was . . . well, it was repugnant. A level only the queen would stoop to, as it turned out, and I couldn't bring myself to do it."

I think of the journals stored away in her attic. Jade wasn't sure why she'd kept them, but I think I understand now. They were an insurance policy against the queen. Zamora must have been truly desperate if she held on to them all those years.

"So you couldn't fight," I agree, "but why didn't you run?"

"I tried to," she admits. "I swore to myself I'd get Jade out, but if we both ran, the queen never would've stopped searching. So I planned to wait until Jade was older, when she could do better on her own. I'd send her away while I stayed. I figured if I was here, the queen might not chase after her. But then the murders started. I grew suspicious, and before I could get Jade out, the queen sent her guards for me. I managed to dodge them, but I went to Johann first."

She bites her lip, a swirl of memories in her gaze. "It was a mistake. I don't regret saving him, but I should've protected Jade first. The queen threatened Jade's life when I didn't comply, swore she'd imprison her down here with me, but it never came to pass. Eventually I called her bluff—demanded to see Jade, but she couldn't deliver." She meets my eyes. "I suspect that had something to do with you."

Minutes ago I would've hesitated, but with all that I've learned, there's no longer any reason to hold back.

"It does," I admit, and I tell her everything, sparing only our kisses and the full truth of what happened the night of Gebreine.

Zamora's quiet for a time after I finish, then meets my eyes. "Thank you for telling me all that. What you and Jade have . . . I'm glad she has you to love her."

"Yeah, well." I'm not sure what to say. It's nice Zamora thinks so, but she's wrong. "Perhaps. But when she needed me, I left."

Something softens in Zamora's gaze, and she grabs the bars of her cell. "Maybe, but you were there for her when I was away, taught her to stand and fight and blaze when I couldn't. That's not nothing."

Her words should warm me, but all I feel is a prickle of frustration that she doesn't understand. "It's not just Jade, though," I insist. "I promised my father I'd protect my family, but I left them. And Lina . . ." I drift off, skin heated, eyes burning. "I let her die," I finally whisper. "I couldn't save her."

I'm not sure why I'm telling this to *her*, of all people.

Her response is quiet. Gentle. "You did everything you could for Lina, but some things are out of our control. Illness, death . . . it's one of those things."

"Not for you." Some of my earlier anger laces my words. "You could've saved her; you just decided not to."

"That's true," Zamora concedes. "But do you know why I didn't help you?"

I squeeze my eyes shut. There's a reason I didn't ask her about this earlier—it's too painful. When she was a monster, my wound had at least scabbed over. Now it's reopened, a gaping, bleeding mess.

"I thought I did," I say, voice trembling.

I'm not sure I do any longer.

Zamora senses what I left unspoken. Though I didn't ask, she answers the silent question.

"I'm sure Jade taught you how thread speaking works. To give, you must take. I chose to let your sister die because gifting her life meant stealing someone else's. Yours, most likely."

It's like a slap, the memory of Zamora's words that night. *I'm sorry,* she said when I begged her to save Lina, *but you can't afford it.*

I always thought she meant I didn't have enough dineda, but really she only intended to spare me.

My voice scrapes, some of my earlier rage returning. "Then you should've taken it. I gladly would've given Lina all the life I had left."

I can't take it, the heartbreak on her face over my sorrow.

"I know," she says. "I could see in your soul that you would've. But you deserve to live too. You always have, and even if you were a cruel, horrible person, it's not my place to decide who lives and who dies. Just because I have this power doesn't mean it should be used like that."

In theory I agree with Zamora. In practice I don't know if I'll ever forgive her for taking that choice from me—taking Lina from me. My next words are sharp. "It wasn't your decision to make. I promised my father I'd take care of them. I owed it to him, to my family, to *Lina*, to save her. Even if it meant my own life. *Especially* if it meant my own life."

For some reason it's become important to me that Zamora understands my duty to my family, because if she does, then maybe it's true. That choosing them over myself has always been the right choice, even when it hurt me. Perhaps it's a foolish desire when living this way is painful, but it's the only thing I know.

She doesn't agree with me, though, asking instead, "Do you know why the queen had me kill your father?"

The words stab. The question crossed my mind earlier but I didn't ask. I'm afraid to know.

"No."

It's all I have the energy to say. Zamora studies me a moment, then shakes her head. "You look up to him. I can see that, and I don't want to take it from you, but you're beating yourself up under a false pretense. Your father wasn't perfect, Lukas. He made mistakes that hurt your family too."

My fire sparks. She sounds like Emma, and I don't want to hear it. "My father wasn't perfect, but it's not easy to settle into a new country. He did the best he could."

"And you didn't?"

She doesn't mince her words. I flinch.

I suppose I always have. Maybe I haven't succeeded, but I've always tried. And maybe that should count for something.

My expression must change, because Zamora warms a fraction. "You deserve the same grace you give your father. Maybe even more." She sighs and tucks one of her curls behind her ear. "I'm not sure how to make this easier for you, so I'm just going to say it: Your father was a rebel, one of the founders of what became a very brief and all-too-quiet revolution. He was horrified by the inequality he saw, and he formed a group with some others who felt similarly." Her gaze turns piercing. "Do you remember when the queen's statue was bombed? That was them, and your father was their ringleader. The queen asked me to kill him discreetly, because she knew the only thing more dangerous than a rebel is a martyr."

I'm going to be sick. In a lot of ways my father has been my role model. He used to tell me that family came first—always. While his cause may have been noble, to learn his guidance was false—

I want to scream at Zamora. To tell her she's rotten and cruel and wrong, and maybe I would if it wasn't for all the memories rising to the surface. My father's night job that frequently kept him away. The way our finances were always bleeding, despite the fact we should've had enough—likely spent on supplies I knew nothing about. The fact that he gave me his pistol shortly after the bombing, just days before he died, almost as if he knew trouble was coming. Emma's insistence that *something* was off, even when I didn't listen, unable to face the possibility my dad wasn't perfect.

I want to rage and scream at a dead man. One who asked me to live up to an example he never met.

All these years I've tried so hard. To be there for others, always. To put my family first and myself last. To never need anything, lest it stop me from being the best caregiver I could be. But with Jade I felt free, because I opened myself up. To those wants and desires, wishes and yearnings. For once, I acted on them instead of simply shoving them down. I wonder if that's how my father felt while sowing his rebellion.

I'm not sure, and I'll never be privy to his motivations. What I do know is this:

My father chose his rebellion.

I chose Jade.

We both acted in our own interests at times.

And perhaps . . . perhaps that's not such a bad thing, after all.

CHAPTER FORTY

JADE

I PRACTICE BREATHING DEEP AND SLOW AS I LOWER MYSELF INTO the sewer, wondering all the while if this is how Lukas felt when he sought Cora Ramos out. Small. Vulnerable. Afraid. *I can't* shrieks inside my skull, but I shut the door on those thoughts and tell myself that *I will*.

Emma wasn't happy when I shared my plan with her. For one thing, she wanted to help, but I refused. I need Lukas's family hidden somewhere safe. I owe him that much. The rest, though, going to Cora . . .

It didn't matter that we'd only just met. Emma lectured me for an hour on how foolish it was. *Look at the trouble it got my brother into,* she reasoned, *no offense.* But I've been dissecting plans for weeks now, trying to think of a better way, and there isn't one. Even the polesa captain—my tutor for years—isn't an option. Not when he reports to the queen. He might help me, but I refuse to risk Lukas's life on a maybe. I need someone with power *outside* the queen's reach. In the end Emma saw that too, and she agreed to wait while I do what's needed.

Which brings me to now, hands trembling as I shift the sewer grate back into place, then pick up my lantern, casting the dark tunnels in a warm glow. It's cool down here, damp in a way that cuts to the bone, and I shiver at the squeaking of rats. I wish Lukas was here, or my mother, anyone friendly.

I'm alone, and for once I have to do this by myself.

True bravery isn't the absence of fear but standing up despite the weight of it pushing you down. I recall Lukas's words, and with that reminder I lift my chin and allow the thread tattoo on my hip to cool. Deactivating, because for this to work, I need to be found.

I'm not sure how long I stumble around. Time's nonsensical in the sewers, but eventually I sense a presence at my back a second before I hear a gun click.

"What are you doing down here?"

The voice is masculine, and I raise my hands, heart pounding. "I'd like to speak with Cora Ramos. I heard she's looking for the Unseen Death, and I know who they are, plus where to find them."

I must've rehearsed those words a hundred times, and I'm relieved when my voice doesn't shake.

A beat of silence passes before the man speaks. "Who are you?"

Nobody important. It's what I want to say, but I need this audience with Cora; I can't defeat the queen on my own. And Cora, though vile, is a strange sort of queen. Her backing will give me the support I need.

So I don't skirt the man's question. "I'm Jade Aguilar, Zamora Aguilar's daughter. I'm a thread speaker, and I was working with Lukas Keller to help him solve the murders."

Though I can't see my assailant, I hear his intake of breath. He must believe me, too, because next thing I know, he orders me to turn around and places a burlap sack in my arms. "Put it on," he tells me. "No one but Serpensas can know the way to the underqueen."

326

I've lost my mind. Truly. That's all I can think when the sack is ripped from my head and I'm left facing the underqueen herself.

I nearly gasp at what I see.

Cora Ramos is gorgeous—like a sinister version of the queen's image on the dineda, with hair so dark it shines blue, and a smile so red it could be painted in blood. It's not her physical appearance that's astounded me, though, but her soul.

I expected a sea of vermillion cruelty, pops of magenta arrogance, and waves of slimy green disloyalty—but while those traits are present, they're mere accents in the constellation that makes up Cora. She's starbursts of violet intelligence, spikes of merlot passion, fragments of emerald beauty, and waves of charcoal strength. And above it all, running through her entire soul, are eddies of icy determination, fierce and unbreakable.

It's enough to make me look at her with new eyes as she lounges across a throne that doubles as a threat, made from all manner of bent swords, old knives, and rusting pistols. Even with her soul laid out in front of me, Cora Ramos is a mystery, her mask perfect.

"Jade Aguilar." Cora flashes me a crooked smile, the kind that makes me shiver. It doesn't help that she's flanked by six Serpensas, each one more menacing than the last. "I'm excited to finally meet you. I always liked your mother."

My mind goes temporarily blank, and for a moment I can't breathe. "You knew my mother?"

"Of course. Who do you think gave me this?"

She lifts her arm to show me the snake there, and I audibly gasp. Because while every Serpensa has a two-headed serpent tattooed onto their skin, Cora's is different. Not stamped with ink, but sewn with thread. *Black* thread, so deep and dark a person could nearly fall into it, and many do. It's the color of misery, sorrow.

Grief.

And she willingly tattooed it onto her body, so much of it I can't imagine the pain she must be in every day, nor why she'd choose to bear such a mark.

My gut clenches. My mother gave her that? She had so many secrets, and I'm about to ask Cora about them when she interrupts my thoughts. "That's not why you came, though. Tell me, what brought you?"

I reel in the urge to ask more about my mother. Because no matter how badly I want this unexplored piece of her, it won't change the fact that she's gone. I can't save her, but Lukas still has a chance, and with that thought in place, I follow Cora's lead.

"I'm here because I need your help. I was working with Lukas Keller. We learned who the killer is, but I can't stop her without you."

Cora's gaze narrows. "Lukas didn't tell me he was working with you."

"I asked him not to."

My words squeak, but that doesn't stop Cora from pushing on. "And why should I trust you, when Lukas is set to be executed for the murders?"

This is it. Everything hinges on this moment, and all my usual messages blare inside my skull as I reach for my pendant, a reminder of them all.

I can't.

What if . . . ?

It's not safe.

RUN.

Not this time. I replace them with an image of Lukas's face, his voice as he told me to breathe, and my own words too, *I will.*

I drop the pendant, look Cora Ramos right in the eyes, then say, "Because Lukas was framed by the queen, the true murderer."

All my focus is pinpointed on Cora, so I don't miss the sudden flaring of her nostrils, nor the flush of her cheeks. Lukas told me about her. *Impenetrable,* he described her. *Nothing gets past her mask.*

But now, with this news, her façade cracks.

"Out," she says, a harsh whisper, then louder, "everybody out!"

Serpensas scurry down the various tunnels, but I remain rooted to the spot. I need to have this discussion with Cora, whether or not she wants to.

She sinks deeper into her throne once they're gone. Before it was an accessory, but now she leans on it for support, almost as if her fire has been doused. I'm not sure what to say, so I wait, my hands clenched to keep them from shaking, until Cora says, voice defeated, "I knew she was horrible, but I didn't want to believe she'd stoop to such levels. Not because I didn't think her capable, but because I doubted my own capability to stop her."

I blink. I've never met Cora, but I had an image of her in my mind, someone cold and ruthless. But she seems truly distressed by the queen's actions.

"Did you try to stop her?"

Her gaze goes distant, and it's a few moments before she answers.

"I tried to learn the truth. First I had my Serpensas look into the murders, and when they became victims themselves, I asked several others. Lukas Keller was only one of them." She sighs. "It wasn't enough. I shouldn't have wasted all that time on false leads when I knew it was Celese. I even brought in one of her guards. When he didn't give me any answers, I took his eyes, hoping she'd see the message and slip up. It wasn't enough, though, wasn't even close to enough."

Nearly everything she's said is shocking to me, but I can't shake one word in particular.

"Celese?" I ask, not because I don't know who she's referring to but because the casual way she used the queen's name, dropping the María . . . it speaks of familiarity.

"Yes," Cora says, and meets my eyes. "Celese. Your queen, my younger sister."

For a moment the world stops. I stand, dumbfounded, unable to process Cora's admission. "But the queen's sister is dead," I finally say. "She died in a fire."

The whole family did, everyone except the queen.

Cora rolls her eyes, but the gesture lacks an edge. "So the official story goes."

She doesn't elaborate, and the seconds stretch between us as I slowly grasp Cora's admission. The queen's sister. The queen's *older* sister—rightful heir to the throne. All these years she's been assumed dead, but the bodies . . . they were too charred to recognize. And even moments ago, when I walked in here, I thought Cora looked like the queen on the currency. The more I stare, the more I realize she does. Not identical, but the similarities are there. The line of her nose, the bow of her lips, the shape of her eyes.

Okay. *Okay.* Maybe she's telling the truth.

I take a breath and meet Cora's eyes. "What's the actual story?"

When I stepped in here, Cora was all sleek, devious perfection, but the mask has fully slipped. Now she looks sad, all that grief in her tattoo flowing through the cracks in her carefully constructed persona.

"The truth is Cel was always ruthless. No one else could see that; she had a way of shaping herself into what others desired, and in turn, most didn't truly know her. She used that to get what she wanted, but there was always one thing just out of her grasp." Cora shudders. "The crown."

A sliver of ice works its way down my spine. "She didn't like that you were first in line for the throne, did she?"

"No." Cora shakes her head. "She hated it. And in all fairness, so did I. The crown was a weight I never much desired, something I expressed to Celese many times. We were close as children, or at least I thought we were, and she became my confidant. It must have been frustrating for her to listen to me complain, when she coveted what I loathed."

Perhaps it was, though I can't find it in myself to summon sympathy for a queen who murdered her subjects and stole their souls. Still, I keep that to myself—it's clear Cora harbors *something* for her sister—and choose a more innocuous direction instead. "Did you know she wanted to be queen?"

It takes Cora a moment to answer, something warring inside her before it settles with a lowering of her shoulders. "Did she ever tell me? No. But was I aware? Yes. She made frequent bids to our mother, trying to prove she was better suited for the throne. Our mother never listened, though, determined to marry Celese off to some foreign dignitary, and I . . ." She absently scratches at her thread tattoo, such a deep and endless black. "I could tell Celese abhorred the idea, but I never asked her about it. At the time, I told myself it was best to let her broach the subject naturally, but in truth the topic simply made me uneasy. I avoided it, and I'll never know if things would've ended differently if I hadn't."

Regret lines Cora's every word, pinches at her eyes and pales her skin. It's an emotion I know intimately, and I have to stop myself from reaching over, grasping Cora's hand, and trying to offer her comfort. I have a feeling she's not the sort who would receive it well. Even so, when I speak, it's with the soothing tone I learned from Lukas.

"You didn't know what she'd become."

Cora meets my eyes, and it's the first time in a few minutes she's really looked at me instead of gazing distantly into her past. "Maybe not, but so much could've been avoided if I'd only guessed."

I'm not sure how to respond to that, so I don't say anything at all. Silence slicks the air, thick and corrosive, until Cora dares break it.

"You can probably imagine where this story is leading. Its bitter, horrid end." She shifts in her seat, and blood drips down her arm where her throne has pricked it, though she barely seems to notice. "After yet another failed bid for the crown, Celese suggested our family take an outing to our summer home. She framed it as a peace offering, an apology for her relentless efforts to secure the throne and an acceptance of her future as some dignitary's wife. My parents were relieved and quickly agreed to the trip."

My stomach curdles. I'm not sure I want to hear where this is going, but if Cora had to live it, the least I can do is listen.

"Our first night there, I approached Celese," Cora continues. "I could tell she was upset about her failed efforts, and I apologized to her. Told her she was right, that she was better suited for the throne than I was. And that moment . . ." Cora reaches for her tattoo again, grasping her wrist in bone-white fingers. "That was the first and last time I ever saw my sister's composure crack. When she collected herself, she suggested I get out of the house that night and visit a nearby tavern. The barkeep was attractive, and the drinks were good. She'd cover for me. A kindness, I thought at the time. Now I'm not so sure it was."

With the way I suspect this story ends, I can understand why Cora would be conflicted. I bite my tongue, though, giving her the space to finish.

"It didn't take much for Celese to convince me to go. I was always searching for little escapes, evenings away from the pressure of being heir, and this seemed like a great one. A night of freedom, I thought. What I didn't know was that in a way, it would be my last."

Cora abruptly drops her tattoo, a flash of something I can't decipher crossing her features.

"When I returned, our home was engulfed in flames, everyone trapped inside. My parents, the servants, even my old nursemaid— they all perished. Not Celese, though. I found her outside, staring at the fire. Covered in blood and smelling of turpentine."

She pauses, her breath a touch ragged, her eyes a shade glossy, though no tears fall. "At first I was relieved to see her," she continues. "I hadn't put the pieces together yet. Then she saw me, and there was something different about her. A chill cruelty she'd hidden from me, or perhaps one I'd refused to see. Regardless, the façade finally cracked, and she threatened me. Told me she was queen now, and if I ever came near the throne, she'd make sure I died a worse death than my parents."

Cora studies her tattoo again, something pained and almost reverent in her gaze.

"Why she let me live, I can't say. I'd like to believe that after all the time we spent together, she held some shred of love for me, but to be honest, I'm not sure she's capable. Regardless, her threats were clear. Make problems for her, and my life was forfeit."

"So you left?"

I don't mean the words judgmentally, but Cora appears to take them as such, her gaze sharpening.

"I didn't want to, but Celese was . . . I couldn't stay there, nor could I bring myself to hurt her. Even after everything, I still loved her then, and a part of me still loves her now, foolish as that is. I still want to stop her, want revenge, but I can't pretend that desire isn't complicated. It was similar back then, so I went to the only person I thought could help me. Your mother."

A stab of surprise pierces my chest, followed by the burning ache of grief. "But she couldn't help you, could she?"

Cora shakes her head. "Her hands were tied. Apparently Celese threatened her, should she get any thoughts of assisting me, though looking back, I don't know what she could've done. She did give me this, though." She gestures to her tattoo. "I asked for it. I didn't want my grief to fade with time, lest I forget what Celese really is."

A wise decision, considering what the queen's done now, and I shudder to think of Lukas in her clutches.

Cora appears contemplative for a moment, her gaze distant, seeing some other place, other time, and her next words hold an unexpected softness. "You know, for all her faults, I truly believed Celese loved me. I saw the way she played everyone else, but me? We were sisters. I thought we had something different." She chuckles. "It shouldn't amuse me, but when we were kids, she used to cheat at cards. We'd play together most evenings, and without fail, she'd try something underhanded. Most of the time she wouldn't even be all that clever about it, almost seemed to relish it when I'd catch her. She'd argue with me, sure, insist on her innocence, but it was always with a sly grin on her face. Something real, I thought. She was so poised, all polished with everyone else, but with me . . ."

Cora wipes away a sudden tear. "But I suppose those moments

were fabrications too. I was just another one of her marks, which is why I went to your mother that night."

My eyes gravitate toward her tattoo, all those ebony threads. I can't imagine what it's like to grieve someone who hasn't passed, who's alive and well but just not at all who you thought they were. *I'm sorry* feels woefully insufficient in the face of her grief, so I remain silent, allowing Cora to continue.

A moment later, she does. "After that, I let myself fade into the shadows," she explains. "I shed the title of Princess Sofia and renamed myself Corazón, after the nursemaid we used to share. Celese must've passed off a different corpse as mine, because the world believed me to be dead, and I let it. Those first few years, I was always looking over my shoulder, waiting for her to find me, but she never came. Eventually I decided to focus on building my own empire." She gestures around her. "Perhaps it's one of sin, but I've found an exaggerated reputation is the best form of protection."

She seems almost sad when she says it, the emotion tucked in the corners of her mouth.

"Why didn't you leave?"

It's what I would've done. My first instinct has always been to run, but Cora stayed despite the danger the city posed.

She chuckles, but there's no mirth in it.

"I wanted to—still do, actually. Believe it or not, I've always dreamed of sailing, even as a girl. The palace never seemed much better than a gilded cage, but the ocean?" A spark glints in her eyes, but then she shakes her head, and it's gone. "I stayed to build up my ranks, an army hidden in plain sight, because I always knew this day was coming."

"What day?"

My chest is tight, and I barely manage to grit out the words. Cora, however, appears to be returning to herself, because her eyes sparkle, and she flashes me one of those wicked grins.

"The day I finally make my sister pay for her sins." She pauses, then adds, "In blood."

CHAPTER FORTY-ONE

LUKAS

I'M GOING TO DIE TODAY.

I lean against the cool stone wall, heart thudding along with that truth as it works its way through me.

Today is my execution.

I can't wrap my head around the fact that in a matter of hours, I'll no longer walk this earth. Won't have thoughts or feelings, because I'll no longer exist at all, not in this world, anyway. I should be scared, but I'm just . . . numb. I've spent the past few days praying to my triple god, asking for strength in my final moments. Perhaps this is how he's chosen to give it to me. A cool absence of emotion so the terror doesn't overwhelm me.

A throat clears in the cell across from mine. Zamora. Purple bags line her eyes, as if she got as little sleep as I did. "How are you doing?"

I meet her silver gaze. Things have been strange between us. I can't say I like her, but we've settled into an uneasy camaraderie, so I'm honest with my reply. "I mean, I'm not great, obviously."

"No. I suppose you're not." A beat of uncomfortable silence

passes before Zamora meets my eyes. "Lukas . . . I wanted to thank you. Protecting Jade like you are, it means a lot."

My throat tightens. "I'd do anything to keep her safe."

I mean it too. It's difficult to measure the passage of time down here, but by my estimate, it's been five days since Zamora arrived and four days since the queen and her tracker started making regular visits.

Apparently the tracker's plan hasn't worked. When he couldn't find Jade, the queen demanded my help. She even threatened to harm my family if I didn't locate Jade, but she could never prove they were alive and unharmed—almost as if she couldn't get to them.

Jade.

She did something—I just know it. Somehow found a way to elude the tracker's grasp and get my family to safety. And perhaps it shouldn't, but it only makes me love her more, that confusing swirl of emotion reaching a crescendo.

It's also why my execution is still set for today. The queen couldn't make me bring her to Jade, so she's forcing Jade to come to me.

I'm bait.

All I can do is pray that Jade stays far away today. She's in Sallenda—I can feel it through our bond—no doubt here to save me. I'd rather die alone, though, than subject her to that trauma or put her in the tracker's range.

Zamora eyes me, intense, almost as if she can see all the thoughts racing beneath my skull. "I have something for you," she finally says. "You'll need to keep it hidden."

Interest piqued, I watch as she dips a hand inside her shirt. When it reappears, there's a needle in her grasp. "I managed to smuggle it away once, when the queen still thought she could force me to make her another sievech. I've stashed it since then, a feeble weapon without my thread, but maybe it can help you today."

She tosses it to my cell, where it lands with a soft clink before I pick it up. It's clean, gleaming against the grime of my hands. I study it a moment: such a small sliver of metal. My only defense.

"Thank you." I close my fist around it. "I'll put it to good use."

Zamora looks like she's about to say something else, but she holds back when the door above creaks open. I immediately tense. Footsteps scuffle on the stone steps, one set light, the other two heavier. I know what it means.

This is it. My escort has arrived. It's time.

My earlier numbness is replaced with roiling nausea as I approach my cell bars. I refuse to grovel, so I'm waiting, my back straight, when the queen turns the corner. She's wrapped in a dress of golden silk, a crown of gilded feathers perched atop her dark tresses. A queen's guard flanks her on each side, blue uniforms pristine.

"Lukas." The queen's smile is sharp enough to draw blood. "How are you?"

I snort at her taunt, refusing to show my fear. "As well as can be expected, considering the circumstances."

"About that." Her gaze flicks to Zamora, then to me. "You'll be interested to know those circumstances have changed, but I'm not unfair. I'll give you one more chance. Lead me to Jade Aguilar, and I might be convinced to delay your execution."

I've dealt with Cora Ramos, leader of a gang literally named the Serpensas, and yet it's the queen who's the snake. She'll never delay my execution, not unless she can use me as a bargaining chip against Jade.

But I'm not a fool. Whatever the queen's referring to, I need to know what it means. She seems to be in a chatty mood, and I do my best to remain steady as I face her. "Tell me what's changed, and maybe I'll consider it."

Zamora flinches, but I force myself to ignore her.

The queen makes a show of looking me over, then shakes her head. "All you need to know is that Jade has her plans for today, and I have mine."

My heart gives a sudden, painful squeeze. So Jade is coming for me—the queen's all but confirmed it.

It's enough to make my eyes burn, a churning mixture of gratitude and horror warring inside me. Because Jade's fighting for me, even with the impossibility of our circumstances. For so long I've been the one protecting others; I forgot how nice it felt to have someone looking out for me. But now, today, it could be Jade's downfall.

I become acutely aware of the needle in my fist, warmed by my skin. It's small, but it's sharp. I imagine all the ways I'd use it against the queen if I could—but if I'm going to help Jade, I need to be smart about this.

"What exactly are you telling me?" I ask, my voice low and edged with ire.

The queen's amber eyes go a bit molten. "I'm saying that it's over. Either you lead me to Jade or I find her myself, but the result for her is the same. The only difference is whether or not you're killed in the process. Help me, and I might be convinced to spare you."

My mind races; my pulse thunders in my ears. The queen wants my aid for a reason.

I don't know how, but Jade must be evading the tracker. Without me they can't find her. And the queen needs Jade not just for her abilities but because she knows the truth. Celese can't have the city find out she's a killer.

No, I realize. I won't do it. It hurts, knowing I won't be around to care for my family, but my dad fought for what he believed in. Now I have to do the same.

And I believe in Jade, so as painful as this may be, that means facing my execution.

I'm about to say as much when Zamora speaks up, her voice high with fear. "Don't do it, Lukas. She's just trying to manipulate you—don't—"

"That's enough. The boy is thinking; let him do so." The queen glares daggers at her, then turns to me. "Well, what'll it be?"

It's not her I look at when I answer, though. It's Zamora. "No. I won't lead you to Jade. Not now, not ever."

Zamora nods, reassured. I can't say as much for the queen. Twin patches of rage blaze in her cheeks; her nostrils flare. "Then you shall die."

Then die I will.

The queen waits a moment, almost as if she expects me to recant, but I stand firm. Not one to show defeat, she sniffs, lifts her chin, and gestures to me. "You know what to do," she says to her guards. "Take him to the dais." She glances at Zamora. "And bring her too. If the boy isn't enough to lure Jade out, perhaps her mother will be."

No. Jade's already suffered enough. Witnessing her mother's death would destroy her. I squeeze the needle, a muscle working in my jaw as a queen's guard unlocks my cell and grabs me roughly by the arm. The other does the same to Zamora, who's begun trembling.

They bind my wrists in front of me and follow suit with

Zamora. Through all of it, I remain still, my muscles twitching. Eager.

"After you, Your Majesty," one of the guards tells the queen, and she saunters past him to the stairs. Zamora shoots me a look as we're escorted a moment later, her eyes wide. I glance at the guards, both their faces turned ahead, and quickly mouth to Zamora, *Be ready.*

She nods, straightens her shoulders, and lifts her chin. The gesture's so reminiscent of Jade, I nearly wince.

Fresh, cool air hits my face as a trapdoor is opened and I step aboveground for the first time in almost two weeks. I breathe it in, quickly taking in our surroundings. We're on what looks to be an abandoned dirt road in that awkward nowhere land that isn't quite city but has been cleared of jungle. Heavy clouds blanket the sky, gray with rain. A glance to my right reveals Sallenda about a mile off, a sprawl of rusty adobe and creamy limestone.

The guard jerks me toward one of the two stagecoaches waiting for us, a pair of guards standing outside it. The queen steps into the other.

I suck in a breath, then carefully inch the needle forward so it pokes out beneath my fingers. This is my chance. I don't intend to waste it.

"Hey." I pull back, refusing to step forward.

The queen's guard faces me, clearly annoyed. "What—"

In one fluid motion, I yank my arm free of his grasp and jam the needle into his eye. He shrieks, hands immediately going to his face. Even with my wrists bound, I'm fast. I reach beneath his coat, rip his gun from its holster, level it at the guard holding Zamora, and shoot.

He screams, dark blood spreading across the arm of his blue coat. His companions lunge for me, reaching for their weapons.

"Run!" I tell Zamora. "Get out of here!"

Her eyes meet mine, just a flash before she takes off, sprinting toward the city. Hopefully she's quick. I keep my pistol raised, intending to shoot the queen right here, right now.

I never get that far.

One of the remaining guards crashes into me. I hit the ground so hard I can't breathe. The next few moments are a blur of limbs as the second uninjured guard joins the pile. I writhe and shake and scream for Zamora to run, run, run, to not come back. To leave me.

It's the only way to save Jade.

Eventually I have no choice but to settle, one queen's guard pinning my arms while the other has my legs. But I can tilt my head. When I do, I'm greeted by the sight of Zamora in the distance, far enough that she stands a chance. I sigh. I did it, then.

The queen appears in my line of sight, crouching down so I'm forced to look at her. Despite everything that just happened, her expression is smooth; even her dress is unwrinkled. The look in her eyes, however, is pure ice.

"I suppose you're proud of yourself."

"I am." There's no point in lying, and I'll do anything to get under her skin.

The queen shakes her head. "Enjoy it, because it won't last." She looks to her guards. "This doesn't change things. Zamora will go to her daughter; we'll simply capture them together at the execution."

She nods toward me, and even though I know I did the right thing, my stomach drops at her next words.

"Bring him to the dais. It's time he learned his lesson."

CHAPTER FORTY-TWO

JADE

THE EXECUTION DAIS IS LOCATED IN SALLENDA'S CENTER. NO DIStrict wanted it, so it became a morbid sort of meeting point for them all. The plaza here is wide and open, paved in lumpy cobblestones, and surrounded by limestone buildings, one of which I lie on top of now, my thread kit at my side. Hundreds of people have arrived, and they mill about on the streets below me, calling for the death of a boy they believe to be a killer, all while cheering on the queen they think caught him.

Their condemnation has me biting my lip, shivers rippling down my spine. It's all so misguided, and the puppeteer behind the curtain has yet to arrive.

The thought pulls my eyes to the queen's box, raised above the ground, the lush throne at its center still empty. Directly in front of it is the dais, its three nooses shifting in the breeze.

I think I might be sick.

Soon Lukas will step on that stage and face a series of false charges. And even though I'm here with a plan, it's no guarantee. Lukas could be dead in a matter of hours.

The panic peaks, a foaming black wave, but I force myself to breathe and focus on the cool limestone beneath me, the chatter below, and the fresh caress of the salty ocean breeze. *Breathe,* I instruct myself, *nice and slow. In through the nose, out through the mouth.*

Gradually, the wave crashes, and I remind myself that I have a plan—*we* have a plan, because I'm not alone in this any longer.

I thought I'd have to beg, grovel, and plead to get Cora Ramos to help me.

I thought wrong.

She's just as eager as I am to stop the queen, and she doesn't even want the throne for her troubles. According to her, that "cushy life" was never "to her taste."

We spent our first day together plotting, and at the end of it I returned to Lukas's family and gave them thread tattoos identical to the one at my hip. They were all so brave—even little Artur—and afterward a few Serpensas smuggled them to a safe house known by only the gang's most elite members. They'll be even more protected there, guarded by Serpensas, until they're smuggled out of the country this evening.

Now I scan the crowd for any sign of Cora. She should be here, having donned the role of returned princess. "If we're going to stop Celese," she said, "the people have to know the truth. We'll need some proof, but they'll have to get it from someone they can trust. Someone they already know of."

Apparently, lost princesses fit the bill.

After that, it was only a matter of tracking down the proof Cora was to share, which arrived with her Serpensas not long ago. Unfortunately, Cora herself isn't here yet, and everything in me tightens more with each passing minute. The crowd thickens, and even though I'm well above it, my breath grows ragged.

Memories of the courthouse steps flash before my eyes, stone digging into the backs of my legs, the crush of bodies, the vivid snap of bone . . .

No.

This is not that day, and I'm no longer that girl. Today, here, now, this is about Lukas, and I nearly yelp when he's led onto the stage, flanked by two queen's guards.

Lukas.

Even from a distance, I can tell he's disheveled, his hair rumpled and clothes dirty. He scans the crowd, and I wonder if he's looking for me. *I'm here.* I think it as hard as I can, hoping he'll sense it through our soul bond. *I'm right here, and everything's going to be okay.*

There's no way to know if it works, but Lukas does seem to stand a bit taller, prouder, in a way that makes my heart blaze. His bravery has always drawn me to him, and now he wears it like a shield. *Keep being brave,* I encourage him, *just a little bit longer.*

Because any second now, Cora Ramos will come out. She'll appear in one of the watchtowers dotting the yard, steal the show, and provide a much-needed distraction.

But the seconds slink by and she doesn't arrive. Not as Lukas is led to the center noose. Not as the polesa hush the chittering crowd. Not as the queen is escorted to her box, smiling and waving, the tracker at her side.

And because the people can't see what I see, they cheer, unaware of the horror standing before them. The wreckage of her soul—not a constellation of rainbow hues, but something rotted, sickly, and decaying. Evil. Only the gold of her life is healthy, pulsing amid the destruction.

I study it, noting the subtle differences between her current soul and the version inside my pocket, safely tucked next to Lukas's and the tracker's. Thankfully, it hasn't changed much, with the most notable alteration being the rot. Most of my work will be subtracting what's already in place, and the decay is so extensive, I won't even have to be delicate.

Satisfied, I quietly reach for the queen's soul and open my thread kit. A steward takes the stage and begins detailing the lengthy—and falsified—investigation that incriminated Lukas. I snip as he goes, pausing frequently to scan the crowd for Cora, but she still hasn't arrived by the time I finish altering the queen's portrait a few minutes later.

She should be here by now.

Where is she? Did she change her mind at the last minute? Was she caught?

Possibilities whir through my mind, each worse than the last, and I'm about to tilt into a full-on episode when I slap myself across the face—hard. For good measure, I do it again, and I imagine the threads of my soul stitched above Lukas's heart. All those streams of sour yellow fear, yes. Those thoughts of *I can't* and *What if,* so many worst-case scenarios. But intertwined with all that fear is courage, and I've never needed to be courageous more than I do right now.

I don't know what happened to Cora, but it doesn't matter, because she's not here. I am, and if I don't do something, Lukas will die.

I stand, my thread kit in hand, a pistol holstered at each hip, and twin knives, both hidden up my sleeves. My cheeks sting as I race across the roof, down the stairs, and to the crowd's edge. Facing the wall of people is akin to being slammed by a tidal wave, and I step back, gasping, automatically reaching for the shell at my chest. *So many people—what if I can't breathe, what if they hurt me, what if I'm trapped—I can't I can't I CAN'T.*

But if I don't, Lukas will die, and I focus on him as I drop my hand and take that first step into the crowd. A shoulder brushes me as I imagine his eyes, vivid and courageous the day we met. I squeeze between two people as I recall that night on the lifeboat, the gentleness of his hands on my calf. Hot breath surrounds me, suffocating, but I push the sensation out, recalling Gebreine and the feeling of Lukas's hands on my body, his lips on mine.

And it works. Step by step, inch by inch, I push my way between the people, growing closer to the centermost watchtower. Thankfully, the steward is *still* speaking, and I swallow, heart racing, as I will the tattoo at my hip to deactivate.

If this is going to work, everyone needs to be focused on me—my actual worst nightmare.

For Lukas, I remind myself, but despite everything, when I reach the steps of the tower, I freeze.

Because the second I get up there, all eyes will be on me. If they don't like what I have to say, there will be no escape. They could drag me to the ground, rip me limb from limb, trample me and—

"Jade."

The voice is breathless, strained, *familiar,* and everything around me slows as I turn and face it. Face *her.*

My mother. Alive. And somehow—miraculously—here.

Everything else drops away, every thought, every feeling, every person and sensation, as I fully tip out of my body before I'm suddenly hurtling back into it, and I'm gasping and I'm crying and I'm panicking because my mother is somehow alive, and Lukas is about to be dead, and I can't contain this emotion any longer.

"Jade." My mother's voice cracks, and then she pulls me into her arms, wrapping me in a fierce hug. "I thought I'd lost you,"

348

she whispers, and all I can think is *Me too* before she pulls away, a tender moment stolen by urgency. "We need to go," she says, voice hard. "The queen, she made threats—I think she knows you're here. We need to leave *now*."

She tugs on my arm, but I don't budge.

"Jade—"

"No." I meet my mother's eyes, unable to believe what I'm saying. "I missed you, Mom, but I can't go with you."

For months the thing I've wanted most was to have my mother back, to be safe with her watching over me. And now that she's here, I can have that dream, but I realize it's not right any longer.

All my life I've viewed the world as a formidable, dangerous place. One that would beat and bruise and break me—and it has. This world has snapped my bones, pointed a gun at my face, and locked me in the dark. It's hurt me, and in doing so, it made me afraid, made me think I was weak.

But that's not true; it never has been. That belief bent me into something small, but it couldn't contain me forever. I've looked into a sievech's eyes and walked away. I've gone head to head with the tracker and outsmarted him at several turns. I faced down a horde of angry sailors, sewed my way across Kabrück, and walked into a den of snakes with my chin held high.

This world will always be formidable and dangerous—that's an inescapable truth. But you know what?

So am I.

And I'm done letting my fear rob me of happiness—starting now. Starting with Lukas.

A quick glance reveals that one of the guards has wrapped the noose around his neck, and everything in me goes still. Not calm, but clear. I know what to do, and no one will stop me from doing it, not even my mother.

"I'm sorry," I tell her. "I love you—so much—but I'm not leaving Lukas."

I don't wait for her to respond as I scurry up the watchtower steps. The tattoo at my hip may be cooled, but the one on my biceps activates, lending me grace and stealth. The polesa officer stationed at the tower doesn't hear me coming, doesn't even turn around before I swing my thread kit into his temple, knocking him unconscious. Later I'll feel bad about that, but not now.

Formidable. Dangerous. *Powerful.*

I'm all of those things, and I feel it too as I unholster my pistol, raise it to the sky, and fire off a single shot.

There's a brief eruption of chaos, of yelps and shouts, before everyone realizes that I've lowered my gun and mean them no harm. And then the moment is here, the one with all the eyes on me, in which the world goes so quiet I can hear my heart beating.

True bravery isn't the absence of fear but standing up despite the weight of it pushing you down.

Lukas's words soothe me even as the terror pounds through my blood, and across the expanse I meet his eyes. So green and courageous.

Now I have to be too.

The people of Sallenda deserve to know the truth about their queen, and I intend to give it to them. Hopefully the Serpensas waiting with our proof will follow my lead.

Cora said that whoever addressed the crowd had to be someone they knew of. I may not be a lost princess, but I am their thread speaker, and I hope that's enough as I face them and say, "My name is Jade Aguilar. Most of you probably know me as Sallenda's apprentice thread speaker, but today I'm here to tell you who the true murderer is."

The hush deepens, and I lift my eyes to the woman behind all this, seated on her velvet throne. Her gaze brims with poison, but I don't look away as I reveal the truth.

"Lukas Keller is innocent," I announce. "Queen María-Celese Ríos, however, is not."

CHAPTER FORTY-THREE

LUKAS

I'VE NEVER BEEN MORE PROUD OR TERRIFIED THAN I AM IN THIS moment. Jade is a beacon, a vision, and a revolution all in one, blazing with the fire I always knew she had. The wind picks up, whipping the curtain of her hair back, but the world is frozen.

"That's preposterous," the queen's voice rings out. When I glance her way, she's still as composed as ever. "You lie. Now get down from there before I order the polesa to do it for you."

Jade doesn't back down. Doesn't even flinch. And *god*, it's not the time to think it, but if we escape this alive, I'm going to kiss her until she sees stars.

"I'm not moving, and I'm not lying." Jade is stern. "I can see it in your soul, the way it's decayed. All those murders—the innocent people, the *polesa officer*, you didn't just kill them, you stole their souls too. Probably to rally people back to the old gods, and therefore back to you. It's no secret your support has been dwindling these past few years."

I overflow with pride. Jade's accusations are right on the mark, and others are beginning to see it too. From my vantage point it's not difficult to make out the polesa officers in their black uniforms with the large brass buttons. They've been steadily creeping toward Jade, but now they pause, their attention captured. Jade mentioned once that their captain was her fighting instructor, and I wonder if he's here, ordering them to wait.

I itch to shout my support, but I'm acutely aware of the noose scraping my throat.

I need to be careful about this.

"I would never kill my people," the queen says, and I nearly laugh.

The crowd bristles, unsure what to think, but the deathly quiet returns as Zamora ascends the watchtower and takes her place next to Jade. "But you would," she tells everyone, "and you have. For years, you ordered me to kill your enemies discreetly, and would threaten Jade's life if I didn't comply." She raises her voice, fully addressing the crowd now. "My daughter speaks the truth. The queen is the killer, not Lukas."

Several polesa officers glare at the queen, cheeks heated, eyes blazing. She notices their ire and chuckles, but it's nervous. The polesa vastly outnumber her guards, and she knows it.

"Preposterous," she says again, loud and clear. "I'm not sure what's gotten into my thread speakers, but they're lying. They probably want my power for themselves."

"No." Jade stares her down. "We're not, and I'm going to tell everyone how I learned the truth."

Her gaze flicks to mine, and I don't miss the meaning there. *Be ready.*

My fingers twitch, anxious for action as Jade spins our story for the crowd. The queen interrupts a few times, but a shift has occurred. Jade's winning the people over. They might not be entirely convinced of her story yet, but they certainly want to hear it, everyone leaning forward in rapt attention. The polesa don't intervene either, as entranced with Jade's tale as everyone else, and the queen's guard don't dare leave her side, sensing the danger about to erupt.

"Now," Jade says as her story draws to a close, "I can't make you all believe me. If you could see the queen's soul as I do, the rot would be obvious, and you'd know I'm telling the truth. But you can't, which is why I brought a witness with me today."

She scans the space before her, looking for something—no, *someone*. The crowd parts as a woman's escorted to the watchtower by two Serpensas, black tattoos poking out from beneath their sleeves. Jade steps to the side once they've reached her, then gestures to the woman, who bears a passing resemblance to the queen.

"Everyone, I'd like to introduce you to Frida Garcia," Jade announces. "The queen hired Frida to impersonate her for a recent meeting with me. She knew if we met directly, I'd see the rot in her soul and realize she was responsible for the murders." Jade turns her focus to the other woman. "Would you like to share more, Frida?"

Frida shifts, obviously nervous, but raises her chin before addressing everyone gathered. "She's telling the truth. The queen didn't share her motivations with me, but she was clear about one thing: Jade wasn't to see her. Now I know why."

A shock wave ripples through the crowd, even as the queen stands abruptly, throne screeching as it's scraped backward. "That's ridiculous!" she insists. "They're lying—they're all lying!"

But the tide is turning against her fast. The polesa look furious, cheeks red, hands on their batons; and the people—well, they look just as angry.

Through all of this I'm so proud I could burst. Of this girl who thought she was nothing but her fear, who is absolutely radiant and incredible and courageous, fear and all. Who stands atop the watchtower—before these people—like it's nothing, when really it's everything. I know how Jade feels about crowds. Her terror over the crush of bodies. And yet she faced her fear anyway, did that for *me*. My heart swells as Jade meets my eyes across the expanse.

"Of course, Frida isn't the only witness." A hush falls as Jade raises her voice. "The accused, Lukas Keller, was with me through the events I've shared, and I'm sure he'll attest that everything I've said today is true. That he's just the queen's scapegoat." She turns her eyes back on me. "Isn't that right, Lukas?"

Her words must be some kind of signal. The queen's guard at my side faces me, warning in his eyes, before he's suddenly tackled to the ground by a horde of people rushing the stage. It's bright, heady chaos, screams filling the air as I rip the noose from my throat. I spin, searching for Jade, when an unfamiliar woman appears in front of me, hands lifted away from her weapons. "It's okay," she says, "I'm here to help you."

She pulls back her sleeve, revealing a two-headed snake. I nearly laugh. I never thought a Serpensa would come to my aid, but when she lifts the knife, I offer her my wrists. Seconds later my bonds fall to the ground.

Free at last.

The Serpensa disappears into the chaos before I can thank her. I whirl to the royal box behind me, but the queen is already gone, as are most of her guards. *Shit.*

But at least the people know the truth now, and I search for Jade among the writhing mass of bodies. In it, civilians scramble for escape while Serpensas take on queen's guards and the polesa try—and fail—to retain some semblance of order. My blood's pounding by the time I spot her, almost at the stage.

"Jade!" I call out, and leap down from the dais. Her eyes whip to mine, and she pushes through the crowd, pale and panting, probably terrified but still here. Still fighting for me.

"Lukas!" My name cracks on her lips. Then we're hurtling into each other, a crash of bodies as I wrap my arms around her, trying to shield her from all this chaos.

"Lukas," she says again, sobbing, and I'm holding her so tight.

"Jade," I say, and nuzzle her brow, inhaling her rosy scent. There are so many things I want to tell her, but this isn't the place, so I drop my arms and take her hand. "Come on—we need to go."

She nods and leans in closer so I can hear her. "Toward the palace. I think that's where the queen's headed."

A thrill ripples through me. Jade must have something else planned, but before we can escape the crowd, a horrible, keening wail pierces the air. The blood drains from Jade's face, and she grips her belly.

"Lukas, something's wrong. I feel sick. Almost like—"

Sieveche. Dozens of them. They appear like wraiths out of thin air.

Howling monkeys. Roaring jaguars. Shrieking crows. I can't see their absence of souls like Jade can, but I don't have to. It's clear in the unnatural way they attack the crowd, clawing at their eyes.

The screams increase, reaching a fever pitch. The crowd's a riotous jumble, people slamming into us as everyone fights to get away.

"We need to get out of here." The words leave me on an exhale, and I tug Jade's hand. "Come on."

She doesn't argue. We force our way through the madness, steadily increasing in tempo.

Soon it's an all-out battle—the queen's guard and sieveche

against the polesa and Serpensas. Jade presses a gun into my palm, and our bullets roar.

At one point a queen's guard lunges for Jade, ripping her back by the hair before I shoot him. Jade returns the favor only seconds later—striking down a frothing dog, its jaws aimed for my throat but set on my soul.

We're spattered in blood by the time we escape the battle, bullets completely spent. My lungs scream as we race down Sallenda's cobbled streets, but we don't stop. Not until we're miles away, the pandemonium a muted roar behind us. I check her for injuries the second we're alone, but there's nothing more serious than scrapes and bruises. Thank god. I pull her close, and her arms slide around me, shaking but solid. Real.

"I'm sorry," I whisper into her hair. "I never should've left."

Perhaps there are more important things to focus on right now, but I can't stop the words.

She pulls back and meets my eyes, her own wet. "*I'm* sorry. I should've told you about your father the moment I realized my history with him."

I'm not going to dispute that. Jade and I both made mistakes, but we're so much more than the ways we've hurt one another. I left her. She lied to me. But we've also saved each other, over and over again, despite the obstacles in our way. We're more than our mistakes, which makes what I say next easy.

"It's okay, I forgive you." And I know the world is falling apart around us, but I never thought I'd have this chance again, so I don't stop myself from saying, "And if you don't mind, I'd really like to kiss you now."

Tears leak from Jade's eyes, but I think they're happy ones. "I don't mind at all."

It's a frenzied, burning sort of kiss. I crush my lips to hers, tighten my arm around her hips, and wrap my fingers in her silky hair. Jade moans into my mouth, and fire erupts inside me as her fingers skate over my back, fisting my shirt. My heart races, blood pounding as I push her against a brick wall. She's breathing heavily—we both are. I wish I could live and die in this moment, in Jade's embrace.

And maybe, if I'm lucky, I will someday. But these seconds, this kiss, it's all stolen. There's quite literally a battle at our backs, demanding our attention. One that won't truly end until the queen is dead.

So I soften my kisses, lift my hands to her cheeks, and cradle her face. Then I pull back, my forehead pressed to Jade's, her breath fluttering against my skin.

"Lukas," Jade breathes. My entire body heats as I recall the last time she whispered my name like that, the night of Gebreine.

Jade brings me back to reality.

"Your family is safe," she tells me, and I still. "I created a tattoo that can make someone untraceable, even to the tracker, and gave it to each of them. Serpensas smuggled them to one of their safe houses, and they're waiting for you there as we speak." She pats her pocket. "I have the supplies, and I can give you the tattoo now. There's a small ship waiting for you in the harbor, the *Guadalupe*. It's crewed with Serpensas waiting to take you and your family home."

Home. There's a tug in my chest, because Jade doesn't mean our hovel in Mugra but across the sea, Kabrück. Just the thought of it, and I can practically taste the strawberries of our garden, smell the pine of the forest, hear Lina's giggles as we wove flower crowns together.

The last place we were all truly happy.

"It's okay." Jade must see the look on my face, and her voice is low. "You can go to them."

And leave her to fight the queen alone—because that's what she's asking.

I see it then, suddenly so clearly.

This whole time, I thought Jade was my freedom, but I was wrong. The freedom I felt was never her but me, finally making choices for myself. For years I've felt that I owed my family everything, and I was willing to pay any cost. My health. My life. My happiness.

I spent so much of myself on others, I forgot my own value. But I deserve to be happy just as much as anyone else, and I'm done *only* choosing others. For the first time, I think I want *balance.* And balance means that sometimes I have to choose myself.

My father did, and now I will too. For him that meant rebelling. For me it means fighting at Jade's side, even if my family is left waiting. I've chosen them for years, and they'll understand that today I need to choose myself. And of course they'll understand. For so long, they've wanted me to be happy. Now, at long last, I can be.

That new understanding is perhaps why there's no twist of guilt as I meet Jade's eyes. "They'll be fine without me, because I'm staying with you." I drop my arm and lace my fingers through hers. "So come on. Let's go finish this." I squeeze her hand. "Together this time."

CHAPTER FORTY-FOUR

JADE

THE QUEEN'S IN THE PALACE.

I can't say how I'm certain, only that I am.

Before I left my mother's side to find Lukas, I gave her some thread-speaking materials, then sent her to the docks, should the queen try to escape that way. But as Lukas and I step into the palace halls—eerily empty and completely unguarded—I sense it.

She's here.

And she's left herself open because she wants me to find her.

I shiver, palms sweaty, and tuck my free hand into my pocket, where my embroidery materials rest. Just a needle, a bit of thread, a pair of tweezers, and my seam ripper. Not much, but it brings comfort all the same.

Lukas, ever watchful, notices. "Are you okay?"

I glance at the halls around us, creamy marble shot through with veins of gold, vaulted ceilings, and opulent pillars with carvings of the gods. Beautiful, perhaps. Extravagant, definitely.

It feels like a tomb. *Our* tomb, if we're not careful.

"I'd be better if we had some bullets left," I answer truthfully.

Unfortunately, we used them all in battle, our empty pistols serving for little more than show now. The only real weapons we possess are a knife each—Lukas's gripped in his hand, and mine is sheathed at my wrist, hidden beneath my sleeve.

"Me too," Lukas mutters.

We're quiet after that, slipping down the wide, echoing halls, and it occurs to me how strange this is. I've always wanted Sallenda's people to be safe, but before, that desire occurred at a distance. I was too afraid to help them if it meant risking myself. Now, though, I'm here, doing the hard thing. Putting everything on the line because it's the right thing to do. And despite the terror, I smile. Perhaps I'm more like my mother than I realized.

It's a reassuring thought as Lukas and I wend our way through the palace, searching for the throne room. Neither of us has been here much, so we're not sure what to expect, but it's obvious when we finally locate it.

Huge double doors span almost an entire wall. They're gorgeous, crafted from deep cherrywood, a perfect contrast to all this pale marble. My gaze drops to the handles sculpted to look like eagles, golden feathers fanned around them, knockers held in their beaks. A symbol of Oro and, by extension, the queen.

A pulse ripples through me, followed by a wave of churning nausea.

"This is it," I whisper. "She's inside. She has—"

I'm interrupted by the unmistakable click of a gun. The voice that follows has my gut roiling for an entirely different set of reasons.

"Ah, little dove. I'm pleased to see you made it this far. Celese will be as well. Now turn around and let me look at your face. You too, Lukas."

The tracker.

I have to clench my fists to keep from shaking, a potent clash of terror and fury racing through my veins. The tracker stands before us, that same haughty sneer tracing his lips, his gun pointed straight between Lukas's eyes.

No, I realize as I stare a moment longer, noticing the pearl inlay gleaming in the sunlight. Not his gun at all. Lukas's father's.

Bastard.

Rage boils in me anew. Lukas must notice too, because he shifts, knife at his side, and the tracker tuts. "Uh-uh-uh, drop your blade, and your pistol too." He glances at me. "You too. Lose the pistol."

Lukas's nostrils flare. "And if we refuse?"

The tracker sighs, bored almost, then swivels the gun to face me. "Then I put a bullet in her—which I'd prefer not to do, but the choice is yours."

I stare down the tracker's gun—his *stolen* gun. Too many times he's had me on the wrong side of his weapon. *It ends today,* I decide. *Somehow, someway, it's over.* I'm done being terrified of this man.

My knife burns, a reminder against my wrist as I unholster my pistol and lower it to the ground. Beside me Lukas does the same. Maybe the tracker's bluffing, but I know Lukas. He isn't willing to take that risk. On his life, perhaps, but not mine.

The tracker's grin kicks up a notch. "Wonderful." He plucks a set of manacles from his waist and offers them to Lukas. "Now use these to chain yourself to one of the pillars."

"What? No!" Lukas splutters. "I'm not leaving Jade!"

"Lukas." He flinches at the resignation in my voice. "Listen to him," I whisper. "It's for the best."

"Yes, Lukas," the tracker mocks. "Listen to me—it's for the best."

Lukas ignores him, those courageous eyes of his fixed on me. I draw from them now, willing him to see the message in my gaze. To feel the resolve through our bonded souls. *Trust me. I've got this.*

Lukas must sense my message, because he appears to calm slightly, and a fraction of the tension shifts off his shoulders.

"Fine," he agrees, swiping the manacles from the tracker. "But don't you dare hurt her."

The tracker's eyes glitter. "It's not me you have to worry about, not as long as your little dove behaves."

Lukas's cheeks tinge with fury, and I feel mine doing the same. Still, he does as the tracker ordered, wrapping his arms around a pillar before he locks the manacles, thoroughly secured.

It's exactly the distraction I need. The tracker watches Lukas, oblivious to the knife sliding into my palm.

"All right, little dove." He turns to me. "Let's—"

I lunge, knife raised, aimed straight for his heart.

The tracker barely has time to react. In his panic he goes for the easiest option: his gun. There's a boom as it fires, and I scream, white-hot pain grazing my hip. I flinch back, and the tracker lifts the weapon. This time it's aimed for my head. A deadly shot.

I don't give him the opportunity to take it.

I lunge again, shrieking. I'm too close for the shot now, crowding his space as I slam my foot on his instep. The tracker howls, instinctively bowing over—the chance I need. I swing my knife for his gut, prepared for the soft give of his flesh.

I never get it. The tracker predicts my move. Quicker than I would've thought possible, he grabs my wrist and spins me around so I'm flush with his chest, trapped in the cage of his arms.

Somewhere behind us, Lukas is putting up a fight, chains rattling as he screams. It's no use, and the tracker drops his lips to my ear, practically purring. "I should've been disappointed when

363

I couldn't find you. All over Sallenda I searched for you, my little dove, to no avail. But you know, it's strange." He squeezes my wrist, applying a near bone-breaking pressure. "I think I rather prefer it this way: the thrill of the chase . . . No one's made my blood race the way you have in years."

He increases the pressure then, and I gasp as my hand flings open, the knife clattering to the floor.

"No!" Lukas cries, but he can't help me, and I force myself to tune him out.

"You're sick," I hiss at the tracker. And before he has time to anticipate my move, I duck my head, then slam it into his face.

There's a satisfying crunch, along with the tracker's shriek. His grip loosens, and it's all the chance I need. I slip from his grasp, but I don't go for my knife—there's no time for that. Not when he still holds his gun.

I charge—straight for his middle this time. We crash to the floor, the tracker's head smacking against the marble, the pistol slipping from his grasp and skidding away. He's a mess, his nose a bloody gush, and I lift my fist.

Hit them where they're already wounded, my fighting instructor used to tell me. *It'll hurt more.*

But the tracker jerks his head to the side before I can connect. I scream, pain erupting in my knuckles when they collide with marble. He takes advantage of my momentary lapse, fingers sifting through my hair before he yanks. *Hard.* He bucks his hips, and suddenly the world's spinning, and I'm the one on my back, stuck beneath him.

"Jade!" Lukas's scream rips the air, his desperation mirrored in the frantic race of my own heart. "No!"

I swing my fist, connecting with the tracker's throat, but he doesn't budge. He's larger than me, stronger too, and despite my struggle, soon he has me completely pinned. My legs beneath his legs, my arms trapped in his. I can't even buck my hips.

A yawning chasm of terror opens inside me, and I fight harder, twisting and turning, desperate to break free. It's no use, though. I'm trapped.

The tracker knows it too, because he chuckles. "Please continue. I like it when you squirm beneath me."

"Stop it!" Lukas shrieks. "Let her go! Jade!"

I freeze. Struggling isn't helping—it's just expending my energy. I need to *think*.

Use the resources at your disposal.

The second lesson my instructor gave me. But what resources do I have? My knife is gone. The gun's too far to reach. All I have are the clothes on my back and the embroidery materials in my pocket—

That's *it*.

"Pity." The tracker frowns at my still form. "It's more fun when you struggle. Now, if I get up, will you come willingly?"

I need my arms free, need him to think me docile, and I will my muscles to go limp. "Yes."

He must see the truth in my eyes, though, because his own spark. "Somehow I don't believe that. There's still some fight in you. No matter—we'll douse it." Fast as a viper, his hands dart for my throat.

And then he begins to squeeze.

I flinch, instinctively reaching for my neck, desperate to relieve the pressure. My side burns, blood soaking my hip where the bullet grazed me, a hurricane of panic unleashing inside my chest.

I can't breathe. Every desperate pull for air is met with the pressure, the tracker's hands around my throat.

Lukas's scream—his *fury*—is absolutely bloodcurdling. But he can't save me, not this time. And the tracker's unwittingly given me what I needed. My hands are free.

I thrash, punching the tracker with one hand, though my hits are weak, my vision tunneling. It's the kind of fight he needs to see. The one he expected, so he believes this is all I have. Doesn't notice my other hand, slipping for my pocket, digging ever deeper, until my fingers graze the handle of my seam ripper.

Just barely out of reach.

I stretch my arm, grasping for the handle . . .

The tracker's grip loosens, his smile slick and gruesome, teeth stained red. "I look forward to breaking you, little dove. Such an exquisite fight you put up today, but you and I both know the truth." He leans close, hot breath fanning my ear. "You're a runner, a thinker maybe, but you'll never be a warrior. Not truly."

Then he squeezes anew, but this time it's different. This time I've reached my seam ripper, steel pulled into my palm. A feeble weapon, perhaps, but a sharp one all the same. And the tracker forgot something about me.

I can be viper quick too.

I strike. Plunge the seam ripper straight into his neck.

The tracker screams, hands going to his throat as he clambers off me. It's all the chance I need. I fling myself backward, eyes set on the fallen pistol. The tracker must see my intent, because he lunges toward me, but it's too late.

In one fluid motion, I've got the gun in my hands, pointed at his heart. So many times I've had the tracker in my sights. On his ship. In Johann's cellar. Beneath a canopy of oak and aspen, deep in Dreiden's forest. Every time, I stayed my hand. Today that pattern ends. His cruelty ends.

Today I don't hesitate to pull the trigger.

I put a bullet straight through the tracker's foul heart.

I'm not sure what I expect. A scream, a cry, a howl perhaps, but the tracker does none of those things. He grunts, a ripple of shock passing through him. His eyes widen, his face whitens, a crimson stain spreading across the pale linen of his shirt. He glances at his chest, as if he can't believe this is happening, that I did this to him, before he finally crumples to the ground.

I stand over him, the gold of his life rapidly fading, but it's still there when I meet his gaze and whisper, "Never a warrior, huh?"

His mouth drops open, coated in blood, and a croak wafts out, some pathetic attempt at last words before the tracker goes irrevocably, permanently silent.

CHAPTER FORTY-FIVE

LUKAS

THE QUEEN'S NOT YET DEAD, OUR TASK FAR FROM COMPLETE. Time is of the essence. I *know* that, but it doesn't stop me from circling Jade in my arms the second she frees me from my manacles. It's impossible to get her close enough. Watching the tracker hurt her was torture, and I inhale her rosy scent, faint under all the blood.

"Are you okay?" I whisper.

I barely catch her words, mumbled into my chest. "Not yet, but I will be soon. I just need another minute."

I'm all too happy to comply. I hold her close, my lips on her brow, her tears soaking my shirt. Eventually she stills, takes a deep breath, and steps back.

"Here."

She extends her arm. I swallow when I realize what she's offering. My father's pistol.

"I checked it," she whispers. "There's one bullet left."

Well then. I'll have to make it count.

I take it from her, reveling in the familiar feel of it in my palm. Jade flashes me a watery smile, genuine all the same.

"I guess it's time," she says. "Lukas Keller. Should we finish what we started all those weeks ago?"

I squeeze her hand. Grateful that if this does turn out to be the end, she's the one by my side for it. "Let's do this."

The second we slip into the throne room, I take stock of three facts in rapid succession.

One, the queen is alone.

Two, she has a gun, which she's pointed right at me.

And three, a sievech is lying at her feet. It's the large black dog Jade shot, the same one that attacked me in the street.

"Lukas, Jade," the queen purrs when she sees us. "I thought you might be the cause of that gunfire. I'm sorry to say, though, your journey ends here." Her voice takes on a lethal edge. "Now drop the gun."

I study her a moment, my pistol still raised. She's seated on a throne of solid gold, in a large, echoing chamber made of ivory marble. Calm. Poised. Familiar. Not unlike another queen I know.

"I'd rather not," I tell her.

A low growl rumbles from the sievech's jowls, while the queen's lips twitch into a jagged smile.

"Please allow me to rephrase. Put the gun down and I'll merely kill you. Keep it pointed at me and I'll take your soul."

I could offer some witty reply or refuse again, but in the seconds I've been standing here, I've been debating. One bullet, two foes. While the sievech terrifies me more, a gunshot moves quicker than a beast. The queen may not remain dead, but if we don't do something about her, we won't remain alive.

For you, Dad, I think.

And then I shoot.

No barb, no warning, nothing to tip her off to my intentions. The queen doesn't even have time to scream before my bullet rips through her chest, straight through her heart. She crumples, dead—for a few minutes at least. Tethering herself to the sievech rotted her soul, and if Jade's right, she can only be killed if Jade unspools her life thread.

"Lukas." Jade's voice trembles as the sievech stands, bares its teeth, and growls. It doesn't leave its position, though, guarding the queen along with her gun.

Shit.

Time's running out. If the queen wakes up before we disable the sievech, we're done.

"We have to attack." Jade echoes my thoughts. "It's not going to move."

"I know." I holster my father's pistol, then unstrap the knife sheathed at my hip. A glance at Jade reveals she's poised, dagger in hand. "You ready?"

She straightens her shoulders. "You go left, I'll go right. On the count of three."

Her eyes burn, level with mine, as she says, "One."

I brace myself, heart pounding.

"Two."

A pause, the sound of Jade releasing a deep breath.

"Three."

I sprint across the throne room, Jade doing the same to my right. The sievech crouches, prepared to spring, but doesn't move as we get closer. Closer.

Closer.

It lunges straight for my throat. I dive to the side, but not fast enough. The sievech's claws sink into my calf. I scream, face connecting with the hard marble, my teeth piercing my tongue. Blood fills my mouth, and my breath evaporates as the sievech towers over me. Hulking. Growling. *Terrifying,* and oh god—

It's about to steal my soul.

I flinch when it unleashes that voice, unnaturally high and eerily chilling. "Fool. You thought—"

Its nostrils flare, and it whirls suddenly to Jade, who's been approaching the queen on silent feet. "How dare you!" the sievech shrieks. Jade skitters backward when it charges her before it stops abruptly. Growling again, hackles raised.

But it doesn't go far. It's unwilling to stray more than a few steps from the queen and the gun in her limp hand, though as I look on, her fingers twitch.

We're running out of time.

I scrabble backward over the marble floor, now sticky with streaks of my blood. Fear squeezes my chest, but I'm determined as I force myself to stand, my calf burning in protest. I ignore the pain and face Jade. Whatever I say, the sievech will understand. If I mouth the words, it'll see. So I think what I want as hard as I can, willing her to feel the message through our soul bond.

Distract it.

Jade nods, and there's a steely glint in her eyes as she faces the sievech.

"I'm sorry the queen did this to you," she says. "I'm sorry she took your soul and made you into this . . . this . . . *thing.*"

Quietly, I step farther from the beast while Jade moves closer. Its gaze bounces between us before landing on Jade.

"You weren't always this way, weren't meant to end up like

this," she says while I take another silent step. "You probably had a good life before she took your soul."

Jade advances some more. "I'm here to undo all that. To make things right."

I take one more step backward while Jade takes another forward. She's on the edge of the sievech's invisible boundary, nearly close enough for it to lunge.

"I know you can't let me," she tells it, "but I want you to know that I'm going to free you from her."

The sievech growls. Jade stares it down. And I take my chance.

My leg screams as I sprint across the floor, using my momentum to take a giant, running leap.

Because Jade and I were never going to get past the sievech, not before the queen woke up. But I figured maybe I could get *onto* it.

The sievech starts to turn, teeth bared, but Jade did her job well. It's not fast enough. I land on its back hard, fisting its hair as the sievech bucks, failed attempts to dislodge me.

"You mongrel—" the sievech cries just as Jade shouts, "Lukas!"

I tune both out and focus wholly on lifting my knife, positioning it right—

The sievech jerks suddenly, and the knife slips out of my grip, clattering to the ground. *No.*

All I can do is hold on as the beast kicks my blade away, still writhing. Still blocking the queen and her gun. Amid the chaos I somehow manage to meet Jade's eyes, fear piercing me at the sheer resolve I see there.

"Jade, no—"

She doesn't listen but sprints straight for the sievech, knife in hand. The monster sees this and settles, preparing to lunge, every muscle growing taut.

"Jade!" I'm not sure what I hope to accomplish by crying her name, but it doesn't work.

Jade meets the beast, but instead of using the knife to defend herself, she tosses it to me. "Catch!"

Everything seems to freeze in that moment.

The sievech tackles Jade to the ground.

I catch the blade.

The sievech lifts its paw, prepared to gouge out Jade's eyes.

I stab it—hard—severing its spine.

I'm jarred violently as the monster collapses, temporarily dead. There's no time to catch my breath. I scramble off its back, heart in my throat when I see Jade pinned beneath its corpse and, oh god—

"Jade?" My voice trembles, my entire world rocking on its axis until she blinks her eyes open and answers me.

"Lukas." She sounds tired, but definitely alive.

"Hang on—I've got this." I'm shaking as I heave the sievech off her, the aftereffects of the battle rushing through me. *She's alive,* I'm thinking on repeat, shock permitting that single thought. *She's alive, she's alive, she's alive.*

I don't realize I'm saying it aloud until Jade finally slips free from beneath the corpse, stands, and brushes her palm to my cheek. "I am. We both are."

I pull her into me then, never wanting to let her go. In these last few seconds I really thought she wasn't going to make it out of this. "I never want to lose you again," I whisper into her hair.

"You won't," she promises, then pulls back. "Now come on— let's finish this."

I kiss her brow, then glance over her shoulder to the queen's slumped body—and immediately freeze.

Because the queen is there, but she's no longer passed out, not limp or dead. She's alive, those light brown eyes blazing, pistol aimed right at Jade's back.

"Very impressive." She grins, but the expression lacks the sardonic edge from before, laced with fury instead. "But I'm afraid I'm done playing these little games."

I don't think. There isn't time. My movements are purely instinctual. I shove Jade to the side, right as the queen pulls the trigger.

At first I don't register the pain, only hear the booming crack. The agony sets in a second later. A burning line of fire, straight through my heart, out my back. I glance at my chest, but it's almost like I'm viewing the world through a different set of eyes, as if the red stain spreading across my shirt belongs to someone else, not to me.

But it's there. It's my chest, my heart, my life slipping away.

"Jade."

I lift my head and meet her horrified eyes. I try to form more words, but I can't get my mouth to work, can't seem to draw air into my lungs and—

Black knifes across my vision, a savage flash, and I crumple to the floor.

CHAPTER FORTY-SIX

JADE

I DON'T KNOW WHY THE QUEEN DOESN'T SHOOT ME TOO, NOR DO I care. My entire world has narrowed to a pinpoint, focused only on Lukas as he collapses. Lukas as he struggles to breathe. Lukas as he lies, *dying*, the golden thread of his life slipping from his soul.

"Lukas!" His name comes out as a sob, but I swallow the rest and lock it down tight. Right now Lukas needs me to be strong, and he blinks as I move to his side, blood pooling beneath him.

"J-Jade."

I take his hand, already horribly cold. "It's okay," I tell him, unable to stop the hot tears running down my face. "It's okay—I'm here. I'm not going to leave you."

He sighs as if reassured, and the gesture fractures my world into millions of tiny fragments. *Hold it together,* I think, *for Lukas,* but the grief is a tsunami rushing for a thin dam. Pretty soon it'll hit, and I'll shatter completely.

"Jade," he breathes again. "I love you."

I hate this. Hate that the first time he said those words will likely be the last time too. That what should've been a tender moment, a happy life, has been stolen by the queen. By death.

"I know, I—" A sob cracks my words, and my tears land on his face. "I love you too. I love you so much, Lukas."

His lips twitch then, the faintest of smiles, and though his eyes have been fluttering closed, he opens them fully now, so I can see all the beautiful viridian. He takes in my features one last time, and there's a faint pressure on my palm as he squeezes my hand and, with the rest of his strength, whispers, "Courageous."

Then the last of the gold slips from his soul, Lukas's eyes close, and the bond between us gives a sudden, painful tug.

Dead.

Lukas is dead.

Lukas is dead.

The realization is the first ripple of a deadly earthquake, and rage unlike anything I've ever felt courses through me, because this isn't fair. Lukas is good, and kind, and brave. He's a deep well of love, the sort of brother who would braid flower crowns with his sister, the kind of person who'd stop to help a terrified stranger on the street. He's the one who made me believe in myself, who saw me clearly before I ever could. It's not fair. He *can't* die.

I won't let it happen.

Instinct bids me to close my eyes and reach for the bond stretching between us. Yes, there was a tug earlier, but it hasn't snapped, not yet. I can feel it, a living cord tethering Lukas and me, and while *his* life may be gone, mine pulses with a hearty strength. *Sustain him,* I urge my own life, and then to Lukas, *Hang on. Just a little bit longer.*

When I open my eyes, his skin is still ashy and his cheeks are still cold. The only reassurance I have is the weathered cord of our bond.

It'll have to do. There's no way to know for sure whether my efforts worked, but even if they did, it's not a permanent solution. I have minutes at best to save Lukas.

I stand. Straighten my shoulders. Lift my chin.

And face the queen.

Good, fierce, brave. Strong, capable, wonderful.

Courageous.

My mother and Lukas believed in me, and now, finally, I do too. I'm all those things and more, and I'm going to finish what Lukas and I started.

"Touching." The queen's words drip with false charm, but her gun doesn't waver, pointed directly at me. "He really did love you. Such a pity things had to end this way."

I meet her eyes, a heated amber. Earlier she looked beautiful, but now she just appears wild, almost animalistic. Blood stains her gown, a reddish brown against the gold, and her hair fans messily around her face.

"As if you care." My voice is quiet, the edge lethal.

"Ah, but that's the thing—I do. Perhaps with him I could've controlled you. Alas, I can see you'll be just as stubborn as your mother. Useless to me now." She gestures to the floor in front of her. "Kneel. I'll make it quick."

The queen is everything Cora said she was, sadistic and cruel. She wants me to see my death coming, just like she enjoyed watching me sob over Lukas. My pain is her pleasure.

I approach her slowly, my steps purposeful. I don't have a knife up my sleeve, nor any weapons save for my will, my words, and my sewing tools. They'll have to be enough, and I'm strangely calm as I kneel before the queen, cold seeping into me from the marble.

Her gun clicks. "Any last words?"

Here goes nothing.

I meet the queen's burning eyes. The cool barrel of the gun presses into my forehead, but I don't let that stop me from saying what I need to.

"You know, your sister told me all about you."

It's fleeting, a mere ripple in the queen's careful poise, but it's there. "And why would I care what my sister has to say about me?"

"Because you love her," I say, and I know it's true. Even eroded, the queen's soul contains a single vein of burgundy love, buried beneath everything else, but it's still there, strong and vibrant. I just hope it's enough. "All your life you've used people instead of loving them, but not Cora, not *Sofia*. You felt something for her. Something true."

The queen stills. She puts on an icy façade, but she's affected by my words, I can tell. She wouldn't be this quiet if she weren't.

"Whatever she thinks about me, I don't care."

She says it all prim, but I don't believe her. Not when I'm still alive. She wants to know more.

So I give it to her.

"I met with her not long ago, and she told me the truth, shared your story. The whole time she was touching her Serpensa marking, a thread tattoo made of her grief for you. Over what you became."

The queen chuckles, but it's brittle, and the gun begins to tremble. "Then she's a fool, grieving someone who didn't exist. Our relationship was never real. She was in my way, an obstacle to destroy. I earned her trust, let her think we were close, but I was just biding my time until I could overthrow her."

"Perhaps," I agree, "but you loved her too. You wouldn't have let her live otherwise. Not with the risk she poses to your throne. I heard Cora's story, see *your* soul. You cared for her then, and a part of you still does."

The gun dips an inch, but the queen doesn't seem to notice. "You're *lying*."

"I'm not," I insist, my gaze still locked on hers. "Everything I've said is true."

The pistol lowers another fraction, and the queen is pale when she asks, voice thin, "What did Sofia say about me?"

This is it. Everything inside me tenses, and I clench my fists to keep from trembling when I say, voice steady, "That against her better judgment, she loves you. Even after the fire, the murders, *everything*, she still cares for you. A complicated, pained sort of love, but it's there."

Shock dampens the queen's reflexes, and I take full advantage of it. I lift my arm and smack the gun from her hand.

"No!" the queen screams. "You—"

Her voice muffles as I tackle her middle, sending us both sprawling across the floor.

It's not a fair fight. I'm not large, but neither is the queen, and I have years of careful tutelage behind me, while it's clear she has no formal training. She thrashes and claws, even bites my arm, but it's fruitless. One punch to her gunshot wound and she screams, hands scrabbling for her chest. I rip her arms up while she's distracted by the pain, then pin them with my knees. The queen howls anew when I sit on her torso, right on her injury, and though she writhes, I've positioned myself well. She could break free, maybe, if she knew how.

But she doesn't.

"You bitch!" she hisses. "My sievech will be up in a minute, and I'll order it to rip away your soul, then—"

"You're going to do no such thing," I tell her, summoning all that artificial primness she used on me earlier, "because you're going to be dead."

The queen's face drains of color when I remove her thread portrait from my pocket, along with my seam ripper and tweezers.

"You're going to pay for what you did," I whisper as I dip a corner of the portrait into her blood. "For killing Lukas," I say as I press the portrait to my hip, where the bullet grazed me. "For hurting me." My blood soaks into the portrait. "All the harm you caused my mother and Johann." I lift my seam ripper to that golden thread. "And for all the people you killed, the souls you reaped."

I carefully slice the first couple of knots of her life, then select my tweezers and begin to delicately unravel the rest. The queen watches in mute horror as I unwind her life—the one piece of her soul not damaged or eroded but strong. She grows weaker as I go, her breathing faint, until soon there are only a few stitches of gold left. I pause then and meet her eyes.

"Most people leave their soul behind when they die. A fading mark, shifting from this plane to the afterlife, where they'll remain forevermore." My voice is low. Grave. "But you damaged yours with all your evil acts, and now you'll pay the ultimate price. Because unlike everyone else's, your soul won't slip into the afterlife, but into nothing. No part of you will remain. Not a single mark." I lean closer, so the last thing she sees is me, and only me. "Everything you did was for nothing, and now you'll be nothing too."

Then I unravel those final stitches, and the queen—the Unseen Death—slips away, swallowed into an abyss even the afterlife can't touch.

CHAPTER FORTY-SEVEN

JADE

THERE'S ONE CARDINAL RULE IN THREAD SPEAKING: TO GIVE, FIRST you must take. Well, now I've taken the queen's life, and I intend to give it to Lukas.

It won't work if Lukas is fully, truly dead. Even thread speakers can't restore life to a corpse, and in the rare instance a life thread is transferred, it's usually to someone who's gravely ill, not deceased.

I have no idea if this'll bring Lukas back. His golden thread has completely faded, but our bond emits a faint pulse, my own vitality tethering him to this realm. *Just a little bit longer, Lukas,* I think as I stand and approach him.

He looks so delicate, pale too, carefully laid out on the ground, haloed in a pool of his own blood. It soaks into my pants as I kneel at his side and kiss his brow. "I'm not giving up on you yet."

Then I remove his soul from my pocket, the one I stitched for him on Gebreine. It's complete, but not active or alive. Not without a piece from us both, and I dip my hand into the wound at his chest, then brush it against one of my many scrapes.

The second I add our blood to his portrait, it comes to life. The colors glow with untamed vivaciousness, while the metallic ones glimmer. Everything's bright and heady, save for his life thread, which has faded to gray.

My grip on his portrait is gentle as I carefully slice through the life thread, all the while holding him tight through our bond. I imagine each of our best moments together as I do, a collage of memories surging through me. The day we met, and not long after, when Lukas arrived at my door and I pointed a gun at his face. Lukas cradling me to his chest after we discovered the soulless body, carrying me to the city gates. The way my heart stammered when I stitched his wounds, and the way it soared when he brought me onto the *Plamara's* moonlit deck, thousands of stars above us. The heat of his body as we shared that small bed, his unwavering belief in me on board the *Xiomara,* our first kiss in the forest, the flower crown and Gebreine, the look in his eyes as I bound our souls together . . .

All of it races through me and down the bond, as if to say *See, you can't give up, not on us, not on life.*

By the time all the gray has been removed, I'm well and truly crying, my shoulders heaving. And though I've never been religious, I pray to the old gods—to *any* god who'll listen. *Please, if you can hear me, help me save him.*

It takes me three tries to thread my needle, my hands are shaking so badly, and the trembling doesn't abate as I rip open Lukas's shirt. The bullet just barely missed our soul bond, passed straight through Lukas and out his back, which is fortunate, in a sense. Now I don't have to fish it out, but I do sop up some of the blood around the wound, then lower my needle to Lukas's chest. There isn't time for a patch; a tattoo directly into his skin will have to do.

I take a breath, an effort to calm myself, because I can't stitch if I can't be still. When that doesn't work, frustrated tears prickle my eyes and anxiety surges anew. What if I can't do this? What if I'm too slow? What if I mess this up? What if—

I cut my thoughts off, slamming the door on those old patterns, then take another breath and urge myself to relax. It helps some, and while my trembling doesn't cease, a memory of my mother surfaces. Of all those times she brought me shortbread, pulled me into her arms, then rocked me as she sang. How truly safe and calm I felt in her embrace.

My mother's not here, but I'll always have her song, and I know what I need to do. I call forth the lyrics and let them wash through me, soothing the panic and stilling my tremors as I lower my needle and begin to sew.

*From the meadows to the mountains, from the valleys
to the sea,
My love for you is endless, eclipses everything for me.
As the sun glides cross the sky, and day fades into
night,
You are always in my mind, shining, burning, bright.
And I wish that I could hold you, I wish that you were
mine,
But should that never come to pass, I wish for you to
find
Happiness for yourself, even if it's not with me,
A love that goes from meadows to mountains, from
valleys to the sea.*

I sing it, over and over, a balm on my bruised heart, sewing as I go. The thread heats to an even brighter gold with each knot I stitch, spiraling through my soul embroidered onto his chest. His new life, his vitality, mingling with my courage and kindness, my strength and ferocity—all those traits he saw before I ever did. And gradually, as I work, a change comes over him.

A flush returns to his cheeks.

Warmth suffuses his skin.

His wound slowly closes.

His eyes begin to flutter.

And finally, as I lay down the last stitch, his heart beats anew.

CHAPTER FORTY-EIGHT

JADE

I CAN KILL A MAN WITH NOTHING MORE THAN A NEEDLE, THREAD, and a lock of his hair.

My skills allow me to stitch love, embroider away death, and unspool memories. Even the most wonderful gifts aren't out of my grasp. Beauty. Courage. Happiness. I can bestow them as I choose, or steal them away as I see fit.

And now, even more wonderful, I can get through tea with the queen—probably anyone, actually—without my hands shaking.

In a strange slipping of her mask, Cora sits not on her throne of rusting weapons but on the floor, just across from me. As it turns out, the day of Lukas's execution, she was captured by the queen, who'd learned of our plans from a mole she'd planted in the Serpensas. By then she knew the tracker couldn't find me, so she sent him after Cora, hoping to disrupt our efforts. We found Cora shortly after the battle, locked in the pit. She was pissed she didn't get to help stop her sister, but I think a part of her was also relieved she didn't have to kill her.

Two weeks have since passed, and until this morning, I assumed Cora had returned to her underworld ways. Needless to say, I was surprised when her letter arrived at the apartment earlier today, requesting our aid. For once, I volunteered to go. My mother and I have been tending to Johann, who was discovered after the battle locked in one of the queen's parlors, and I didn't want her to leave him. After he was forced to make all those sieveche, he'll need a lot of love, help, and time to heal, and he does best when my mother's with him.

Besides, I'm strangely happy to see Cora, and I stare at her tattoo, that two-headed serpent of ebony thread—the reason she called me here.

"Are you sure you want to do this?" I ask.

She glances at her forearm, expression unreadable before something inside her softens. "I am. I got this so I'd never forget Celese's monstrous acts, nor what I had to do. But now . . ." She swallows. "Celese is dead, and I can move on."

I glance at the chambers surrounding us. Last time I was here, they were an odd clash of decadence and odiousness, but now they're just bare. Cora's throne is all that remains.

"Is that why you cleared everything out?"

"It is." Cora studies her empty surroundings, as if seeing them for the first time, while I lift my seam ripper and slice the first couple of threads on her arm. "I've grown tired of this city. I only stayed because I knew that one day I'd have to do something about Celese, but now that she's gone, there's nothing keeping me here."

I select my tweezers and begin the slow, delicate process of unspooling thread from her flesh. If it were a simpler procedure, I could easily cut through the fiber, but Cora requested that I return it to her soul. She didn't want it gone permanently, but instead wished to restore her grief so it could evolve naturally. Normally, an operation like that wouldn't work—you can't stitch new traits into souls, only skin—but since this grief originated within Cora, I promised to try.

I don't lift my eyes as I respond. "Where will you go?"

"Here, there. Everywhere." When I glance up, there's a spark in her hazel eyes. "I'm done being the underqueen, but sea queen has a nice ring to it, don't you think? Why govern Mérecal when I can rule an entire ocean?"

If I couldn't see Cora's soul, her words might terrify me, but the truth is written in that rainbow aura. Cora Ramos isn't necessarily a good person, but neither is she evil, which is perhaps why I chuckle. "What, like a pirate?"

"Exactly like a pirate," she says as I return my focus to her arm. "But instead of one boat, I'll have an entire fleet."

I imagine Cora at her ship's helm, wind tousling her hair, no worthy adversaries save for—maybe—the ocean.

And that's a big maybe.

My lips twitch. "And where do you plan on getting this fleet?"

Her answer is quick. "There's a man operating out of Kabrück, Richard Beck, who owns a shipping empire. Twelve boats, all of which he uses to transport goods *and*"—she pauses for emphasis—"blitz. It's a dangerous drug, one he tried to introduce to Sallenda three years ago, but I burned his ship in the harbor. It sent quite the message."

I remember that. Cora's signature snake had been carved into the pier, furthering her reputation as a tyrant, when really she'd been protecting the city. And like that, another fissure splits her mask.

"So you burned one of his ships, and now you're going to steal the rest?" I ask.

Cora's grin is downright serpentine. "Of course. Now that I've set my mind to it, Beck doesn't stand a chance."

I privately agree, and Cora shares more as I unravel her tattoo. Apparently she purchased a ship of her own—the *Corazón*—to begin her travels. She sent for my mother today, because she leaves tomorrow with no intention of returning anytime soon.

"It sounds like you have big plans," I say as I finish my task. "Congratulations." I lift the thread, which I carefully spooled as I went. "If you give me a lock of your hair, I'll bring this home and stitch it back into your soul tonight. I can even bring you the portrait before you set off tomorrow, if you'd like."

Cora studies me a moment, gaze assessing in a way that makes my skin prickle. "Actually, I have a better idea. Come with me, tomorrow, on the *Corazón*."

The air whooshes from my lungs. Lukas and I haven't gotten a lot of time together these past two weeks. I've been helping my mother and Johann, while he's been getting his family settled in the home they purchased with the funds I gifted Emma. In the moments we've stolen, though, we've talked about leaving Sallenda. Packing our belongings, stepping onto a ship, and seeing the world. Not because we have to, or because people will lose their souls if we don't, but because we *want* to.

But those desires never felt possible. Like an *eventually* sort of thing that would fade as the years passed. Now Cora's offering me the chance to turn that *eventually* into a *right now* opportunity.

"Wh-what? I mean—*what?*" I stumble over my words but don't let that stop me. "And be a pirate? Be your thread speaker?"

As terrifying as her offer is, it's also thrilling, but not if I have to do Cora's dirty work. Now that Celese has fallen, things are changing around Mérecal, starting with the queen—or lack thereof.

Fortunately, when Celese died, so did all the sieveche along with her. Johann was able to confirm she was the only one he ever tethered them to, and so that problem was remedied with her passing. The trouble with Mérecal's government, however, hasn't been fixed with quite the same speed, though efforts are being made.

The people were already unhappy with the monarchy, and the Regela quickly stepped up. The council's taken over the aspects of ruling she handled, at least until a more permanent solution can be found, and our country is beginning to heal from all the pain and injustice fostered by a vengeful queen. For the first time we have a minimum wage, assistance for the hungry, plans to make healthcare accessible, and—most wonderful for me—thread speaking has been affected too. Already a motion's in place that would end its use for punishment in the criminal justice system.

The changes have been a huge relief to me and my mother both, though that didn't stop her from marching into the Regela chambers and renouncing her position.

She couldn't do it with Celese alive, but with our government in flux, she saw her chance. My mother didn't want that for herself any longer, and I don't want it either.

Cora must see my hesitation, because she shakes her head. "On my ship you can be whatever you want. I won't force you into anything like my sister did your mother."

Warm relief floods me, but there's a trickle of cool unease beneath it. "Then why ask me?"

I'm not exactly pirate material.

Cora's returning look is long and hard. "Because," she eventually answers, "you took down my sister. That takes guts, and I could use that on my crew."

"Oh." I blink. I hadn't expected that. Perhaps I'd make a better pirate than I thought, though I'm still not sure if it's for me. "And if I decide to go, but later I want out?"

Cora doesn't hesitate. "I'll drop you off somewhere nice with enough dineda in your pocket to get you wherever you want to go." She sighs. "Look, Jade. This isn't a trick. I could use you, and I think maybe you could use this."

It's true—I could. I've spent most of my life sequestered away, too terrified of the world to really enjoy it, and while that fear hasn't left me entirely, I'm done letting it rule me. I *want* to enjoy the world now, but I can't do that if I stay here.

"Could Lukas come too?"

I'm not sure if he'd want to, but I refuse to accept Cora's offer if he doesn't have the option.

"Of course," Cora answers. "He's got guts too. He wasn't the only one I had on the case, but of everyone, I had the best feeling about him. It's why I asked him to help solve these murders. I'm not sure he ever saw it, but I did."

I did too, that first day in the alley. The courage in Lukas has always been part of what's drawn me to him.

"Okay." I nod, still processing, though I already know what I'm going to do, regardless of what Lukas chooses. "Okay, I'll let him know." I shake my head, dispelling all the thoughts crowding in, and face Cora fully. "I'll be at the ship tomorrow morning."

I don't specify whether it's simply to drop off her portrait or join the crew. Cora must sense my answer, though, because her crooked smile quirks. "Perfect. I'll see you then."

I stand to go, but Cora's voice stops me.

"And, Jade?"

I glance her way, waiting.

"If you tell anyone about this—that I was kind—I'll spill your guts and use them as chum." She sits back, eyes twinkling, and winks. "I can't risk my reputation, now, can I?"

CHAPTER FORTY-NINE

LUKAS

I CLUTCH THE NOTE IN MY HAND, MIND NUMB AS I READ OVER Jade's words for what must be the hundredth time. In it, she details her meeting with Cora, along with the underqueen's offer and Jade's decision, spelled out in black and white.

> *I'm going. I have to do this, I think. For myself. If I need to, I'll go alone, but I'd much rather take this adventure with you. Regardless, meet me at the harbor tomorrow at sunrise, for what will either be a bittersweet goodbye or a boundless hello.*
> *I love you.*
>
> *—Jade*

My hands tremble as I set the note on our kitchen table—a new addition along with, well, *everything*. The past two weeks have been a flurry. First with buying this house, a nice little two-bedroom in

Sallenda's Comerqueda District. Then there was moving, followed by the realization we had nothing to fill our new home with. So now Emma and I have spent hours shopping together—though *together* is an exaggeration. I offer her my opinions, which she quickly shoots down, then picks out whatever she likes most.

And I let her. Perhaps I should be annoyed, but I've enjoyed watching her transform this house into a home. It's not overly large, but it's cozy with soft rugs, a quaint kitchen, and a couch you can absolutely sink into. We were just out purchasing new quilts, and when we returned an hour ago, Jade's note was on the kitchen table.

I have to do this, I think. For myself. Of everything Jade wrote, those words sprint through my head on repeat, not simply because they're true but because I feel it too. For years my sense of self was based on serving others, but no more. It's time for balance.

It's time for me to live for myself.

My family will be okay without me. They still have a chunk of Jade's funds left, and I'm sure if I ask, Zamora will keep an eye on them until I return. This doesn't mean I don't care about them—quite the opposite. I'm a better brother and son when I take care of myself too. I can feel it in my heart: This is right.

Now I just need to figure out how to tell them, which I'm still contemplating when Emma sidles up behind me and plucks the note from my hands.

Her eyebrows rise. "What's this?"

I let her have it. Emma's features shift as she reads, moving from mirth to something serious, her mouth settling into a line. By the time she looks up, a severe expression has eclipsed her features. I brace myself for the admonishment. *You can't leave,* I imagine her saying. *You know that.*

But that's not what she says at all.

"I'm going to miss you, you know. Every single day. I'll deny it if anyone asks, but it's true."

My mouth drops open, and Emma's lips crack into a smile. "What? Did you think I'd yell at you?"

"Well . . ." I shrug. "I mean, yeah. Just hours ago you lectured me for ten minutes when I suggested we should get the yellow quilts. That's nothing compared to this."

Emma rolls her eyes. "Firstly, I didn't lecture you—I kindly suggested the yellow would clash with the room's color scheme, which it would have." I snort, and Emma wisely ignores it. "But secondly . . ." She looks at me, and my heart does a strange sort of flop when I realize her eyes have gone misty. "Look, Lukas. Don't think I haven't seen all the sacrifices you've made. But we're fine now, and you deserve to be happy."

"What about you?" My voice scrapes, and my eyes are wet too. "You've done the same, Em. Deserve the same."

"I do." She straightens and wipes away a tear. "But I'll be happy here. You won't, not if Jade leaves."

"Emma . . ."

She's never been the touchy-feely sort, but Emma doesn't object when I wrap her in a bear hug. "I love you and I'll miss you," I tell her, "and I promise I won't be gone forever."

She chuckles, but I don't miss the way my shoulder has gone damp with her tears. "That's a shame. I thought I finally got rid of you and your terrible taste in quilts for good."

"Nope." I pull back and meet her eyes. "I'm going to sail the world, and when I return, I'll have a quilt from every country—yellow too, just the way you like them."

She slaps my arm. "You're the worst, but fine. I love you too."

"Good." I take a breath, step back, and steady myself. I haven't even packed yet, and I'm already struggling. "You're sure you'll be okay without me?"

"Lukas—" Emma begins to answer, but she's interrupted.

"We will."

I whip my gaze to the stairs, where my mother's perched on the landing. My throat tightens then, because she's not quite the same. Ever since my father passed, something in my mother has been quieted. A good, beautiful, loving piece. When Lina died, it only got worse, to the point where she wouldn't leave her room for weeks at a time.

Something has shifted in her, though. Her silver hair is washed and combed. Her apron dress is simple but well fitted and clean. Her posture is straight, and most encouraging of all, there's a slight sparkle in her brown eyes, almost as if she's finally woken up.

"Mom?"

I barely squeak the word past the ball of emotion in my throat, and my mother smiles. Actually *smiles.*

"You know," she tells me, "the loveliest girl stopped by today with a note for you, and we got to chatting."

"Yeah?" My throat aches a bit, imagining Jade and my mom together at this table, hot mugs of champurrado in their hands.

"Yes," she confirms. "She told me about her adventure. How she was hoping you'd join her on it." A weighted pause descends. My heart surges to my throat, but my mom's lips part in a soft smile. "I told her I'd make sure you did."

I don't get the chance to respond, because that's when Artur vaults down the stairs and launches himself into my arms. Something crinkles in his hand, scraping against my waist.

"Hey, buddy." I pat the space between his shoulders. "What's going on?"

He leans back, hazel eyes taking me in. "Mom told me you were leaving for a while, so I made you this."

He waves his hand in front of my face, revealing the crinkling object—a card. *Goodbuy* is misspelled across the front in large green letters. When I open it up, a message is carefully written there in Artur's wobbling script:

Have fun! I hope you see some sharks.

Love,
Artur

It's wrinkled, poorly folded, a little wet in one corner, and absolutely perfect. My eyes burn as I scan the words, and I have to blink a few times before I can face Artur without crying. "Thank you, bud, I love it."

His smile flashes as he spins away, into my mother's waiting arms. "Mom said you would like it."

"She was right. I do."

Silence falls, though it's not fraught with anger but ripe with possibility, excitement, and love. My family watches me a minute, and I study them right back. My mother with her glossy eyes, Emma's smile wobbling, Artur still looking one hundred percent pleased with himself.

"Go," my mother whispers. "We'll be okay."

Emma glances at her, a tear tracing her cheek before she furiously wipes it away and faces me. "She's right—you deserve it. Go. Let us take care of you for once."

Artur, not one to be left out, adds, "Mom said if you leave, I get to be the man of the house, so I think you should go too."

I chuckle, a hoarse sort of laugh, and then I'm enveloped in their arms.

For years I thought I had to be impenetrable, strong, perfect in the way I cared for them. That anything else was selfish. All I achieved, though, was isolation—from this, the warmth of their compassion. Now I let it wash over me, filling my cup to the brim in a way it hasn't been in years.

Receiving, after all these years of nothing but giving.

And there, as I'm cloaked in their loving embrace, it happens. Something intangible shifts back into place. Something that's been off for years is finally made right, and I grin at them as I pull back, my vision blurred with tears.

"Thank you," I tell them, heart warm and cup full, "for taking care of me."

CHAPTER FIFTY

JADE

I DON'T THINK I'VE EVER SEEN A SUNRISE QUITE SO BEAUTIFUL. IT'S not the most dramatic or extravagant, but a gradient of rosy pink, pale green, and crisp cerulean, stretching over a boundless ocean. Pleasant, and certainly pleasing, but what makes this particular sunrise so breathtaking is the sheer possibility of it.

Because it's my last sunrise in Sallenda—at least for now.

Water laps against the *Corazón*'s hull, the name printed in glittering black letters, with the tail of the *n* giving way to Cora's signature twin-headed serpent. Nearby, sailors bustle about the ship, but I stand alone at the bow, a welcome breeze kissing my cheeks and a burn in my throat from an evening spent crying.

Yesterday was a whirlwind, especially after I told my mother I was leaving. She didn't try to stop me but pulled me into her arms and cried, telling me how proud she was.

We chose to say our goodbyes last night, but this morning when I crept downstairs, there was a parcel of homemade shortbread, a note pinned to it in my mother's even script.

*Baby girl, I wish that you could stay, but you're right.
It's time. You've found your meadow mountain love,
now go find your happiness too, even if it's not with me.
I love you.*

—Mom

Just thinking of the note has my eyes burning again, and I instinctively reach for my pendant. The shell is cool beneath my touch, and I'm reminded of that day at the beach, of how terrified I was to simply step onto the sand.

And now look at me. About to set out on the ocean.

A bittersweet smile tugs my lips as I carefully unclasp the chain and study the shell, but before I can do anything further, a voice sounds from behind me.

"You weren't really going to leave without me, were you?"

"Lukas!" I turn and fling myself into his arms. He's so warm and solid and *Lukas,* and I melt into him. "I was scared you weren't going to come."

He chuckles, and his breath dusts my hair. "Did you honestly think I wouldn't show? Not even to say goodbye?"

No, I didn't think that, but I've still been terrified my decision may have hurt him, even if he understands it.

And of course I'm terrified he won't come with me. Not because I can't do this on my own, but because I'd rather do it with him. My life's better with Lukas in it.

I pull back, chest a bit tight as I meet his eyes. "So?"

He grins. "So let's do this. You and me against the world."

I squeal when he picks me up and spins me, giddy peals of laughter, and he doesn't stop until we tumble onto the ship's deck, a dizzy mess. "I was nervous," I admit, the cool floorboards beneath my cheek, my gaze deep on Lukas. "I didn't want to hurt you, but I was also scared you'd stay here."

Lukas traces my cheekbone with his thumb. "Where you're concerned, Jade, I've never been able to say no. I've never wanted to."

I shiver, from both his touch and his words. "I love you."

He stills and meets my eyes. "I love you too."

He kisses me then, long and deep, and I wrap my arms around him, holding him as tight as I can. By the time we break apart, my skin is sparking, and Lukas kisses me once on the brow before he asks, "What are you holding?"

"Oh." I pull my arms back and open my fist, revealing the shell. "My pendant."

"Hmm," he murmurs, and I know he's giving me the space to say what needs to be said.

So I do.

"All my life, I've been so scared of the world that I've never been able to experience it, but I'm ready now. There are so many things I want to do and try." I glance at the shell, chest tight not with fear but with possibility. *Excitement.* And when I meet Lukas's eyes again, I'm smiling. "I want to get really, really drunk," I admit. "Not just tipsy like at Gebreine, but stumbling drunk."

"Yeah?" Lukas chuckles. "Okay. We can manage that. What else?"

I think it over a minute, all the possibilities whizzing through my head until they tumble out in the span of a breath. "I want to ride a prizewinning horse as fast as it can go. I've always been scared of breaking my neck, but not anymore. I'd like to go to a show, too, one with music, where I could sing along. Generally, I'd like to see new places, try new foods and . . ." I sigh, a slight weight to my next words. "I want to make friends. I've never had any before you, and now I want more."

Lukas takes my hand, covering the shell with his palm, and squeezes. "We'll do all of that, I promise. Especially the last part. You're wonderful, Jade, and anyone would be lucky to be your friend. I definitely am."

Gods. This boy. Love flares inside me, and another idea flashes to the surface, something else I'd very much like to try. I grin, mischievous, before I whisper it into his ear.

"Oh." Lukas coughs, a scarlet tide crawling up his neck. "*Jade.* We—I, well, *yes.* Of course we can do that. I mean, I would love to."

I giggle. Lukas is cute when he's flustered, but slowly my amusement fades, and I look down at our joined hands and the shell digging into my skin. "I think it's time for me to get rid of it," I whisper. "Time to find my own. I'm ready now."

"You are," Lukas agrees, then adds "my courageous girl."

I blush, silent as Lukas stands, gently pulling me up with him. The moment is drenched in possibility, and my breath tightens as Lukas guides me to the boat's edge, to that endless expanse, nothing visible but ocean and sky.

So beautiful. So big. So much to see and do, so much living to be done.

And I'm finally going to do it.

I pull my arm back, then hurl the shell as far as I can. It makes a tiny splash, but that's it. It's gone, the weight finally lifted.

And that's when it happens. When the Serpensas on board— now sailors—begin shouting orders. A second later the ship hums to life, cloudy steam billowing from the smokestacks, and soon we're pushing away from the docks, setting out at last.

Lukas's eyes burn when he faces me, a brighter viridian than ever before. "You ready?"

I grin back, so wide my cheeks hurt. "I am."

And I mean it. Meeting Lukas, solving the murders, overthrowing the queen—that was all the beginning.

My adventure has only just begun.

ACKNOWLEDGMENTS

Oh my goodness! Acknowledgments. I never thought I'd get to write these!

First, to my agent extraordinaire: Sarah Fisk! Thank you for your belief, insight, and advocacy. You continue to be an absolute rock in the messy storm that is publishing, and I'm so glad to have you in my corner. Finding an agent is HARD, finding a great agent is harder, and it's a little unbelievable to me that I somehow got so lucky as to land one of the greats.

To the best editor in the history of editors: Gianna! I'm eternally grateful that you decided to take a chance on me. Your vision and expertise are unrivaled, and from the start, you've made me feel safe and welcome as I take these first steps as a professional author. I'm still so touched that you sent me books for my daughter when you learned about my pregnancy. What kind of editor does that?! (Answer: the BEST one.) So thank you—not just for your feedback and guidance but also for your kindness.

To the wenches: Erin Rand, GW Prouse, L.J. Thomas, Michelle Tang, Olivia Woods, Johanna Randle, Lily Mehallick, Erin, Tami, Cate, Carlin, Rosa, and Jason. There's no doubt in my mind that I wouldn't be here without you. The query trenches would've claimed me as their victim. Thank you for keeping writing fun, making me a better author, and just generally being awesome and getting me through Covid times. I'm so glad to call you all friends!

To Brittney Arena: You were the first person to pluck me out of a slush pile and make me feel like my writing had value. You are truly the best mentor I could've asked for, and *AEOS* wouldn't be where it is without you. Thank you for your friendship and guidance and for being the amazing human that you are. The world is a better place with you and your stories in it. <3

To Marie Pennamen: You've been such an incredible cheerleader and friend, and I'm so glad the Goodreads Beta Reader Group brought us together! Thank you for your help with *AEOS* and for being a part of my life. You're one of the kindest, most thoughtful people I know, and I had no idea how lucky I was when we first connected.

To Maria Heater, your feedback has been invaluable and your friendship even more so! It's been so wonderful to have a friend who's also navigating publishing as a Latine author. Thank you for all the chats on everything writing, publishing, and parenting. (And thank you again to Brittney for introducing us!)

To all my incredible beta readers (who are all mentioned elsewhere): You rock, and this book never would've made it this far without your help. Thank you for putting up with my obnoxiously long sentences, endless grammar mistakes, and tendency for melodrama. Your feedback and suggestions all made this book so much better.

To all the spectacular publishing professionals at Random House—marketing, publicity, production, design, sales, everyone working to make *AEOS* a success: THANK YOU. A special shoutout to Cynthia Lliguichuzhca for your incredible publicity, an area in which I'm woefully incompetent, and also to my copy editors, who saved me from many embarrassing typos and inconsistencies. (Truly, y'all are the unsung heroes of publishing.)

To Anna Stead: The cover you made for *AEOS* is gorgeous. Thank you for bringing my work to life in such a beautiful way.

To Elizabeth Lim, Angela Montoya, and June Hur, it absolutely blows my mind that authors as talented as you took the time to blurb my book. Thank you for using your platform to support a newbie like me! I'm sorry I'm so awkward on social media (full disclosure: Instagram gives me terrible anxiety), but you're all amazing, and I'd love to return the support and connect more if you're ever interested!

To the Indies Introduce program, each panelist, and especially Keeley! Thank you for believing in my book and choosing to uplift it. We need more people to love and support books, and the work you're doing is so important. Thank you for letting my story be a part of that!

To my parents: Thank you for always supporting me and my creativity and never pushing me into a more traditional career path. I would've made a terrible doctor or lawyer. And to my brothers, you didn't really help write this book, but I love you, and your support for me on this new adventure has been so heartwarming.

To my Cohen crew, thank you for your love and enthusiasm for me and for my book! It means the world. I'm so grateful that Natan brought you all into my life and that you welcomed me into yours.

To Brita Larson, Sarah Nasgowitz, Roxie Dobbs, Evelyn Sadlowski, and Sarah Ladousa, thank you for your friendship, for always taking the time to ask about my writing, and for your excitement as I go on this wild publishing journey. I can't believe an introverted couch potato like me gets to have friends as incredible as you. Thank you for letting me be a part of your lives! <3

To my mom's book club, who read the first book I ever wrote (which we shall never discuss again) and, even though it was TER-RIBLE, lifted me up instead of knocking me down. Thank you for giving me the spark I needed to keep going.

To every person in my life who's shown interest in, asked to read, and given *AEOS* love, thank you!

To Lilah. You make me want to be the sort of mother you can be proud of, and you inspire me to keep following these dreams. I love you.

To you, reader, because without you this dream is impossible. Thank you for giving my book a chance!

And finally, to Natan. Even as an author, I fail to find the words to properly convey what you mean to me, so please allow me to fall short now: Thank you for supporting me always, in all ways. For insisting that my writing was "eh-mazing" every time I said it was just "eh." Your encouragement, love, and belief are what's kept me going. I love you, now and forever.